A duel to the death in space!

Shabir turned and floated the few feet to the Zhukov Control Panel to prepare for his final tasks. Suddenly he froze, for there, clearly on the radar screen, was a 'target'! He kicked desperately towards the screen, overshooting in his haste and taking several vital seconds to steady himself in front of the brilliant white dot moving towards the centre of the screen.

He could hardly believe it, but it was there. A huge target, far bulkier than the bomb, and approaching at two miles a minute. With feverish movements he set about the task of gathering the target in his sights.

'He's seen us, Mike, he's seen us!' screamed Pete. 'The thing's turning round, for God's sake!'

The Hunting of Salyut 7

Guy Alimo

CORGI BOOKS
A DIVISION OF TRANSWORLD PUBLISHERS LTD

THE HUNTING OF SALYUT 7

A CORGI BOOK 0 552 11620 3

First publication in Great Britain

PRINTING HISTORY
Corgi edition published 1981

This book is set in 10/11 Bodoni

Corgi Books are published by
Transworld Publishers Ltd.,
Century House, 61–63 Uxbridge Road,
Ealing, London, W5 5SA

Made and printed in Great Britain
by Hunt Barnard Printing Ltd,
Aylesbury, Bucks

CONTENTS

1

Dawn

She could feel the pain acutely now. Like two hands splitting her apart. She'd never believed it would be this bad. Her mother had warned her but she was always one to exaggerate; not this time though. She felt sticky all over, bathed in sweat, her knees and thighs trembling with the strain.

'Relax Alia, breathe deeply, try to relax, you're doing well . . . doing well. Keep pushing, I can see something now . . . Push . . . relax . . . push . . . relax. Good girl, good girl . . . now push hard . . . Yes, yes it's coming . . .'

And she pushed again and this time felt a difference. The muscles were taking over without her involvement. She gripped her mother's wrist till it was white and her face creased into a grimace that camouflaged her normally soft schoolgirl features. She had lost all sense of shyness now, nothing was as bad as the pain.

'It's coming, I can see its head, keep pushing, Alia, keep pushing . . . I've got you, little one, I've got you, don't be so reluctant, it's warm out here as well . . . come on now, come on . . . there, there, come to me, little one.'

And Alia started to scream as the shoulders slipped through, behind the glistening head.

'Good, good, beautiful, beautiful, well done, well done, careful now, hold the cord, nurse, not there, woman, *there*.' And the big hands turned the tiny creature over onto its head and gave it a sharp pat on the back. The infant screamed more loudly than its mother, breathing air was its first traumatic experience.

'Alia, Alia, quiet my dear, quiet now. God is good . . . your first-born is a son!' And no matter how many times he had said it before, the good doctor's eyes always shone and his bearded face would beam like a clown whenever he uttered those simple words. Alia heard them and started to weep . . . after the tears of anguish her face was flooded with joy that trickled into her black hair and spread wetly into the sheets.

Mohammed would be so proud, so proud; God had given them his greatest gift, a son, a beautiful son.

And through the tears she saw the good doctor hand the precious one to the nurse who cradled him and wiped him while he attended to the afterbirth.

Mohammed was only allowed into the bedroom after what seemed like hours and he moved shyly, awkwardly, to see the miracle. He kissed his young wife with great tenderness and their tears mingled and he was like a boy again, shy and clumsy but so proud of being a father for the first time. His long, thin fingers caressed her hair and hovered nervously over the tiny face and fingers of his son.

'Shabir, my son, Shabir, you are our gift from God. Welcome to this world.'

The doctor crept out quietly, his job done, his body aching with the strain of the past hours. A walk would do him good, dawn was breaking, it was a new day, a good day for coming into this world, no matter what its troubles. He walked quietly down the steep path, and then it came, sure enough as it always would on every day's dawn. The call of the Muezzin, from the Holy Mosque.

'Good morning, Doctor Fahzi.'

The greeting surprised him slightly, as he hadn't noticed anybody in the street. He turned and there, emerging from another door, was the baggy-suited figure of his friend, Dr Stern.

'Ah, Stern, how are you, working as well, eh?' The two old men smiled at each other from an acquaintance that had survived every twist in the progress of their lives.

'Yes, I'm too old for this of course, but the father is my nephew,' and he shrugged as he closed the door quietly behind him.

'Everything all right with the patient?' They started to walk slowly down towards the Western Wall.

'Yes, no sickness, just a delivery, no problems,' Stern replied, his eyes slowly adjusting to the brightening sky.

'Good, what was it?'

'A boy, another Michael. Fine parents. Their first, very happy, makes you feel good.'

'I had a boy too, Shabir, screamed me half deaf, not that it would make any difference. It was their first also. Quite a coincidence in this little place, eh?'

And he thought how little the place was, The Old City of Jerusalem, the heart of Palestine.

2
Soyuz 47

'Ladies and Gentlemen of the broadcasting services and of the Press—my name is Konstantin Kulikov and I am responsible for directions of various aspects of Soviet space research and exploration. I welcome you to the Kalinin Mission Control Centre on what is an historic occasion.

'At 11.23 Moscow time today, the Soviet Union launched into Earth orbit the three-man spacecraft Soyuz 47, in preparation for an automatic rendezvous and docking with our Salyut 7 orbiting space laboratory.

'The Soyuz vehicle is in a 100—mile x 101—mile orbit inclined at 51.5° to the Equator. The purpose of this latest flight in the Soyuz/Salyut programme is to extend further our knowledge of operating space stations in orbit, to improve our techniques for processing and assembling material in space and to carry out observations of our Earth, particularly with regard to mineral content, hydrological features, pollution measurements and snow and ice forecasting.

'The crew of Soyuz 47 consists of Flight Commander Valentin Karpov, age 38, from Leningrad and a Hero of the Soviet Union.

'Flight Engineer is Boris Tsiolkovsky, age 40, from Kiev. He is a holder of the Order of Lenin.

'Finally, Soyuz Pilot is Shabir Al Timimi, age 33, from Jerusalem, in what is now Occupied Palestine.

'The crew is reported to be well and . . .'

But Kulikov never finished the sentence. The roar of exclamation from what was already an expectant audience drowned the words of the speaker.

Within seconds the assembly changed from a hushed group of professionals to a crowd scene transplanted straight from the terraces of a football stadium.

The Arab journalists literally threw themselves into the air, releasing simultaneously their note-pads, pens, lighted cigarettes and other paraphernalia which could in any way impede their expressions of delight. They shouted themselves hoarse above the growing applause of the Communist press who to a man stood and clapped in recognition of the greatest KGB propaganda coup since the announcement of the launch of Yuri Gagarin as the world's first spaceman.

The seven men on the podium, a mixture of spokesmen, interpreters and space scientists, kept their gaze on Kulikov and maintained their detached calmness amid the cacophony of whoops and cheers that filled the conference room.

Kulikov, his bald head perspiring freely under the concentrated illumination of the TV lights, scanned the scene like some ageing reptile, the heavy bags of his cheeks casting strong shadows in spite of the make-up artist's vain attempts to soften his features.

His glasses sat precariously on his long nose and reflected a scene of near hysteria.

The 'On the Air' sign showed that this was a live broadcast transmitted via Molniya satellite throughout the Soviet Union and relayed via Intelsat to the United States. The huge audience of 800 million viewers would be treated to a jerking, breathless image as the prime cameraman tried to ignore the dynamics of the Arab journalists adjacent to his equipment.

Kulikov looked straight at his audience whilst his peripheral vision perceived a tall grey-haired man standing close to the emergency exit, scanning the assembly, never moving his right hand from its constant residence in his jacket pocket. Kulikov knew also that behind him stood the 'grey' one's sidekick from D7, assigned to 'protect' him every moment of his life.

By now, individuals in the audience had ceased to react and were slipping back into their 'professional mould', many flourishing press kits towards the podium in attempts to catch the famous Russian's eyes.

The first to succeed was a tall, blonde female, her face almost totally hidden behind an enormous pair of quite unnecessary sunglasses; she did what everybody else was not doing and sat down.

This signal hit Kulikov between the eyes, and her next a good deal lower. She started to undo her blouse. Two empty button-holes brought her the ear of the Soviet Union's most heavily guarded scientist who indicated her with his ever-smouldering cheroot.

'The young lady in the front row appears to have opened the conference. Will she please stand up and will the rest of you please be seated so those at the back may see more clearly. Thank you for your co-operation. Now, you were asking?'

'Director Kulikov, Pauline Foster, *Daily Telegraph*, London.'

The audience reluctantly accepted the prejudice of the chair and listened hard to the dialogue.

'Does the Soviet Union consider that this announcement could be construed as an obstacle to current attempts for a Middle East solution; and may I ask a supplementary afterwards? Thank you.'

There was relief as the professionals recognised one of their own kind and listened for the answer.

The Chairman tapped out a length of brown ash before replying.

'My function as Director is for certain space activities of the Soviet Union; it does not embrace the political field in any way. I will ask for your supplementary before moving on.'

Their mutual gaze never faltered as she responded to his evasive reply.

'Was the non-Russian cosmonaut selected for his ability or his nationality?'

This brought an immediate protest from the reporter from *Al Ahram* who waved the remnants of his press kit in an attempt to gain the Chair's attention. He need not have been concerned.

Kulikov's reply was powerful enough in volume and cold enough in tone to be acceptable as a genuine response.

'I can reassure the reporter for the *Daily Telegraph* that if and when the British Government demonstrates its ability to launch one of its own citizens into space, then the Palestinian people will be well prepared to teach them how to become good cosmonauts.'

There was a moment's subdued chuckling before Kulikov squashed the reporter flat.

'When she was your age, Miss Foster, Valentina Tereschkova, as she was then named, was flying jet fighters in preparation for her own flight into space. The Soviet Union is not subject to the same prejudices as are many of your readers.'

The blonde English girl flushed with embarrassment, fumbling to do up her buttons and feeling as if she was a child who had just been scolded by a parent in front of a roomful of her classmates.

The *Washington Post* came to her rescue in the shape of the well-seasoned James Holloman, whose question diverted both the audience and the Chair.

'Mr Kulikov, I am sure that my Government will be pleased to accept your implied assurance that the selection of—if my hearing is correct—of Mr Shabir Al Timimi, was based entirely on an assessment of his skill rather than as an attempt to obstruct the Middle East peace initiative.

'However I would like to ask you to describe more of his background and in particular how he came to be a cosmonaut in the Soviet Space Programme.'

Holloman folded his six-foot-three frame into the plywood moulded chair seat which creaked slightly under the load.

The timing of both Holloman's and Foster's questioning

had to be admired. They had cut through the emotional group reaction to the news and beaten the others off the blocks. It was Hollman who was powering away now leaving Foster sprawled flat while the rest ignored her, their eyes first on the big American and then on the little Russian.

For the first time in many years of attending conferences or gatherings of one kind or another, Kulikov was seen to show real emotion. He took the bait proffered by 'Big Jim' Holloman and approached his target like a chainsaw operator taking on a gnarled old oak.

The first cut was a marker.

'In all my years of working with cosmonauts there had never been a better example of sheer talent and bravery than that of the late Comrade Komarov, who perished on the first test flight of the Soyuz spacecraft when his parachute lines became entangled.

'Now we have another, one of the few among that elite of cosmonauts and astronauts to be born with a similar gift.

'He is nothing less than a true spaceman! He excelled in all his physical, psychological and intellectual testing. He established at Baikonur the new standard for excellence which all his colleagues attempt to emulate. His people should be proud of him, the first Arab cosmonaut.

'Regarding his background, Shabir Al Timimi was born in Palestine in 1947 shortly before his people commenced their war of liberation from Zionist oppression. His father gave his life in that struggle for his family's future. He was as great a hero as any Hero of the Soviet Union, and now his son Shabir has received his mantle. His mother too was killed by the Zionists in 1957 when the Israeli Air Force attacked a camp of refugee women and children. She has no known grave.

'He was selected for training as a pilot and went to an airfield in the Soviet Union where he first demonstrated his ability in the air by flying aircraft of the PVO Strany, our Frontal Aviation.

'He was then offered the opportunity to train as a cosmonaut. He was shown no favours. He speaks fluent Russian and of course has an excellent command of the recognised international language of the air, namely English, and . . .'

At this moment, *Le Figaro's* man timed his interruption precisely by addressing one of the other Russians on the podium. He selected the man on the extreme left of the front row, the veteran cosmonaut, Andrei Nikolosky, another Hero of the Soviet Union and Deputy Director of Cosmonaut Training at Baikonur.

'Senor Nikolosky, can you give us more details of the training programme adopted for this, your star cosmonaut?'

Kulikov almost spluttered into his microphone at this calculated slight at conference procedure, but before he could say anything all the lights went out.

When they came on again some three seconds later the atmosphere had completely changed. Everybody but Kulikov appeared to be relaxing. A general murmur of conversation spread through the body of the hall and washed around the small rock of humanity in the centre of the podium.

The tall grey-haired man appeared at one side and moved forward to the centre, respectfully acknowledging Kulikov with a deferential nod of his head.

He carefully extracted the concealed right hand and lifted it, complete with its metal claw, stretching the shoulders of his American-made suit. It always worked. Everybody stopped talking and listened respectfully.

He looked at them from a vantage point three feet above the floor, with the knowledge gained from forty years of experience in every continent on Earth. Boris Masursky stood six foot four inches high in his heavy black shoes, but here looked twice human scale to his listeners.

His brain had survived repeated traumas, first as a young farm boy in the Ukraine and then when Operation Barbarossa extinguished over ten million Russian lives, but spared his.

He lost his hand in a gutted arms factory in Stalingrad, to a piece of German mortar shrapnel that took it off so cleanly that he only knew it had happened when he placed the now phantom hand on the trigger of his machine gun. He was carried off the T34's turret by a woman, who then drove the brand new tank straight off the production line. She had fired as she drove, like the other women tank drivers in front and behind her.

'Big Boris' never looked at his audience but through them. They always looked at him however, and listened attentively to his 'requests'.

'Comrades, that was a hopeless performance. How can you expect Director Kulikov to behave realistically if you cannot act like a bunch of real Western journalists. You have now seen umpteen films and video tapes of typical Western press conferences and today you behave as if you were in a Hollywood studio.

'It will not do. In deference to the good Director here I suggest you listen to your teacher, Colonel Rominsky, who will remain with you until you appear to be less intelligent, less provocative and more respectful. Remember, for the past eighteen years we have rehearsed all major press conferences before the real thing so as to ensure that this, our most vulnerable and exposed situation, is controlled according to the rules *we* set, not those of NBC, CBS or the BBC. Let's maintain our record.

'Now I want no unbuttoning of blouses or hot flushes from you, Lt Pomonova, and you, Captain Gorodni, are playing the role of an alcoholic journalist who gave up fighting for the truth soon after our men at Sverdlovsk introduced Gary Powers to our courts, so no more bright questions.

'As for you so-called Arabs, remember: a real Arab would not behave with indignity at such a historic moment for his people.

'Replay the interviews of Mohammed Heikel of *Al Ahram* and then try to behave as he would on such an occasion.'

There was a rumble of approval, straightened backs and shifted chairs as 'Boris Karloff'—as he was affectionately known—slid the claw back into its specially tailored pocket.

The giant Russian then turned to his assistant standing at the side of the audience and delivered an unspoken order; within two minutes the room was empty except for the

Director and his colleagues on the podium.

'Karloff' respectfully stepped down from the temporary wooden platform and moved into the empty auditorium. He turned to Kulikov and waited for him to open the dialogue.

'Boris, it gets more difficult every time we do this, my friend. That 'Holloman' got to me. I took it to heart; that was the real me, he was the actor. I must remember not to show such personal involvement.'

'Director Kulikov, sir, I'm grateful for your candour and I would ask you further not to refer to the Palestinian's flying of Soviet Air Force planes; say only that he was flying aircraft provided for his people to defend themselves against Zionist aggression. The Americans will use any reference which directly links our Air Force and the Middle East struggles with that of other examples of so-called Soviet aggression. They in turn will then find excuses for training more Luftwaffe, Saudi, and Formosan pilots in response to a so-called Soviet threat.

'Will you also not refer to Baikonur in your reference to the Palestinian's training.'

As if to soften his criticism the giant lowered his voice, shifted his weight, smiled very slightly and said in a more friendly tone:

'All references to the Palestinian's performance are of course perfectly acceptable and, as you are the greatest judge of all, perfectly accurate; so please, sir, give him the best references you can on the day of the actual announcement.'

3
The Hunter

The watch sat in the folds of his palm and fingers, slightly tilted away from the vertical. It was a soft round solid silver lump with a ballooning glass cover that invited frequent polishing. Women admired its silver sheen, men its strength and absence of fussy engraving.

Mohammed Al Timimi liked the beautifully made hinge and spent hours opening and closing its protective face with a careful squeeze of his fingers. It was a full 'hunter', its simple message concealed by a hinged face-plate which opened to reveal the faultless dome of optical glass that protected the black Roman numerals encircling its pure white face. Mohammed never ceased to admire the clarity of the face and the status afforded by its maker's name—

'John Harrison, Watchmaker, London'

The man who had left it to Harrison lay buried a few hundred yards away in the British Cemetery of Jerusalem.

Colonel James Ogilvy had brought his father's pocket watch with him in the year of the Balfour Declaration when, on the orders of the King, he rode into the Holy City after disembarking from his troop ship at Haifa.

Twenty years later he was dead, shot through the neck by a mere boy of sixteen who approached him from behind while he was shouting at an Arab for letting his donkey pee on his shoe.

Ogilvy had fallen flat on his face into the dirt, his blood and brains seeping fast into the absorbent earth of the Holy

Land. The boy had disappeared at once and the mixed Arab and Jewish crowd simply evaporated as if into the masonry, leaving only the donkey sniffing nervously at the dead Englishman.

It was only after the incensed British had collected the body of their dead officer and vented some of their wrath on any passing Arab or Jew that Mohammed Al Timimi ventured closer to the scene.

In the dirt he saw what the Army had missed in their fury: a dull metallic object that lay under the tethered donkey. The Englishman must have dropped it as he collapsed. It could be a spent cartridge, in which case he would not touch it for fear of being incriminated.

For an hour the donkey's owner was interrogated where he stood by a British officer, who was in turn guarded by four soldiers with Lee Enfield rifles and fixed bayonets.

The man was led off, protesting, by his armed escort and the inevitable crowd flowed back to the spot.

Al Timimi moved quickly to the donkey's last position and straddled it with his abayah. He squatted down for a few minutes, scratched his buttocks and palmed the object.

By the time he was home on his rooftop sleeping space over the Wall he was consumed with excitement.

The object was some kind of locket as it was inscribed on both sides and obviously valuable. An experimental squeeze was sufficient and the face opened to reveal the time. It was 4.27pm on a hot afternoon in Old Jerusalem, Palestine, in the year 1947.

Al Timimi held the watch in his right hand while his son Shabir attempted to catch the sunlight reflected off its face. The baby sat comfortably in the father's arms, happily gazing at this handful of magic, his little fingers unable to span the smooth glass face.

A year later Mohammed and his son stood in the crowd by the Dome of the Rock in the Old City of Jerusalem and waited for history's latest war to begin. It was a foregone conclusion; the Arabs would at last control Palestine and the pathetic Jews and their terror gangs would be forced to surrender and accept Arab rule. Never in history had a minority so small succeeded in resisting the might of a majority in whose land they lived. Palestine would be no different.

Mohammed proudly held his son as a gift to God and a sign of his faith in God's will. In spite of the entreaties of his mother, the baby was taken out into the fierce afternoon sun.

Within hours, thousands of Arabs, many carrying weapons of every kind, had congregated in the centre of the City to await the call of the Mufti. In deference to parental responsibility Mohammed ventured only a few yards from his house and his anxious young wife.

The watch signalled its historic message to Mohammed as the hand passed through 4.00pm on 14 May 1948, Friday, 5th Day of Iyar 5708: Israel was born and the infant state started its fight for life.

The crowd roared its support for the Mufti, Haj Amin, and his proclamation of the start of a Jihad, a holy war, to drive the Jews from the City.

Firing broke out among the crowd as the Mufti's exhortations raised its expectancy to fever pitch.

Mohammed felt his blood racing and clutched his son tighter to him, protecting him in an enveloping embrace, scared for the first time by the sheer weight of the crowd.

Before he could take a step, automatic gunfire broke out all round the square, followed by the 'crump' of explosions. The crowd started to run in confusion, screaming as it flowed out through the City, hunting for Jews, the enemy, the invaders, the usurpers, the non-believers.

Mohammed found himself back in the house where his wife of only two years clutched him till the blood ran from his back.

Alia sobbed hysterically on his chest, the baby wrapped in their joint embrace, now crying in fear of the riot. The watch pressed uncomfortably into her shoulder but she in turn was oblivious to the pain.

Then with a deafening crescendo a bomb or shell exploded above their roof shaking the entire structure. Objects crashed to the floor all round them as the air quickly became a nauseous cloud of grit mixed with every other ingredient of a human habitation. It was like a soup of dirt that condensed over them completely, blocking their ears, suffocating their mouths and nostrils, and blinding their eyes.

All three humans screamed together, their animal conditioning relieving the sheer terror of the experience. A few thousandths of a second later they were literally blown out of the building by the shock wave which ironically saved them from being crushed beneath the lethal debris of their disintegrating home.

As so often happens in bombings, effects are difficult to predict; the freak action of heat, blast and shrapnel do bizarre things to humans, animals and buildings.

The entire family landed, still clutching each other, on the only soft surface in their path.

The camel was dead already but its soft body saved the mother and baby.

Mohammed lay with lungs totally punctured and collapsed. He died without being conscious of his injury while his wife and baby screamed at the horror around them. The watch lay undamaged in the palm of the dead Arab's hand.

It was 5.14pm in Jerusalem, the Holy City.

At the same moment that Shabir Al Timimi's father became one of the first victims of the War for Palestine, another family living less than a hundred feet away also suffered the consequences of war. The blast from the same explosion blew the Allon family, consisting of Ruth and her husband Benjamin holding baby Michael, flat against the pile of blankets and cushions that they had erected around them. This time nobody was hurt seriously but Benjamin suffered a perforated eardrum which made him half deaf for the remaining years of his life.

Their home was smaller and lower than the Al Timimis and escaped some of the blast that killed Mohammed. The effects were just as terrifying for the three humans who cowered in a contorted heap, waiting for the end.

A burst of heavy machine gun fire ricocheted in the house,

blowing off fist-sized chunks of hard masonry and supersonic shards of glass that embedded deep into any soft objects. One piece half an inch long hit Ruth in the thigh an inch from the main artery. All three were peppered with tiny pieces of glass that caused excruciating pain whenever movement was attempted.

As they lay recovering from the automatic gun fire nobody spoke. Ruth sobbed silently while Michael lay in shock, unable to move his baby eyes which stared unblinking at the sunset outside.

Benjamin started to move his trunk but screamed out in pain as he felt the glass cut in to his flesh.

All six members of the two families had been the victims of a single heavy mortar bomb fired at them by two nineteen-year-old Arabs recruited into the Mufti's army.

They were attempting to kill Jews and believed that more Jews lived close to the Western Wall than Arabs. Accuracy was not their forté but they felt that any explosion was better than none in this, their first real war.

They were soldiers fighting the enemy and, as they were ready to accept death for the life of their own people, some innocent people were bound to die in the process—such is the way of God.

They could see the devastating effect of their first mortar and hastily loaded the second shell. Their youth, inexperience and enthusiasm killed them. The tall one slipped backwards on the loose earth and the bomb fell three feet, nose down, onto its impact fuse. Nothing remained within a hundred feet of the centre of the explosion and they were reported missing believed killed at the final count, many deaths later.

The War raged around the two families who crawled their way to the nearest protective structure as close to the ground as possible, while others fought to ensure their freedom.

Both were sustained by a sheer animal desire to survive and protect their infants. Alia cried her little one to sleep during the bouts of firing, and covered her dead husband with a tattered remnant of rug from the dead camel.

She kissed his still face and then his hands. Here she found the watch and prised it carefully from his stiffening fingers. She held it to her face and then showed it to the baby. Her actions were entirely by reflex, her normal sensitivity held in suspension until her body gradually absorbed it in waves of screaming sobs. The baby had no conception of his loss and so recovered more quickly from the shock.

The watch became his plaything and assumed a permanent place in his mother's memory. As the hours went by, Alia saw only the watch and the baby and she found all other sounds were in a different world, as if she was experiencing a waking dream, just as she had when she was a child in Amman, before Mohammed brought her to his home in Jerusalem.

The night was very cold and Shabir started to cry with distress until his mother covered him with her body gently like a cat with a kitten, accommodating rather than pressing. It was the longest night of her life.

When the morning came she was shivering uncontrollably. Her brother recalled later how she had to be dragged away from Mohammed, fighting for her husband's body like a woman possessed, before she finally collapsed unconscious across his chest.

On the other side of the wall the Allon family never moved from the floor for four days, while the battle for the Old City waged around them. They survived on the emergency rations piled up in anticipation of a war.

Ruth and Ben were trained survivors. They had both suffered the carnage of the Jewish experience in the other war; the one in Europe that had ended only four years before.

'Ben, we are going to live, aren't we? For Michael's sake we will live no matter what happens around us. If the Arabs win we will still survive. We will keep together, won't we? Please. Please say yes.'

'God willing there will never again be a time as bad as that, Ruth. Never. This is also war, but we are now fighting with weapons. We expected the worst and planned for it.

The two aren't the same. The other time we had nothing. We had no weapons. No planning. We had no homeland. We were split up. Now we have a land to fight for. Michael will be safe when we have won our land; see how quiet he is, darling. He knows that we are safe here. He has eaten well, he has slept well. He feels us next to him; he is happy, eh? Look, the cuts are healing and he can hear and see properly. Don't you think God saved him for a reason?'

Ruth closed her eyes to hide the fear from Benjamin. What if they lost, what would the Arabs do to them, and Michael?

As she lay there the memories of the Holocaust fought their way back into her consciousness. It was the longest night of her life and all the time Benjamin stared at the decorated cushion near Michael's head. He tried to memorise every stitch in it. He might have to use it to suffocate his own little boy, rather than leave him to the legendary wrath of the Arabs.

They lay in the cover of the wall below the window-sill for a further three days, not daring to emerge during the fighting which burst out day and night. The worst time came during the second day when they heard whispering directly outside the door. It was a soldier, they thought. They could see what might be a boot through a splintered crack in the door panel.

'There must be at least two, Ben,' mouthed Ruth and she carefully slid Michael under the pile of cushions into a little protected shelter they had formed. Ben nodded gravely towards her, paler than she could ever remember. With slow, silent movements he raised one knee to his chest and to Ruth's growing alarm started carefully to assemble small, unrecognisable bits of metal on a cushion. Within a minute he had a revolver in his hand, a gift from the Irgun resistance movement for services she had never known about.

From a caddy of tea in their dwindling pile of food he extracted a handful of small, chunky bullets. There were five and each slipped silently into the revolving chamber. This he spun, adjusting the worn handle to his grip. No sooner had he done this than the door scraped inwards slowly. A complete boot, then a trousered leg and finally the lower half of a crouching body appeared until the door pressed against the table.

Ruth and Ben knew no Arabic but it was obvious from the whispering that there were two people by the door.

Ben slowly covered the Webley pistol with a pillow while Ruth clenched her ears and eyes to keep out all sound and sight.

Suddenly the Arab stood up and turned to look into the protecting shelter. He must have been only sixteen and could not adjust his eyes from the brilliance of the morning sun to the shadows of the room, before Ben fired through the pillow.

The heavy bullet lifted the boy off his feet and he pitched against the wall, the quizzical expression turning to surprise as he slid down the hard wall like an imitation tin soldier.

The puppy burst in after him and Ben stifled Ruth's scream with the smoking pillow.

Ben shook involuntarily, then vomited when the Arab's shirt turned from green to rust.

By the time they emerged two days later, on hearing a crowd of Hebrew voices outside, the body was covered with flies.

They helped bury the boy along with many others indistinguishable in the bloating form of death. The puppy ran away that same day.

Ben and Ruth never talked about the incident again.

Gradually a semblance of normal life returned to the City over a period of months, then years.

Amazingly, the daily struggle for existence in the shadow of the Western Wall had its compensations. They began to feel special, part of a tightly knit group, the rare survivors of both the Holocaust and then the birth of Israel.

Ben worked at the Hebrew University in a quiet section devoted to research into desert crop diseases. His work gained sufficient recognition for him to be given his own small laboratory where Ruth often came to visit him with Michael in tow.

The little boy would run around the forest of benches and stool legs while his mother played hide-and-seek and his father sat quietly watching him through his own private clouds of pipe smoke.

Ben sometimes complained to Ruth about her mollycoddling of the child but, whenever tempers got too frayed, somehow she managed to slip in a smile, cock her head to one side and then say sternly to the boy:

'Your father, Michael Allon, thinks I'm too fussy with you so I think we'd better go, eh pardner, and then you can escort me home like the big man you are.'

By the time Michael could see over the tops of the benches he was being accompanied by his sister, Liza; the two children always drew favourable comments from grown-ups they met or passed in the streets.

The boy developed a wide grin that always seemed to be ready to break through his soft pale face and light up his grey-blue eyes. He laughed a lot but never said very much except when he was alone with Liza. Her little face was sharper, after her father, and what she lacked in stature she more than made up for in vocabulary.

The two were inseparable and whenever Michael found himself in an argument or affray with his peers, Liza would muscle in no matter what the odds or the justification.

They were in a fight the day their parents died. Michael was on his back with a bigger boy in the same class sitting on his chest, and Liza dragging at the assailant. Then with hardly a sound the bigger boy slid free and ran back to the classroom. Liza collapsed breathlessly across her brother's legs and both were looking up into the sun when it was blocked by the face of their local Rabbi. Standing slightly apart from him were Michael's and Liza's teachers. Both looked concerned but the children's fears were dispelled by the reassuring smile that parted the Rabbi's heavy beard and moustache.

He stooped down and his strong arms heaved them to their feet. Michael stood, head bowed, while Liza glared defiantly at the 'old' man. Rabbi Groman was in fact in his early thirties but had prematurely greyed after the experience of seeing his parents and eighty-two other Jews hanged at Treblinka in a mass execution—a birthday gift to the Camp Commander from the head of the local Waffen SS unit.

The only way he could live with the memory and stay reasonably sane was to embrace death wherever it touched him or his people at the Yeshurun Synagogue near the Dome of the Rock.

'Michael, Liza, please come with me for a while. We are going for a walk to your aunt Elizabeth's home in Hayehudim Street. No, don't be worried, Liza, everything will be explained when we get there, but come now, your teachers have to return to their classes.' he said with a slight turn of the head.

'Liza, hold Michael's hand and I will hold yours, eh. That's it, now, wait, no running . . . I'm too fat for that.'

The three of them went straight out of the yard without reentering the classroom. As they left, the classes grew very quiet and then almost out of earshot Michael thought he heard them chanting something rather dreary.

The little group threaded its way through the Street of the Chain and then climbed wearily up to Hayehudim Street. The journey took a mere six or seven minutes but in half that time Michael had concluded that something was wrong. The Rabbi was too friendly and talkative and he put up with Liza dragging her heels or balancing on any convenient rock or wall she found in range. When he saw Aunt Elizabeth he was convinced. She had not come to the door but Rabbi Groman went straight in without knocking.

The 'beautiful lady' as Michael always described her was sitting hunched at the table. She had obviously been crying and her wonderful, tidy hair was awry. She did not look at him and Liza as they ran to her, abandoning the Rabbi in the tiny hall, like a big black Michelin man.

Elizabeth grasped the two children almost fiercely to her hips, pressing their faces into her soft cotton dress. Neither child spoke and then they heard the Rabbi approach them and go down on one knee softly touching their shoulders.

'Michael, Liza, you are almost grown up now and you must learn to be brave. Your aunt Elizabeth will love you more now than ever before. I have some sad news for you both that I, to my sorrow, must bring you. Your dear Mama and Papa have been taken away by God today for a long, long time. They asked me to tell you they love you both with all their hearts and will watch over you as you grow up. But you will not be able to see them, but you will feel their love around you always. Michael, my son, you must look after Liza even more now . . .'

The two children cried on and off until they slept and then woke and cried again for many days. They would never know exactly how their parents died, but Rabbi Groman told Elizabeth the truth some days later when she too had overcome the first shock of her sister's death.

'Elizabeth, you have ridden the worst part of the storm and now you can feel it becoming calmer. If you are ready to accept the truth I will tell you how Ruth and Ben died. Then I must hand over to you their personal effects.'

Rabbi Groman's voice was low, it was evening and the children were asleep. Elizabeth looked ten years older, her hair lank and still untidy, with lines under her once perfect eyes and her nose, red from constant blowing. She, who had never been able to have children was now the adopted mother of two. This and the pain of losing her only living relations had changed her overnight. The once extrovert flirtatious girl of 24 was now a resigned, exhausted woman. She asked for the truth to be told, nothing could affect her much more.

'Elizabeth, Rabbi Schulman's brother David was there when it happened. Ruth and Ben had driven out to see the Kibbutz at Tel Ahad. They went in the bus. It's about twelve miles or so.'

'Yes, I know, they told me first the other day that they were thinking of joining the kibbutz. Ben wanted to see his preventive techniques properly taught to them. He thought the crops would not be so vulnerable to disease. He felt he should be there on the spot,' she said calmly.

She clenched her hands to stop the feeling of sickness then she waited for Rabbi Groman's reply.

'Good, so you understand why they were on that bus then. You see I wasn't sure myself, Elizabeth. Anyway the bus journey was fine and they stayed an hour and a half with the kibbutz leader, Yigal Ariv. They took the next bus back to Jerusalem. Three miles or so from the kibbutz the road is very treacherous because of the slope and the weak soil there. The bus driver went off the road but nobody was hurt.

'Ben volunteered to walk back to the kibbutz for help and needless to say Ruth insisted on going with him.

'They hadn't walked more than a hundred yards along the shoulder of the road from the bus when there was an explosion. The bus driver saw everything. Nobody in the bus was hurt.

'Ruth and Ben were both dead my dear. They could not have felt anything. They were holding hands. You saw them at the morgue. They were at peace, weren't they?'

Elizabeth let the tears stream down as she recalled their dead faces, expressionless on adjoining tables. The sheets covered what remained of their bodies.

The mine was one of the first types supplied by the Russians to the Arab guerilla forces.

Rabbi Groman waved a big pudgy hand over the arm of the chair trying to find the handle of his small brown suitcase.

He lifted it reverentially onto his lap, then decided to place it on the table by Elizabeth. He stood up and Elizabeth followed him silently with her eyes.

She would remember that moment forever. They both heard the call of the Muezzin to the mosque as Rabbi Groman slid the two catches apart.

The case was lined in dark red satin worn thin over many years and inside lay a shawl.

Elizabeth recognised it as Ruth's favourite and almost thought she heard her sister say, 'Oh, that's where I put it.'

The Rabbi's hands were surprisingly deft at undoing the

knot and pulling aside the four corners of the Tallis, Ben's long prayer shawl.

Jumbled in a heap were a handful of diaries, bundles of paper, rings, a man's watch, a small gilt mirror with pearl and ebony frame, a bracelet and a child's painting.

'Thank you, Rabbi, thank you for these few things.'

Rabbi Groman left Elizabeth gazing at the humble pile, happy to be returning to his own room near the synagogue.

He saw Michael the next day waving the watch around his thin little wrist and proudly signalling with the mirror. Elizabeth soon took them off him and kept them in a safe place until the children were older.

4

The Camp

The sun was obviously hurting his eyes so his cousin folded up the torn poster and made it into a crude sun shade.

She tied it on his head with a piece of string—difficult as he would never stop moving for more than a second or more —and tilted his brown face to ensure that the shadow cast by the paper covered his eyes.

He squinted up at her then pouted his lips, his 'kiss kiss' as she called it.

Leia kissed her cousin's head, then stepped out of his 'camp'.

Shabir was always building little fortified 'camps' in the mud near the water pipe whenever he had a chance. It was his favourite game, one which had lasted the eight years he had lived at the camp with his mother and her sister's family.

He was content to play by himself for hours, living in his own private world that shut out the harsher realities of camp life. Leia, having been born five years before him, could remember her home well enough to miss it.

'Shabir, what is this one called, eh?'

No answer.

'Come on, is it Camp number two or three? It looks like the other one.'

'Two, but it's based on the big one we visited before Ramadan.' he said.

'That wasn't two, it was three and it was after Ramadan.'

'It doesn't matter.'

'What's this?' she pointed at a squared off lump of mud with a squat tin on top. The tin had a nail pointing out through a hole in its side.

'It's the command post and that's the mortar coming out of it.' He never lifted his eyes but kept fashioning round lumps of mud as big as his thumb.

'What's that?' Leia asked, not understanding what he was talking about and pouting at the lumps.

'Bombs.'

'Ours?'

'Theirs.'

'Why not ours?'

Her questions were getting him down. Girls of Leia's age were stupid.

'Because we don't need them.'

'Oh! Why not?'

'Because we can carry them ourselves without planes.'

'What's this, a tank?'

'Yes, a T34.'

She picked up two lumps stuck together with another nail pointing at an angle from the smaller one.

'Ours?'

'Of course, it's Russian.'

'Who are these two?'

'Egyptians, they drive the tank. We don't need tanks but the Egyptians need them to kill the Jews. You've just trodden on the plane.'

Leia did not know she had destroyed a 'Mystère' but Shabir retrieved the squashed lump and reshaped it.

The day had started well. There was a great atmosphere of excitement in the camp. The old HMV radio in the UN tent had crackled out the latest news. Nasser was defying Eden. The British had been thrown out of Suez and now it was time to start on the Israelis in earnest. Sinai would end it all at last.

Alia Al Timimi sat outside her tent on a Red Cross box

cooking the meal for the family, keeping an ear open to the constant chatter of her older sister Farah. As she sat up to stretch her back she saw that something was happening by the UN tent. Then she heard cries and shouts. People began running in every direction, clutching each other and obviously anxious to tell the latest news to their families and friends.

'Alia! Alia!' It was her brother-in-law running towards her and shouting wildly.

Arshad arrived panting at her tent, a wild expression on his face, clutching a folded piece of paper to his stomach while he regained his breath.

'They've attacked, Alia, the Imperialists have attacked Suez. The swines have cooked it now. We can fight now, eh? Oh, what a day! . . .'

As he recounted the news he reached down into the hot pan and grabbed a lump of meat.

'Yowee! Ouch!' He popped the lump into his mouth as Alia reached forward to cover the stew. 'It's good, eh, Alia? At last, after all this time we can fight the swine face to face. Nasser will mop them up. It'll be over in a few days, you'll see. Here, what do you think, eh? And look, I've got the notice ready to pin up. I wrote it myself. I was in the UN tent when it came through.

'You should have seen that bastard's face . . . sorry, but he was scared, I tell you. He actually called me Arshad, you know, not just Al Azawi, eh? The bast . . . oops!'

Alia did not speak, just looked out towards Shabir and Leia. She put the spoon down and stood up, her face ashen.

'Leia!' she called, 'Leia, come here, bring Shabir too. Your food's ready. Come now. And you, Arshad, don't put any more ideas in Shabir's head until he's eaten. You know what he'll do once you start talking about fighting and battles. He'll drop everything and listen. I want him full before the UN people find excuses for stopping the food. Talking about food, keep out of that pot until I've given you a plate.'

She loved Arshad dearly as a brother. He and Farah

had taken her and Shabir under their wing the day Mohammed died. They had seen her through the worst and kept her spirit alive when all she wanted was to be with Mohammed.

'Farah, please call Leia. She won't listen. Leia, come here at once and bring Shabir.'

The children disentangled themselves from whatever they were doing and ran up to eat. Shabir beat Leia to the fire.

The meal passed quickly. Shabir asked about the news his uncle had brought, while Arshad told him he must finish eating before he would tell him everything.

The three females started to clear up the few utensils as Arshad collected his nephew and walked back to the boy's 'camp'.

Alia watched them and soon released Leia who bounded off to find out what she had missed.

No more than an hour had gone by when they suddenly heard a dull explosion in the distance somewhere. It was followed by several more. It sounded like artillery fire but nobody could really tell.

They were close to the border here and it was a common occurrence, so normal activity resumed without too much obvious interference.

The shelling lasted for at least an hour before much more happened.

Alia noticed faces turning up to the sky and then heard the sound of aircraft. They were jets, flying too high to pick out easily but for the contrails which slowly formed into ragged lines across the southern sky towards Israel. Leia was leaning over the walls of Shabir's fort as he fashioned more 'equipment', as he called it, all the time listening to his beloved uncle's stories of the brave Arab soldiers he was training with. Shabir too looked up, his eyes shaded by his cousin's 'sun hat', and gazed at the sky.

Suddenly the siren started and he saw Arshad stand up quickly and signal something to his mother and aunt. He could see over the walls of his fort as people started to move more quickly, more fearfully; Leia leaned over to pick him up.

At that instant everything disappeared in a thunderclap of sound and he fell back, flat onto the mud. The air was forced out of his lungs as if by a huge hand and he lost his vision and hearing. In complete, deafened silence he lay there as things started to fall on him. Mostly it was dirt and rubble, bits of paper, mud and other odd bits of rag and things he could not recognise. Shabir lay there knowing this had happened before, but when and where he could not remember.

He was terrified. He could not scream because he could not breathe and he could not move because he felt paralysed. He lay there and the sky went grey, then black, for what seemed like a long time. His eyes started working first. The blackness started to dissolve and he could feel he was breathing. Within a few seconds he saw the colour of the blue sky: still there, but more ragged, were the pretty white trails in the sky. He could not move though, and could not hear, but he felt no fear as a face filled the sun in his eyes.

It was an old man's face. He was talking because his lips were moving and Shabir felt the earth leaving him behind. He was being lifted. The world spun past his fixed eyes and he was looking over the man's shoulders.

He could not recognise anything at first but then felt a flood of joy as he glimpsed Leia's face smiling at him. She was lying down on the other side of the fort's wall and was staring straight up at him.

He started to mouth her name and then saw something odd about her body. Her feet were pointing straight down at the ground, but that could not be right somehow.

He was carried away from his dead cousin and laid onto a blanket by the Red Cross doctor: there he was left until it started to grow cold and dark around him.

By the time he could see the stars he could pick up sounds again, and then somebody bent over him again and kissed him.

It was a woman he recognised from the camp. Her people lived a few tents away. She had been crying.

Shabir could hear himself speak now.

'I am Shabir Al Timimi and I want my mother please. I think my cousin is dead. We live near to your tent.'

The woman said nothing, just sobbed and hugged him closer to her face until he started to weep. Their tears mixed and dried stickily on them both.

5
Golan

Michael lay on his back looking hard at the sky. He could hear the noise but could not see the plane.

'Mystère.'

'How do you know? You can't see it.'

'I know the sound of the engine.'

'Clever, clever.' Liza taunted Michael about his prowess in aircraft recognition. Her uncle had once whispered to her that her brother was more than often right. He should know. He was a pilot in the Air Force.

'There it is, look, follow my finger, not there . . . *there*.'

Liza squinted awkwardly along her brother's arm until suddenly she saw it, a tiny fleck of silver, hard and bright, but nowhere near the apparent source of the noise.

'It's a glider.'

'No it's not, Liza, it's a Mystère. It's one of ours. The noise takes a long time to reach us, so the plane has moved away from where it was before.'

They watched it until their eyes lost focus and only saw the floating dust on their own lenses.

Michael loved aeroplanes more than anything he could think of. If he heard one fly over he would rush out just to identify it and if he missed it he felt an odd sense of loss. To him they meant one thing—freedom. Freedom to exist in another world, another dimension, to fly away from Golan into his waking dreams.

Liza loved Michael, and of course thought he was silly,

but did not care so long as he asked her to come with him.

They closed their eyes and waited for the next one. They were always somewhere in the sky, especially here in their kibbutz at Ramta below Golan.

They lay at the mouth of the concrete shelter and could hear a tractor working the fields around them. It was Daniel's turn to drive today, and to be scorched by the blistering heat of the armour-plated cab.

Nobody had complained about the conditions after what they had all seen a month back when a Syrian shell had exploded a hundred feet away from Joseph Ariv. A lump of shrapnel had literally cut the seat away from beneath him. A very shaken but uninjured Joseph had later claimed that if it had gone six inches higher he would not have been able to carry on ploughing because of the tears in his eyes.

The shells came over at least once a day now since the end of the Sinai battle and the British withdrawal from Suez. Three kibbutzniks had died in a month and there was talk of raids on the guns to silence them permanently.

Today, Michael and Liza were two of many witnesses to a typical incident of the continuing war.

The plane, or one similar to it, came back. Michael noticed a vapour trail coming from the sky above Golan and, within a minute, two others appeared approaching the first head-on. At the last moment these two split and turned two perfect half circles to appear alongside the original.

The three flew in formation until suddenly all three dived down as if they were aiming for the kibbutz.

At that instant, the klaxon started to scream and the children prayed that they would not be forced to miss what might be a battle developing over the Heights. They could hear the jets now: three sonic bangs were followed a moment later by the secondary cracks. Their curiosity overcame their fear as Michael carefully stood up to look over the edge of the shelter wall. He saw all three jets were much closer now and a moment later the vicious hammering of cannon fire cracked the air. The three fighters had now separated by several hundred yards and were screaming in at different angles to confuse any anti-aircraft fire.

Michael watched fascinated as a line of small explosions erupted and tore through the brown rocky hillside about two miles to the North.

The lead aircraft was definitely a Mystère; its short but graceful body with curled upper lip and blister canopy followed by swept fin presented him with an easily identifiable profile.

The aircraft whined over to his left, banking steeply towards him, then flying hard right before diving down to skim over the rubble-strewn ground.

It disappeared for two seconds and then shot up into a climbing, rolling turn that put it onto a giant circuit for a second straffing run.

The boy whisked his head back to see the second aircraft, lower this time and coming obliquely towards him from the left where the leader had turned. He saw two small black objects lazily detach from the aircraft and arc towards the smoke trail from the cannon fire.

The pilot pulled hard away to his right and shot straight overhead at less than a hundred feet, rolling as he went, while Michael spun round to follow him, and looked straight into the sun. Before he could shade his eyes he heard the third aircraft making its attack behind him and he turned again to see it release two long silver cigars that lazily tumbled end-over-end towards the target area.

But the ground erupted first in two huge bursts from the leading jet's high explosive bombs.

The napalm canisters struck a few seconds later and spewed out the flaming petroleum jelly in a ribbon-like inferno of oily fire.

Vast black gobs of smoke poured out in a rising pall; it was the most vivid sight of his life.

The sense of sheer gut-shaking power expended by the aircraft coursed through the boy's body—and it was not over yet.

The leader had returned with a shattering roar over Michael's head and he smelt the rich sweet smell of cordite as the pilot fired further short bursts of cannon towards the heart of the fire. The aircraft flew straight into the smoke and disappeared somewhere behind it when the two others, also Mystères, flew over the target in line astern, dipping and weaving as they fired in bursts that formed a border of smoke, like white flowers erupting out of the rock.

Suddenly the wingman pulled up sharply into a spiral climb while simultaneously there came the sharp crackling of gun fire. Michael could not believe his eyes as he saw a stream of white and green tracers tracking the fighter in its victory climb. In a moment they struck and Michael saw distinctly metallic fragments 'flake' off the port wing of the aircraft, followed by a stream of white smoke.

The aircraft must have been about three thousand feet above Golan when two large pieces detached themselves in dividing trajectories. One streamed a parachute that brought it instantly to a halt where it looked as if pinned to the deep blue sky like a silver butterfly.

Behind it the empty fighter flew on but spinning faster and faster until it abruptly exploded into a mile-long streak of flame that blew it to a huge, tattered shower of metal.

The parachute swung very slowly down and with growing horror Michael saw it head for the pall of smoke as powerful convection currents from the heat of the burning napalm sucked back new air into the vacuum it had just created.

When the parachute was almost into the cloud it suddenly started to rise, until Michael could see it suspended directly over the heat of the smoke.

Suddenly a line of tracers spewed out from the ground ahead of the fire zone, seeking the fragile target.

And then Michael cheered, for out of the sun behind him came the two remaining Mystères, wing-tip to wing-tip and both firing like mad, at the base of the deadly line of tracer.

In a moment they broke in opposite directions, visibly slowing down, and flew in a protective circle round their helpless colleague.

It was over in a few moments: the pilot's canopy started to

turn grey and then evaporated into nothing, dropping its load into the smoke.

Michael was stunned. He had never seen a man die before, but what impressed him profoundly was the way the two remaining pilots kept flying for a further two or three minutes as if mesmerised and unable to break the circle.

Then, almost reluctantly, first one and then the other glinted its wings and arced back towards the sun.

Michael heard no more firing and stared at the flames, his eyes bright with the imagery imprinted on his brain.

He felt the pressure of Liza's hand on his elbow but would not turn around.

She soon relaxed her grip and put her hands back over her ears. For the first time he realised she had been shouting at him to get down below the wall. With a feeling of extreme irritation bordering on anger, he strode up the ramp from the shelter and started to run across the field towards Golan, but David caught up with him and dragged him back to the tractor.

The shelling resumed within an hour but more fiercely.

6
Kibbutz Ramta

The next day there was a meeting at the kibbutz office attended by all the kibbutzniks. The children ran around the central trestle table playing 'tag' until sufficient grown-ups had arrived to usurp their territory. Liza had succeeded in outrunning all but two of the boys and was now ensconced under the table, refusing to move.

Even the appearance of the leader Shimon Yariv failed to impress her so it was Michael who broke the stalemate. He simply whispered in her ear and a grin broke over her rather grubby face. She could hardly wait to get out from underneath and disappeared out of the room with her brother following behind her.

The room was filling now with people of all ages and appearances, dressed in an assortment of working clothes, mainly denim or rough cotton that tended to hang loose with lots of useful pockets. The women were tanned, not unkempt but certainly devoid of make-up, their femininity taking a backstage role in the everyday drama of surviving among their hostile neighbours.

They could have been and certainly were from many different countries. Daniel Perès, the kibbutz's leading intellectual and practical joker, had once declared that there were twenty-three nationalities and nine major language groups present at last month's meeting. Unfortunately all of them usually tried to speak at once. He had quipped that the meaning of the title 'the Chosen Race' was God's way of selecting the noisiest elements of mankind whom he could then tuck away in one of the most inhospitable areas of the world; by giving it the grand title of the Holy Land, God, who was obviously the original Jewish Entrepreneur, could get rid of the least valuable piece of real estate in the world. After all, 'who would want to plough through rock in 100 degrees Fahrenheit where the biggest lake was full of salt and the neighbours hated your guts?'

Daniel's humour was not always appreciated by the more orthodox kibbutzniks and there was a definite antagonism developing between him and Shimon Yariv. The two were often called David and Goliath, with Daniel's six-foot-four frame suiting the part of Goliath admirably, whilst the small, handsome Yariv moved around him like a bantam-weight boxer. Intellectually there was little to choose between them; both had PhDs from respectable universities, Daniel's from Princeton where he had studied Engineering Science and Shimon's from Oxford where he had read Classics.

Shimon's aggressive personality was tempered by a sense of fairness that was often utilised in disputes between kibbutzniks. He had founded the kibbutz, being among the first to arrive after the Holocaust and leading his little band of dazed humanity to a rocky hill overlooking Galilee.

He had picked out Daniel as his personal human power-house capable of translating paper plans into the solid floors, walls and roofs that sheltered 'his' people. The democratic principles of the kibbutz itself had enabled him to excel in the many debates and to decide what to plant, how to irrigate and how to defend their tiny patch of soil.

Daniel, with the self-confidence of a man who knows he is strong, fit and attractive to women, accepted his position with equanimity, getting on with the job of building a home in the desert.

Neither man was married now. Nobody knew what happened to Daniel's wife—if he ever had one—but respected the evasive lighting of his pipe as a sign reading 'No Trespassers'. Once, Michael's aunt Elizabeth, had found him weeping quietly out near the generator at night. It was her concern and tenderness then that had won him to her and brought her a degree of contentment she had never known from any other man.

Daniel and Michael respected each other, enjoying being buddies, as Daniel called them. It was Daniel in whom Michael had confided after the incident of the dead pilot. The boy had wept tears of anger and frustration, his wet face pressed into the big man's stomach, repeating the statement:

'I want to fly, Uncle Danny, I want to fly.'

Daniel had said, 'You will, Mike, you will,' and pressed the boy's face to him. He'd heard him say this so many times before.

Shimon had never married, for time had been against him; while he was studying at Oxford, Hitler had invaded Poland and Shimon had joined the British Army as a volunteer officer of the King's Own Rifles. He had served as an Intelligence Officer at Alexandria and then as an aide on Montgomery's own staff. Shimon went with the 7th Army across the deserts of North Africa, then embarked for Sicily and finally Italy.

At Anzio he had been hit in the hip by a piece of shrapnel and was invalided home to England in time for Normandy. He then met up with Montgomery in Germany and was in the tent on Luneberg Heath when Field Marshal Kesselring surrendered to the tough little Englishman who loved killing Germans.

Shimon had been given the harrowing task of interviewing survivors from Auschwitz in preparation for the Nuremberg Trials. Only then did he become a Jew, never having bothered to attend his synagogue before. He cut his ties with England and the Army but personally exported Montgomery's approach to life, here in the Promised Land of His People, with the passion of a zealot in the body of an Englishman. This extraordinary cocktail of personality, attitude and experience, so typical of Jews in Israel, made Shimon Yariv into a natural recruit for Mossad, the Israeli Intelligence Service under the legendary Isser Harel. He was unaware until one day many years later, at the Western Wall in Jerusalem, that Daniel Perès was a Mossad agent also.

'May we start please?' Yariv's sharp voice cut through the chatter as people settled expectantly on their wooden benches and stools.

'Today's meeting will be opened by Rabbi Groman who is kindly visiting us for the day.'

The Rabbi led a prayer of thanksgiving and then sat back and looked intently at the assembly around him.

'You will all know of yesterday's attack on Syrian positions on Mount Hermon and the loss of one of our pilots. I hope it will bring to all of you a sense of responsibility to the Military Commanders and an appreciation of their task.

'You, David, did well to protect Michael Allon and bring him back to the shelter.'

The youth grinned sheepishly, basking in this little spotlight of publicity, nervously adjusting his yamulka and glancing sideways at his admiring girl friend, a stunning raven-haired creature from Haifa by way of the Warsaw ghetto. He could almost feel her now caressing him, mumbling quiet words of praise, just like last night in the hut.

'However, David, don't do it again, ever.'

The grin vanished in the face of the harsh tone of address.

'Michael Allon, as all young members of the Kibbutz know, is responsible for his own safety and that of his fellow kibbutzniks. He endangered two lives, his own and David's. Never do that again.'

Michael, standing in the doorway by Liza, blushed scarlet whilst Liza stuck out a tiny tentative tongue at the table.

'The Syrians are firing anti-personnel rounds using 152mm D-20 Howitzers embedded in fortified positions. These shells will kill any exposed human target, that's all of us here, at a distance of five hundred feet or more.

'Only authorised tractor drivers and observers may leave the shelters during an alert or shelling.

'Furthermore we have been told by Captain Lod at the

Military Post today that the shelling will intensify during the next few days.

'Ploughing and seeding will be restricted so food stocks will be further rationed.'

There was a general murmur of annoyed resignation at this worsening of their beleaguered existence. It meant more fish-heads and less green vegetables for everybody but the younger children.

'The future position here at Ramta will be one of increased shelling and tension so we are required by the military to reduce our population to the minimum necessary to protect our land allocation and to maintain food production . . .'

There was a restless murmuring among the assembly that conveyed a sense of failure, even betrayal, at hearing Shimon Yariv's sombre announcement.

'. . . as previously planned. Furthermore, before we discuss our response I wish to call on our visitor, Rabbi Groman, whom many of you know from Jerusalem. Rabbi, please.'

The fat, black-garbed cleric leaned forward and nervously pulled at his beard, the sun catching his thick pebble lenses and making it difficult to see his expression.

'Kibbutzniks, bless all of you and thank you for this opportunity to speak plainly. I have come from Jerusalem where I attended a joint meeting of the Rabbinical Council and the Military Command Council. The objective of the meeting was to establish a plan for the maintenance of a Jewish position in world affairs with particular regard to the security of Israel.

'As you all know, the United Nations is changing its position, under the influence of the Soviet veto, from a favourable to a hostile attitude towards Israel.

'This strategic development has been accompanied by a measurable increase in tension and Arab military action.

'You of the kibbutz are the front line of Israel and the first to experience this in reality. So far three kibbutzniks have died in a month due to artillery fire by Syrian guns on Mount Hermon.

'Further, you know that yesterday saw an escalation of firing in spite of air strikes by the IAF. Elizabeth Allon had the distressing experience of seeing her late sister's boy exposed to artillery fire; bless you, David, for your lack of caution.'

He smiled slightly through his beard, looking over his glasses at the young tractor driver.

'It is going to get worse before we can reduce the effects of Arabs shelling. It could be years before a ceasefire is effective, if ever. The Arab nations are continually threatening war and the destruction of Israel. The Soviet Union is providing arms and equipment in support of Arab policy and has placed in Nasser's hands a huge array of aircraft, missiles and tanks. I need not go on about our position, I'm sure.'

His audience waited respectfully for the message he was bringing today.

'We must respond in a logical manner that will ensure our survival and improve our diplomatic position. The key to our future is in the hands of two states.

'The first are the Jews of Israel, ourselves. The second are the people of the United States.'

Another murmur broke the silence: some eleven kibbutzniks had previously been American citizens.

'We are the nut in a nutcracker having one American and one Russian lever.

'Pressure by both superpowers is being constantly applied on us as we are at the centre of the modern industrial world's major oil fields and sea route through Suez. We, allies of the US, are the front line against Soviet Communism in the Middle East which has now dominated Egypt. Witness Nasser's Aswan Dam and Soviet military control of the Egyptian forces. Iraq and Syria are our enemies here in the North, dedicated to complete Hitler's programme.

'All this we know but now we have a strategic policy to follow which, God willing, will ensure our survival into the twenty-first century.

'The secret of survival is very simple. We must go back to

being Jews as we have been known since the destruction of the Temple. We must wander the Earth again, while retaining Zion as our home and our political and religious heart. There will be no surrender, no withdrawal, no military defeat here in Israel. The state will prosper but for the next twenty years or more we will have to fight the entire Arab world and the Soviet Union.

'How will we do this, you may ask? The answer is by alliance. We will adopt the United States as our benefactor, our arsenal, rather as Britain did during the desperate years of 1939 to 1942. We will build a bridge so strong between our two communities that no propaganda, no staged incident, no diplomatic game will break it.

'In turn we will do the fighting and the dying and the sowing and the reaping here in Israel. We will give America our loved ones, our children, and we will ask her to train them in those skills we do not possess here in Israel. We will select our best and we will send them to America where they will have the facilities for further education, research and development. Then at the hour of need we will bring them back to defend our State in any future war.

'We are naming it the Abraham Policy.'

Rabbi Groman waited for a long half minute, but nobody spoke; he had their attention. Even the children had stopped fidgeting.

'My friends, I have come to ask you for one of your sons. He has been selected from many, many possible names provided by each leader of each kibbutz in Israel.

'He will be offered a passage to America where he will be cared for by a Jewish family. There he will receive the best education and training the United States can provide. There will be no official recognition of his training programme. He must succeed by his own ability and application.

'He will have the greatest support anybody could wish, for he will go with our blessing and the love of his kibbutz.

'Michael Allon, will you please come here,' he said gently.

Elizabeth brushed the tears from her cheeks, squeezing Daniel's strong hand where it rested on her right shoulder.

Michael came slowly, reluctantly through the closely packed group and stopped opposite the Rabbi. He looked slightly alarmed, his hands clasped behind his back and his hair falling forward over his face.

'Round here please, Michael' said Rabbi Groman beckoning him to the other side of the table.

The boy almost tip-toed around until he stood awkwardly by the Rabbi, staring down at the table as if he had seen something there to catch his attention.

'Kibbutzniks, Michael Allon is the son of this kibbutz accorded the privilege of the Council and our blessing. Please acknowledge his merit.'

There was a burst of applause led by Liza who was delighted with her brother's achievement. It would only be a few hours later that she would start to cry at the realisation of their forthcoming separation.

The Rabbi stood up and led the assembly again in a short prayer before Shimon Yariv addressed his people.

'I think this calls for a celebration, so may I ask if someone will propose the appropriate motion?'

A babble of support carried the motion and the place took on the atmosphere of a Barmitzvah—for Michael, still two years away.

Elizabeth and Daniel held their two wards close to them as their friends came round to offer their blessings and congratulations.

Rabbi Groman found an excuse to leave the hut early and walked out into the dusk of Golan.

He went as far as it was safe to do so, away from the noise and singing.

When he found the quiet he was seeking he pulled the tallis over his shoulders and commenced reading his Talmud. His concentration was only broken twice by the whine of shells followed by the echoing boom of their explosions, too far away for him to be concerned for his own safety or that of the kibbutz.

The following week Michael Allon said goodbye to his aunt Elizabeth, her lover Daniel and his sister Liza and climbed aboard the bus with Rabbi Groman for the twisting journey to Haifa. He took with him a suit of clothes and some personal effects that his weeping aunt had sealed in a small travelling box.

The kibbutz had collected sufficient food to keep him fed on the journey to the port until he came under the care of the ships's captain and crew. The vessel took twelve days to bring Michael close enough to America to see the Statue of Liberty rising out of the sea mist, a giant green sentinel guarding the edge of the New World.

It took him two full days to clear immigration at Ellis Island assisted by his new found guardians, a young American family named Cohen, relatives of Daniel from New York City.

Judith Cohen was a short plump woman with bright auburn hair that never seemed tidy. She was always caught in a panic and smoked at least thirty cigarettes a day. Her husband John, short and stocky, taught in the same University that Daniel had attended and their home in Princeton came as a revelation to Michael who spent several days discovering the wonders of a modern American home. His investigations encompassed the television, electric toaster, ice maker and everything Judith and John took for granted.

To have his own room, decked out with giant posters of unfamiliar football heroes, film stars and a cartoon of Bugs Bunny chewing a carrot while riding backwards on a motor bike, was to him the biggest piece of luck in his eleven years of life.

The Cohen's own eldest boy, John Junior, had a couple of years over him and could tuck Michael's head just under his chin, an advantage which would be reversed by the time Michael was fifteen.

The first night in 47 Orchard Drive, Michael ate himself stupid on a concoction of food such as he had never experienced.

'Go on Michael, have a try. It's a turkey roast. Uncle John will cut you couple of slices, won't you, honey. There, that's nice, isn't it. Now you try some of these potatoes, huh? Your aunt Elizabeth told me in her letter you love them mashed. Spread a bit of butter on it, that's right. Johnny, you help Michael now.'

John Junior took after his mother, feeding his face as often as possible and a complete stranger to comb or hairbrush.

He bombarded Michael with offers of various dishes, all of which the boy accepted with a nod, a grin and a polite 'thank you'.

In between the offers of new gastronomic experiences he told Michael of all the plans he had ready for them together, including going to a football match with his father, riding an older friend's motor bike as passenger, of course, he added hastily for parental reassurance, and making various contraptions in the rumpus room out of his hobby kits.

Throughout this dialogue Judith fed her husband both with food and all the information she had gleaned from Elizabeth's, Daniel's and Rabbi Groman's letters.

John provided the appropriate responses to his wife's stream of family data while attempting to check off in his own mind the list of things he would have to follow to get Michael into school and on the right course.

He had cleared matters with the PTA, the Principal of Waverly School and his Rabbi, Joseph Rabinowitz, who had been briefed independently by Rabbi Groman and the Rabbinical Council.

John Cohen felt the responsibility more than Judith of ensuring that Michael had the best possible security at home to enable him to concentrate on the task of achieving the goals set by the Council. Later that night, after the meal had rendered both John Junior and Michael speechless in front of the television, he had written a reassuring letter to Elizabeth Allon telling her of Michael's safe arrival and his future plans for him and wishing her, Daniel and Liza his love and good wishes for the future.

The maternal feeling in Judith contributed to her own sense of well-being and she accepted her husband's approach to her in bed that night like a contented cat.

In the room at the end of the hall, Michael lay awake

absorbing his new surroundings in sleepy awe. For the first time in days he was alone with himself. The past few weeks had been a kaleidoscope of novel experiences; the tearful parting from Liza and Aunt Elizabeth, the theatrically proffered handshake from Uncle Daniel. The trip to Haifa with Rabbi Groman had saturated him with images and sounds of a noisy, hot, busy people. Somehow he had gazed the voyage away, staring out across the blue Mediterranean past dirty steamers, the occasional dhow, the curious, threatening warships that cruised out of nowhere, winking urgent messages at the bridge high above him.

And always there had been Uncle Daniel's gift to go back to, hidden there under his bunk but now, safe beneath his bed.

Michael rolled over, his arm stretching awkwardly as his delicate fingers groped for the box. They found and gripped its corner, dragging it out and placing it alongside him on the bed. For the hundredth time at least he prised up the cardboard lid and peered in. Sure enough it was there, safe and undamaged, a perfect silver-painted replica of the same Mystère he'd seen flying over Golan.

Michael stroked the hard, polished wood marvelling at the beauty of the thing, the sweep of the wings, the matching tailplane and the curious fishlike mouth of the air intake.

He imagined himself sitting inside that swelling canopy, surrounded by switches, levers and instruments that would push, roll and spin him free of the dusty earth and the ponderous, rolling ocean to swoop above all things, master of his machine, king of the sky.

And when he felt afraid, alone at night and prey to his fertile imagination, he would hug the thing to him, cover his head completely with the blankets and pretend he was high, high in the sun, free to fly where he wished.

Many times he had told Liza how one day he would become the greatest pilot in the world, greater even than Mordechai Hod or Douglas Bader or Guy Gibson or Charles Lindbergh. He, Michael Allon, would be quite simply the best pilot on Earth.

His last thought as he fell asleep was of that day on Golan, and of Liza shouting in his ear. Before he could feel the first pangs of homesickness, he picked up the plane and brought it close to his face, squinting up its tail as if he were flying in battle formation close behind it, weaving and thudding through the heavy air of Palestine.

And there below him he could see Liza's stern little face, screwed up in the blazing sunlight, waving at him, calling him to take her up, up into the scattered powder-puff clouds where they both could escape into the absolute freedom of the great blue sky.

He was asleep in seconds—a quiet child in the night.

Unknown to him, Liza too would soon be asleep. She was in fact finishing her lunch of meatballs and latkes with her classmates, before resigning herself to the most boring part of her day—having to sleep for an hour in the dormitory while the sun burned down outside.

It was David's turn again to drive the tractor that day and as Liza dropped off to sleep, as she did in spite of her reluctance, her ears received the sound of the armoured tractor clattering away monotonously at the foot of Mount Hermon. Her last thoughts were invariably of Michael. Today was no exception; but what happened twenty minutes later was.

She, like her friends around her, was suddenly awakened by the continuous roar of exploding metal, earth and glass as Russian-made Katyusha rockets straddled the kibbutz in a haphazard grouping. The sirens broke the shocked silence which followed the explosions, and everybody started to move fast for the shelters.

Liza fought off sleep, rose from her little camp bed and ran along with her friends to the shelter.

As she filed in amongst the chattering, excited children she glanced out towards the mountain and saw a dirty smudge of smoke rising from the middle of the fields. Something was dead out there and she heard the crackling of flames and smelt the burning oil of David's funeral pyre, the shattered remains of the armoured tractor.

7
Guerilla Camp

Shabir sighted along the familiar shape of the AK-47, gathering his target first with both eyes open, as he had been taught, until the bead covered the figure's chest.

With a slow, controlled adjustment he brought the back-sight below the bead and gently squeezed, not pulled, the trigger. The single shot cracked out across the scrubby range and reacted against his right shoulder, kicking it back like a muffled hammer on his bone. His body trembled as he lowered the ten-pound rifle, put the safety catch to 'on' and rested it in his now relaxed hands.

'Good. Well done Al Timimi, excellent attempt, not too slow or hesitant and not too fast to over-react. Now, on my command to commence firing at will, you will switch to automatic, sweeping very slightly right to left to counteract the pull. Do you understand?'

'Yes, Captain.'

'Good. Now raise your rifle, safety catch off. Steady, steady, wait for the target to be gathered and fire at will, full cyclic rate.'

The noise burst out as a stream of high velocity bullets seared through the wooden effigy of an Israeli soldier.

As six hundred rounds per minute seared through the wood, Shabir's tracking kept the vicious energy on a concentrated band across the target's chest.

The burst lasted less than a second, followed by continuous echoes in the Syrian hills of Golan.

Then there was a gentle splintering sound as the head and chest fell forward at a drunken angle to the lower torso.

Shabir felt a shiver run down his spine as he imagined what reality must be like, the sight of one of them, the hated ones, folding into a messy sack of tattered khaki and spewing guts. His brow broke into beads of perspiration.

'Excellent concentration, my boy, excellent. Safety 'on', gun rests. Withdraw, keeping flat and then stand up to attention. Pull your scarf down from your mouth and let's see if your cheeks are bruised.'

The Russian held the Palestinian boy's head firmly in his pudgy hands, tilting it to its left to see if the rifle had been held too tight to the right cheek.

'No, you're OK. Good shooting, very good shooting.'

Turning to the Palestinian youth on his right, Captain Yeliskeiv gave him a stern look and said with a firm, loud voice and excellent Arabic:

'Comrade Al Fahed, your platoon does you credit. The best I've seen of its age group during this inspection. I congratulate you, particularly on your training approach and dedication. Young Al Timimi here should be given a sniper's course after the next move and in two years he will be ready to send on a raid.'

'Thank you, Captain,' said the sixteen-year-old Palestinian, his voice constricted with emotion in response to the high praises of the Russian.

'You, Al Timimi, have a special role ahead of you, I can see. We will keep an eye on your progress, won't we, Al Fahed, and shape you into a platoon leader, and who knows what after that.'

'Thank you Captain Yeliskeiv, I will do my very best.'

'Good, now let's take a break. Captain Kerensky will take over in fifteen minutes to give you a little talk on demolition techniques under fire. Dismiss your platoon, Comrade Al Fahed.'

The Russian stood respectfully as the youth dismissed his class of eleven- and twelve-year-olds. The Palestinians always demanded respect and Al Fatah ensured they got it by maintaining a raiding sortie rate that ensured a continuous flow of new recruits and weapons.

Yeliskeiv was typical of the thousands of Soviet and East German military advisers operating in both the conventional military bases and guerilla camps.

He had a two-year posting from his base in the Czechoslovakian border district and had completed the first month, very much to his own surprise, with satisfaction.

Ever since he had arrived here in the Golan, via Al Fatah Headquarters in Beirut, he had drastically changed his attitude towards the Palestinians.

His impression of Arabs—both of their temperament and their fighting ability—had been sceptical to say the least. But here in Golan with the Al Fatah groups the nearest description he could give of them was, ironically, 'They are like the Jews.'

'They're dedicated, clever, innovative and tough, Colonel,' he remembered saying to his CO on the line to Soviet Headquarters in Cairo, the previous week.

'I think they will surprise us yet. No, I'm not joking, your Egyptians are different, I've no doubt; but here is a group of guerilla soldiers as good as any I met in Poland, Yugoslavia or Czechoslovakia during the Patriotic War. . .

'Yes, they accept us with contempt concealed behind an obedient face. They can't understand our philosophy, only our arms and military experience. Only the most communistic ones are atheists otherwise they all vary in the degree of their Muslim faith . . .

'No, they're not all thieves here, Colonel, they've lived virtually on nothing for ten years now; their food is bullets, shells, rockets, mines, you name it . . .

'Yes, forty Katyushas were fired this week in my district. They even shot down a Mystère some days ago with a Shilka . . . no, the Israeli was killed before we could interrogate him. I think he deliberately steered his parachute into the flames from his attack rather than be captured. It's a shame, I'd love to have had him for a few days . . .

'Yes, the Mystère was partially recovered. I had the IFF

transponder sent to Moscow for inspection and we found a modification plate attached to the gun-sight. It's probably a dual-purpose sight now, for bomb laying as well as air-to-air combat.

'No, the body was too badly burned but we're having the teeth sent to the Pathology Lab in Alexandria to check his dental records. We'll probably be ready to broadcast his name and family background over Radio Moscow by the end of the week. We'll certainly transmit to their airpatrols next week from the Cairo transmitter . . .

'Yes, the Americans flew an RB57 over us yesterday—about 55,000 feet, I believe. We followed instructions and never had a go. They're going to get one hell of a shock soon when our new baby comes into service, eh? Any chance of having a few launchers up here? We'll blow the bastards out of the sky . . .

'No, the '15s' and '17s' are too slow at high altitude and we've not got the training right yet. The Israelis are too good. They're like the Palestinians, they use their brains. They caught three '17s' last week and it was over in four minutes flat. They're using Super Mystères for top cover and standard Mystères for ground attack now. The '19s' will set it right, I hope, but we've got to improve training or they'll carry on shooting us out of the sky every time . . .' There had been a pause and change of tone by the distant Colonel. Yeliskeiv had responded.

'Oh, I'm sorry, we weren't told. When was he posted out here? My, my, I thought he was a District Commander. What aircraft was he flying? A 19! What happened? . . . couldn't he turn onto the Israeli . . . no! Was it a Sidewinder? It must be a new version. Usually if he turns into the sun he can confuse it; the infra-red signal's too strong for the missile to discriminate so it chases the sun until it runs out of fuel.

'Who saw it happen? Oh. Any film record? I've made three requests this trip for ground-based combat cameras. I think we ought to fly a camera plane marked 'International Press' to record all the dog fights we keep losing, and then play them back to our pilots and the Arabs so they'll learn what to do right next time. By the way, when is his body going back to Russia? Next week, that's fast . . .'

A further pause had given Yeliskeiv a chance for a scratch, then . . . 'The Israelis are using high explosives on the fortifications now, followed by napalm once the cracks provide sufficient openings for the flames.

'The Golani unit lost twelve on the last raid, only the Commander survived long enough to hit the Mystère. The Israelis got him on the next run. I'd met him the first week here. He was a short, fat fellow, never thought he could do it. Amazing people, as I said, just like the Jews.'

The Russian's thoughts were interrupted by a gentle voice low down by his side.

'Excuse me, Captain Yeliskeiv.'

'Oh, Al Timimi, it's you, what's up, eh?'

'Forgive me, sir, but Comrade Al Fahed told me to ask your permission to speak to you about a private matter.'

'What's that then? Girl-friend trouble, eh?'

The boy's perplexed look almost embarrassed the forty-year-old Russian, so he adopted a more formal approach.

'Something serious, Al Timimi?'

'It is, sir. I'd like your permission to learn Russian.'

The Captain was amazed. No Arab had ever asked him for permission to learn Russian, although many attempts were being made to get them to use Russian military phraseology.

'Why, Al Timimi?'

'I believe that I must understand Russian to be able to fight better with Russian equipment and Russian advisers, sir.'

The Captain wondered at the boy's maturity and obvious intelligence. Here was a very special case.

'Admirable. Yes, quite admirable. I'll arrange for one of our interpreters to visit here and teach you himself. Well done, Al Timimi. I'm going to report this to my own Commander in Cairo so don't let me down, eh? This *is* a serious request?'

'Yes sir. I will try my best to understand your terms and intentions. It will be for the good of all Palestinians.'

The boy walked away briskly to join his comrades sitting round the other Russian, Captain Kerensky, who was about to show them how to blow up an Israeli Centurion tank with a cola bottle and two pounds of plastic explosive coloured to look like the dark brown liquid. A child simply stopped the tank by offering a few bottles to the tank commander who, taking the first real bottle, would then pass the next down to his crew inside. Within fifteen seconds all would be blown apart, inside the solid steel cauldron of the turret.

'You need not even take cover—unless you want to save yourself from being covered by bits of burning flesh,' Kerensky had said, grinning at his boys.

Captain Yeliskeiv left Golan a month later to report back to his Colonel in Cairo and to place on his desk a file, complete with photographs, on Shabir Al Timimi, the gifted young Palestinian.

'It's remarkable, I agree, Yeliskeiv. How's the language course progressing?'

'Well sir, his vocabulary has developed considerably and it seems clear he has a scientific mind as well as maturity beyond his years. He's a first-class sniper and competent with small explosive charges. I'd say he has the dexterity of a sixteen-year-old, rather than an eleven-year-old.'

'Right. I've brought in Captain Mendeleiv here from Dzershinsky Square who will study your report and work with you on a plan to utilise this boy to our best advantage. We must take the long view. A time will come—maybe in twenty years, who knows—when he will be of use to us. So I'll expect a planned proposal and programme from you both before you return next week. Thank you for bringing this matter to my attention.'

The three Russians stood up and exchanged salutes; then the two Captains walked out of Soviet Military Command Headquarters in Cairo, to travel to their base near Alexandria.

Their passage, like that of all Soviet military personnel

visiting the Headquarters in Cairo, was logged by the three major Western intelligence services and of course by Mossad, whose agent was at that moment busily engaged in trying to interest two Russian ensigns in the services of his 'cousins, nieces or nephews'. He was a familiar figure, squatting outside the compound and accosting the odd Russian soldier or prosperous-looking Egyptian; a typical Arab pimp of the 'nuisance variety' worth the occasional curse or a boot up the backside.

8
The Plan

Captain Mendeleiv of the KGB, the Committee for State Security, lay back on the bed in his office overlooking the Port of Alexandria and listened as his military counterpart, the stock, bald Captain Yeliskeiv, filled him in on Shabir Al Timimi.

'So that's what I propose, Mendeleiv. Let's groom him for possible leadership of Al Fatah after he's tried a few safer raids to gain experience and some sort of record. Meanwhile we'll programme him with Soviet thinking. We'll make him our man in Al Fatah, loyal to us even above his people.'

The young KGB man took time before replying. He brushed his blond hair back off his face and scratched his slim, aquiline nose. The two men were the extremes of Soviet military training. On the one hand was the overweight forty-year-old veteran, popular with his men and noted for his humanitarian approach; on the other, Mendeleiv, who had been trained in the new school set up by KGB officers in the Urals.

There, in a complete mock-up of the centre of Jerusalem, he had been taught Hebrew and Arabic, how to listen and observe, how to survive among Jews and Arabs, and lastly how to kill with minimum effort when necessary.

He had been a gifted schoolboy, like Shabir Al Timimi, and anxious to fight for his country against the threat of Western Imperialism. He was interested in the subject and agreed with the GRU man Yeliskeiv, but something kept flashing weakly in his mind like a distant beacon on a clear night in the mountains.

Suddenly he knew what it was. Yes, he had it. The key to Shabir's role. The most important and secret new project ever undertaken by the Soviet Union. He and a handful of selected officers knew only the vaguest outline. It was something to do with a place near the Caspian Sea. What was it called now? He had heard the name mentioned by a slightly drunken KGB General after a heavy celebration to mark his grandson's birth.

'Mark my words, gentlemen, you will hear it soon enough. We're going to surprise the entire bloody world soon. So save a little of this excellent vodka and put it away until you hear one day of a place called Baikonur.'

'Baikonur,' declared Mendeleiv.

'What is that?' asked the puzzled Yeliskeiv.

Mendeleiv immediately regretted his indiscretion. 'Oh, nothing, sorry. Forget it,' and he turned away to pour himself another drink of anis.

Yeliskeiv knew it was best not to pry too much, Mendeleiv was an odd bird.

'Oh, but what do you think of my proposal?' he said quickly, looking for safer ground.

'Excellent, Captain, excellent. Let's draft it right now, just as you propose. And to save you the bother of travelling back to Cairo, I'll deliver it to Colonel Kerensky myself the day after tomorrow.'

In spite of Yeliskeiv's slight suspicion of this offer they prepared their report, entitled 'Future of a Palestinian Guerilla', and typed it up next morning.

The two men parted at Alexandria's military airfield, the KGB man on an Ilyushin 14 back to Cairo and Yeliskeiv on the big Antonov transport back to Golan via Damascus, capital of Syria.

On 4 October of that year, 1957, Yeliskeiv suddenly remembered the name Baikonur when he read of the launch of the world's first artificial satellite by Vostok launcher from Baikonur cosmodrome near the Caspian Sea. But he still did not understand why Mendeleiv mentioned it in regard to Shabir Al Timimi.

By that time, however, the boy's future was being planned for him by the KGB Headquarters Staff in Dzershinsky Square, Moscow. The first thing they decided was to try to keep him alive. But it was necessary that he gained the respect of his fellow guerillas. There was only one way, he had to go on a raid.

It was easy enough to arrange, or so they thought. All raids had to be approved by a joint Palestinian and Soviet command, and the Russians fed appropriate data to influence their nature and timing.

It was well they did so for within two years Shabir Al Timimi was leading his own platoon on his first raid, accompanied by an eighteen-year-old Palestinian of considerable experience—he had survived four raids uninjured.

Their objective was an Israeli observation post recently established between Mount Hermon and Galilee, covering the supply road from Masadeh to Nafakk near the Jordan Valley. Eight Israelis were believed to be manning the post that week.

The party of eight guerillas had moved under cover of darkness along a previously reconnoitred approach route that gave them the best chance of cover in the event of star shells, which would expose them to bracketing by Israeli mortars.

Shabir was now just thirteen and respected by his platoon for his skill in night movement, sniping and explosives. All his colleagues were between sixteen and twenty—average for guerillas—and all were willing to die for their cause, so long as they killed Israelis.

Shabir carried the familiar AK with NSP-2 infra-red sight while his adviser, Al Azawi, carried an RPG-7V rocket launcher slung over his back. Another member of the team, an eighteen-year-old girl named Fatima, held an American-made Thompson sub-machine gun in case of close range combat and carried two HE projectiles in the standard canvas rucksack.

The remaining members carried standard AKs. Each had been supplied with 100 rounds of ammunition and rifle-fired flares to illuminate the target, plus hip-slung fragmentation hand-grenades for use against counter-attacking Israeli troops.

It took them four hours to cover the three-mile approach route, the white cloths on their backpacks helping to keep them together.

They had no radio as the Israelis were getting too good at locating them by DF techniques, even in the heat of an engagement.

Shabir led the way, crouching, as far as a man-sized lump of lava and signalled his party to fan out to provide enfilading fire.

Within minutes the post had been partially surrounded by a fire arc of two hundred degrees at a radius of two hundred yards.

Shabir placed his RPG in the clearest sighting position and as close as possible to the agreed withdrawal route, allowing for its weight and bulk restrictions during the withdrawal.

The night was completely clear, the stars forming an elaborate canopy overhead and providing sufficient light for the sniper scope to be effective.

The bulky sight on Shabir's AK-47 gave him a restricted but illuminated view of the target.

He loaded the first flare grenade quietly into the muzzle and sighted at the target. All he could see in the green imagery was a slight protuberance in the ground marking the sandbagged entrance to the post.

He looked at his watch. The luminous dial told him it was four minutes to H Hour.

He heard nothing from his comrades—a good sign—and felt his heart beating heavily in his chest and his palms sticky with sweat despite the cold night air.

Then something suddenly puzzled him: he could see an HF aerial sticking out from the post's position and as he turned up his infra-red sight he saw what appeared to be about a dozen ribbons radiating out from the aerial to a radius of about twelve foot. None of his previous briefings had told him of this obvious communications device. As he had insufficient data with which to modify his plan, he remained puzzled.

But it was now only twenty seconds to H Hour so he carefully brought up the weighted barrel and gathered in the target.

Again he felt the killing spasm, that delicious wave of excitement that washed over his back bristling his hairs like a breeze. He counted off the remaining seconds in his head and squeezed the trigger.

The grenade thudded into the night, followed a second later by an incredible cascade of white light as it struck something.

Precisely on cue the rest of the team opened up in sequence. The first HE rocket seared towards the target, exploding in a ball of flaming debris ripped apart by the dry crackle of automatic fire. The sensation of sheer destructive power nullified Shabir's fear as he switched to semi-automatic bursts that poured into the gaping mouth of the post. In a few moments, blown apart by a second round from the rocket launcher, it was unrecognisable. He thought he heard a low moaning, but it could have been his imagination. Slowly he started to run in a crouch towards the smoking pyre.

The rest of the team moved up cautiously, covering the target while the two flankers held their fire, their night sights aimed at the flames, ready to annihilate any survivors.

The return fire did not come and it was the big Palestinian who got there first. He tossed two grenades into the entrance and ran back for cover.

Two dull thumps shook the ground and everybody waited vainly for a long half-minute.

Still there was no response so Shabir threw two more grenades into a second, smaller hole and again hugged the ground for protection.

After a further echoing minute, he signalled for three of

his team to move forward and inspect while scanning the surrounding ground for an ambush patrol attracted by the son-et-lumière in the invisible hills. For the first time Shabir noticed he'd voided in his trousers. Like a child, he thought, and he almost savoured the hot wetness in the cool night.

He suddenly looked at the girl as she sprayed the site with her Thompson and saw her pause on seeing the tapes.

He saw her bend down, her slim body filling the overtight jeans, her adolescent figure silhouetted by the flames and Shabir instantly started to warn her not to touch them in case they were booby-trapped. He dived for cover as he screamed 'No, no, no . . .!'

They were!

There was a momentary whining as camouflaged mines sprang waist high, spinning at phenomenal speed before exploding a hypersonic expanding disc of steel razors that sighed into the horizon.

The girl fell in half, her torso neatly severed, the head and breasts toppling with a dull thud onto the collapsing legs. Shabir vomited.

A few seconds later there came the whine of a shell from somewhere to the south-west and suddenly a brilliant starburst blew the night apart.

Shabir lay bathed in the pure white light of burning magnesium flares, almost paralysed with fear and sticky at crutch and face—but alive.

Numbly he rose and began to work his way back before the Israeli gunners straddled what was obviously a carefully planned killing ground. His wide eyes noted a series of heavy lumps lying in neat piles around the post. All were dead. As he moved, shells glowed like meteorites as if they were coming from the stars themselves. Detonation after detonation ripped the rocks of Golan apart as he crouched each time for cover.

Somehow he did not stop moving, although he could feel neither the ground nor his legs beneath him. Within thirty seconds or so he was clear and running upright along the escape route. The image of the slaughter danced ahead of him as he broke into a sprint.

With a scream an armed figure emerged suddenly in his path and he knew he would be impaled on the man's bayonet. But it was one of his team, a flanker, who dropped his rifle in fright. He was as surprised as Shabir and both stared at each other for a moment before grabbing the gun and running away to the pre-arranged rendezvous point, two breathless miles to the north-east.

By four o'clock that morning three of them were standing by the camouflaged East German truck, dazed by the adventure.

They hardly spoke until Shabir said, 'OK, dawn is breaking, we must go. I'm certain the others were killed.'

Dejectedly they got into the truck, and the driver, an 'old' man of thirty, drove them back along the open hillside until they joined the road to Damascus.

Shabir sat uncomfortably in the corner by the tailgate, his incontinence no worse than that of the others. They'd get used to it, like growing up.

They turned off north and arrived at their supply camp at seven in the morning.

Nobody spoke until they had eaten; then Shabir again led the team as they were debriefed by their Palestinian Commander.

'The target was an ambush, sir, and it was booby-trapped. The Israelis set it up for us and we walked in,' Shabir said.

The Commander asked them for their independent reports, then hurried off to signal the news to Damascus.

Within hours, they knew about it in Moscow; and they knew it was time for them to act.

All camp commanders were notified of the Israeli booby-trap, namely an imitation HF aerial with false metallic tapes radiating from its centre connected to an anti-personnel minefield.

A number of these were observed, distributed around Israeli border posts soon afterwards; none was touched by the guerillas.

This was how the Israelis were able to lay a series of automatic listening posts along Israel's borders which would not be interfered with.

They had waited a month for the Golani guerilla units to observe the new target and prepared it accordingly. They had then broken the Palestinians' code and monitored the warning signal sent by Shabir's Commander.

It was Daniel Perès' idea. He always was a practical joker.

Shabir's next raid was a comparative success. Their target was a supply truck that had been observed along the road from Jerusalem to Haifa.

The road had been mined sporadically for many years and a number of people had been killed or crippled. As the mines were not discriminating, some were Arab villagers, but this was a price paid in the struggle, and the guerillas went on planting the mines.

The raid would be a risky operation: it would be in daylight when Israeli patrols could operate more effectively and call in air strikes against retreating groups.

This time Shabir played the part of an Arab boy, who would appear to be 'run over' by the truck thus appealing to the driver's conscience or that of the inevitable armoured car patrol that accompanied the truck everywhere it went.

This diversionary ploy would catch the patrol off-guard, and allow the surrounding 'sympathetic' Arab villagers to infiltrate the scene innocuously and place sticky plastic charges on each vehicle.

As the day came, Shabir felt the growing excitement, the quivering in his legs, the shortness of breath, the lightheadedness of the approaching killing. Fear was there, no doubt of it, but so also was another strange sensation, a feeling of pleasure.

The team passed through the Israeli checkpoint with comparative ease, their weapons already smuggled in ahead in the Arab donkey convoys of food for the markets in Jerusalem. The donkey inevitably grew 'lame' near the appropriate arms cache and was unloaded by local villagers, members of Al Fatah or sympathisers, ready for collection later that night.

By dusk the team had collected its weapons and then established an ambush position in the hills before nightfall.

Next day, at dawn, Shabir moved into the village and waited for the trucks. His compatriot, a girl of fifteen from Hebron, carried the two plastic charges. The Israelis were less likely to check a girl as thoroughly as a boy, all of whom were suspect.

The first sign of the truck was a column of dust climbing slowly up the steep hills forming the valley road to Jerusalem. Shabir remained inconspicuously sitting on the doorstep of the last house out of the village. The girl pretended to be playing alongside him and the two chattered on in as free a manner as they could muster.

Soon the truck appeared, but ahead of it came not one but two Israeli vehicles, one an armoured car, the other an open jeep complete with a 0.5-inch heavy machine gun on a steel mounting bracket.

Shabir could see the 'crowd scene' moving quietly out of the fields toward the village and waited for the truck to be almost on top of him. Then he clenched his fists, and ran away from his friend the Arab girl, straight into its path. It looked very nasty.

The boy timed it perfectly, apparently bouncing off the front offside wheel, screaming and landing in a heap on the road side.

The effect was immediate. The truck driver slammed on his brakes and jumped out. The two military vehicles came to a halt, the soldiers suspicious but primarily concerned for the boy.

The Commander, a young Lieutenant, jumped out of the jeep and ran to join the driver. All attention was focused on the victim.

Meanwhile the 'villagers' slowly infiltrated the scene and took up positions with good cover and field of fire.

The girl started crying and stood by the truck, shrugging

off all attempts to comfort her by the Israeli soldiers. They turned to the accident.

In a moment she had deftly placed a primed charge and detonator directly under the chassis above the fuel tank.

Moving 'haphazardly' to the armoured car, the girl pressed her remaining charge of soft, sticky plastic underneath the pronounced flare of the nearside front wheel arch.

Both charges had five minutes to run.

Slowly, Shabir got up in a daze and tottered groggily down the village street refusing all help.

The truck driver, obviously relieved that the boy appeared to be alright, climbed back into his cab, started up and moved jerkily forward.

The Israeli officer walked quickly back to his jeep and ushered everyone to their positions.

The convoy moved off as the 'villagers' took up firing positions ready for the charges to explode. The first charge went off early, blowing the back of the truck clean off in a ball of fire. This saved the driver's life; he remained shaken but uninjured in the cab section, which lay on its side in the road.

The jeep and the armoured car immediately spread out and, to Shabir's dismay, the three soldiers in the armoured car jumped out and ran for cover, knowing instinctively that an ambush meant rocket projectiles against which even tank armour was useless.

The jeep drove straight off the side of the road into cover behind a group of thorn bushes, its gunner hastily composing himself for returning fire.

At that instant the armoured car blew up, the entire vehicle rising a good ten feet off the road and landing on its side. Simultaneously the guerillas on the hills opened fire, followed by the 'villagers' a few hundred yards down the road.

The sound was deafening as shells and bullets ricocheted off the road. Then there came the heavy hammering of the jeep's machine gun as the remains of the truck and the armoured car crackled into flames.

Shabir saw one Israeli fall like a sack from the jeep and concentrated fire now struck the thorn bush, blowing it about like the wind. The surviving Israelis were laying down controlled fire towards the village.

Suddenly the man next to Shabir choked and fell forward, the top of his head blown clean off. Shabir pulled back into cover, watching fascinated as the bright red, oxygenated blood slowly spread fragments of glistening pink brain tissues in a sunburst of colour over the Arab's pure white abayah.

He moved to another corner and saw the three Israeli soldiers from the armoured car moving at a crouch towards the hill from which the Arabs were firing.

Having no weapon the boy could do little but observe the action, ready to warn his compatriots. This was as well, for suddenly he saw two tiny specks, coming out of the valley to his right, flying low in a circling approach to the village. They were almost certainly Israeli aircraft. The jeep commander had obviously called up an air strike.

With a scream and a desperate wave of his headdress, Shabir pointed towards the valley. One of the crouching Israelis turned and aimed at him from a range of three hundred yards or so. Little spurts of earth erupted a few feet ahead of him and he pulled back into cover as the bullets suddenly shattered the corners of the building above his head.

The burst ceased in a couple of seconds as the Israeli turned back to fire toward the hill. The guerillas were breaking cover and running now as the sound of the two jets boomed up the valley walls.

The Israelis responded to the open targets with a continuous volley of small arms fire directed at the hill, and the occasional burst toward the village.

The boy moved back cautiously to the dead guerilla and pulled the AK-47 out from under the heavy weight of the body. Slinging the rifle over his shoulder, Shabir moved back to the other corner and prepared to fire.

Checking his magazine and selector mechanism in one

deft movement he poked the muzzle round the splintered stones and brought his head into view. Taking quick aim at the three running Israelis he fired a burst of automatic fire and withdrew. No answering fire came so he changed position again, moving to the corner of a low wall overlooking the valley. He rose, the rifle along his cheek, and fired a full clip at the distant figures.

One fell flat on his face and started to slide back down the gravelly slope until he came to rest against a low bush. He did not move.

At that moment the top of the hill erupted under a massive burst of cannon fire as the lead aircraft opened fire on the exposed guerillas running down its far slope. But the jets were too fast and low for sustained accurate shooting and the entire guerilla team started to disperse down the village road and across the hills.

Shabir started to run, unable to prevent the manic grin that split his face and made his breath rasp through his teeth. He wasn't wet or sticky this time, he'd killed a Jew, he was triumphant, he was a man now—a man at thirteen.

The Israelis could do little to pursue the terrorists and immediately grouped to prepare for the remote possibility of a counter-attack. One of them reported to his officer that he had seen an Arab boy running down the road out of the village. He was too small and distant a target to hit with his UZI machine gun, however, but he was certain he was the same little bastard who had faked the accident.

The entire jeep crew was safe, including the gunner who had been ordered out as he was too exposed to the elevated firing positions of the guerillas. The crew had hidden in the shelter of a culvert running beside the thorn bush; the jeep, however, was a write-off. The concentrated fire had burst it open like an exploded tin can, and now it looked like a clown's car in a circus, its innards spewed out in every direction.

As the jeep's crew waited for the men from the armoured car to rejoin them, they heard a burst of expletives from the cab of the truck and a foot appeared from its upturned side window. Then two hands gripped the door frame and out came the tousled head of the truck driver, Yuri Dan, showering obscenities on all about him.

They helped him out of his awkward position and finally sat him on the edge of the cab. He was covered in olive oil from his shattered cargo, looking like a giant, blotchy sealion floundering on shore. Bits of vegetables were stuck to him like seaweed and he smelt awful. He had been carrying two thousand eggs, most of which appeared to be spread under the oil.

'All those bastards wanted to do was make me into the biggest fucking meatball you've ever seen!' he shouted, shrugging off the various comments of his grinning and relieved comrades.

But the grins stopped as they saw two of the armoured car crew struggling down the hill with the limp body of their driver.

They all ran to help and gently lifted the young soldier under his arms keeping the body as level as possible. When they reached the road again they placed him gently on the dirt. He was quite dead.

The whole of his right side and shoulder had received at least half a dozen rounds of high velocity ammunition and was a mess of ruined flesh. He was eighteen years old and this had been his first action, having only recently emigrated from Italy.

'Poor Pietro. Poor little sod,' said Yuri Dan.

'Yes, and the guy who shot him must have been at least four years younger. He was that fucking kid. You should have driven over him, Yuri, and squashed the bastard flat. Dirty bloody Arabs. Even using kids. Never again. Next time run the bastards over, don't stop.'

It was the armoured car's sergeant, a veteran of the Sinai campaign and many years with the Haganah. Suddenly, the memory of a day long ago when he was a child in Jerusalem came back to him; a momentary scene, the weight of the revolver as he placed it against the English Colonel's neck and squeezed the trigger . . .

At that moment the jets roared over, rocking their wings and entering a circular run directly overhead. The sound drowned the image.

'Shit, I forgot about them. Anybody got a radio still working?' It was the jeep's officer.

'Yes, in the armoured car. I called up the air strike, sir, sorry. I didn't have time to get permission. It was a feeling I had when we entered the village. I could have been wrong. As it was we were lucky.'

The sergeant had noticed the villagers coming from the fields. At that time of the morning the men would still be at the cafe, only the women would normally have been out. Also, there were simply too many of them.

'OK, Sergeant, you were right, but next time try telling me about your feelings, eh? Who knows, I might have been calling one also and we'd look bloody fools with a squadron of Mystères circling round one bloody little supply truck.

'Check the radio is still working and send off an all clear signal with thanks. If not, report back.'

The radio did not work so they spread out in a line and waved hands down crossing their chests as the jets came over again.

The leader waggled again and broke away from the circle followed by his wingman, relieved that he could get back to refuel at his home field.

'Lucky bastards, all they do is fart around the sky like a couple of fairies, press a little red tit and blow up a fucking mountain, bless 'em. Now which one of you is going to find an honest truck driver some nice soap and water so that he can return to his dear wife and kids in time for an evening of conjugal bliss, eh?'

Yuri Dan did not get his bath until very late that evening, after they had wrapped up young Pietro Farnese in a plastic body bag and put it in the relief armoured personnel carrier that arrived three blistering hours later. And the interrogation of the villagers was pointless also—nobody had seen anything. They put the dead guerilla in another body bag and the Arab and Jew rested against each other in permanent isolation until they were placed in two adjoining refrigerated drawers in the morgue at Jerusalem's Military Hospital.

Pietro was collected by his parents and buried in the Jewish Cemetery in Florence. The Arab was never identified by Israel but Al Fatah knew he was Aziz Al Azawi, age twenty, from the Old City of Jerusalem. It was his sixth raid.

9
Olga

Nearly two hundred miles east of Moscow and near the boundary of Moscow and Volga Military Districts was a village of 4,200 inhabitants; a small community, tightly knit together by common purpose and outlook. The village had a central square, shops of a kind, a cinema, a clinic-cum-social centre, and air-conditioned accommodation for all. It was self-sufficient and, indeed, virtually independent of the capital. It was also unaffected by the weather, for the village of Arzamaska was 480 feet under granite that was a billion years old, and thus isolated not only from the vagaries of Russian winters but, more particularly, from 'Blast, Heat and Radiation'.

Its people worked for the First Directorate of the KGB—Foreign Operations. It was linked by landline with the Personnel Directorate in Moscow on whom it depended for raw data and standby processing power.

The 'villagers' of Arzamaska were essentially a simple folk: they all did one job and they did it as well as they could, twenty-four hours a day throughout the year.

They remembered people.

They remembered people of every kind, of every race and creed. They remembered their lifestyles, their hobbies, their medical histories. They remembered their ages, their physiques. No matter what their identity cards, passports, birth certificates, employers' references or examination papers might say they all came under one group classification—'Politico-military subversives'.

Arzamaska was the world capital of terrorism.

Here was the well into which the masters of the First Directorate dipped their cups to draw on fresh supplies of reliable disciples who could be counted on to spread the word —by deeds.

Here was listed every known 'peoples' liberator', freedom fighter, guerilla, and commando from every operational area of interest to the KGB.

Its data bank in the central square swept the alphabet of nations from Afghanistan to Zambia and unerringly came up with the finest sniper, the cleverest saboteur, the quietest assassin, all available for use by the local branch or residence.

Here was stored the name and description of Aziz Al Azawi and, twenty-four hours after he ceased to be a terrorist, so was he shifted, electronically speaking, out of the 'Dynamic' to the 'Static' data bank, ready for further use. Nobody, alive or dead, was wasted; nobody was forgotten once they had been registered in the village records.

Theoretically speaking, three billion individuals—the world's entire population—could be 'stored' in a room thirty feet square.

And it was here in the supermind of 'Olga', as the bank was affectionately known, that Al Azawi's fellow commando, Shabir Al Timimi, had his destiny shaped. Not by an individual or a committee, subject to the whims and fancies of humanity, but by a wall of integrated circuits, the best that KGB money could buy.

Olga was efficient, ideally suited to her purpose. Her chassis was made in Cracow and her software from a variety of sources, as far afield as Sunnyvale and Osaka, for like her subject matter she had international origins. She respected no borders, boundaries, cease-fire lines, declarations or disputes. For five more years 'Olga' stored Shabir Al Timimi's data as the humans supplied it and gradually assembled a picture, a 'scenario'.

She noted his growing weight, his height, his stature. She

even reminded her operator when to congratulate Shabir, for of course she could never forget his birthday. She recorded his increasing achievements in sniping, sabotage and unarmed combat, and his developing skills in language, political theory and science at the PLO school in Beirut.

She noted his strong Muslim belief and now and then received fresh insights into his character. His determination to succeed, on a raid, at a rally, in a dispute with a visiting East German journalist.

Under 'Political Development' she noted the twin belief in Marxist principles intricately interwoven with his interpretation of the Koran. 'A potential stresspoint here, something to keep an eye on', thought her operator as he underlined it in red ink on the teleprinter facsimile.

Then one day she made a bold statement. Her operator almost let out a whoop of delight when he read it on the monthly print-out. The machine had come to the same conclusion that he had in 1957. But Olga had taken five long years where he had taken days. Whoever said machines will replace men was wrong, he thought as he copied the facsimile.

A—SUBJECT	: AL TIMIMI, SHABIR MOHAMMED
B—DATE OF BIRTH	: 8-11-47
C—REFERENCE	: TPPLO 1392-7A-'DYNAMIC'
D—STATUS	: ACTIVE UNDER TRAINING
E—RECOMMENDATION	: NOW SUITABLE FOR ADVANCED TRAINING IN LINGUISTICS, COMPUTER SCIENCES, MATHEMATICS OR SIMILAR SCIENCE—BASED SUBJECT: GOOD SUBJECT FOR SCIENTIFIC/ DYNAMIC SCENARIO:

F—POSSIBLE ROLES	: 1) PILOT 2) TANK OFFICER 3) DESTROYER OFFICER 4) INTELLIGENCE OFFICER 5) SUBMARINE OFFICER 6) INFILTRATOR—MILITARY 7) SUBVERSIVE—POLITICAL
G—PSYCHOLOGICAL PHENOMENA	: SUBJECT SHOWS AGGRESSIVE BEHAVIOUR IN STRESSFUL SCENARIOS WITH STRONG ROLE IDENTIFICATION: EVIDENCE OF SADO-SEXUAL RESPONSE WITH PRONOUNCED HOSTILITY SET. SUBJECT DISPLAYS CONSISTENT ALLEGIANCE TO SUPERIOR COMMAND STRUCTURE WITH MINIMUM DIVERGENCE . . .'

And so he read on, the high speed typewriter chattering away at him in his individual cell. Nearly twenty years with the Centre still left him uneasy, the back of his neck conscious of the unsleeping eye of the video camera recording his presence and enquiries. Olga watched everybody she talked to, and never forgot a face.

The operator knew that fact better than anybody; he had helped create her, when fresh out of training school. He had conceived the need for a machine like Olga, had submitted his proposals, had seen them accepted with quizzical regard by his superior officers in 'The First' and now was reaping the rewards of his efforts.

He stood up, switched off his terminal, and exited by the heavy steel door marked: 'Director's Terminal Only—Strictly No Admittance—Security Protection—Lethal'. As his limousine emerged from the simulated barn in a field half a mile from the rocks of Arzamaska, the Russian closed his eyes, relishing the plan that would fulfil another of his growing ambitions.

'Where to, Colonel?' his driver asked, leaning back to catch the reply above the din of the accelerating vehicle.

There was a pause before he answered.

'Tyuratam, Baikonur Cosmodrome.'

'With respect, Colonel, that will take us at least two days.'

'We have years, Petrov, years.'

And the driver stared ahead, silently cursing the man he served and feared, above all others in the KGB.

•

The Aeroflot TU-104 from Damascus landed at Moscow's Domodedovo Airport at 8.12 in the evening.

The young man walked self-consciously towards the customs and immigration point; he was familiar with the Russian accents he heard around him, but had a curious feeling that something was different. They were more relaxed of course. The first immigration officer, in a baggy blue suit with black shiny gunbelt, asked for his passport in Russian. The young man was confused for a moment but long enough to hear the second immigration officer say quite clearly:

'Bloody incredible, he knows how to wear a suit, eh? Normally come in pyjamas from there.'

The first grinned slightly and asked again, 'Passport.'

In deliberately broken Russian the man fumbled for his necessary documents and maintained the performance until all his papers appeared to be in order.

The second one stamped his 'new' passport, issued in the

name of Sadi Al Azawi, and said clearly in Russian, 'Go suck yourself', much to his comrade's amusement.

Shabir replaced the documents in the heavy overcoat he had put on before disembarking, smiled at the two customs officers and walked over to the nearest Soviet police officer he could see, addressing him loudly and in near-perfect Russian:

'Lieutenant, may I request your assistance in charging those two mindless oafs called immigration officers, with gross abuse to an invited guest of the Soviet Government's State Tourist Bureau.

'Furthermore I will point out that as a citizen of Lebanon my country enjoys excellent relations with yours. Those relations will be endangered until these two gorillas here immediately apologise for their extremely hostile and inaccurate description of my country's customs of dress and address.'

The Lieutenant was amazed, and so were the two men, their grins long vanished at the sound of the competent verbal onslaught launched by a very fit looking young man less than half their ages.

'Finally, I will advise you that unless these men get down on one knee, which is the custom of supplication in my country, then I will knock their stupid teeth out into the dirt where they are obviously more at home.'

The loud protest had stopped a number of people in transit and brought over two policemen, who stopped on seeing the Lieutenant's wink aimed obviously at them.

'You two gorillas, I am reporting your behaviour to your superior who will know exactly how to deal with you. Meanwhile, as this young man is an honoured guest of our State, I suggest you accord him the custom *his* State would require. Unless you wish to be charged with causing a Diplomatic Incident.'

The two nervously exchanged glances and shakily bent a knee whilst muttering mumbled apologies to the Palestinian.

Without a further backward glance, the young man thanked the Lieutenant and walked with dignity out of the

6

immigration hall, and directly to the men's toilet, straight out again via a door marked Store, through the store and out into a yard where the big black Zil was waiting for him, exactly as drawn on the map in his jacket pocket. He was driven straight to a KGB-run students' hostel in suburban Moscow.

The following day Shabir Al Timimi enrolled under the name of Fayez Mahmoud in Moscow's vast State University; he was one of its youngest-ever students. He became pupil DZ 98349 in the Faculty of Engineering where he embarked on a systems engineering course with specialist classes in electronics and astrophysics, thereby firmly placing himself also on the road to Tyuratam, exactly as his 'operator' had hoped.

10
Colorado Springs

'Michael, Michael, you can't stop now, for God's sake . . . oh . . . oh . . . oh . . . my God . . . oh . . . oh . . . oh . . . Oh . . . Oh . . . Oh . . . Wow . . . oh, my . . . mmmmmm Oh, you bastard, you lovely bastard.'

She kissed him sloppily as she felt him relax his weight onto her and squeezed his buttocks so that their pelvic bones pressed together.

God, she adored the fellow she thought as she lay back looking at his smooth, strong face and wavy dark brown hair. What a boy, and me two years older too. Who would have thought at nineteen that I, Jennifer Selway, would have fallen for a guy two years younger than me. Still, he's leaving school soon. Oh, shit!

She suddenly thought. He's going all the way to Colorado for goodness sake to that damned macho pile in the middle of the goddam desert. Oh, I must stop swearing, I know he doesn't like it.

'Michael.'

'Yes, Jenny.'

'Was it good, uh?'

'Beautiful, baby, fantastic.'

'Mmmmm, you were good, good, good, ummmmm, oh, oh.'

'Hold on Jenny, just wait a bit, I'll be right back, wait there.'

'Well, where the hell else am I going, for gosh sakes?'

'Just hang in there baby.'

Michael slid out gently from the beautiful warm body of his Uncle John's secretary.

Wiping himself dry on a paper tissue he slid off the bed and made his way downstairs to the hallway.

There were two letters, one from his college and the other marked United States Air Force Academy, Colorado Springs. The second envelope was thick and therefore promising; thin ones only said 'no'. He rushed up the stairs, to enjoy the freedom of being alone at last in his Uncle's house with Jenny.

He came in the room and found her spread-eagled lying on her stomach winking at him over her right shoulder.

'Let's try it this way, Mike, eh? S'beautiful, I promise.'

'Hang on baby, here I's a comin'!'

He dived for the bed, landing between her legs but with his arms keeping his weight off her. She giggled excitedly.

'Wait a minute, now wait a minute.'

Within half a minute he was deep inside her, moving gently while he slowly opened the important envelope.

'For God's sake, Michael, am I just a sex object to you? What're you doing?'

'Opening up the future honey; it's the letter.'

'Oh no. That's you well and truly hooked, eh?'

'Wait. You do the moving, I'll do the reading. Mmmmm, that's nice . . .'

So it was that Michael Allon, gifted son of Kibbutz Ramta, read the news of his acceptance into the United States Air Force Academy at Colorado Springs for the class of 1965. Jenny thought of that day as the start of the end of her first love affair. Michael thought it was the beginning of his life. At last he was going to fly.

'Gentlemen. As cadet officers you will be trained first and obtain primary flying experience on the Cessna 172; then, subject to inspection, you will fly the T37 trainer, also made by Cessna.

'You will then progress to the T38, the Air Force's twin jet trainer, in which you will learn how to handle a supersonic aircraft. Now, the Northrop people over at Hazeltine built a really fine plane here. It's so slick it'll drop through the sky like greased lightning, so don't scratch your ass too long or you'll spread yourself sunnyside up over the desert.

'The one you've got to master first is this little fellow, he's the 172 made by our old buddies in Kansas. They don't pay me so I'm not going to tell you what a strong, easy critter this is to fly, but it is.

'He's got good flying characteristics when you need them, and a few funny ones to keep you on your toes . . .'

The Air Force instructor went through the same patter every year to every new class but they all felt they were the first. Colonel James McConnell was retired from first-line flying; during his career he had flown P51 Mustangs on long range escort raids into Germany where he had downed two Messerschmidt BF109-Gs and a Focke-Wolfe 190, and been shot down in turn by an ME262—the Luftwaffe's first jet fighter and the world's first operational jet aircraft.

He was embarrassingly kitsch, an obsolescent character out of a Hollywood movie with credits such as:

'This story is dedicated to the men of the United States Army Air Force, on active duty, somewhere in Europe.'

The Cadets called him 'Jimmy Mac', and some of them liked him. Michael brushed with him the first week of his course.

Michael climbed smoothly into the T38 as it stood parked in the hangar. He nestled into the little grey pan of steel and cushioned black plastic until he felt the ejector seat taut and snug around him.

Without his bone dome he had plenty of headroom and felt unrestricted by the beautifully tailored form of the enormous plexiglass canopy that rose above his head.

His hands deliberately rested in his lap as he closed his eyes, then opened them to absorb the magic of the plane. Before him lay the tiny panel of instruments, all logically laid out in groups so that his hand would not move too far or work too hard when he needed speed to save his life.

On his left and his right, parallel with his forearms and the horizon, lay clusters of switches including the throttles for the twin turbojets.

Directly in front of him were the flight instruments, radio switches, gyro compass and, like a crude slab of glass, the gunsight, fitted here for air-to-air gunnery training.

Down at his feet lay the rudder pedals: push left, rudder goes left, aircraft swings left, and vice versa.

Right in front of his crotch lay the most important device of all, the control column, the big, knobbly, black plastic switch, gimballed at the base; when pulled back the column would raise the nose of the aircraft and, if he had the power, the plane would climb like a rocket on rails in a beautiful curve to eight miles above the earth. Just a gentle pull, never force it, like a woman.

If he did not have the power, like a car in too high a gear, it would get mushy until finally a stall warning horn would buzz out its strident alarm in his ear and he would know he had to push the nose down to buy more airspeed.

The beautiful thing was that if you let the bird fly herself she would tuck her nose down, gain airspeed and glide, as long as he had trimmed her correctly.

And rolling: he would just nudge the same stick over to left or right and over she would go, a full circle in a blink of an eye.

'What the hell do you think you're doing, cadet?'

Michael literally jumped an inch out of the seat as the voice, focused by the curved canopy and echoed by the hangar building burst his day-dreams apart.

'Uh, sir? Nothing, sir. Sorry, sir.'

'Get out of that aircraft only when I tell you cadet, but don't move an inch or you'll be dead, got it.'

'Yes, sir.'

'Good, now don't move a muscle.'

Jimmy Mac's head appeared over the edge of the canopy side rail and a big hand followed it carrying a long steel pin with a little red flag.

Carefully the officer slid the safety pin into its hole thus making safe the ejector seat mechanism.

'Now, Cadet Officer Allon, you may slowly vacate your seat without touching any switches.'

'Yes, sir.'

The young man climbed unsteadily down the access ladder and skipped lightly to the floor where he stood rigidly to attention by the veteran flyer.

'Allon, if you ever live long enough to have the privilege of learning the dangerous art of flying from me or any other unfortunate instructor, then the first thing you must never, never do is climb into an aircraft, A, without permission, and B, without checking that all safety pins are safely stowed.'

'Yes, sir.'

'Good, now tell me what were you musing on as you sat in the lotus position in Mr Northrop's little baby.'

'I was just sitting, sir, just feeling the cockpit, sir.'

'Feel women, feel yourself, but don't ever feel a cockpit, OK? It's for working in. It's your office, right?'

'Yes, sir.'

'Now, tell me what you know about this aircraft, Cadet Officer Allon.'

'It's a Northrop T38, sir, twin jet aircraft for advanced training, sir.'

'And how well does it perform?'

'838 miles an hour, sir, at 36,000 feet; rate of climb is 32,500 feet per minute with 50% fuel; dry thrust is 5,000 pounds total . . .'

'OK, OK, Allon. No prizes here. Now, why do you want to fly it?'

'I've always wanted to be a pilot, sir.'

'Since when?'

And of course Michael knew when: the day he saw the Israeli die in the flames at Golan.

'Since I saw some flyers.'

'Where was that?'

'Golan, sir.'

'Where?'

'The Golan Heights, sir. In Israel, or on the borders, sir.'

'What happened?'

'I saw three Mystères attacking a Syrian artillery position. They destroyed it but one Mystère was hit. The pilot ejected and parachuted into the flames. The two guys with him just flew round and round afterwards. Then they flew away.'

The description reminded McConnell of a similar event he had seen in Korea.

He had been flying with three other F86s again in a combined air-ground strike. They were trying to protect a platoon of Marines who had been surrounded by a battalion of North Korean regular troops. The thing went on until just one guy remained; they could see him waving at them as they flew over, each aircraft carefully separated so as to keep up a constant barrage around the target in spite of the heavy small-arms fire.

The survivor was obviously terrified and the nearest Koreans were only about two hundred feet from him. Finally the planes ran out of ammunition; they kept flying low enough to suck in dirt and the smoke from their strikes but they were helpless, and then the third pilot, a quiet Texan, came in very low as the Koreans reached the Marine.

The Texan hit the hill at five hundred knots and spewed a huge ball of screaming, burning metal and fuel all over those Korean mothers. Must have killed a hundred at least.

The Air Force gave the Texan a medal and they had named a shopping precinct after him.

McConnell felt he would like Allon.

'OK, Allon, I get the story. You saw one guy get zapped so you have a death wish. Now understand this: with me you have only one motivation, a life wish, OK? There's no glory in being spread over the ground like peanut butter. It looks ugly and it's rarely necessary. You can outperform anybody so long as you keep training and you do one thing. *Think*. Use that brain, don't perform aerobatics until you have to lose sky or energy to save your life. When you're flying combat air patrol keep high, always; height is energy, always use the sun, it's your friend. Fly out of it when you're attacking; look around it till your eyeballs fizzle and fly into it if you've a missile chasing your tail.

'Your neck is for twisting, your eyeballs are for swivelling, your hand is for controlling and your feet for pushing but most of all, your brain is for thinking.

'Remember, even IBM doesn't make a brain as good as yours, and the Russkies sure can't beat IBM, so don't get all worked up about electronics and radar fire control. Those are the last things you need to finish the job. The first is what God, who was one of the all-time great flyers, put on your shoulders, OK?'

'Yes, sir.'

'Now, tomorrow we're going to commence flying training and I'm going to make you into the best, OK? I know why you Jewish fellows want to fly, just to shoot down A-rabs and Russkies, but over here you're going to be trained to do one thing, fly, and only the US Government is going to tell you who they want shot down, bombed, strafed or snapped, got that?'

'Yes, sir.'

'Good. See me at 07.30hrs with the rest of your circus at the flight briefing room. Dismissed.'

'Sir.'

Michael could feel the backs of his eyes twitching. He had never felt so excited in his life before.

Michael Allon flew so damn well that within eighteen months he was asked to fly regularly with the Commanding Officer of the Academy.

The 'Old Man', as he was known, enjoyed the experience of talent such as Michael's. Michael had what could best be described as 'perfect co-ordination'. The closest the General had come to it before was on a rare visit to England when, much to his annoyance, his wife had obtained two tickets for a performance by Yehudi Menuhin of Brahms' Violin Concerto.

What started as a 'bit of a damned nuisance', dressing up and all that 'junk', ended with him spellbound, the tears brimming over his eyes and a memory he would treasure to the end of his life.

It was Michael's perfect co-ordination that saved both their lives a week before the final passing-out ceremony before they were assigned their squadrons.

They had taken off at 08.30hrs on a one-hour air patrol and simulated combat sortie; Michael was scheduled to fly against experienced instructors.

The first target co-ordinates were fed to Michael by the Fighter Director and he climbed on a stern chase course that would bring him out onto the tail of the target, an Air Force F4 Phantom flying at 40,000 feet.

The target appeared high and to their right as Michael climbed up using the sun and the blind spot of the big fighter. But the Phantom was being flown by a first-class ANG Instructor who kept weaving and bobbing to maintain rear surveillance.

Michael could not avoid being seen, and the fighter turned on afterburners and entered into a high-speed diving turn before attempting to come up behind his assailant.

Michael immediately rolled onto his back and pulled a beautifully co-ordinated 6G turn that put him perfectly on the inside of the Phantom's radius with sufficient 'lead' and height to keep an energy advantage over the much more powerful jet.

The Phantom saw him, however, and rolled back again, spiralling down to the deck for safety, using his power and weight to gain airspeed. Michael followed, the manoeuvrability of his light fighter enabling him to cut corners and counter the power difference.

The desert was coming up closer and closer now as the Phantom pulled out of its dive and shot up in a vertical rolling climb to bring it into a head-on, snap-shot collision course. Michael broke instantly into a vertical dive knowing that the Phantom would try to track him down but would have the disadvantage of greater weight and inertia.

He rolled the T38 through 180°, approached the deck at 800 knots pulling 8G until he shot up in a perfect slingshot manoeuvre that bought him all the energy he needed and there he was, slap on the tail of the still turning, diving Phantom.

At three hundred yards the target filled his sight totally as he fired the camera gun, the Phantom desperately twisting to evade what in real combat would have been certain destruction.

'Phantom, spotted,' Michael announced crisply. He'd 'shot' him down. It had taken two minutes. The F4 pilot rocked his wings and climbed; he was dead and knew it.

It was a great moment in Michael's life. He had been pitted against an experienced Phantom jockey, a man with 1,200 hours of flying F4s around the sky, and here was Michael, a student jet pilot, accomplishing a feat only squadron pilots achieved after many hours of training.

Michael felt the thrill wash over him, conscious of his CO just three cramped feet behind him, remembering his growing ambition in Israel and his daydreams in New Jersey. Now the dream had become reality.

He was a pilot, a fighter pilot, this was only the beginning. He wished Liza was there, down in the desert, waving up at him.

His thoughts lasted a second or two before he lifted the long, elegant nose and pointed the T38 towards the safe blue skies of Arizona. That's when he nearly died.

There was an almighty 'bang' and Michael's vizor turned red with blood. Fantastically he thought his brains had exploded, that his eyes were registering the last, dying vision of life. He heard an excruciating screaming in his ears and instinctively brought up one gloved hand to wipe away the redness. He stared around him in disbelief through the smeared vizor—the canopy had gone. All that remained was the splintered front windscreen and the jagged fringe of perspex embedded in the framing.

The cockpit was a horror. It was covered in blood and gore —and feathers.

'We have a birdstrike, sir,' Michael snapped over the intercom. 'Report your status. Over.'

There was a pause before a weak voice came back, '. . .

Think I'm OK, can't see anything, think it's blood.'

'Just wipe your vizor, sir. It worked for me.'

Another pause, then:

'No good, Allon, my vizor was up when it happened . . .' and Michael felt the implication of that remark sear through his head. He licked his bone-dry lips.

'No sweat, sir, I have control, we'll clean you up soon as we're down . . .'

But at that instant the plane lurched, then started to roll. Michael immediately corrected it whilst his eyes scanned the instruments. They told him he was losing power on both engines as well as airspeed. He automatically corrected with a push on the stick to put the nose down, and checked his fuel status. He had more than enough, enough to burn.

Almost simultaneously the engines flamed out and the fire warning lights came on. He throttled back and punched the extinguisher buttons. The lights kept on glowing red. He was burning.

'We have a fire in both engines,' he said. 'Prepare for ejection,' as he initiated the emergency procedure to inform the Flight Director at the airfield.

'May Day, May Day, May Day. This is T Bird Five Nine Five, at height one nine zero, course two seven nine, estimated position ten miles due west of Luke Field, Runway two seven zero. Do you read, over?'

'T Bird Five Nine Five, this is Luke Field. We read you strength five. We have you on radar. Your position is ten miles due west of the Field. You are clear for a straight-in approach. Please state your damage and fuel condition. Over.'

'Colorado Field this is T Bird Five Nine Five. We have a birdstrike and double engine failure. Our windshield is obscured. Passenger is blinded. Will attempt to eject, please confirm our position. Over.'

'T Bird, this is Luke Field. We confirm your position at nine miles due west of Runway Two Seven. We are ordering out search aircraft. We confirm ejector message understood. Understand your crew is CO, Colorado Springs.'

'Luke Field, affirmative. CO preparing to eject. Over.'

The aircraft was now starting to buffet alarmingly as the airflow broke up over the shattered canopy and the damaged intakes.

The engine-bay fire warning lights still glowed, and soon Michael could see through his single rear-view mirror black smoke trailing behind them. The plane was going to burn, then it would explode.

'Pilot, this is number two, I'm ready to eject. Over.'

'Number Two, eject on the count of three, now. One, Two, Three . . .'

But there was nothing! The passenger's seat had failed to fire.

Michael instantly stopped his ejection sequence and spoke calmly to the CO.

'Number Two, I understand the seat has failed, check your parachute again and prepare for me to tip you out, do you understand? Over.'

'Affirmative, I'm preparing now.'

The aircraft started to oscillate wildly as parts of the tail-pipe broke off and the entire swivelling tail surface started to flap alarmingly.

'Hold it, Number Two. Are you ready to go as I roll?'

'Affirmative. Let her roll, Number One. Good luck.'

With the stick and rudder pedals shaking crazily, Michael Allon rolled the bucking, crippled machine onto its back and saw the CO fall out cleanly from the empty ejector seat. He didn't have time to watch for a 'chute.

'Luke Field, This is T Bird Five Nine Five. Number Two crew is out, altitude one five zero. Am leaving myself. Over and Out.'

'T Bird. Good luck. Over and Out.'

Slowly Michael pushed the stick over to the left, no response, then the right, still no response.

The controls were useless.

The flames enveloped the entire tail section now and would reach the fuel tank in seconds.

Michael pulled the yellow and black ejector seat handle—

and shot out straight down towards the desert below.

He was numb with the shock and speed of it, then still unable to breathe, he felt his tumbling stop as the drogue chute arrested the spinning seat. There was a massive bang as the main chute opened, pulling him sharply away, leaving the seat to plummet on its own tiny 'chute down to the desert floor.

The sky and desert spun crazily around him, then steadied as the canopy filled. He might just do it. The desert screamed up towards him like a great wall of rock, then almost stopped. He was floating. He'd made it by a good three hundred feet.

Glancing briefly to the horizon, Michael watched fascinated as the T38 arced over for another second before suddenly exploding in a huge ball of glistening fire and black smoke releasing a shower of debris into the sky, fluttering down like a giant cloud of metallic confetti. He had another hundred feet to go, he looked back in the other direction and could see a small white parachute in the distance heading for the desert.

For an instant the image of the Israeli pilot floating down into his own funeral pyre came to him.

The incredible shrieking of the wind had ceased and he was alive and floating not into black smoke but onto the hot, baking desert of Arizona. He hit the hard ground and rolled over breathlessly.

The silence was exquisite, but it only lasted a few seconds because there was the Phantom, his 'victim', screaming over in a high-G turn, watching his fallen adversary. He circled the way they did that day in Golan. Michael unclipped his harness, drew up his aching legs and put his domed head between his knees. He felt he was going to faint.

Within ten minutes, two 'search and rescue' helicopters were roaring overhead, checking for safe ground before alighting in the firm sand beside the two isolated figures.

Michael stood up slowly and started to roll up his parachute and with the help of the winchman made it into a bundle which he stuffed into a locker in the 'Huey's' cabin.

The two helicopters took off in a clattering whine in near unison and made their dipping, noisy way back to the field.

'How's the CO?' Michael shouted to the winchman as he lay firmly strapped into the pannier.

The masked man didn't know.

They flew on. The Field was ten long minutes away before the two Bell helicopters slapped the air over the emergency medical unit.

Michael refused to be carried and walked groggily out onto the blinding white concrete apron.

The other stretcher was out of the helicopter in a few seconds, fussed over by three medics. It disappeared through the flapping grey doors. The body was spattered in blood.

They gave Michael an empty ward and pumped him asleep.

For twelve hours he flew into wall after wall of blood and granite, he floated in clouds of silver confetti and choked in palls of black, oily smoke.

All the time his body kept falling towards the pyre, his pyre, his own funeral pyre. He twisted and screamed, desperately contorting himself in repeated attempts to avoid the globs of liquid flame. Each time he succeeded he would start to fall again.

When he woke up it was the evening of the following day.

He'd lost five pounds in weight. The bed was damp with his own sweat. He felt as weak as an infant.

'. . . How is he?' Michael asked of the CO.

'He's OK,' the male nurse replied.

'Alive?'

'Yup. He made it.'

'Can I see him?'

'No. It's too early.'

'Oh.'

'He's lost both eyes though . . . broke his legs too, in the fall. He'll live. He checked on you soon as he woke up from the operation.'

Michael felt relief and sadness at the same time.

'He wants to thank you, when he's ready.'

And Michael closed his eyes and started to float again.

Lt Michael Allon was awarded the Air Force Medal in recognition of his outstanding airmanship and quality of leadership. He graduated top of his class and was posted to the Operational Conversion Unit for combat training on the same type of fighter that he had shot down, the big F4E Phantom.

If the T38 had been about flying, the Phantom was about war—future war, total war, the Third World War. The aircraft was an airborne tank but travelling at fifty times the speed and five times the distance, carrying sufficient firepower to sink a battleship or, in its nuclear role, to wipe out a small city.

The Phantom created many new experiences for Michael: thundering power with breathtaking acceleration; sustained, tortuous, high-G manoeuvring that required him to wear an extraordinary water-filled corset to squeeze his blood back to his emptying brain; air-to-air refuelling in cloud and at night that soaked pounds off him in sweating concentration; violent take-offs on full afterburners through eerie tunnels of dusky fog; emergency arrests that slammed him into his harness till he felt he would burst through in a nightmare extrusion of arms and legs; and sunbursting zoom climbs that flung him towards the infinity of space until, for one glorious pause, he hung utterly weightless nearly twenty miles high on the peak of an invisible parabola.

And to find his way through this new world he had to understand a new language of symbols and mnemonics like Big Wham, CAP, Stab-Aug, RAT, INAS; an entire dictionary that welded him and his WSO—his weapons system operator—into a team, totally enveloped in their twenty-ton, drab green cocoon.

The strange electro-mechanical creature that was the Phantom possessed one giant 'eye' staring ahead under a massive, drooping nose, searching for invisible targets, night and day, in every weather that its human crew had ever avoided before. The Phantom killed things with an awesome array of weapons that streaked for miles under the radar 'eye' through rain and pitch-blackness, finally to blow up in a fantastic detonation of blast, fire and shredding steel rods. And when it was clear it launched long white heat-seeking tubes that snaked crazily through the sky, hunting for glowing jet pipes and then blowing out the innards of its quarry.

Above all, Michael preferred its gun, the incredible six-barrelled revolving cannon with which he could kill at 500 yards—eyeball to eyeball—simply by pressing a little red button on the control column whenever the target filled his gunsight.

He was the best marksman of his new pilot group, the one to beat on the range. He was the one confident WSOs asked for and nervous ones avoided because above all things, he was a flyer. He was not reckless though; he flew just above the limits, always with a margin to spare, trying not to frighten himself or his WSO, but he was determined and skilful. And he hated losing.

With the Phantom he noticed that he himself was changing. Flying was his life and he intended to do it better than anybody; everything else was of secondary importance. He knew this was selfish so he avoided intense relationships with people, and particularly the girls he met.

Jenny he had liked and written to for a few months. Then there had been a friend's sister whom he'd dated; the affair had turned bitter as she fell more deeply in love with him and he felt his only love threatened—but nothing could be allowed to interfere with his flying. There had been an unhappy break-up and Michael had realised that he had been cruel, allowing things to develop too quickly. Tessa had packed up and gone the day he told her he wasn't in love with her. She'd returned, desperately hoping he'd change eventually but he'd told her it was no good, he was too young, he needed more time, more of life, more flying, before he could ever settle. It had hurt her, but it was honest and he was right. She'd gone and never written; then he'd heard she'd met somebody, and married. She lived in Canada now.

And always there was Liza, counselling, admonishing, encouraging at a distance. Far enough away for him never to feel threatened. He looked forward to her letters, thick bulky ones marked 'Private and Confidential'. And he'd write back with the latest happenings at his base; his flying, the trips he was doing and always questions about the kibbutz. But when he wrote about 'home' he meant Princeton. For Michael realised beyond doubt that he was firstly a pilot, secondly an American, thirdly a Jew and finally, an ex-kibbutznik.

The photographs he sent to Liza invariably showed a smiling young man of medium height and build, usually clad in flying overalls or peering over the side of a cockpit. When he wasn't festooned in the paraphernalia of jet flight, free of oxygen mask, straps, bone dome and vizor, his hair could be seen black and straight, blown across his face, his eyes dark grey. His nose was fine, slightly chiselled, certainly not recognisable as 'Jewish', whatever that meant. His forehead was high and square, his cheekbones slightly raised, adding tension to his slim, wide mouth. His chin had a slight cleft that he tended to squeeze together when distracted. His eyelashes were long, almost feminine, his ears only slightly lobed.

Liza's favourite photograph of him was the one in his graduation uniform. Many copies had been made by her, unknown to Michael, and distributed among her girlfriends and 'interested' good Jewish mommas. 'Such a fine boy,' they had all said, clucking as they sized him up for their daughters.

And Michael was proud of Liza too, whose photograph he carried in his wallet, useful sometimes for putting off unwanted admirers.

'. . . Oh her, she's my girlfriend.' And invariably they'd retired, their confidence evaporating at the sight of such a face; a renaissance face, a pear-shaped, honey-fringed face, like a nymph from a Botticelli. A face that might have looked at you from expensive, fashionable magazines left casually on coffee tables. An 'impressive' face that actually graced a seventeen-year-old, denim-clad kibbutznik who thought make-up was 'tacky' and could never understand why old men stopped and stared and young men's conversations ceased as she walked by in the streets of Jerusalem.

All except one, that is, and he had never stopped talking but simply peeled off from his cronies and literally walked with quickening strides into her life.

Mordechai drove the very kind of machine that Michael's plane could destroy with a single obliterating fusillade. He commanded an up-gunned Centurion tank which he loved and hated while adoring Liza. He wrote her short, heavily censored postcards, everyday, 'from Ghaza' or 'near Tel Aviv'; these she kept in an album in her satchel of college textbooks, along with the letters from her brother in the United States.

The two men in Liza's life were at that moment sitting in their respective vehicles filling in that hollow time familiar to all young front-line officers, waiting for combat orders.

Mordechai's tank lay hull-down behind the dunes, one roaring, grinding gear change away from war. All he had to do was give the order and his driver would engage the first range of cogs that would turn the sixteen wheels of his Centurion, and send the tank charging to the crest of the rampart where his gunner would slew the awesome barrel of the 105mm gun, lock on the first Egyptian target and blow it into a smoking ruin.

But not today, or so he'd been assured by his Brigade commander. So he watched the sun setting over the limitless desert, occasionally scanning the sky with his binoculars, picking out the high flying solitary IDF Mirages streaking westward on lonely, dangerous reconnaissance missions over Egyptian territory.

Mordechai read for the third or fourth time the words of his sweetheart, hastily scribbled on a postcard of the Western Wall and signed 'Your ever loving, Elizabeth' while half a world away Michael Allon watched the same sun rising high in the east and catching the flimsy corners of the lengthy airmail letter from the same girl, but signed, in his case, 'From Liza—with love'.

Michael usually saved her letters for the times when he had to sit for hours on Alert, waiting to be scrambled from his concrete pad to intercept 'hostiles' threatening his patch of Florida sky.

He was strapped, buckled and clipped by a variety of devices to his ejector seat and plugged and connected to the life-saving, life-giving, life-supporting fabric that made him an integral part of the entire weapons system.

He'd completed his ritual walkround, peering, kicking, thumping, noting, comparing new leaks with old, examining pins, doors, flaps and pipes. He'd touched each one of the Sidewinders, the Sparrows, the long-range fuel tank. He had climbed the ten feet to the cockpit satisfied that all he and his crew chief could do had been done. He'd grinned at the vizored face of his WSO, back in his own rear seat, who'd already run through his checklist and switched the two generator switches on the starboard front console from 'Off' to 'Ext On', feeding the Phantom's nervous system with life-giving electrons.

So Michael sat contented in his three-foot by five-foot office, his pre-start checks completed, ready to face a very different enemy from Mordechai's, a Russian rather than an Egyptian, anywhere within twenty billion cubic miles of sky.

The long flowing script with its confident curling loops flowed easily past his eyes.

'Dear Michael,

Aunt Elizabeth and Uncle Daniel are very well but Daniel is away often now that he's a company salesman. Elizabeth is looking a little older, she worries a lot about Daniel and of course is terrified of you flying aeroplanes, especially after that medal business that Rabbi Groman told us about. Remember, you promised you'd tell me everything about you, so tell me first when you win your next one. OK? Promise?

Rabbi Groman has lost a lot of weight and spends a great

deal of time with Daniel and with the Joint Council in Jerusalem.

Shimon Yariv, our kibbutz leader, also works more in Jerusalem but a friend told me she'd bumped into him in the Negev of all places (near Dimona). I think it's something to do with solar energy or something.

I still go to the Wall for David's memory. I feel it is my way of thanking him for keeping you alive the day that pilot was killed. Do you remember David's girlfriend, that beautiful one from Lebanon, well she joined the army and is now in DELETED, I believe. She married another pilot, he flies DELETED, like DELETED, possibly.

The terrorists raids are DELETED our boys are very successful and I think the Fatah will have to give up soon. They won't have enough men left. They are using a lot of kids now. Two DELETED were shot last week near Haifa by a patrol.

There was a DELETED bombing the day before yesterday on the road where dear mother and father died. I still think of them every day and most Sabbaths I put a prayer in the Wall.

Why can't the Arabs leave us alone and let us all live in peace together? This is such a tiny land and they've got all those deserts. We could show them how to irrigate and plant them so they will never have to worry about food. Aunt Elizabeth was saying that it was the British who were to blame. Before they came to Palestine, Arabs and Jews lived well together but of course Jerusalem was very tiny then and there weren't many of us here.

I'm studying my history now because I believe we should all understand why we're in this situation today.

Daniel says that it isn't the British but the Communists who are to blame and they're stirring up the Arabs so they can destroy us, then they'll take over and the Russians will control the oil fields.

The Egyptians and Syrians are screaming abuse at us everyday now. It's as if they want their people to believe that once Israel is destroyed then everything will get better. If the

Arabs couldn't have improved their standards before 1948 why do they believe they can do it now?

Thank goodness the United States supports us; the French are DELETED and the British are DELETED. Don't they ever remember the war and what we fought for and how much we lost.

When are you coming back home, Michael? I've missed you so much and I'd love you to meet Mordechai. You'd both get on so well together, I know. He commands a DELETED tank. He's very good and he says he'd love to have a go at the Russian T54s or whatever they call them. He says the Arabs can't fight with modern weapons so all they can do is throw in thousands of soldiers. Sorry to go on about the war, but I know you are interested.

I'm going up to the kibbutz tomorrow to show Mordechai where we used to live. He's from Tel Aviv. His parents died in Warsaw, so I think it would be nice for him to feel part of a family . . .'

He never finished the letter that day. The alert cleared his introversion in one, crackling blast through his helmet:

'Zulu Foxtrot, Zulu Foxtrot, this is Big Wham, prepare to scramble—Bogey One at bearing one fiver niner—range two niner eight miles—closing at four hundred knots—believed Soviet.' As Michael's vizor snapped down, he tucked the letter back into his knee pocket, and his hands and eyes started flicking, pressing and turning switches, buttons and knobs.

Again, the strident voice, 'Zulu Foxtrot, Zulu Foxtrot, Scramble, Scramble, Scramble.'

'Big Wham, this is Zulu Foxtrot, we are scrambling. Over.'

'Zulu Foxtrot, you are cleared for take-off and intercept of Bogey One This is no exercise, repeat no exercise.' It was a statement Michael wouldn't forget in a hurry.

His left hand held the twin throttle levers and smoothly pushed them forward to the spring-loaded gate, as the turbojets blazed into whining life. With a positive leftward pressure Michael snaked them to one side as they entered the AB slots.

There was a new note, a low rumbling that cut in as the afterburners lit, belching out twin plumes of blue-white flames that matched and quickly outshone the blazing sky. The airframe shuddered as the power reached a screaming crescendo and Zulu Foxtrot rocked on its wheels, held to the earth for one more second before rolling faster and faster straight up the centreline of the long, shimmering runway. The noise rocked distant windows as it screamed out of the jetpipes at over 700 miles an hour.

Zulu Foxtrot lifted its nose, tucked in its gear and shot towards its true domain, the dark blue, icy stratosphere, in one barrelling, curving climb.

Michael Allon and Joe Kennedy were about to come face to face with the Cold War.

'Zulu Foxtrot, Zulu Foxtrot, target is hostile, possibly Soviet Air Force Recon flight. You will intercept, identify and escort. We have a KC135 vectored to you in ten minutes. Over.'

'Big Wham, this is Zulu Foxtrot, understand we are to intercept, identify and escort possible SOVAF Recon Flight. Thanks for the gas. Over.'

With hardly a touch on the controls, Michael Allon pulled his twenty-ton fighter into a 30° right-hand turn through Mach One on a collision intercept course for the as yet unidentified Soviet aircraft.

Joe Kennedy fed him steering and speed co-ordinates based on the constantly changing data from Big Wham's search equipment, while setting up the proposed air-to-air refuelling plan which would enable the Phantom to escort its target as long as possible.

The Fighter Director simultaneously dispatched a Boeing KC135 Stratotanker from its patrol point ten miles south-west of Paradise Island in the Bahamas to meet and rendezvous with the target aircraft and interceptor later in their journey.

'OK, Joe, let's check our weapons status,' Michael called out.

They were carrying four medium-range Sparrows and

four short-range Sidewinders plus a centreline fuel tank and twin inboard wing tanks in view of the over-water nature of their sortie. Michael powered up the gyros on the Sparrows so that they would be ready to launch at optimum range.

'Weapons status is go for all systems, check master safety,' Joe Kennedy announced.

'Master safety is on,' said Michael, as he ensured that the weapons could not fire unless positive action was taken by both crewmen, via the fire control system.

And all the time the two aircraft approached each other at close on 1,500 miles an hour. Within five minutes Joe had the target on his airborne radar, its beam shaped to 'tracking mode'. Two minutes later he switched to 'intercept mode' narrowing the beam into a cone of radar energy which could be used by the Sparrows for homing into the target.

Michael saw the aircraft ten thousand feet below and crossing him from east to west; he cruised round and down into a stern chase, giving himself the optimum pursuit condition.

As he checked his speed, with throttle and air brakes, he identified the distinctive long, swept wings of the Tupolev TU20 Bear, four massive Kuznetsov turboprops projecting from its slender silver fuselage. The red stars on its wings and fuselage were visible now as he approached within Sparrow range. Joe came in tersely:

'. . . I have an ECM status check. The target has us on his own radar and is sweeping.'

The Bear's fuselage was blemished by several small 'blisters' concealing aerials, transmitters, radar warning receivers and any other development in sensor technology that would enable it—when the day came—to see, jamb, fly and fight its way through US air defences.

'Check camera status.'

'OK, Joe, gun camera is ready, how's the Brownie?'

Joe Kennedy checked the airborne 16mm camera used for filming interceptions such as these. The developed film would be interpreted by Photo Intelligence officers attached to the squadron.

Michael rode slowly down on the Bear, flying level with its nose before carefully sliding below and behind its elegantly swept wings. All the time the Bear tried manoeuvring to offer its upper wing and fuselage before — then suddenly it dived steeply towards the sea. From here the sight was every bit as dramatic as he had imagined. Just a few feet from them flew Russia's largest bomber but to Michael's amazement and immediate concern instead of a long, smooth, silver belly, there, like a giant pilot fish under a great silver shark, hung suspended a dirty, black weapon. No wonder the Russian never wanted Michael to see his belly. The two Phantom crew were the first US pilots to photograph at close range Russia's most advanced stand-off missile.

The missile was thirty feet long with swept wings and tail and a long snout through which it would suck air on its solitary flight to Armageddon. NATO called it Kangaroo and it was a jet-powered thermonuclear bomb wrapped in the wings of a fighter but carrying a million tons of explosive force in a four ton package.

'Joe, have you got that? It's a Kangaroo, I think.'

'OK, Mike, I'm shooting, put it on the gun camera. After I've finished cross directly below so I can see its belly, then over to its left. Finally I want to study its intake.'

'OK, here we go.'

The Phantom was following the diving bomber like a shadow, the Russian pilot desperately attempting to prevent filming of his very secret cargo.

'Joe, send a signal to Big Wham on the "War" cypher. This is an order, copy this on the voice recorder for replay, ready . . . OK, start transmitting, *now*!

"This is Phantom Zulu Foxtrot, on air intercept of Soviet Bison Bomber Number Zero Four, time 12.01 GMT, 45 miles due east of the Bahama Banks. This crew confirm positive identification of aircraft which is carrying a 'Kangaroo', repeat 'Kangaroo', stand-off missile. We're photographing with both air-to-air and gun camera for records. Request orders, will maintain stern chase position at six miles range in accordance with nuclear blast avoidance profile. Over." '

The Phantom carried a very special electronic cypher machine that encoded and decoded signals of a 'nuclear' or 'war' status which then could only be decoded at North American Air Defence Command Headquarters at Cheyenne Mountain.

The signal automatically went out on the status boards seen only by senior staff of the highest security clearance. Within thirty seconds NORAD Command had alerted a squadron of Phantoms to close on the Bear at long range. There was a special reason for this extraordinary action which Michael had immediately assessed and acted upon.

The 'Kangaroo' had never been photographed at such close proximity before; it was thought never to have been flown into a position whereby its 400 mile range could directly threaten the US mainland. In this case the Russian Bear could have selected Galveston, Miami, Houston or many other U.S. cities and bases to attack on a pre-emptive strike.

To ignore the possibility was too great a risk no matter how unlikely. Michael heard a new voice break into his helmet. 'Zulu Foxtrot, this is NORAD Command, maintain contact at six miles, stern chase and report any changes. You will receive escort assistance in twelve minutes from F4s out of McGill AFB in full NBC status. Keep filming and report every minute, commencing now.'

NBC stood for nuclear, biological and chemical warfare. Michael was relieved at the speed and seriousness of the response as it vindicated his decision to us the 'war' cypher.

Still the 'Bear' kept weaving, descending closer and closer to the water. Michael slowly moved back out of range of a possible thermonuclear blast in case of an accident or if he were ever to be ordered to destroy the Russian with a salvo of Sparrow missiles.

At a little over two hundred feet the Russian levelled out to maintain a constant height above the waves with Michael tracking him as he followed. He could just see the gunner himself in his tiny isolated position below the massive fin.

The pale blue waters of the Grand Bahama Bank flashed by underneath as Zulu Foxtrot rocked about in the turbulent air above the warm ocean.

It was an incredible chase, the giant silver bomber sweeping over the ocean like some great bird rocking its wings from side to side, rising then dipping in violent wave-skimming swoops that forced the hunting fighter to twist and turn dangerously.

The Russian was superb, and not once did Michael get an easy 'shot'. His Sidewinders would be almost useless, their primitive brains easy prey to the dazzling, enticing sunlight off the rolling waves. The Sparrows would find it difficult too, their tiny radar receivers desperately confused by the scattered radar energy bouncing off the ocean.

Only the gun could work so long as the Russian hugged the waves but Michael knew that the Russian had two further advantages.

First, he had twin, radar-directed tail cannons that followed his every movement—rarely was Michael out of their cone of fire.

Second, he had fuel enough to leave Michael riding an empty, silent plane, hours before he need bother even to check his own fuel gauges.

But Michael was determined to stay, he wouldn't let go of this one.

'Big Wham, this is Zulu Foxtrot, we have Bogey One ahead and in range, where's the Cavalry?'

And, suddenly—as if John Ford himself had directed it—there they were, a gaggle of four Phantoms, mean looking objects diving straight out of the sun.

Like hawks plummeting from the sky, they rocketed towards their prey, ignoring the lone Phantom and flashed across the nose of the giant.

The four broke into two battle flights sweeping a ten-mile racetrack low across the sky, worrying the Bear with constant nips and swoops that deflected it more and more to the west, away from the mainland until finally it began to manoeuvre.

The creature, for that's what it had become in Michael's imagination, banked and yawed violently from side to side, trying desperately to throw off its tormentors. Many times it ejected glittering clouds of chaff, tiny strips of metallic foil, breaking the lock on the Westinghouse radars.

It tried jamming, sweeping the radar spectrum with hurricanes of invisible electromagnetic pulses that left Joe Kennedy and his fellow back-seat riders cursing softly at their useless displays. Had it not been for the clear skies of the Caribbean it might well have succeeded, diving into cloud banks, or hugging a blanket of sea mist. But in these clear skies it could do nothing about the most important sensors of all, the pale grey eyes of a determined fighter pilot.

With a final flurry of rocking wings, the Bear lifted its long nose and roared in a smooth, soaring climb up to the quiet, safer air of 15,000 feet, from which it could see the familiar distant outline of Cuba. But still the fighters followed, stacked in two battle flights above and below the bomber with Michael hugging closely to its belly like a remora, still photographing until his camera indicator flashed: 'Exhausted'.

Ahead of and above them appeared a further flight of four fighters while somewhere in the distance Big Wham had placed a third line of defence, just in case the Russian ever fired the 'Kangaroo' in anger.

Zulu Foxtrot broke formation on the orders of NORAD and climbed steadily and economically on the next essential part of its flight, the rendezvous at 28,000 feet with the circling Stratotanker now twenty miles from Paradise Island.

Michael and Joe started to breathe properly again.

Big Wham took over and within seven minutes the Phantom was carefully nudging up to the flying boom hanging from the big Boeing. The sight was impressive: the two aircraft had to fly until the tanker's boom engaged in a fuelling receptacle in the Phantom's shoulder and the two dissimilar machines had to keep station while the boom operator, sitting in his central blister, pumped the fighter full of fuel. The dynamics involved could only be mastered by sheer flying skill and Michael had never yet aborted an air-to-air.

The crew of Zulu Foxtrot felt the boom engage with a satisfying clunk and then Michael adjusted power and trim as his aircraft virtually doubled its weight in a matter of minutes.

But when it was over, the Phantom carefully withdrew and the boom rose on its little V-shaped wing, nestling back against the tail of the tanker, and left a fine spray of jet fuel threading the sky for miles behind it.

Then with a positive rocking of its wings the fighter winged over and headed for home, its young crew the latest participants in a Cold War incident which could so easily have gone wrong.

'Big Wham, this is Zulu Foxtrot, tanks full, returning to base. Over.'

'Zulu Foxtrot, good work, I'll buy you both a beer. Out.'

What had seemed like hours had actually been nine minutes, but in the world of afterburners that's too long and Michael knew how close he had been to ejecting, once again.

Zulu Foxtrot roared down to a smooth touchdown on McGill's runway, streaming its brake chute to reduce its landing run. As it came to a halt at its own blast-proof revetment, an Air Force jeep was waiting for the precious load of film. Ground crew men unclipped the camera hatch from the nose, slid out the film cartridge and placed it in a polished metal carrying case. Joe handed out the air-to-air camera and as a bonus, his small movie camera.

'Tell the General I wanted some shots for the kids and happened to have it along. Careful now, that's private film you've got there.'

As the three cameras were loaded into the jeep the pilots suddenly noticed that they in turn were being filmed by a civilian in a grey suit who climbed back into the jeep and left with Air Force Photo Intelligence Officers without saying a word.

A crew van arrived and conveyed Michael and Joe to the debriefing room where they must have gone over their description of the encounter half a dozen times to the senior Intelligence Officer and two men they had never seen before.

It was a week to the day, over a large breakfast of hash brown, eggs and tomatoes that Joe suddenly swatted Michael with a copy of his paper: it contained a photograph of the tail of 'Bear 04' 15,000 feet over the Bahama Banks. The headline splashed:

'US DEMANDS CURB TO CUBA PROBES.

'Air Force pilots Allon and Kennedy snap the Russian Bear on the Miami run.

'Two Air Force pilots flying a McDonnell Douglas F4 Phantom jet off Cuba snapped this single shot of a Soviet 'Bear' long range bomber.

'A Soviet spokesman refused to discuss the incident in detail when pressed today, claiming the US is using fabricated evidence to conjure up scare stories about Soviet flights.'

The two men were even more amused when the man in the grey suit came by their mess that evening and advised them to maintain a relaxed, ignorant posture regarding the incident.

Finally after two months had elapsed Michael and Joe were cordially invited to meet General Wheeler, chief of USAF Intelligence, down from Washington.

The two pilots were ushered into the Commanding Officer's main office where they were introduced to a dapper, tailored man of fifty or so on whose heavy-jowelled face sat a pair of rimless glasses serving a pair of bright glistening blue eyes.

The introductions over, the Base Commander sat back as General Wheeler leaned forwards in his chair to dash out his pipe. He sucked on it a couple of times to make sure it was clear then looked hard at the two young men.

'Allon, Kennedy, gentlemen, I would like to thank you on behalf of the Air Force for the finest close-up shots ever taken of a modern Soviet military aircraft in flight. What's more your coverage of the Kangaroo was exceptional in quality and the wealth of details you revealed. It may interest you to know that your single flight has advanced our knowledge of the Soviet military capability by a significant amount.'

The two men listened with growing interest and surprise as Wheeler described his findings.

'You see, we've examined every frame of film as well as the ephemoral tape; also the voice recorder, your signals, the Soviet's ECM response, their signal traffic, your flight data recorder and the radar coverage of the entire flight.

'Believe me, it's taken us a whole month to analyse a few minutes of recorded time. You two fellows, if asked, could describe say fifty separate sections or minor events during your interception. We've reached over three-quarters of a million data bits already.'

The two crewmen looked at each other with silently mocking expressions.

'Let me explain to you what our approach is,' the General continued.

'Firstly, because of your excellent shadowing of the Russian, we have a good idea of his manoeuvrability envelope, his diving acceleration and drag, his control response and so forth.

'Secondly, we recorded his electronic emissions via your ECM recorder. Did you realise he kept losing lock on you? He's got a big weakness there.

'Thirdly, we tracked his gun-laying ability from the films and he's got excellent tail-borne radar. We now know its frequency range so we'll be able to jamb it, possibly.'

Wheeler took another suck on his pipe.

'Then we recorded his response to your signals and here we got a hell of a shock. He can read our 'war' cypher. We recorded a definite rise in signal traffic at Soviet Defence Command Headquarters directly relating to our 'war' cypher traffic. So we've changed all our cypher codes.

'And we analysed the frequency of his transmission and reception of signals to abort his flight and we may have understood part of his long-wave radio code. He got that signal from Russia, not Cuba.

'We also know his aerial types and some of their frequencies. We noticed that his radar does not have clutter suppression of radar waves bouncing off the sea but he does have height hold over the sea. He never saw the Navy F4s on his air-to-air radar until they were within fifty miles—and so it goes on.

'The most important thing however is that we know that Kangaroo must carry a two-megaton warhead because we built a computer model of the Bear with Kangaroo attached, fed it with the data of your flight and thereby measured the mass of the missile. That took two weeks of continuous refining, by the way, a slow job. Having obtained the mass, we found its density.

'We also recognised the engine type from a number of photographic details and so we know how much fuel it carries to confer its range. The result of that little teaser is that the total warhead mass is not one but two megatons and this ties in with seismic and high altitude sampling data from a series of puzzling two-megaton tests held last year.

'See my drift? Good, then I won't bore you any further except to say that it was the most beautifully co-ordinated chase I've ever seen and for you two there is a special job that I'll only give to the best because it's a lot harder than intercepting an old Russian Bear.

'I've asked your Commanding Officer, the Colonel here, for authority to place you on a 'Special Status' list we keep for guys like you two who do an exceptional job.'

Wheeler smiled, and returned to puffing contentedly on his pipe.

Michael looked at Joe, then at the Colonel, then back to the General before breaking into a grin.

'Thank you, General, we'd appreciate that, wouldn't we, Joe?'

'Yessir.'

And for Joe, that was a dramatic emphasis.

11
PVO Strany

'Gentlemen, the two of you have been selected for your high degree of proficiency shown during your initial squadron deployment.

'You have now both completed your first tours and you have been selected for special service. You are no doubt wondering why you were brought here in the cargo hold of a transport aircraft and were prevented from viewing outside. The reason of course is security, for what you are about to see is unknown to all but selected aircrew throughout the country.'

The instructor signalled the engineering officer to operate the huge blastproof doors which rumbled to one side of the camouflaged steel and concrete hangar.

The daylight slid over the humped form of the aircraft sitting menacingly inside the otherwise empty space.

The latest F4E Phantom, resplendent in its Vietnam camouflage and tiny low-visibility Air Force insignia, was fully laden with centreline drop tanks, Sparrows and Sidewinders. The paintwork looked and smelt new, a blend of dark olive drab and brown that was highly effective when viewed against the jungles of North Vietnam.

The three men walked slowly towards the aircraft till they could touch the barrel of the 20mm rotary cannon emerging at a shallow depressed angle from under the nose.

They walked, talking quietly as pilots do when examining a newly delivered aircraft, checking the fit of the inspection panels, examining the undercarriage for oil leaks, and inspecting the many red safety flags dispersed around the missile pylons.

They noted the long, thin, aerodynamic slats that projected from the leading edge of the wing, these recent modifications smoothing the airflow as the aircraft manoeuvred at high, nose-up angles and tight turns, critical to survival if a Mig 21 was on its tail.

They ducked their heads under the tailpipes and reached up to touch the drooping tailplane. The only sign of its country of origin was the tiny US Air Force insignia and the various instructions in English and Vietnamese on the inspection panels.

One by one they climbed the access ladders and peered into the tandem cockpits under their individual rearward-hinged canopies.

The two young men slid into the Martin Baker Mark H5 zero-zero ejection seats that would blow them out of the aircraft even at nil speed and height, such as in a runway emergency. The controls came easily to hand, the view through the glass reflector plate of the gunsight improved by the steeply sloping nose, derived from the plane's original role as a Navy carrier-fighter.

The two men swapped seats as the third man, the Colonel, sat grinning at their enthusiasm, straddling the hump of the big fighter.

'Well, gentlemen, what do you think of her.'

'Incredible, Colonel, I never thought I'd sit inside a Phantom. The closest I ever got was over Haiphong one night last year, but he was a hundred feet in front of me before he went down. So this is how they build them. It's beautiful, magnificient engineering, but it must be very heavy on the controls. No, give me a Mig 21 any time for close-in combat.'

Shabir Al Timimi slowly hauled himself out of the front seat and climbed down the ladder to the hangar floor. He strolled backwards until he could admire the 58-foot-long fuselage, towering sixteen feet from the top of the fin to the ground.

He was dazed by the sight. Here he was on a Soviet airfield examining America's most advanced fighter. Not bad for a Palestinian boy from the camps, he thought.

His crewman, Viktor Belishek, emerged from the rear seat and skipped down the second ladder. Within a minute he and Colonel Yeliskeiv had joined Shabir out on the apron.

The older Russian clapped them both on the shoulder. 'Well, do you think you can fly it?' he asked, never doubting their abilities for a moment.

'Colonel, we will fly it better than the Americans,' Shabir replied unhesitatingly.

'Good, because in six weeks from now you will be flying against dozens of them. You've both been selected for combat flying in Vietnam!'

The two faces were a picture of incredulity, the dark aquiline features of the Arab contrasting with the pale round, slightly boyish face of the Russian. They glanced at each other as if in slow motion, then back to their Commander.

Belishek's jaw lifted, his mouth spreading into a grin as he clapped his comrade on the shoulder. Shabir never took his face off Yeliskeiv as he felt that old familiar tingling sweep over his back. He suddenly felt hot, his stomach muscles constricted and he clenched his fingers into two solid fists.

'Well, Al Timimi, what do you have to say to our plan, eh?'

Yeliskeiv looked into the black, sparkling eyes, knowing Shabir would always respond in measured tones, no matter what the circumstances.

'Thank you for the trust you have placed in me . . . us, Colonel. It is an honour.'

Turning to his wingman he said, 'Well, Viktor, at last we have the chance of a good fight, eh?' This time he too smiled, proffering his firm grip which Belishek returned with enthusiasm.

Later, as the two left to return to their base, Yeliskeiv watched the aircraft depart, and he remembered that day long ago in the guerilla camp when he'd first seen the Arab boy firing at the wooden target. The boy was now a man of quiet determination, and popular, not because of any flamboyant traits or extrovert behaviour but because his record commanded respect.

Colonel Yeliskeiv was a proud man; the Alexandria report on the Palestinian had changed the life of the boy from Jerusalem, he had lived up to his promise. At Moscow University Al Timimi had graduated first in class and been accepted into the special Zukhovsky Academy of the Soviet Air Force, the equivalent of the British Royal Air Force College at Cranwell or the US Air Force Academy at Colorado Springs. Now he was a pilot in PVO Strany, Frontal Aviation.

Al Timimi had trained first on Mig 15s, the two-seat version of the Soviet counterpart to the US Sabre Jet in use during the Korean War. He had graduated to the faster Mig 17 and the supersonic Mig 19 'Farmer' (as it was known under NATO classification coding), and was currently flying the nearest Soviet equivalent to the US Phantom, the Mig 21. Yeliskeiv knew that Shabir loved and hated the aircraft. It was completely different to the highly sophisticated Phantom and yet was the Phantom's most frequent antagonist in the skies over Israel and Vietnam.

As the Colonel looked back to the American aircraft, expensively salvaged from the remains of six shot down over North Vietnam and cannibalised to create a single plane, he knew that the very cutting edge of the Cold War was expressed in these two weapons.

The Mig was nearly half the weight of the F4; it was powered by a single Turmansky turbojet which sucked in air over a central, pointed nose cone containing interception radar. The single seat nestled beneath a classic bubble canopy from the rear of which ran the control circuits to the sharply swept tail fin. The fuselage was supported in flight on a pair of small mid-mounted delta wings and a conventional swept tailplane. The entire aircraft was so simple that several thousand had now been produced for all Eastern Bloc countries; Finland, Egypt, India and China assembled their own versions under licence, the last known as the Shenyang F6.

The Mig, being lighter than the Phantom, could usually out-turn it at low or medium altitudes and also offered a smaller target. Its main weaknesses, however, were its lack of range due to its small and badly located internal fuel tanks, its limited firepower, incomparable to that of the Phantom, and its unsophisticated radar and electronics. The extraordinary thing was that in the hands of certain dedicated skilful pilots over Vietnam it had proved to be a highly lethal interceptor and had brought down Phantoms flown by Air Force, Navy and Marine Corps aircrew.

The key to the Mig's success was its ability as a hit-and-run fighter under good ground control, when used against heavily loaded strike aircraft attacking the most heavily defended target in the history of warfare: Hanoi, capital city of North Vietnam.

The entire defence system of North Vietnam was designed by the Soviet Union and General Giap, the North's military leader, as a gigantic interlocking killing ground for American aircraft operating north of the demilitarised zone, the DMZ.

Yeliskeiv suddenly felt a premonition of disaster; the risks were high. The Arab had survived a harsh upbringing, a true offspring of the Cold War who would soon be flying for his life against the most sophisticated Air Force in the world. He hoped 'Olga' was right, for after all it was she who had selected him.

The fat, balding Russian pulled out the folded paper that had told him that Shabir Al Timimi was ready for combat flying against US pilots in Vietnam. It listed his entire operational background, both as a commando and as a PVO Strany exchange pilot. It recorded his successes in simulated combat, dog fighting and interception. It listed his scores at the various ranges in the Moscow Military District.

Al Timimi was ready. The Palestinian would fly against Americans, Mig against Phantom, over the saturated battleground of South-East Asia.

12
Tonkin

'We have four minutes to target, you are go for one pass.'

'Roger.'

'I have weak radar responses over 240°.'

'What kind?'

'Two kinds, SA-2 and ZSU. Also a strong, broad-band jamming sweep.'

'Are you jamming?'

'Affirmative.'

'Any IR?'

'Negative.'

'Report any launches of infra-red. Watch out for SAMs.'

'Roger.'

The Phantom was rocking uncomfortably in the turbulent air over the hills and sudden valleys. One hundred and fifty feet was as close as Allon could get, allowing for the undulating topography, and at 600 knots IAS he couldn't afford the risk of striking a hill or alternatively offering himself as an exposed target to the concentrated fire of NV cannons.

Only last week the squadron lost an F4E over the North. Its wingman had seen the trail of a Soviet SA-7 heat-seeking missile emerge from the jungle at frightening speed and fly straight into the jet's starboard tail pipe before exploding.

The tiny five-pound warhead had blown out the fuelpipes and ignited the highly volatile fuel in the starboard drop tank. It was over in two seconds: the Phantom bloomed into a streaming comet of flame ahead of which rode the still intact cockpit complete with its two crewmen. The wingman had heard just one desperate plea on the emergency wavelength, 'Jesus, please don't . . . .', and then it was over as the coffin tumbled into the jungle at more than 500 miles an hour.

Tears of frustration trickled into the wingman's oxygen mask as he screamed obscenities down the silent microphone.

'Bastards . . . filthy, fucking, bastards, fucking Red bastards, why don't you die, you vermin! Die, die, die, you evil race of filthy Red bastards!'

He'd banked round in a sharp 6G curve that brought him back to the flaming debris of his buddy's beautiful machine; then he guessed where the 'Grail' missile had come out of the green floor and fired burst after burst at the trees, which soaked up the cannon fire and simply withered and shook and carried on growing and covering what was to him the most evil race on God's earth: the filthy North Vietnamese.

Allon heard him talk that night in the tent they had rigged up as a bar and which they moved from time to time in case the VC planted a demolition charge under it or zapped it with mortars. With so many Vietnamese working at the base it was impossible to trust anyone; anyone could be a 'Gook' spy.

Allon had shut himself off from the South Vietnamese, especially the senior officers. He despised their corruption and the way they treated their soldiers, and he had the professional flyer's detachment from their 'petty' day-to-day problems of guarding aircraft, stores and huts and living in a homeland savaged with war.

'Two minutes to target. Maintain this heading.'

The Phantom roared along. Suddenly the firing could be heard and Allon knew they could be hit on this run. Then, just as predicted on the combat model, the target—the Lop Nol railway bridge spanning the Red River to the west of Hanoi—appeared on the horizon.

'We have TV lock.'

'Roger, climbing to launch height.' The Phantom

suddenly lifted its nose and climbed sharply to give its Maverick TV-guided missile sufficient height to hit the target without clutter from the ground.

'Missile away, break, break, break.' The aircraft screamed over into a brain-numbing turn that took it away on an escape trajectory out of the killing zone around the bridge. The big white missile almost loped off its pylon, its long, steeply raking, cruciform wings and tiny tail tabs controlling its altitude. Its soft, round, glass nose had a cyclopian television camera that acted as the missile's 'eye', and the WSO behind Allon saw the TV's field of view through a miniature television monitor in his cockpit. He held a tiny remote-control joystick between right thumb and forefinger and watched the target rapidly filling the graticule in the centre of the monitor. He was flying the missile while Allon bore the plane round to safety.

The bridge was clearly visible now as the missile thrust its camera and warhead unerringly towards the central steel truss spanning the river at its deepest point. In a moment Engstrom couldn't believe his luck as a blurred image of a locomotive resolved into the missile's view. Then the screen was full of steel. Then nothing. Blank.

They wouldn't know until they landed and received the reconnaissance photos whether the missile had been on target. All the time, Allon kept the fighter's nose down, weaving around the hills and hugging the ground for safety, as he beat south towards the DMZ and home.

'First turning point in one minute.'

'Roger, steering order please.'

'Steer one four two when confirmed'.

'One four two when confirmed.'

The aircraft approached the imaginary point on the map where it had planned to turn, on a route selected after careful study of known North Vietnamese anti-aircraft batteries, which changed daily by means of their clever Russian-designed mobile transporters. The entire killing machine of North Vietnam could move almost at will, always trying to fool the high flying U2s, the Blackbirds, and even the spy satellites 120 miles above them.

'Turning point ten seconds ahead, eight, seven, six, five, four, three, two, turn NOW!'

Allon rocked over crisply, and headed straight for the Gulf of Tonkin where he would be safe from little peasants in plain black pyjamas who could kill him in at least four different ways even at this height and speed.

'Nice turn, eight minutes to next turning point, maintain this heading.'

'Roger, eight minutes.'

They'd made that one too and now the coast was only ten miles ahead. But that was when the Mig got them.

'BREAK RIGHT, BOGEY, BOGEY!' Engstrom shouted suddenly.

Allon's reflex cut the Phantom over to the right and he saw the white streaks of two Atoll air-to-air missiles flash past him.

'Still behind us, break left, then right and hold.'

He followed his buddy's instructions, but still the Mig was there. He was good. Allon hit the afterburners knowing that a Mig 21 usually carried only two missiles, which would have had an easy job if he'd been on 'burners before.

The surge of acceleration and the additional lift from the wings raised the nose, and Allon started a gut-twisting, neck-straining climb for Jim McConnell's blessed height while he tried to locate the Mig over his shoulder or in his rear view mirror. Suddenly it was there, but only for a moment, the circular black hole of the nose, the tiny mid-mounted wing and a hint of fin and then, amazingly, a glitter of red flashes below its belly.

The twin NR 30mm cannons ripped the heavily ozonated air, blasting shells at 100 rounds a minute towards the Americans. Allon pulled hard left as the shells burst past him in a solid stream of fire. At the same time he jettisoned the twin 370-gallon fuel tanks which brought him down to fighting weight.

'Jamming now.'

'Keep at it.'

Engstrom swept his tail with a band of radio energy designed to break the lock on the Mig airborne-interception radar. The Cutler Hammer jamming pod did its job, but the Mig pilot had taken over, using pure flying skill to set up what must be his final attempt before the ocean appeared and his minimal fuel supply ran out. The Phantom skidded into a rolling, climbing turn to the left, desperately trying to get into its ideal energy band—where the Mig couldn't touch it—and flew straight into a burst of accurately placed cannon shells!

The force was like a hammer and both crewmen looked at their starboard wing. The entire tip had gone: the big canted slab had been blown clean off at its junction with the neutral mainplane. The Phantom started to roll faster and faster as Allon and Engstrom pulled the ejection handles desperately before they hit the sea.

The Martin Baker rocket-powered seats fired fractions of a second apart flinging first Engstrom then Allon out into the air over the Gulf of Tonkin. The rear seat left the aircraft almost vertically in roll, but 28 degrees backwards and Engstrom's canopy ballooned out a thousand feet over the China Sea. The pilot's seat roared out of the dying aircraft, flinging Allon almost horizontally over the waves. His parachute opened at 400 feet and Allon hit the water a good ten seconds before his crewman.

The Mig screamed through their last point in the sky, tracking the empty hulk of highly sophisticated junk like a shark after a dying fish, as the jet fell with an enormous splash of foam and spray into the Gulf. Engstrom hit the water hard, 200 yards from his pilot, and lay in shock as his bright orange life jacket inflated, tipping his head towards the horizon.

The Mig was coming round now and hugging the waves; the Americans could both see it aim directly for their patch of sea and then roar overhead so low that they both ducked instinctively. Finally it climbed towards the shore and rotated very slowly in a beautiful victory roll until it became nothing but an invisible distant noise in the Asian sky.

Allon and Engstrom were very lucky. Within fifteen minutes they were being circled by three Skyhawks returning to the carrier *USS Hancock*. The planes had been vectored over the floating airmen by the high-flying Grumman Tracker constantly stationed over the Gulf to watch over downed airmen and co-ordinate their search and rescue.

Allon felt an immense sense of relief sweep over him as he bobbed quietly, almost happily, on the swell of the ocean.

'Mike! OK, Mike?' the shout sounded tinny and desperate.

'Joe! Fine, fine, you OK?'

'Phew, thank God, thank God. Oh Jesus, I thought you wouldn't make it at that height. Wow! God bless Mr. Baker, wherever he may be.'

'He's in England.'

'No kidding. Say, any injuries?' the Texan was relieved.

'Nope. You?'

'Nope, your beacon OK?'

'Guess so, they're our buddies up there.' Allon looked to the sky.

'Not quite, they're Navy.'

'Bless 'em just the same.' Allon started paddling gently with his arms.

'Hey did you see that mother.'

'Not a thing until he hit.'

'Must've been sitting in a tree.' The Texan was mystified.

'Any contact on radar?'

'Not a thing.'

Then Michael thought he remembered a small black tube under one wing. A jamming pod? 'I think I saw an ECM pod under the port wing.'

'That's the only explanation unless he took off vertically as we flew over,' the Texan replied.

'Not a chance, only the Marines and the British do that, with AV-8s.'

'There again, it could have been a Marine, huh?'

The two of them laughed, desperately, and all the time a Jolly Green Giant clattered steadily towards them, its radar operator locked on to the beacon which flashed its signal like a tiny lighthouse in an electronic ocean.

'Here they come. Wowee, a free ride in a Giant!' The Texan was delighted.

It took only eight minutes to haul them up, one by one, to the huge green Sikorsky CH 53, hovering like a tornado 30 feet above them. As the chopper lifted away to its base, south of the DMZ, four sharks that had also picked up the floating distress signals swam impatiently away.

Michael lay in the hospital bed and thought of Liza. It was the kind of drowsy afternoon heat he remembered as a child when they had to go to bed after the midday meal in the kibbutz. He closed his eyes and willed himself back almost fifteen years. Yes, President Kennedy was killed ten years ago this week and America had now been nine years in Vietnam. He'd flown his third tour and now he'd been shot down for the first time. A week ago today he was floating in the Gulf of Tonkin and tomorrow he'd be out and back to the States for 'R and R' after the operation. He was lucky, so very lucky.

He held his hand up to the ceiling, stretched open his fingers and counted off the lucky breaks.

One, he hadn't been killed.

Two, he hadn't been made a prisoner.

Three, he'd survived the ejection in spite of the altitude.

Four, he hadn't drowned.

Five, he'd been picked up.

Six, ditto all these for Joe.

Seven, he hadn't broken his back, only strained it.

There were three fingers to go. I've got three pieces of luck left, he thought. Then there are my toes, of course.

'Colonel Allon. Colonel Allon, sir, are you in pain?'

Michael blinked and turned towards the voice.

'Are you alright, Colonel?'

He looked straight into the prettiest face he'd seen in Vietnam. His hands fell with a slap to the bed and he sat up, leaning on his elbows, and grinned.

'I'm fine, thank you, nurse. Just counting my blessings.'

'I'm sorry, I didn't mean to interrupt. I thought you were signalling for a nurse.'

'Nope . . . I mean, yes, um . . . I mean, I'd like some assistance with this belt nurse . . . what's your name heh, you know mine?'

'I'm Nurse Koh, Colonel. Will you please lie down while I check your corset, sir.'

'Corset? This is a body belt, not a corset, sister.'

'It's a medical corset, Colonel, we use them on patients of both sexes. It performs the same function, it keeps your back straight.'

'Oh, Joe Engstrom told me it was the latest ground-level G-suit, to protect me on high G-turns in the wheelchair, stop me from blacking out, hold my gut in and . . . hurt like hell.'

'It's probably the hard edges making you sore as you move, Colonel, you should be lying still, certainly not leaning like that.'

Nurse Koh moved to his pillow and placed one hand under his back while dropping the pillow support to ease him flat.

'Just relax, Colonel, and please lie flat as much as possible. When they fly you back home you'll have two further days on your back then.'

'Anything you say, Miss Koh, so long as you ease my corset.'

She was used to the suggestive approach. It mattered less in his case, he was interesting. The three ward sisters had all admired him when he'd arrived.

He was quiet but not dull, his eyes sparkled and he laughed a lot. Diana Koh watched him become part of the ward, his easy relaxed manner attracting the injured pilots around him. All had shared a common experience, they'd all ejected from crippled aircraft. Two had broken backs, one being totally paralysed from the neck down, the other suffering from permanent nervous spasms as his twisted ganglia touched the jumbled vertebrae caused by a through-the-canopy ejection. Four had varying degrees of burns; a fifth had died, mercifully, the day before. One had lost his jaw, wiped clean off by a 23 mm cannon shell fired by Vietcong out in the Delta. The remaining twelve had various broken limbs, mainly resulting from hard landings as they came down through the tree canopy.

All suffered from shock. Some would never completely recover; none would forget.

Nurse Koh had seen more than four hundred of them in four years. They were a minute fraction of the war's casualties and were treated like royalty compared with her own people. She felt no bitterness, though—rather, a feeling of gratitude. Like most Vietnamese, she couldn't understand Americans; she didn't know why a rich, secure country with a million times the wealth of Vietnam bothered with a poor one where your enemy was indistinguishable from your friend and killed you day and night in the most varied and painful ways.

Here was a room full of foreign young men, injured by her own people. She did not understand it, but she knew the reality was pain, pain in every clever way imaginable. Like the phantom pain of a missing limb, the pain of newly burnt flesh like crackling on pork, the pain of lacerated skin with thousands of tiny pieces of metal, and the pain of blindness, the effect on the optic nerve and the effect on the personality.

Nurse Koh felt that she must try to alleviate the suffering around her. Regardless of the complex reasons, the politics and the corruption, her job was quite simply to give help to the injured, be they Americans or Vietnamese.

No doctor in the world could find any medical difference between a Vietcong or a South Vietnamese. When the clothes were stripped in the mortuary they were identical. All were dead. The war fed on death: it craved armies of young men, but for every soldier it required an old woman, a pregnant girl or a baby. Nurse Koh had seen every form of injury, every messy limb, head, eye, hand or glistening intestine, and she ceased to be amazed at anything men might inflict on each other.

And here was this good-looking young American, a flyer,

no less: a modern man, a technocrat with a simple, strained vertebra, ready to go home and leave it all behind. In five years' time, she estimated, the Americans would be gone, tired of the game, disillusioned and bitter. The Vietnamese would still be there fighting among themselves as they had been for centuries. Nurse Koh was tired and dispirited, and her instructions to the Colonel were perfunctory but not impolite.

'Lie still, Colonel. Now where does it pain you?'

Still grinning, he pointed to his exposed right hip: the flesh was red and sore where the corset had chafed him.

'Right, I'll put some powder on it, but you must remain still or the powder will rub off.' She disappeared for two or three minutes as Michael watched her go, her black hair tied up in a neat bun and tucked under her starched white nurse's cap, revealing her slender neck. He fantasised briefly on her sheer stockings and slender but well-proportioned legs, and he suddenly felt very frustrated. Here he was, 25 years old with a healthy bank account enhanced by his 4000-hour flying pay; he was attractive, well-proportioned and very fit —and my God, could he do with a bit of ass right now.

Nurse Koh reappeared by the nursing station carrying a pink plastic bottle of medicated powder; in the other hand she held, lightly, as if it were an invitation card, a long buff envelope. He looked hard at her, imagining the light tropical outfit sliding off her shoulders to reveal what must be a beautiful, buttermilk-tinted body with small, pert breasts and pinky-brown aureoles.

She walked with her head held slightly to one side, her thighs brushing together, rustling the flimsy dress, in tiny beige shoes with heels that clicked on the glistening vinyl floor. He closed his eyes slowly as if to fix the image in his drowsy mind before it dissolved too soon.

'Colonel, this letter was just handed in by courier, Matron asked me to give it to you.' She handed him the official looking envelope and started to powder him with smooth, firm, circular pressure using her free hand. The massage was beautiful. He lay there 'umming' and 'aahing', his eyes closed, willing her to move her searching fingers to his front, to his groin, to fondle him while she undid her shift and he slid his hand up the back of her thigh and cupped her soft buttock, then reaching forward deeply into that warm, moist heaven that opened into her beautiful body.

'Colonel, will you please stop that.'

He opened his eyes and looked down to see his penis erecting below his pyjamas and instantly cupped it in his hands with a mixture of embarrassment and pleasure.

'Sorry, Nurse, it's been a long time since I had a pretty girl massage me. Pardon me.'

He smiled softly, but she never flickered an eye and pushed him onto his left side so that she could rub the small of his back. The envelope crinkled as he turned and brought it closer to his face where he awkwardly tried to read the postmark. It didn't tell him much.

PRIORITY—US Government Official Telegram
FOR NAMED ADDRESSEE ONLY. DO NOT BREAK SEAL UNLESS IDENTITY CARD AND SIGNATURE ARE IDENTIFIED WITH THOSE OF ADDRESSEE. INFRINGEMENT WILL LEAD TO PROSECUTION.
COLONEL MICHAEL J. ALLON, USAF
293rd FIGHTER WING
DA NANG MILITARY DISTRICT
SOUTH VIETNAM
US MILITARY POSTCODE MBD19982AD.

He slit it open with his little finger and held it upside down, shaking out the folded white letter. He unfolded and spread it till he could read it clearly, angling it so that the Nurse couldn't read its silhouette in the glare of the afternoon sunlight. The message was clearly printed below the USAF franked insignia.

THIS ORDER SUPERSEDES ALL PREVIOUS ORDERS.

FOR: COLONEL MICHAEL J. ALLON, USAF No. 198892173
THIS ORDER CONFIRMS YOUR CLEARANCE TO RETURN TO CONTINENTAL US ON MILITARY CHARTER RT 177 DEPARTS TAN SON NHUT DEC. 3 1972 WHERE REPORT 11.30 HOURS SAIGON TIME. COLLECT TRAVEL WARRANTS AT AIRPORT AND AWAIT FURTHER ORDERS.

BY ORDER
LT. GENERAL HOGAN
USAF
MILITARY AIRLIFT COMMAND

'Well, it's official, Nurse Koh. I'm going home for good,' and he closed his eyes and savoured her stiffening fingers.

Suddenly he sat up, much to her confusion, surprise and annoyance.

'Hey! Have you been to the States yet?'

'No, Colonel, and if you do that again neither will you. You could have displaced the vertebra completely and then you'd be here for another month. Now just lie back and co-operate, will you?'

'Just a moment, please. *Have* you been there before?'

'I said no, but the way this war is going I'll probably have to, no doubt.'

'Hey, wait on there. Do you mean that?'

'Anything is possible, Colonel. You see the fighting, I only see the wounded and the dead. If the Americans decide to leave, thousands of us will die. I will either be killed or imprisoned. I could never accept that. So I would leave, no doubt for America, if she will have me.'

'Hey, that's pretty sorry talk there, Nurse Koh. Nobody's leaving, and the bombing's going well. I know that for a fact.'

He was partly right. President Nixon had ordered a dedicated strategic bombing offensive of North Vietnam literally to blast the Communists to the peace table, and it was to succeed in that limited objective. Fifteen B52s were lost in the heaviest surface-to-air missile salvos ever recorded, but the rate of loss—a little over two per cent—demonstrated to the Vietnamese and the Russians that the country could be flattened by conventional weapons long before the Americans lost all their bombers. Michael himself had flown top cover for many of these raids as well as low-level strike against isolated strategic targets.

The Nurse continued. 'When we sign the peace treaty, your dignity will be saved and then you will leave. It will still mean war, this time between the South and the North, without the Americans. The South will lose, because it cannot fight without the Americans and so I will leave. I have made plans, Colonel.'

'Miss Koh, that's ridiculous. But look, I tell you what, if you do have to leave call me up, will you?'

'Colonel, please lie down while I finish.'

'No, you give me your address and I'll give you mine. Then you can call me, eh!' He laughed, never believing that every word she said would prove to be true.

'Colonel, if it makes you lie down then you give me your address and I will contact you.'

'Is that a promise?'

'Sure.'

And he did.

And she did.

13
Home

The flight in the Pan Am 747 Military Charter brought the Israeli boy out of South-East Asia and home for Christmas. John and Judith Cohen were there and so was John Jr, now an executive in a real estate company and married with a two-year-old daughter. Other friends of Michael watched him from a distance as he walked down the big Boeing's steps at Los Angeles International Airport, twenty miles from their new home in California. He blinked in the sunlight, looking marvellous in his Air Force Blue, scanning for the welcoming party he knew would be there.

A military band suddenly blared out and brought home to him the fact that he was a warrior, home from the wars at last. But the welcome couldn't compare to the victory parades he'd seen in documentaries of airmen returning from Europe or the Pacific in 1945. The Air Force had to follow strict codes from the Government: nobody could go overboard, press could not ask embarrassing questions, family reunions were encouraged only as long as they were kept discreet and homely.

Michael saw them, a shouting waving bunch of tiny figures out by the terminal buildings; then he recognised the black-hatted, rounded form of a familiar figure. 'It must be Rabbi Groman. My, my, all the way out to meet me, would you believe it,' he said to himself.

Then he was running from the Transit bus, up the escalator, and into the military reception area; in twenty minutes he was out and there they were: they all screamed together and everybody cried, even Michael—because waiting, like a beautiful mannequin, in front of all of them was Liza, his beautiful black-haired sister Liza, who held him tight like a vice and sobbed into his chest and couldn't say anything but 'Michael, Michael, Michael'. Then he felt the Rabbi embrace them both and they all wept because they suddenly felt so very, very close.

For a week they celebrated. It was like a week-long Bar-mitzvah with people arriving from towns called Schenectady and Sioux Falls and Santa Clara, who slept on the floor or the sofa or with the neighbours. People Michael couldn't remember, mamas who hugged him and sheepish middle-aged fathers who pressed gifts of money into his hand and clapped him on the back. People who remembered *their* war and how none of their families welcomed them home because they'd left them all behind in the ground and in the air of Europe.

Michael and Liza and Rabbi Groman talked for hours, soaking up each other's presence, like heat from a glowing fire when you've been out in the cold too long. They went for walks and to synagogue and out to eat with the family. Liza wept on the anniversary day of the death of her beloved Mordechai, killed in the War of Attrition. Michael felt awkward for having survived, but she was 'fine, just fine' in another day and said she was sorry. They'd never had time to marry, she said, but they'd made love and that made him special. Liza talked about the kibbutz and how well Elizabeth and David were when she'd left them a week ago, after the Government had telegrammed her with the news of Michael's repatriation. Daniel was away for long periods now, travelling around Europe on sales visits for his firm, a Rotterdam-registered shipping company. Elizabeth was quite grey, and slept only with the aid of tablets. Liza and she had grown further apart during the years as her aunt withdrew more and more into her own private world.

Shimon Yariv, the kibbutz's original leader, now lived permanently in Tel Aviv where he had gone back to teaching.

Archaeology was his latest interest, taking him on long journeys into the Sinai and the Negev, surveying Biblical sites. Somehow he'd wangled an old American-made half-track out of the IDF commanders; into this he piled two or three research colleagues, his camping gear and a massive ice box full of cheap Israeli wine. Michael laughed at the thought of the serious, now completely bald Yariv, half drunk, driving a half-track at night in some of the most rugged deserts in the world; then he frowned when he remembered that Yariv never drank.

The victory of the Six Day War had suddenly expanded Israel's borders as far as Suez and the Gulf of Eilat, and given her total control of Jerusalem and the Holy Places. The hardest hand-to-hand fighting had been won by the Golani Brigade who had taken the infamous Golan Heights near Kibbutz Ramta and forced the Syrians back towards Damascus where they dug in behind vast Soviet minefields and tank traps to replenish their shattered divisions with thousands of Soviet artillery pieces, tanks and armoured vehicles. The talk in Israel, however, was of possible peace.

Few Israelis with whom Liza had spoken believed that Egypt, under the conservative Sadat, would launch an attack against Israel. The cease-fire to the War of Attrition had come into force in August 1970 and since then action had been confined mainly to anti-terrorist raids into the Lebanon. The worldwide hijacking and bombing outrages had been the major expressions of hostility towards Israel, thus keeping the conflict on the front pages of the world's newspapers.

Liza herself was living in Jerusalem near Rabbi Groman and both would often visit the Western Wall to pray, and to remember their parents. Liza placed her message on a tiny, fluttering slip of paper which she would then fold and slip into the cracks of the Wall of the Temple.

'Michael,' she said, one lazy afternoon by the pool, 'what did you do with Papa's suitcase, the one Elizabeth gave you when you left for America? I'd like to see it again.'

'It's upstairs, Liza. I'll fetch it down later when Rabbi

Groman visits. Funny you should ask about it, I was thinking about it only yesterday when I was reading Daniel's letter from Munich.'

'Couldn't you fetch it now? We could dust it off before he arrives?'

'OK. Let me finish my drink and I'll fetch it. Want to give me a hand?'

'No, I'll mix another drink. Same again?'

'Please.'

The cocktail slipped down easily, reinforcing his feeling of contentment. It was a beautiful California day and few things could be nicer than lying here on a very comfortable leisure bed by a blue, blue pool. He slipped into a doze and thought again of the Vietnamese nurse, the lovely Nurse Koh who'd fill a bikini as well as Liza any day. Before he felt himself stiffening he rolled off the bed, stood up and stretched his tanned frame while yawning at the sky.

'OK, Liza, back in a minute.'

The grass felt delicious under his bare feet as he loped to Uncle John's house and made his way to his room. It was cool and quiet inside, everybody out for the day except Liza and himself.

He owned few things, as is the way of operational pilots; he spent his money mainly on casual clothes, the very best electronic audio-visual systems and his pride and joy—a metallic-brown English Lotus Esprit S2 which he maintained in perfect order for racing in and out of town on the odd casual date.

He opened the big built-in wardrobe and looked up to the top shelf. The suitcase, its brown leather still strong and supple, lay under a pile of old aviation magazines. He pulled it out, balancing the magazines still on the lid and placed the lot on his bed. The magazines started to slide off and he gathered them into a tidy stack which he put on his chest of drawers. The suitcase lay in the afternoon sun, its neat brass catches reflecting the warm California sunshine. Michael paused for a moment, gazing at it, then picked it up by its soft leather-covered handle and carried it, cool against his bare legs, out to the pool.

Liza broke into a wide grin when she saw the case.

'Hey, it looks almost new! What did you do to it, Michael?' They both knelt down in the grass, touching it reverently.

'I polish it now and then, after all it was Mama's and Papa's gift to us. Looks good, doesn't it? Liza, you open it.'

She opened it to reveal the red satin sack with its two long sash cords. Inside were the Tallis in its brown velvet bag and the small boxwood picture frame with its double portrait of Benjamin and Ruth Allon, taken in 1939, in their last summer of peace. There was a little Tunbridgeware jewel box, a gift to Ruth from Benjamin on their first anniversary. There was the little hand mirror that Michael had used as a make-believe semaphore when playing in Jerusalem before moving to the kibbutz, and there was his father's pocket watch, its glass cracked and the hands frozen at 11.32, the instant of his death on the road to Jerusalem.

In a plain, black metal tube with an airtight cap, Liza found a bundle of papers including the family birth certificates and her parents' educational diplomas. A copy of their will and a number of private letters completed the written records of the Allon family up to the time the landmine killed Ruth and Benjamin.

Liza started to hum to herself as she always did in times of deep emotional disturbance, and Michael suddenly felt a wave of sadness and nostalgia sweep over him. He felt strangely homesick for Israel after fifteen years away, and he remembered the anger he felt towards the Arabs. But he felt a far greater anger towards their armourers, the Russians, for the murder of his parents.

'Michael, I must go back soon, you know. Israel's my home; yours is anywhere you can fly. Could I take the case back to Mama and Papa? It ought to be close to them. It'll be safe there, I promise'

'Of course, Liza. It's the right thing to do, I'm sure. Just one thing, would you mind if I kept father's watch?'

But Liza said nothing; she just smiled through the tears,

rocking gently on her haunches and humming her song to herself.

She stopped as a shadow covered the case, and both of them looked up at the silhouette of Rabbi Groman. For a moment, all three felt as if they were back in the schoolyard in Jerusalem, the day Michael and Liza lost their parents.

'Michael, Liza, forgive me for interrupting you, but I came round the side of the house so as not to get you out of the pool. I should have rung the bell.' He looked embarrassed and fidgeted.

'Not at all, Rabbi, it's always good to see you. Your timing couldn't have been more auspicious, we were looking at the case I brought with me to America; you remember, the one Aunt Elizabeth packed.' Michael was standing up, now taking the man's coat and drawing up a garden chair.

'Thank you, Michael, it's hot out here after the synagogue.'

'A drink?'

'No thanks, I'm off the liquids, you know. This kidney trouble.' He patted his side, smiling gently at Liza. 'It's good to cry, my dear, never be ashamed of tears, I've seen every kind. Tears of happiness, of grief, of laughter, of relief. You name it, Groman's brushed them away. Now, what are those tears for, if you don't mind telling me?' He touched Liza gently on her shoulder and she smiled up at him, blinking them away and rubbing her eyes clear.

'They were happy-sad tears Rabbi: happy to see Michael and sad to say goodbye.'

He looked surprised. 'Never! Why goodbye, Liza?'

'I'm going home, that's all. Home to Jerusalem,' she said.

'In that case, I was meant to come, because so am I. I've just been recalled by the Joint Council. Could we travel back together?'

'Oh, could we!' and she jumped up and hugged him, then lifted his hat and planted a big kiss on his balding head.

'When are you leaving?'

'Within the next couple of days.'

'Fine, I'll book the flight tomorrow when we're in town,

but I'll ring the airline now. Any preference?'

'Economy, my dear. Make it El Al, will you—the food you know.'

'OK.'

'Liza, this is the best news I've had today.' And he clutched her warmly by the hand.

Michael felt relieved. He knew Liza was homesick, but he was worried about the long flight back. The hijacking was very bad at present, but El Al was the safest way to travel, as security was very strictly enforced and everybody and everything was searched before each flight.

'Say, dat's fine, you two guys are goin' to be jawing all the way to Jerusalem, leaving poor little me with my ears burning, dat's not fair. I think I'll come along and make sure there's no funny business goin' on. You like my sister, mister? Den you treat her like a lady and dat means you make her respectable, huh, and—' Liza pushed him backwards into the pool and started to bombard him with ice cubes from their unfinished drinks. Michael raised an arm straight above his head and sank like a stone, leaving a noisy track of bubbles. He jack-knifed and swam underwater in smooth strokes to the bottom, and then porpoised out in a powerful vertical thrust that splashed Liza and the Rabbi and forced them both, laughing and spluttering, away from the edge.

Liza turned and ran at full pelt over the edge, tucking her legs beneath her, pinching her nose, her eyes shut tight. The splash came like a crack and Michael immediately dived to intercept her, but she was too quick and thrust away, her slender legs powering her around the edge. Michael let his arms relax and followed her like a seal after a fish. She was a fast swimmer and in a moment dived down to the deepest part of the pool, where she held her breath as long as she could before surfacing again.

'Hey, you were a time, you had me worried. What were you doing down there?' Michael said.

Liza said nothing, just smiled and lifted herself out of the water. Then she pattered onto the grass where she lay face down letting the water soak into the California soil. She began to hum softly to herself. Michael had turned to float on his back, his eyes shut, facing the blue, blue sky. The lapping water slapped gently against his ears, and he felt calmer than he could remember. He closed his eyes and thought of Diana, as he often did now. Rabbi Groman put his hands on his hips and gazed at them both affectionately as he thought back to the day he found them playing in the school yard in Jerusalem. He picked up his coat, slipped it on and walked quietly away, not wishing to interrupt their thoughts.

Liza Allon and Rabbi Groman left America and Michael for the very last time, flying home to Israel one day in January 1973. As the big Boeing rose into the California sky for the long flight, Michael stood slightly apart from the rest of the family, looking at the plane's disappearing silhouette and listening for every last trace of its vanishing roar. The tears lay brimming on the edge of his eyelashes and he had the distinct feeling he would never see either of them again. He was right.

The twenty-mile drive back to the house was quiet and reflective. Aunt Judith lay asleep in the back seat luxuriating in the now uncrowded wagon. John Cohen sat next to Michael on the front bench, staring, but unseeing, at the flicker of passing lights.

Ahead of them in the little Pinto were John Junior and his family cruising along the freeway.

'Michael, when we get back home, can you spare me an hour out on the porch? We've got things to discuss and it's best we do it now while everybody's flaked out by the TV.' John kept staring out the side window in his quiet way, Michael glanced over but couldn't see the expression on his face, just the whitening of his knuckles on his safety harness.

'Sure, any problem?'

'Later, Mike, at home, eh?' and they drove on without another word.

The sky was crystal clear, the way it can be when you're out of the Valley and half way up the mountains. The two of them stood side by side staring out at the twinkling lights of the large city while above them swept a carpet of stars like a million fireflies that fooled you into believing that you could see the Universe when all that was there was a minute part of an insignificant galaxy among millions of others.

'Michael, Rabbi Groman asked me to give you a letter after Liza had gone home. It's from your Uncle Daniel. I suggest you talk about it to nobody but me ever, then give it to me, I'll destroy it myself. Whatever you decide will be respected and you will never be asked again. Here, take it, it's been giving me the first sleepless nights in years.' He offered the puzzled young man a sealed envelope.

They walked over to the pool and switched on the soft blue lights and finally the outdoor lamp by the barbecue pit. The cicadas were noisy out here which helped to fill their silence. John took out his pipe, settled back in his garden chair and closed his eyes. Michael sat in Rabbi Groman's usual chair, illuminated by the light.

The envelope felt heavy; it was made of thick, parchment-like paper, and had no mark or seal on it that Michael could discern. He opened it at its short end and was surprised to feel another sealed, black polythene wallet inside. The plastic was very tough and he was forced to slit it with his pocket knife to avoid tearing the contents. Inside was a single flimsy square of very thin paper, very much like rice paper. Michael frowned and looked up towards John.

'Hey, this looks edible. It's so thin.'

John kept his eyes shut and carried on puffing away. Michael opened the single fold and sat back, the empty anonymous envelope lying on his lap, and began reading. There was no preamble.

Michael,

You are the son of the Abraham Policy and you are now being asked to return to your homeland. We believe that the State of Israel will be in greater danger in 1973 than at any other time since its birth. Information has reached us of a massive Soviet plan to destroy our state in a co-ordinated assault through the Bar Lev line in Sinai using Egyptian forces. Simultaneous attacks will be launched on the Golan by Syrian forces backed up by a worldwide propaganda campaign to discredit Israel whilst maintaining the oil threat discreetly in the background. Huge investments are being made by Arab countries in Western industry which is becoming dependent on Middle East orders for development contracts.

For the first time since its creation there is serious reason to believe that Israel could be abandoned by the United States! We will receive no support from the EEC countries who are totally dependent on Arab oil. The United Kingdom will as usual maintain a 'discreet' profile, rather like a duck, composed on top, but paddling furiously underneath.

America is now importing 50 per cent of its oil from the Arab world, Nigeria and Venezuela. Its major corporations do not even know how many shares are owned by Arab clients who are also becoming major customers.

We have definite proof that the Soviets have established nuclear parity with the US. Read the papers during the next few months. The Soviets are using this situation to stalemate any US involvement in developments in the Middle East. The Russians have served notice on the US that any use of 'non-conventional' weapons in Vietnam will result in the supply of equivalent weapons to the North.

President Sadat is anxious to establish an honourable peace in the Middle East, but is being pressured by enormous KGB efforts. For the first time since 1945 there is a joint KGB-GRU Planning Council operating under Lt. General Mendeleiv; this reports directly to Minister of Defence Grechko, and to Brezhnev who controls the CPSO, the Central Committee of the Communist Party of the Soviet Union. This means nothing less than supreme priority in Soviet planning, second only to conditions DURING a nuclear war.

War in the Middle East will start by the end of 1973, possibly earlier. It will bear no relation to the Six Day War because this time the Soviet Union has stalemated the entire economic and nuclear power of the United States and Europe by using a) the Arab oil weapon, b) the so-called Vietnamese 'peace' talks in Paris with the US, and c) world opinion by manipulation of the media who, in any case, are preoccupied with an amateurish burglary in Washington.

The position regarding military power in the Middle East as of December 1972 is as follows:-

a) Sadat will be forced by the Soviets to attack using his totally re-equipped forces relying on a missile umbrella to protect his troops and tanks when crossing the Suez Canal. We observed a total rehearsal of this plan in 1968.
b) Syria have over 1000 T54 and T62 Soviet tanks within twenty miles of Golan.
c) The Russians will make a series of feinting moves particularly at the SALT talks in Helsinki, which have achieved nothing for the US but have bought five years for the Soviets.
d) We in Israel must win the war in no more than 15 days or our economy will be destroyed.
e) The United States must maintain resupply of our losses in aircraft and missiles until we have achieved a cease-fire.
f) We will be fighting Russian pilots air-to-air and Russian ground controllers operating new missiles and radars.

These are sobering facts and I know you will be disturbed by this news so soon after returning from Vietnam.

We have watched your progress every day since you left Israel and seen you develop into the man we respect and love. We have no ties over you and know that the bond between Abraham and his son was not as strong as his respect for the Creator. You must choose your own Master, and perhaps you already have.

I myself asked the Joint Planning Council to recall you; I begged Rabbi Groman when last I saw him in Tel Aviv to intercede personally and ask you to come home where you could instruct our young pilots and aircrew on the latest Soviet weapons, missiles and tactics before the War begins.

The good Rabbi declined; he said that we Jews have fought for thousands of years; that we have wandered in the desert and been led to our Zion by the Creator's own prophet Abraham and only a prophet will lead us to final victory.

He believes that you have a rare gift in life which is God-given. You are an innocent abroad, a happy child in a world of devious plots and intrigues. I disagreed, for I believe that your gift is flying, and your love is the sky. We need experienced, gifted pilots more than any other kind of skill in this coming War.

You will ask, why do the Soviets want a Middle East War, why is the defeat of Israel so important to their world strategy, this tiny nation of four million people in the middle of a desert land? Nobody knows the truth, but the record of history tells an extraordinary story.

Since the end of the Second War there has been mounted a pogrom in Russia worse than any in history. Why? Since 1945 the Soviet Union has waged a ceaseless war against Israel, creating conflict between Arab and Jew. Since 1948 the Soviet Union has shipped more arms to Arabs for fighting Israelis than to the rest of the world, including Vietnam and Cuba. In 1967 the entire Arab war plan, which we pre-empted, was prepared by active Russian military commanders while their Air Forces, tanks and infantry were trained by the best Russian instructors.

In one year the Russians replaced the entire Arab front-line forces which we had destroyed in six days, at a cost to them as great as the whole of the NATO Central Forces.

For 25 years the Palestinians, with whom we had previously lived in intimate contact, have been trained and armed by the Communist bloc under orders from the Soviet Union.

WHY, we ask, WHY?

Forgive me expressing my own opinion, but I sincerely believe I know the answer. It is the Communist leaders' fear of the TRUTH. Communism was created by men who saw around them appalling squalor, deprivation, corruption and inhumanity. A Jew, Karl Marx, in a relatively tolerant kingdom called England, wrote a book about the abuses and how ordinary people could defeat the tiny powerful minority by working together. His words became the Tora, the Bible, the Koran of the twentieth century.

By extraordinarily complex circumstances his book was adopted by a group of people, primed and ready to fight. They won, because the capitalist West was involved in its own World War which exhausted it of weapons, money and men. The Russian people defeated a crude, corrupt, evil, ignorant class who had tried to stop the progress of history.

The next twenty years saw the conventional struggle for power among the leaders of the Communist Party who fought a huge civil war whilst the rest of the world turned its back and struggled for power. The Russians lost fifty million dead between 1917 and 1945.

We Jews lost six million in ten years.

All of Russia was controlled by one political party, which could only maintain power through terror, a fact which Stalin recognised and exploited continuously. The environment of terror has a disastrous effect on reason, debate or discussion. Stalin made terror work until the day he died; thus was Communist power maintained.

The moment even the tiniest hint of democracy was introduced, with Krushchev, the Russian people started to question Communist Party doctrine.

The leaders of the 'dissidents' were mainly educated people and a very high proportion were Jews.

Even the chief scientist of the Soviet thermonuclear programme, André Sakharov, was a Jew.

For the Communist Party to maintain power there was always one simple solution: kill intellectuals, kill thought. They knew that the most powerful weapon on earth is thought converted into the written word; witness the power of individuals with no weapons but words; Jesus Christ, Mohammed, Buddha, Marx.

So the Russians embarked on a war against free thought, and the free thinkers of the Western World have so often been Jews. If the words of one free-thinking Jew, a refugee in London, could create the Communist world, then imagine what four million Jews could do with their homeland, if they were to focus their thoughts.

The Russian people are no different from any other cross-section of humanity, but the leaders of the Soviet Communist Party are totally different. They are dedicated to holding on to power and so they must fight any individual or any state who could threaten that power.

So many Jews came from Russia, witnesses to the total power of the Communist Party's secret police, the NKVD, now the KGB; and the KGB know it. So long as the witnesses are free to talk, to tell of their experiences, to ACCUSE, then the evildoer will try every way to destroy them before they can expose the evil.

Can you imagine then, the gift to the KGB of the Palestinians; for here is another group, another oppressed people who can be used as pawns in the game to kill the Jew, the free-thinker. And what a bonus, to control the fuel of the modern world, oil. Ally with the Palestinian, keep him in squalor so that the world's press can be manipulated, as it always has been, to portray human suffering. Forbid free discussion of alternative solutions. Refuse to discuss how the huge ransoms of Arab oil money could be used to assist the truly poor Palestinian or Bedouin or Egyptian in a peaceful co-operative development of the millions of acres of desert. No, the KGB must focus all attention on the struggle against the Jews.

And meanwhile, Michael, what is happening in the rest of the world? Soviet Communism under the control of the KGB is winning the battles and losing hardly a man, exploiting every avenue and creating new ones to achieve their single goal, world domination.

Finally, while they manipulate Arabs, Cubans, Vietnamese and so forth, they prevent any free thought or discussion among their own people, surrounding them with an army bigger than NATO whose guns and minefields are designed to keep their people IN.

Forgive the rambling, Michael. I am not a philosopher,

just an ordinary free thinker with my own opinion and interpretation.

I respect therefore, totally, your freedom to choose your answer and even your silence. But remember: we only have one year at the most.

Sincerely,
Daniel Perès
Tel Aviv
December 1972

He felt a shiver run down his back, his fingers went clammy, and he noticed he was holding his breath. A slight breeze appeared to be shaking the letter, making it difficult to focus on the abrupt, nearly illegible signature; but the night was still. It was his hands that were trembling. He willed himself to relax and found he was stooped forwards, taut as a bowstring. Slowly, he lay back in the chair again, dropping the featherlight paper softly to his lap as he looked straight up to the glittering blackness.

It became still and silent. His eyes absorbed the history above him while his brain began recalling images of the past: playing amid a forest of table legs with Liza, staring at a Chinese-white canopy drifting inexorably towards treacle black smoke, the smell of crackling metal heaped in a half ploughed field, the tremor through his bare feet as the ship's horn groaned, and freshest of all, the sound of Liza's flight being called at LA International.

'Will those passengers travelling on El Al Flight 201 to Israel please report to the departure gate.'

Michael stared down at the letter again for a moment then turned towards John Cohen with a new respect. He said softly, looking at him with affection:

'Uncle John, I feel very humble. This must have been a burden to you, especially as Liza was here, and Rabbi Groman. Thank you for waiting until they had both left for home. I have an answer which I'm sure you can convey in your own way to Daniel, wherever he is.

'I love my country more than anything in my life, even more than flying. I can enjoy my flying because I have been given the training and the equipment with which to do a good job. I am not a political person at all, except that I do have a feeling of patriotism. Israel was my cradle if you like, but you and your family have made America my home. I cannot serve two masters; I've chosen mine and that's why I will not go to Israel.

'However, I believe as an American that we are the sole guardians, embarrassing as it may sound, of freedom. Whatever that may be—I only know what it isn't. It isn't lies, propaganda, regimentation or dictatorship. In America I believe I can express my opinion more freely than most men, and I value that.

'America took me in, a ten-year-old boy from a tiny country 5,000 miles away, and gave me a home. It asked for nothing back. I volunteered to be a pilot; nobody forced me. I believe my skill will help my country to help other countries like Israel. Now I know this must sound stilted and naive compared with Uncle Daniel's reasoning, but that's the way I am. I won't go back to Israel, unless America sends me.

'I don't ever regret my job in Vietnam, though other "free thinking" Americans would say I was one of Uncle Sam's hired killers; at least they can express that opinion. I believed, and still do, that I was fighting the spread of Soviet Communism; maybe I was misled. All I know is that I was shot at by Soviet Migs, hit by Soviet cannon shells, tracked by Soviet radar and heard a lot of Soviet controllers on the radio. Finally, I believe, I was shot down by a Soviet pilot.'

But he was wrong. It was a Palestinian.

14
Blackbird

Wheeler read the transcript again, the occasional thread of pipe smoke obscuring his vision like a theatrical gauze. His large farmer's fingers drummed softly on the ancient wood, interrupted by the occasional creak of his arthritic leather chair. The three components—man, desk, chair—made up the unique entity known to his staff as 'The Office'.

It was here they came for the final approval of all important work, to see it flourished with an antique black-and-gold 'Parker' that still flowed as smooth as velvet. In thirty years that signature had initiated some of the most secret operations of the Cold War. From the first brilliant analyses of Nazi 'V'-weapon development through the totally ignored prediction of Soviet ICBM research, the forgotten paper hastily resurrected from the vast files at the Pentagon. The 'Wheeler Report' as it was later called had won him grudging respect from earthbound militarists and pushed him rapidly through the cogs of the US military machine to lead larger and larger efforts in the long Cold War with the Soviet Union.

Wheeler looked up from the paper, his eyes scanning across a wall of photographs taken in every continent on earth; in strange places with names like Totonicapan, Maquinchao, Baraukura and Ayagh Kune Kol. He needed no photograph to remind him also of the searing heat at Woomera, the saturating humidity at Bien Hoa and the throat-cutting dryness of the Kara Kum desert.

Scattered around, like a theatrical agent's wall, were faces of every age and colour. A young Chinese farmer, a beautiful Malay girl, three laughing Cubans on a burnt-out tank, the bleak profile of a Texan, his prisoner-of-war number never forgotten by the General. Most of them were dead now but none forgotten: Wheeler's family of man. His eyes and ears, his friends and enemies.

And in the middle, like a burgled gallery, nothing but a blank space, 'Reserved'. The one face Wheeler wanted more than any on his wall but did not know, could not identify—his other self, his alter-ego, his counterpart in the Soviet Union—the Head of Soviet Air Force Intelligence.

Wheeler's staff had invented a name to give him substance. They'd called him 'Moriarty', after Sherlock Holmes' arch rival, the evil professor of fiction. They'd even given him a birthday, October 4th, the date of the launch of the first Sputnik; one young idiot had actually posted a card to Moscow during a vacation in Europe, addressed to:

Professor Moriarty
Head of Air Force Intelligence
Moscow Military District
USSR

The card had been returned within the month, directly to 'The Office'. It hung there, next to the 'Reserved' space, its only endorsement—a short, handwritten note that read,

'Returned to Lt. General Adam Wheeler
With kind regards
Professor Moriarty.'

And that had pleased Wheeler; someone out there was human. It still didn't stop him from ordering a full laboratory analysis of the paper, the ink, the glue and the handwriting style of the joker.

The paper was standard Soviet Government Issue, the handwriting was probably a woman's—the ink was East German. The saliva that had licked the stamp and sealed the air mail envelope was that of a man of blood group RH negative, probably impotent and certainly older than 40 years. He had contracted at one time in his travels sickle cell anaemia and licked from right to left, holding the envelope in one hand, probably the left. The inevitable cartoons had circulated resulting in an office 'identikit' character resembling a cross between the hunchback of Notre Dame and Mae West. Wheeler reckoned it was good for morale and had let it run its natural course.

The other wall, the one by the airlock door, had but one picture, three feet wide and two feet high. It showed what can only be described as some kind of space plane, a mixture between air- and space-craft. It was big, black and to Wheeler beautiful. It might have appeared fantastic but it was very real: it stood on a baking concrete apron in the middle of a desert in California.

Beale Air Force Base was the home of the world's fastest operational aircraft. The Lockheed SR71-A was known as the Blackbird because it looked black although it was painted a dark-blue indigo to merge with the near blackness of space as it flew over war zones at a height above 80,000 feet and at a speed in excess of 2,000 miles an hour. The entire machine measured up to the schoolboy's fantasy of a space plane; its 107-foot fuselage blended perfectly into a curiously rounded delta wing plan from which in turn there emerged two huge Pratt & Whitney J58 turbojets specially designed to suck in the massive volumes of air needed for fuel combustion at high rarefied altitudes. Even the fuel itself was a uniquely blended hydrocarbon which wouldn't be affected by the extremes of temperature encountered by this extraordinary machine.

Wheeler's most expensive toy, the brainchild of Lockheed designer Kelly Johnson, was about to be assigned a new crew, as long as Wheeler agreed.

'Yup,' he said to himself, 'looks OK to me,' and the famous pen crossed the mere square inch of paper leaving behind the unique pattern.

Michael Allon was going to fly the Blackbird.

Michael and 'Pete' Peabody, his electronic systems officer, sat enveloped in astronauts' clothing on rocket ejector seats packed into the two tiny capsules crammed full of the very latest electronic sensors. In front of Michael was the curious windscreen with its central razor-sharp leading edge which sliced up the air at more than 2,000 miles an hour.

For Pete, the view could not compare however with the clear canopy of a Phantom. To achieve the incredible speed and altitude necessary to avoid Soviet or Chinese missiles and radar, windows were virtually non existent. Peabody's view of the world was confined to two tiny observation panels set into the sloping sides of the craft, but where he missed out on the visible spectrum his array of electro-magnetic sensors gave him the most comprehensive view of the invisible energy of the earth that any human had experienced before.

He could select a range of wavelengths sweeping through a 'rainbow' millions of times more 'colourful' than that normally visible to the naked eye and with his array of forward-, downward- and even sideway-looking radars he could pick his way across the Earth at any height, weather or position, regardless of deserts or mountains, rivers or oceans. To navigate the Blackbird in this near-space environment Pete had mapping and Doppler radar, triple inertial gyros and Starfield sensors, supported by a bank of miniaturised computers. The best spies avoid confrontation and Blackbird was the best spy aircraft in the world.

The men who flew Blackbird were all members of the USAF's exclusive 9th Strategic Reconnaissance Wing, Michael Allon being their latest recruit. They were the élite pilots and electronic systems operators in the United States as their primary task was to fly over hostile countries or war zones gathering intelligence on everything that happened beneath their electronic sensors. They were the primary source of aerial intelligence for areas such as Cuba, China, Vietnam, the Soviet Union and the Middle East.

The Blackbird was part of an extraordinary aerial team whose job was to keep America and the West informed about Communist military activities anywhere in the world. The other elements were the well-known U2s and other electronic intelligence or ELINT aircraft working with the Big Bird reconnaissance satellites and remotely piloted vehicles or RPVs.

What made Blackbird special was that it flew in comparatively high-risk environments, directly over battles in progress, fooling hostile radar and missiles with fake electronic signals or powerful radar jammers. It depended on the reliability of its engines to keep out of the battle and the skill of its crew to conserve fuel and avoid interception by Soviet missiles or aircraft.

When Michael arrived at Beale in the first week of January 1973, Blackbird had been in front-line service for seven years and not one had been shot down.

Before he could fly Blackbird, Michael was subjected to the most stringent medical examination and performance tests ever used in the Air Force. All Blackbird pilots were required to have a proven record of high-speed jet experience in a combat environment and to attain astronaut standards of performance for they would have to wear full spacesuits while flying in a near-space environment, 25 miles above a very hostile earth. Composure, calmness and skill were needed, as well as enormous stamina. Some flights took several hours, with two or more air-to-air refuellings from the slow Stratotankers, the same ones Michael had used every time he'd flown on a combat sortie over Vietnam.

Michael had no trouble with the medical and performance tests, having fully recovered from the strained vertebra he'd experienced when ejecting into the Gulf of Tonkin. And so he was cleared for his first technical briefing prior to his first flight.

The facilities at Beale were designed to cover all aspects of flying, operating and maintaining the world's fastest operational aircraft. Michael was one of four new aircrew being trained for the job, two pilots and two Reconnaissance Systems Officers or RSOs. Pete Peabody was a small Pensylvanian with sharply crew-cut hair and a pale white baby face that belied his thirty years and gave no indication of his outstanding flying record.

'OK, gentlemen, welcome to the Blackbird briefing. You fellows have joined the élite: we believe we're the best and this aircraft is the best. I won't bore you with things you know well enough already but I'll just hit some of the essentials before we start following our course notes.'

The Colonel who addressed them was one of the original Blackbird development pilots working with 'Kelly' Johnson out at the 'Skunk Works' as the secret facility was known, in Burbank, California. Louis K. Sharpe was a mild-mannered silver-haired career pilot with more than 9,000 hours of flying behind him. People listened when he talked, he had that kind of way. He never smoked or drank, but played the pan pipes of all things for relaxation. He and his wife had a home near the field, they kept to themselves a lot ever since their boy had died in Hue at the age of nineteen. It was his first time away from home. He'd been flown back and was buried at Arlington with several thousands of other victims of Vietnam. He was lucky, some were never found, neither dead nor taken prisoner.

'This aircraft is capable of cruising at Mach 3.2 at 114,000 feet. It's 107 feet 5 inches from nose to tail and 55 feet 7 inches across the span. Don't fall off the tail because that's 18 feet 6 inches off the ground. It established the world absolute speed record as the A-11 prototype back on 1 May 1965, when two of my friends Stephens and André recorded 2,070 miles per hour. It's a hot ship. The twin engines are Pratt & Whitney J58 Turbojets delivering 32,500 pounds of thrust, each, when the 'burners are on. They'll drink 8,000 gallons of our own special brew, each hour, so check your consumption rates.

'Peabody and Davidson, you'll be very busy because your sensors will cover 60,000 square miles in an hour, and that's a lot of country. Allon and Hoverman, you will both have to rethink your flying because there's no tight turning like an F4 in this bird: she takes a good twenty miles to turn at low speed, and that means 1,000 miles an hour! You two crews will first fly the simulator and then complete ten flights on the specially built trainer out on the field. She's got a raised cockpit for the instructor, looks mean.'

Beale meant Blackbird and that meant sweat. The four crewmen worked hard at the multi-million-dollar simulator, mastering the concept of energy management by balancing height, speed, fuel and altitude to achieve the most efficient flight profile. Few references were made to the purpose of their flights at this stage, and nobody had time to ask.

It took two weeks before Michael was ready to fly. The flight started from the moment he and Colonel Sharpe put on their spacesuits, which is exactly what they were: almost identical to the Apollo crew suits with several interlayers for waste management including underpants and urine tube; a complete body-hugging, water-filled, heat-absorbing rubberised vest; an all-body G-suit for withstanding high acceleration or deceleration forces in emergencies at low altitude; and a portable air-conditioning unit connected to the aluminised outer layer for the ride to the aircraft.

The bus took them the three miles across the baking apron to the trainer. It looked incredibly lethal, painted in the special matt coating that visually pulled together the extraordinarily long flattened fuselage, like a gigantic stretched power boat whose crisp flared edges blended into a curiously cambered delta wing that wrapped round the two huge engines. Each had a giant conical centrebody that moved on tracks backwards or forwards to allow more or less air into the gulping turbojets. Its twin fins reared up like black monoliths, looking all of their eighteen feet in height.

Michael, used as he was to complex machinery, was still in awe of this near-spaceship. He climbed the platform to his tiny cockpit, unclipped the air conditioner and checked to see that his suit was still under pressure, then stepped into the new world of the Blackbird. He plugged in his umbilical, which would feed him air, water, power and sound before commencing his pre-flight checks under the guidance of Colonel Sharpe.

'OK, Colonel, we'll test our suit system first to make sure we're still breathing and I'll ask you to refer to your checklist.'

'Roger, I have checklist open at page one and commencing.'

It took them 35 minutes to make sure that the aircraft was safe before turning on the power.

'Canopy one closing now. Seal effective. Check Two.'

'Canopy two closing now. Seal effective. Over.'

Michael, in Crew One position, could see directly ahead and to each side through four multi-layered optical panes.

Everything fell to hand as he expected after flying the simulator, and at three minutes to take off Blackbird T-One-Four started to roll under the power of its J58s. The nose was nearly 60 feet ahead of the main wheels, so turning was a novel trick in itself.

'Beale Control, this is Blackbird T-One-Four ready for taxi. Over.'

'Blackbird T-One-Four, this is Beale Control, you are clear to taxi, you will take off on Runway Two-One, take off when ready. Over.'

'Beale Control, this is Blackbird T-One-Four, understood take off when ready. Over'.

Then the noise really hit them as Colonel Sharpe poured on the full afterburning thrust of the J58s, holding the shuddering, dipping aircraft on the powerful brakes.

'Beale control, Blackbird T-One-Four rolling. Over.'

'Roger, Blackbird T-One-Four. Over.'

The roar was enormous as 30 tons of thrust thundered out into the California air and suddenly they were moving, faster and faster.

'Crew One, I'm checking the rudders gently. Over.' And the aircraft wavered slightly as Sharpe checked rudder effect then ran at maximum acceleration along Runway Two-One on its way into the deep blue California sky.

'V1 . . . V2 . . . Rotate . . . Lift off, cleanly, cleanly, she does all the work, there she goes.'

And Michael felt the thrust pushing him into the seat as they climbed at a steady 28 degrees best climb angle, and long after a Phantom would be decelerating she was surging ahead, leaving all recognisable landscape . . . twenty,

twenty-one, twenty-two miles below her. It took just over five minutes from roll out to achieve her planned cruise height, this trainer version was slower because of the additional drag of the raised instructor's canopy.

It was the most beautiful flight of Michael's life, flying in a near vacuum at 180,000 feet and a speed approaching 2,000 miles an hour, now in virtual silence. He felt a sense of isolation looking straight out at true infinity, knowing that he was riding nearly 100 feet ahead of the tail pipes with nothing below him for over twenty miles; the realisation could have disturbing psychological effects on even the most experienced 'conventional' pilots.

'OK, Colonel Allon, we're going to fly an energy management profile with two turns as in our flight plan zero four nine. This will give you the feel of turning the Bird at 2,000 miles an hour. Your G-force should never exceed 3G on this manoeuvre or you burn up too much fuel. Over.'

Again, it was easy for Mike with a few thousand hours of flying behind him. The Bird banked ten degrees to port in a controlled turn that brought T-One-Four onto a new heading of 175 degrees.

'Colonel Allon, I'd like you to commence a simulated air-to-air refuelling in accordance with section three of your flight plan. Over.'

'Roger Two, understand section three, air-to-air refuelling commencing two minutes. Over.'

Michael turned to his flight plan checklist specially prepared and printed by the IBM computer for this one flight. It was two inches thick, containing a complete statement of every single action to be carried out, noting its time, ground position, altitude, heading, thrust setting and fuel state.

The aircraft's brain, a triple-redundant computer system, could fly the entire mission automatically, including preprogrammed evasion manoeuvres against Soviet interceptors, missiles and electronic jammers. As this was a test flight, however, it was necessary for the new pilot to be able to maintain total safe control of the operation in case, in the future, his flight control system was damaged or failed, for any reason.

To ensure the most efficient use of the energy of the aircraft, namely the combination of its dynamic horizontal speed component or velocity (VH), and its potential energy component or height (H), then Michael would 'shape' his flight profile to follow a ballistic curve, exactly as if he were riding the nose of a ballistic missile.

For him it was the first extended experience of weightlessness, zero G, the permanent condition that astronauts experienced in earth orbit.

'Number Two, we will enter descent profile condition Beta in fifteen seconds. Over,' Michael informed his instructor.

'Roger One, she's all yours. Over.'

'Here we go: B minus ten, nine, eight . . .' and Michael nudged the complex control column, its matt-black grip festooned with sculpted switches, gently forwards. Within seconds the crew of T-One-Four had lost their entire body weight as they floated over a parabolic curve down to their simulated refuelling point, fifteen miles below.

The air density increased as they went down and the drag on the airframe caused a build up of heat that would have literally melted almost any other aircraft made. But Blackbird was the largest, most complex titanium airframe in use, the exotic metal well able to withstand the enormous heat load of re-entry into the atmosphere.

Below them stretched the fertile acres of Southern California down to the borders of New Mexico, while on the horizon lay the birthplace of the weapons they were trained to hunt for, the spawning ground of Armageddon, Los Alamos. From the blackness of near-space they curved down into the blue light of the filtered sun, continuously monitoring their velocity, height and fuel state, playing the complicated and novel game of Energy Management.

For the first time, Michael Allon was learning not how to fly but a skill completely new to mankind. He was joining that handful of human creatures created only in the last twenty years—spacemen.

'Number Two, we have two minutes to rendezvous. Over.'

Michael did it beautifully, his natural, inbuilt skill and judgment brought the massive vehicle to a stable nose-up position at a steady 420 knots, 31,000 feet above New Mexico, well away from the restricted area of Los Alamos where, unless he'd obtained flight clearance beforehand, he would have been intercepted by the same type of Phantoms he'd recently left behind in Vietnam.

The space plane maintained a twelve-degree angle of attack to the dense air, balancing on the lift from its extraordinary wing-body blended form that was generated in turn by the idle thrust of its huge twin turbojets.

'Number One, assume full tanks and break off, check completed; now let's move to section five in your flight plan, commencing when you receive my intercept alert signal. Over.'

'Roger One, received and understood; section five to commence on your signal,' and Michael grinned from ear to ear because this was the moment he'd been looking forward to throughout his training. He remembered the description from the briefing lectures:

Section Five. SIMULATED THREAT SCENARIO. Assume detection by hostile radar and five targets at 125 miles, closing from two stern areas. Targets correlate with Mig 25 Foxbat A interceptors armed with four AA6 'Acrid' air-to-air missiles each; two radar, two infra-red all-under 'Barlock' GC1. After 30 seconds assume launch of four SA2 Improved Guidelines accompanied by heavy jamming.

Suddenly, there was the signal, a strident intermittent buzzing in his headset followed by a flashing red, 'Attack' light on his panel. Michael's job was to fly the plane out of range whilst giving his RSO, in this case his instructor, the best chance of evading interception.

The secret of survival had changed since old Jim McConnell's days; now there was insufficient time to gain height and furthermore height would hold no security because he was faced with the greatest high-flying interceptor ever built, the Soviet Foxbat A, the only operational aircraft capable of flying to 100,000 feet and shooting him out of the sky at a range of fifty miles with one of its four, 21 foot missiles, codenamed 'Acrid'.

Michael rolled the Blackbird on to its wingtip and screamed down for the deck. Within seconds he'd accelerated from a little over 400 to 1,000 miles an hour, indicating Mach 1.8 and pulling 2Gs in the process, while reeling off his intentions to his RSO.

'We're going for the deck, Number Two, jam and advise heading. Over.'

'Roger, Number One. I am jamming on Barlock Foxbat AI and SA2 Radar frequencies. Head 192, descend to 200 feet and maintain vertical separation. High ground to 8,000 feet in twelve minutes. Over.'

'Roger Two, understand jamming, heading 192 at 200 feet; advise pull-out time. Over,' and the Blackbird thundered down to 200 feet above the desert while the RSO fought an invisible electronic battle.

'We have no SA2 threat now, Number One, but two Foxbats still tracking and closing from port and starboard. Port Target is 60 miles at 175 degrees relative bearing, closing speed 400 knots; Starboard Target is 80 miles at 57 degrees relative bearing, closing speed 450 knots. Over.'

'Turning eight degrees port, using full combat thrust. Over.'

Michael instantly rolled to put his aircraft on an escape vector while checking for frontal threats or unmarked vertical hazards.

'Number One, we have Target One now at 167 degrees at 40 miles. Over.'—then suddenly—'Target One has fired two missiles,' and Michael knew that his RSO's radar screen would be showing two white floating dots creeping across the eight-inch-square television tube.

One missile could be radar-guided, the other heat-seeking, that was standard Soviet interception procedure; he'd seen it all before in Vietnam. But those giant AA6 missiles, the largest in the world, had to be beaten.

'Number Two, Chaff when ready. Over.'

Sharpe prepared the automatic chaff dispenser that released a cloud of flimsy metallic strips, each cut accurately to correlate with the known wavelength of the missile's radar beam.

'Chaffing commencing now,' and out of the jet flew a cloud of brilliant strips that would drive the missile's brain crazy, like suddenly being given a million targets.

'Number Two, commence flare drop. Over.' The second missile would home in on the incredible heat of the J58s on full afterburn and the Blackbird's speed gave it a little over a minute to create decoy targets for the missile to destroy. The flares were housed in the weapons bay originally designed to accommodate nuclear-tipped missiles for the YF12A Interceptor version of Blackbird.

'Number One, flares armed. Tracking on IR sensor. Over.' And the RSO had to wait until the missile was near enough to be fooled by the aerodynamic flares which would trail out from the fuselage.

The first dot suddenly disappeared from the display screen by the RSO, its warhead theoretically detonated in the cloud of metal strips. The second rode on until it was less than ten miles from its target.

'Flares deployed, commence 5G turn, cut afterburners. Over', and Michael banked over 30 degrees, simultaneously cutting the afterburners while raising the nose to maintain lift. The effect was to leave the missile a hot flare radiating at the intensity and wavelength of the afterburners while the real aircraft turned its heat source away from the target as its tailpipe temperature cooled. They called it the 'now you see me, now you don't' manoeuvre; it was more like hide and seek at 1,000 miles an hour and 200 feet.

It worked. The simulator registered a second 'detonation' and Michael was clear to concentrate on maintaining an evasive flight plan using the approaching mountains as a natural screen to hostile radar scanners.

They flew for a further seven minutes after the five minute engagement and Sharpe took over command.

'Good work, Colonel, now let's see you on combat thrust, buy some height, flight level eight zero, on this heading. Over.'

The aircraft lifted its nose and resumed full afterburners as it roared up to 80,000 feet, rolling every fifteen seconds to give the pilot a view of any undetected visual targets ahead of him. Within four minutes they'd reached their cruising altitude with Mach 3 reading steady on the Machmeter: Blackbird was at home.

The sky up there was the very indigo the aircraft was painted, a deep rich blue-black that washed over Michael's head like a solid canopy. It was a breathtaking day, gin-clear to the distant horizons, making it difficult to believe he was actually flying.

Michael felt as if he were suspended from the solid ceiling above him, an encapsulated observer of some vast model map with the thin converging ribbons of Interstates 40 and 15 nearly twenty miles below him. To his right was San Bernadino County, next the Devil's Playground, an ancient dune field at the foot of the Providence Mountains.

They tracked rock steadily towards Fort Irwin with its ancient granite mountains, far, far below them, mere wrinkles in the wastes of the vast Mojave Desert. They could see the tiny jewel of the Goldstone Deep Space Tracking Network, sleepless listener to the invisible signals of the interplanetary probes.

Michael was momentarily startled as the sky rolled steadily to the right, the Bird's brain guiding him unerringly to the south-west, clearing Fremont Peak, normally an exhausting 4,500 foot day-long hike, 80,000 feet below him.

Isolation, that was the feeling, total isolation from the real world. Like gliding in a Rolls Royce after years of riding in a dune buggy. Not that the Phantom was rough, it was just that the Blackbird lived in a different dimension, a world of space-time. Where the Phantom hung for a few giddy moments, the Blackbird soared like a black queen, gliding above the common order, aloof to the problems of day-to-day flying, never in danger of colliding with anything but air itself.

Viscous, invisible, pure clear air. A virtually unknown phenomenon only encountered by very-high-flying aircraft. Those pilots who'd experienced it, and survived, had likened it to hitting a wall that slammed them around in their harnesses like a crazy roller-coaster, shaking the airframe with a series of jack-hammer blows.

There'd been the occasional mysterious disaster, the inexplicable accident on a bright clear day when an experienced pilot would simply disappear with his aircraft off a lazy screen, torn to a cloud and scattered unrecognisably over a thousand square miles of baking desert. Clear Air Turbulence, CAT they called it—the CAT that got the Bird, as one grim-humoured investigator had observed as he sat amid the confetti of a dead Blackbird.

Michael switched off, and deliberately forced himself to concentrate on his flight plan; it was easy to spook yourself in that world. The brain played strange tricks on the eyes which countered with a few of their own, like 'phantom spots', 'defocussing', 'white-outs'. UFOs too were commonplace, high up in the lonely reaches of the Blackbird's flights. Strange lights, shimmering haloes, unexplained 'targets' that suddenly appeared and followed you, dancing ahead in balls of light before zipping away at 'silly' speeds that knew no limits.

Michael consciously pressed himself against his harness, shaking off the dreams and the fears, and scanned his incredible office with its banks of switches, knobs, buttons and levers that gave him the power to operate only the flying part of the awesome device. Its real magician sat behind him: the RSO, feeding its multiple brains, interrogating its myriad eyes and ears and most of all telling him, the mere pilot, where he was going.

'Number One, let's head for Edwards, bearing zero two five. Over.'

'Number Two, understood, zero two five, turning now. Over.'

The nose slowly swept the horizon until it was aimed for their landing field, the famous Edwards Air Force Base deep in the Mojave desert. Of all the strips of land on earth that have recorded the progress of aviation none compares with Edwards, the greatest experimental airfield in the world.

Michael started his landing approach from 200 miles, sliding down the 'Energy Ramp' towards a final approach from 25 miles. The strip came up faster and faster as the big Bird moaned its way back to the desert floor, its corrugated skin crinkling under the change of temperature.

'Three Greens. Over.'

The gear was locked securely, the nose at the correct angle of attack to generate the ideal lift vector, balancing the drag of the airframe. Blackbird T-One-Four almost glided in at 180 knots over the threshold to touch down in a spurt of tyre smoke and trailing runway dust, held altitude to create a braking drag, then gently lowered its 40-ton mass onto the tiny twin nosewheel.

The big Bird rolled, decelerating slowly, 6,000 feet along the runway to its allotted turn-off point where Michael nudged it along on a few tons of thrust.

The 'ramp' was attended by its ground crew who always celebrated a first flight by a trainee pilot with an assortment of rude placards prepared for the occasion.

The largest and most alarming read: 'Welcome to New York, Kennedy.'

Others said: 'Bye, Bye, Blackbird.' 'Don't look now but your fly is undone.'

'Will Colonel Allon please phone his wife, he took the car keys.'

Michael grinned from ear to ear while Sharpe wrote in his 'Instructor's Notes' under Initial Impressions:

'Potential—Excellent ability, could be suitable for specialised missions.'

His full report went into the Allon file which had expanded steadily in its data bank at SAC Headquarters in Omaha and in the very special safe in General Wheeler's office.

The next day Michael went out to watch 'Pete' Peabody go up for his 'first' this time sitting in the rear seat, the magician's throne. He didn't stop talking for an hour when he returned to Edwards the following day. For him it had been the answer to all his prayers. For the first time he could take a real grandstand view and select any one of a dozen different sensors to map the ground below. The most outstanding system was the radar mapping, its clarity was so good you could photograph it and it would be pin-sharp at 25 miles.

The jamming power was ten times greater than anything he'd used before and he received an automatic read-out of priority and secondary frequencies to jam; all of this was then carried out instantly unless he overrode the system.

His electronic data bank held a master file on all Soviet and Chinese radar systems giving their frequency band, power, range signal characteristics, and associated weapon systems. All this data had been collected by satellites, U2s, EC130s and many other ELINT aircraft on continuous patrol of areas under Soviet influence or control. Every bit of data was transmitted to SAC HQ where it was analysed before being stored against the day it would be needed either to win a battle or prevent a nuclear war.

Few of the men at Beale knew how many times their intelligence data had prevented escalation and threats while saving enormous sums of money on unnecessary responses to hypothetical Soviet weapons.

Within three months, that is by April 1973, Michael Allon and Pete Peabody had achieved a performance standard sufficiently acceptable for them to be placed on the pre-operational list in case of a major emergency. The Allon/Peabody crew combination had to work well on the ground too, as both of them spent many hours attending intelligence briefings on different areas of the world, their political status (ie. friend, foe or neutral), and their individual radar, electronic and weapon status. The complex picture also embraced communications and cypher systems which enabled the Blackbird to receive and send data only when it was safe and secure. They learnt how to track and communicate with defence, listening, warning and communications satellites and what to do in the case of an attack or systems failure which required them to eject over hostile territory. Then they had to learn how to evade capture, survive in remote or hostile environments and, in the event of capture, to withstand interrogation, staged press conferences and forced confessions.

Both of them attended SAC War Planning conferences to understand how their data was incorporated with the other major intelligence services such as the National Security Agency reporting directly to the Secretary of State and the President; the controversial Central Intelligence Agency, responsible for overt and covert foreign intelligence operations; and the Military Intelligence Directorate at the Pentagon.

They were amazed at the extent of Soviet involvement throughout the world, shown clearly on a daily 'World Status' board at Omaha and just as impressed with the vast quantity and excellent quality of data on the Soviet Union's defence systems, its naval strength and its highly co-ordinated Air Force.

The most impressive data form of all was the photography achieved at day and night, and in bad weather, the sensors being specially designed to cover wide windows in the electromagnetic spectrum. At 25 miles they could photograph the number plate on a car, with great clarity, and identify individual faces that might be viewing the sky for the silent, invisible Bird.

Their favourite 'pin-up' in their ready room was a photograph of Miami beach taken on a clear summer's day where each of the sunbathers was recognisable. Successive crews had ringed their particular choice, which a kindly Air Force photographer had then enlarged for the price of a bourbon.

Beale was the most demanding and enjoyable posting of Michael's career to date and from April to September 1973 he graduated from domestic flights over the continental United States to 'foreign' missions. He and Pete Peabody flew regular runs over Cuba, maintaining surveillance of the Soviet naval base and airfields on the island. They flew long, double-refuelling missions across the Pacific to Guam and along the west coast up to Alaska, filtering the air for tell-tale nuclear debris from Soviet or Chinese tests. On two occasions they flew from Alaska straight along the Kamchatka Peninsula, the impact area of Soviet long-range missiles fired from their test site at Tyuratam in Central Asia.

In May 1973, the Russians tested four missile types, all of which were photographed by a combined team of U2s, Blackbirds and ELINT aircraft with overall coverage by a Big Bird reconnaissance satellite. The same team would later photograph 371 rocket launches in 1973 alone and the extraordinary sight of the previously unknown SSX19 liquid-fuelled missile as its warhead split into three separate sections after travelling some 4,500 miles. The photographs enabled the Air Force intelligence group to estimate that each nuclear warhead had a power equivalent to 200,000 tons of TNT. What is more, the impact points or 'footprint' coincided very accurately with the deployment of the US Minuteman ballistic missiles in their triple groupings.

The three other missiles included the gigantic SSX18, carrying up to eight thermonuclear warheads each seeking a different target; alternatively it could carry a 50 million ton warhead. The SSX16 and SSX17 used a special 'cold-launch' technique whereby the missile was fired from its site like a cork from a gun, by gas pressure. This had the effect of cooling the missile's exhaust gases, thereby reducing its infra-red signal to fool US reconnaissance satellites.

On June 21st, 1973 Leonid I. Brezhnev met Richard M. Nixon in Washington where the two leaders agreed on objectives for the second strategic arms limitation talks, SALT II, planned for early 1974 in Geneva. Nixon's staff had the latest Blackbird photographs on their files. The crew were quietly marked down for special missions requiring high accuracy in a hostile environment. They were Michael Allon and Pete Peabody.

15
Omaha

On 10 September, Allon and Peabody were called to a briefing at SAC headquarters, Omaha, Nebraska, their short flight in an Air Force Phantom recalling for both of them the days of 'conventional flying'.

The briefing was held deep inside Cheyenne mountain, a natural shelter of high density granite which protected the headquarters of the American nuclear forces. They travelled through the familiar underground labyrinth, designed to drive all claustrophobes insane, passing successive security checks until they came to their destination. Chamber 'C' was their briefing room, its walls painted in pastel shades (to reduce visually induced tension) and bare except for ten plastic chairs, a display panel and a map unit.

'Remember me, Michael?' and it was General Wheeler, in full uniform, stretching out a firm broad hand from his stocky frame, the soft voice sounding rather like Ed Murrows. His short hair was even greyer now but he still wore the metal-rimmed spectacles, and still held the briar in his left fist.

'It's a pleasure to see you again, General,' Michael beamed, anticipating what was likely to be an interesting meeting. Peabody just nodded briefly, shook hands and listened.

'I've been keeping an eye on your progress, Colonel, and you, Colonel Peabody. You fellows have been earning quite a reputation lately; I saw those shots of the Kamchatka tests on the President's desk. He asked me to extend his good wishes to you and your team at Beale. He said it gave him great confidence negotiating from a position of detailed knowledge rather than hearsay or rumour.

'Before you meet some of my associates in a moment I want to formally advise you of your position here today.

'Make a note of this, Linghorn.' He turned to his tall, thin aide who accompanied him at every meeting, noting conversations discreetly by the simple expedient of listening hard. Linghorn, known affectionately as 'the hat stand', was always to be found standing rigidly in a corner, his Air Force hat resting precariously askew on what someone had suggested was a hook on the top of his head. He had perfect recall and hypermetropia, all visual information being passed through a pair of bottle-like lenses to be stored permanently in his prodigious brain.

Like a benign Dr Johnson, Wheeler continued. 'The information you will be receiving today is of the highest security classification. It will be part of a briefing for a mission of extreme political sensitivity and potential danger.

'If you, Colonel Allon, and you, Colonel Peabody, accept it, you will be required to exercise high standards of skill and judgment above and beyond your normal flying duties, and there will be substantial risk to your own lives. You may wish to consider this fact before we proceed. You may withdraw now and it will have no detrimental effects on your careers. What do you say, gentlemen?'

'After that build up General, we couldn't refuse,' Michael replied steadily.

'I agree, General,' said Peabody.

'I knew you would, but I had to ask formally. Now, meet a few friends. OK, Linghorn, show 'em in.'

The second door was opened and in filed three men in civilian wear. The first was medium height, thin and grey-haired, aged about fifty. The second was short and stocky like Wheeler but bald. The third was a complete shock—it was Michael Allon's 'uncle', Daniel Perès, all six foot four of him, grinning with pleasure at the stunned expression on the face of the boy he'd helped to rear in the kibbutz. The two men ignored all formalities and hugged each other with the joy of reunion after so many years.

'Well, well, well, Michael, what a man you've become, or should I call you Colonel Allon, eh?' and he slapped him on the shoulder before standing back and addressing the attentive audience.

'Gentlemen, this is my 'boy' in whom I am well pleased,' and gave a laugh that echoed in the corridor; like his heart, Daniel Perès's voice was a big one. Michael adopted a quizzical expression, arms akimbo, his mind full of questions.

'Uncle Daniel, I never dreamed I'd meet you again inside a mountain. This must be one of your practical jokes. What did you do, tell them you were in the Israeli Air Force?'

'No, it was easier than that, I told them I was in Mossad,' and the grin slowly disappeared leaving a twinkling pair of blue eyes set in a rugged, determined face.

'You in Mossad? Oh pardon me, General.' Michael dropped his arms to his sides.

'That's OK, Mike, we sure had you surprised there. Would have done exactly the same thing myself. Now, why don't we all introduce ourselves and you two gentlemen can jaw away after our business is concluded.'

Not for the first time, Chamber 'C' at Omaha served as a meeting place between the agents of Israel and the United States. They settled into the proffered seats and quietened down as Wheeler took the floor.

'Well gentlemen, you're all known by name to each other now,' which of course wasn't wholly true. Michael only knew Daniel's name, the other two were covers. 'So let's get down to the job in hand. Lights please, Captain.'

The lights went out and the screen came brilliantly to life. Michael was soon to feel himself returning home again, a very odd sensation.

'This is a general satellite view at 500 miles of the area in question. Israel's military occupied areas are defined here, here and here', as Wheeler pointed with his light-arrow to the Suez Canal, the northern border with Lebanon and the eastern border with Syria and Jordan.

'We have reason to believe that there will be a war within 28 days, the object of which will be to destroy Israel. We intend either to prevent it or to change its result. Our problem is that the United States Government is actively attempting to achieve a cease-fire in the area and we cannot condone another pre-emptive strike by Israel as occurred in June 1967. This time we are adopting a 'pragmatic profile'; we intend to provide massive aerial reconnaissance of the borders to enable both sides to recognise the futility of a war and thereby force them to the conference table.

'We will mount continuous flights along these corridors or fire zones. He turned to the map using a telescopic pointer slipped from his inner pocket. Suez, from Port Said, due south to Suez Town. Lebanon, from the sea to Mount Hermon. Syria, Jordan, from Mount Hermon to Eilat and finally the Gulf of Eilat to the Red Sea.

'The purpose of these flights, which will be co-ordinated with satellite passes, is to give the Soviets evidence of the scale of our monitoring, which we believe they will consider as rendering impossible any surprise attack by either side. At the same time the US Government will furnish the United Nations with photographic evidence of violations of the 1967 cease-fire lines. Finally, all photographic intelligence with associated interpretive accounts will be given totally unofficially to the Israelis, which is why these gentlemen are here today. This intelligence will balance that being provided by the Soviets for the Arab forces.

'The United States Government will do everything in its power, short of direct military intervention, to prevent a war; but in view of its domestic political situation vis-a-vis Watergate and its military commitment in Vietnam our options are severely reduced.

'Your job, Colonel Allon, will be to co-ordinate with Daniel Perès and his colleagues so that both sides get the sensor data they need to achieve those stated objectives.'

What it came down to, in Michael's estimation, was that he and Peabody would have to fly better than he'd ever done, to help avoid a major war. The plan involved a complex system of bases in Turkey, Cyprus and Iran which formed a staging triangle for the Blackbird crews and U2s acting as the primary surveillance aircraft, which in turn would be supported by US Navy and Army installations.

The choreographer of the whole show would be General Wheeler while the chief leads were Michael Allon for the US, and Daniel Perès for the Israelis. Perès' two colleagues would feed Peabody with detailed Israeli Air Force and Mossad Intelligence data assisted by General Wheeler's staff and the other intelligence branches. The operation was called 'Jericho'.

It started the minute the meeting ended.

16
Jericho I

Two Blackbirds arrived at the huge Royal Air Force base of Akrotiri, Cyprus, on 16 September 1973 and were instantly parked in hangars normally used for the RAF Vulcans that patrolled the Mediterranean looking for Soviet submarines. Wheeler had to obtain the approval of the British Prime Minister which was achieved after promises had been made to share the data with RAF Strike Command at its underground headquarters in High Wycombe. The U2s were sent to Turkey and Iran so as to disperse the force around the war zone.

At Vandenberg Air Force Base on the west coast of California, a series of spy satellites were made ready and the biggest of all, Big Bird with its eleven-ton 'eye', was launched by Titan 111B on 20 September into a polar orbit complete with two electronic ferret satellites and two low-pass satellites, making up the space-borne contingent.

By 20 September, the team was ready and Blackbird Two-Seven, piloted by Colonels Allon and Peabody, thundered off at 08.00 hrs to spy on the most embattled area on earth, the Holy Land and the great Nile Delta. The most dangerous corridors were over Suez and Golan, the main points of confrontation, bristling with radar, surface-to-air missiles and interceptors. All 'Jericho' aircraft were fitted with special IFF transponders, electronic devices which told the Israeli Air Force that they were friendly, in the unlikely event of a successful interception by Israeli Phantoms.

Within half an hour of leaving Cyprus the boy from Israel was 25 miles high above Kibbutz Ramta on Israeli occupied Mount Hermon; Michael Allon had come home in style.

'Pete, make sure these are the best photographs you ever take, because straight down there is where your pilot first decided to become a flyer.'

Michael felt the strangest sensation. He'd never considered himself as having any strong belief in his faith. Judaism was more a way of life to him, a social behaviour rather than a religious practice. And yet he felt the first vague stirrings of premonition.

Flowing below him, faster than a rifle bullet, was the land of his birth, the home of his sister, the resting place of his parents. He was back to defend his heritage, riding a space plane like some prodigal of science fiction. He was the peacemaker, the watcher in the night, the guardian of the Promised Land. Upon him, the Jericho team and the Mossad agents, rested the fate of Israel. Without them the tiny garrison could not see what the enemy was preparing and would be forced to expend their slender resources on fighting deceptions, diversions and feinting manoeuvres.

One Blackbird flight was worth a division of armoured troops, for its electromagnetic eyes and ears could see through the camouflage of war and reveal fresh underground workings, new power lines, the heat trails of tanks and aircraft, the babble of electronic data that welded a modern army together.

Michael recognised the feeling more acutely now as they sped towards the south. Destiny, that was the word he wanted, destiny. Maybe he *was* there for a reason.

'OK, Mike? You've gone very quiet.' Peabody's voice broke his train of thought.

'Oh, yes, fine . . . just admiring the view. I reckon we could see Lebanon, Syria, Jordan, Israel and Sinai from here if only it wasn't so hazy.'

'Probably, trouble is they can probably 'see' us too on their radar,' Peabody replied, optimistic to the end.

'What's our threat factor here?'

'Pretty low, nothing to worry about, I don't think they could touch us up here.'

But Peabody was wrong.

Cairo West Airfield was one of the major Soviet airfields in the Middle East. Its importance was gauged by the fact that sitting in the biggest, most closely guarded bomb-proof aircraft shelters ever seen in Egypt sat two of the most sought after prizes of Western Intelligence. A brace of Mig 25R Foxbat aircraft. What the Lockheed SR71 was to the US, the Foxbat was to the USSR. It could fly at 2,100 miles an hour—3.2 times the speed of sound—cruise at 80,000 feet and carry four AA6 missiles. And it did it every month, over Israel.

The Russians had invested huge quantities of weapons and radar in the hands of the front-line armies of Egypt and Syria and they were absolutely determined that Israel would be destroyed or defeated by the end of 1973. To do this they had launched a massive satellite and aircraft surveillance of Israeli forces since June 1967. By 1971, two pairs of Russian-piloted Foxbats were flying regularly over Israel and Iran, out of reach of the Phantoms equipping both Air Forces.

The Israelis attempted to destroy or damage a Foxbat over Israeli territory to prevent the Soviet incursion and to serve notice on the Russians that they would resist all threats or overflights. They didn't succeed: the Mig 25 was simply too good a plane and it continued to fly with impunity, photographing airfields, supply routes, storage depots, command posts and any other installations of the IDF, the Israeli Defence Forces.

Pressure had been brought to bear on the US Government by the Israeli Government to supply the Israeli Air Force with the Phantom's successor, the McDonnell Douglas F15 Eagle, but the first test aircraft had only flown on 27 July 1972 and deliveries would not commence to Israel until 10 December 1976. The US Government had responded to Israeli pressure by promising to provide intelligence as good, if not better, than that collected by Foxbat. The answer had been Blackbird.

'Crossing Mount Hermon, height of peak is 9,219 feet, heading 182 degrees. I'll call out landmarks as we go. On the east we have Syria, west is Israel. Directly below now is Hadar, heavy Syrian tank concentration at Harfa, Hales, Maaz and Han Arnaba on the Kuneitra-Sasa road. On our right is Masada in Israel on the main supply road to the Hermon stronghold from Nafakh in the south. We'll be crossing Kuneitra in fifteen seconds, with Nafakh, Israeli headquarters to our right, that is, true west. We're now over the Syrian 52nd Tank Brigade at Um Butria with the 43rd, 33rd, 1st and 51st dug in between Tel Hara and Tel Kudna.

'We've just crossed the Hashnia Road at the border and we'll be over the Gamla Trail in eleven seconds. Rafid in Syria is to our left on the main road to the south-east. Joining that road at Rafid is the Gamla Trail, now, and the South Road, in fact south-west of the southern end of the Sea of Galilee in Israel.

'Below us now are the Syrian 46th, 112th, 47th, 132nd and 61st Tank Brigades, I'm getting heavy IR response, somebody's moving along down there.

'It's going quiet now, we have the Yarmuk River directly ahead, change heading to 215 degrees in seventeen seconds.

'Just crossing the north Jordan-Syria border and entering Jordan . . . now.

'Steer two one five degrees now,' and gently Michael banked the aircraft towards Israel.

For the entire sector of the Syrian-Israeli border Blackbird had been taking infra-red, visual, radar and electronic 'photographs' of one of the largest concentration of tank forces ever assembled. Peabody continued his epistle of mechanised warfare:

'Sea of Galilee on our right with Tiberias on its central western shore in the distance there. Prepare to head due south in ten seconds . . .' and over she went, banking to port to resume her flight path along the Jordan, across the full length of the Dead Sea and then on across the wastes of the

Negev and Sinai over the Israeli port of Eilat and out into the Gulf of Eilat and the Red Sea.

'Refuelling in seventeen minutes, I have our target on radar. Over.'

'Roger Pete, let's go down the Ramp. Over.'

And for the 152nd time Michael flew Blackbird down the Energy Ramp to rendezvous with a KC 135 Stratotanker. They met at 32,000 feet over the southern tip of Sinai, the big tanker having flown from the huge military base in Iran at Shiraz. Within fourteen minutes they were replenished and the Bird wallowed, heavy with fuel, as it broke off from the life-giving boom before rocking its wings in appreciation of a fine 'boom operator' and gently soaring off to the deep blue over one of the most desolate areas of land on earth, the Sinai Peninsula.

'We have 102,000 feet, heading three zero five. Gulf of Suez on our left, that is west, Suez Town is at the head of the Gulf. Look out for hostile response, over,' and Pete Peabody checked his ECM status for the fifth time since refuelling. He knew from Israel of the incredible missile defence network that the Russians had built along the Suez border and there had been reports of a new missile and radar possibly installed already. Furthermore, Foxbats had been photographed by lucky chance by Big Bird, taking off from Cairo West. It was believed they were the Mig 25R (reconnaissance version), but one or two may have been replaced by the A version, the interceptor.

'Ras Masala in fifteen seconds, then Suez itself, sensors operating . . . now.'

Below them the Gulf of Suez came to an end at one of the most evocatively named towns of the Middle East. It was the gatekeeper to the Suez Canal, that incredible system of waterways that linked two cultures, that of the Indian Ocean and that of the Mediterranean.

'Head due north in five seconds . . . now,' and Michael banked over to fly directly along the Suez Canal at a height of 100,000 feet.

'On our left is the road to Cairo, Egyptian territory, on our right is the road east through the Mitla Pass, Israeli-occupied territory.'

We are now crossing the Egyptian 4th and 25th Armoured Divisions with their 7th and 9th Infantry Divisions. The Israeli Bar Lev line runs continuously from here to Port Fuad on the Mediterranean.

'Crossing the Little Bitter Lake in five seconds, head three four zero, now.'

The Blackbird banked gently to port to fly along the north western axis of the interconnecting Little Bitter Lake and Great Bitter Lake.

'Kabrit in Egypt on our left and the whole Egyptian border has a major rail and road system through Faid and Duweir Suweir at the north end of the Great Bitter Lake to Ismailia. Major Israeli fortifications on our right.

'We're now flying over the administrative border between the Egyptian 3rd Army to the south and their 2nd Army to the north. The line crosses the east-west axis of the Great Bitter Lake. On our left are the Egyptian 21st Armoured and 16th Infantry Divisions.

'Head three five zero . . . now.' Blackbird rolled gently to starboard to run along the next section of the Canal before its long, final section from Ismailia, through Kantara, to Port Said.

'Over Ismailia now, we're crossing the major road from Cairo in the west across the Canal, then due east to the Israeli-occupied town of Tasa which tracks across Sinai to Bir Gifgafa. Directly below are the Egyptian 23rd Mobile Division and 2nd Infantry guarding Ismailia and the El Firdan Bridge. The road to the left, running due north-south, is the main Egyptian supply road for their Canal forces.

'Head due north now, we have Kantara ahead and then a dead straight run along the Canal to Port Said. The Egyptians have the 15th Armoured and 18th Infantry Divisions around Kantara, the Israelis have fortifications at five points north of Kantara.

'We're crossing the road from Kantara north-east to

Baluza and Romani, Israeli points on the southern shore of the Mediterranean.'

The Egyptians, 25 miles below, felt just as frustrated as the Israelis had, for their radar confirmed that the Americans were flying along their entire Suez border, but there was nothing they could do unless they could persuade the Russians to attempt an interception using Foxbats from Cairo West.

'Port Said coming up directly below us, the Manzala Delta over to our left, I think we made it, Mike.'

'Must say, I never thought that I, a good kibbutznik, would be flying over the whole Egyptian Army in less than an hour and without being fired at. Bless you, Blackbird.'

'OK, Mike, take me home to sunny Cyprus and lets get these shots developed, just hope I didn't keep the lens cap on,' and Pete grinned at the thought of even holding the massive protective doors that slid open to reveal the incredible battery of lenses, photomultipliers, infra red sensors and radar antennae that hung in the cavernous 'Sensor Bay' set in the belly of the Bird.

The distinctive silhouette of the SR71 was caught clearly by a host of cameras on US, Soviet, British and even Israeli naval vessels crowding the eastern Mediterranean as the aircraft came down to land at the huge airstrip at Royal Air Force Akrotiri.

As the strange plane taxied towards the black shade of the bomb-proof shelter Lt. General Mendeleiv of the KGB-GRU Joint Planning Council pondered on the significance of the report sitting on his desk, deep underground at Egyptian Military Headquarters. He strummed his fingers nervously on the top of his steel desk, leaning back in his padded armchair whilst his team of advisers waited for his response. It felt like an hour but it was in fact little over 30 seconds.

'General Yeliskeiv, according to this report from the Joint Intelligence Unit it appears that the Americans have commenced detailed surveillance of the war zone as we expected.

It's interesting to note that they're using so many systems, including the SR71, U2s ánd Big Bird.

'Will you please summarise your findings?'

'Yes, General, we have reports from Turkey, Iran and Cyprus confirming a committed surveillance team, it's called operation "Jericho" and its objective is, I believe, to prevent a surprise attack by Arab forces on the Israelis and vice versa. I further believe that Israel will receive the intelligence data gathered during the operation and respond accordingly.'

'Thank you, General, any further conclusions?'

Mendeleiv looked straight at the report, waiting for the answer.

'Yes, I believe that we should do nothing to prevent the Americans from maintaining "Jericho", thereby deluding them and the IDF into believing that only a madman would attempt a surprise attack.'

'What about observation of our preparations, will they encourage a pre-emptive Israeli strike?'

'No, General, I believe not. Both the Americans and the Israelis have an excess of confidence in their own technical equipment; their failing is psychological, not military.' Yeliskeiv spoke with confidence.

'How do you mean, psychological?'

Yeliskeiv felt it was just like a test for cadet intelligence officers, but Mendeleiv was Chairman and his superior in this operation.

'The War of 1967 won Israel a massive victory because everybody assumed they'd play fair and go down fighting. They didn't, they used their brains and bravery, they seized the initiative.

'They believe that no enemy could risk suffering a second defeat no matter how well prepared. They underestimate the Arab will to fight for his land and they underestimate President Sadat.

'They are mesmerised with the passing of Nasser—Sadat is nothing but Nasser's deputy, made good; just as if Ford succeeded Nixon. Sadat is a man of conservative manner, unlikely to take the initiative in war or peace.

'The Israelis are totally wrong.'

'As we know, General, Sadat is the greatest Arab leader of this century. He has established a fanatical respect in Egypt that even Nasser could not emulate, but it is of a different style. Sadat is the wise and reasonable man, Nasser was the great warrior leader. Sadat is the conservative, introvert; Nasser was the extravagant extrovert.

'Since 1967 we have re-equipped and retrained the Egyptian forces, but most important of all, Sadat has created an intelligent, educated officer class, not unlike the Israelis. His "favourite sons", as he calls them, and one of them is in fact his youngest brother, are dedicated men who use reason and logic, inspiring obedience and devotion from their men.

'This is why Israel will be defeated; the leader, the men and the equipment are utterly improved. The Israelis will never accept this change, even if we wrote to Golda Meir herself, and soon they will be caught with their pants down, as we were in June 1967.'

Yeliskeiv sat back, looking directly at his cleverest and most despised colleague.

'Thank you, General. I accept your analysis; however, there is one thing we will do: we will intercept an SR71, just to show the Americans that they can fly over Egypt, but never over the Soviet Union. Select your best pilot, but I want no weapons, this will be another psychological blow. Report your flight plan to me at 08.30hrs tomorrow. Who knows, the Americans may decide to restrict their involvement even more once the War has started. Good day, General. Good day, gentlemen.'

The tall, thin, blond Russian strode quietly out of the room, acknowledging the salutes of General Yeliskeiv's staff while savouring the obvious awe and respect in which he was held. He almost heard the sigh of relief as the armoured steel door closed behind him.

On 2 October 1973 at 09.30hrs, Allon and Peabody turned due north over Suez towards the Little Bitter Lake. Their two previous flights had revealed one chink in the Egyptian armour: it was an invisible flaw, so minute that the Egyptians were not aware it existed. It was a simple failure of judgment by an army commander patrolling the defence line at Deversoir on the northern tip of the Great Bitter Lake, the boundary of the Egyptian 2nd and 3rd Armies. He believed that the area east of the Great Bitter Lake could be guarded solely by mobile patrols. The effect of this was quite simply to leave a gap between the two armies.

The absence of equipment had been revealed in the sensor print-outs and photographs; a simple lack of energy response had to be investigated.

'Head three four zero, now. Great Bitter Lake below,' and all the time the shutters clicked whilst the sensors hummed inaudibly in their myriad grey boxes.

'OK. Head three five zero, now.'

For the third time Michael headed towards the now familiar town of Ismailia, but at that instant Peabody interrupted his thoughts.

'Heh, we've got a contact, most positive, we have him on radar. Switching to track-while-scan. Over,' and Peabody switched his radar from mapping to tracking mode whilst maintaining a scanning sweep.

'Target is approaching from three zero five, closing speed, Jesus . . . 3,000 . . . hey . . . it's a missile, they've launched a missile! Over.'

'Check for Foxfire radar, Pete, it could be a Foxbat. Over,' replied Michael tensely.

'Checking now, . . . Yup, it's Foxfire characteristics, could be a Foxbat. Over.'

'Give me its height. Over.'

'Target is climbing at 40,000 feet per minute he'll be within AAC range in 30 seconds. Over.'

It was incredible; after all the simulations reality was different; you could never fool a good pilot into really believing he would die when intercepted in the simulator. Allon and Peabody knew they could die within two minutes at the most.

'Jamming Foxfire. Over.'

'Prepare for combat descent, and arm flares and chaff. Over.'

Michael readied himself for the violent manoeuvre he would have to enter once a missile had been launched on a head-on chase. Chaff and flares were far less effective and he knew he was going much too fast to turn in time to present his tail to the hostile interceptor. All he could do was wait till the other guy fired.

Suddenly he saw him. A tiny, silver dot, about twenty miles out and five miles below, lit by the brilliant morning sun like an incredible flying diamond over Egypt.

'He's turning and closing, no missiles. We're over Kantara. Over.'

The target kept disappearing as the sun caught its changing profile and then in ten seconds it was much closer, flying almost level but still at a dangerous 30 degrees towards his tail, directly behind his shoulder.

'Jesus, look at that mother,' exclaimed Pete. 'I can't see his number, I'm photographing now. Over.'

'That's some aircraft and some pilot,' agreed Michael in reluctant acknowledgement of the skill of the flying he'd seen; at no stage had the Americans had a reasonable chance of escape, all the emergency doors were firmly shut.

'God, he's coming closer,' Pete almost shouted with a strange feeling of admiration and fear.

And he was: very steadily the lethal silver craft edged towards and alongside the Blackbird. Michael could see its massive engine fairings from between which emerged the long, beautifully pointed nose. Hugging the top of the fuselage directly above the sharply swept-back intakes emerged the tiny canopy in which both Americans could clearly see the head of the single pilot. His visor was down, but not heavily tinted and Michael prayed that the camera would reveal his features. The aircraft's nose was chiselled with tiny cuts to accommodate optically flat cameras and sensors similar to Blackbird's, there were no missiles under the wings and the shoes were empty. The twin outward sloping tail fins raked back at a steep angle. This Foxbat was definitely an R version and its number was painted out to prevent unit identification.

'Give him a wave Pete and let's get home.' Michael said, the tension leaving him, 'Shame we can't ask him back to the Mess. We could do a swap even; you know, just between flyers.'

But before they could, the silver craft banked over in a long gentle curve back to its field at Cairo West; unlike Blackbird the Foxbat had limited range and poor air-to-air refuelling facilities in Egypt.

For the first time in months, General Yeliskeiv saw his KGB 'Chairman' smile.

'Magnificent photographs, General. The best air-to-air shots I've seen. You can even see the crew's faces. What did you say the altitude was?'

'100,000 feet, General Mendeleiv.'

'Good grief, how did he do it?'

'Sheer flying skill: he flight-planned the whole thing himself and timed it perfectly. He flew what is known as a Parabolic Interception Climb, the Americans call it a "Zoom" climb. He knew he could only stay up there for three to four minutes, so he hit it perfectly. Of course he was helped by the fact that the Americans were flying a repeat flight plan and not taking evasive action.'

'Even so it was a great achievement. This will make the Americans think hard before assuming technical superiority in every field. How many Blackbirds do they operate?'

'Two squadrons, mostly reconnaissance, they have a few YF12A interceptors available also.'

'And we have over 200 Foxbats already. When will the Americans learn that we are no longer a country of hard-pressed ignorant peasants . . . there again, I hope they maintain their delusions. It will be to our benefit when we fight them face-to-face. By the way, General Yeliskeiv, who was the excellent young Russian who took these excellent photographs?'

'He isn't a Russian, sir, he's a Palestinian, his name is Al Timimi.' and Yeliskeiv couldn't help but grin with pride as he shattered Mendeleiv's composure.

At Jericho headquarters in Akrotiri, a very worried General Wheeler addressed an emergency meeting of the Joint Team.

'Gentlemen, today's interception of the Allon/Peabody aircraft over Suez has altered our plan somewhat. After conferring with the Joint Chiefs in Washington by phone an hour ago, we are instructed to avoid a face-to-face conflict between US and Soviet air crew. I believe this decision may cost us dearly and play into the hands of the Soviets, but I have been over-ruled. All further surveillance will be carried out by Israeli Phantoms on their own side of the border while we will maintain satellite surveillance as before. The Blackbirds will fly no closer than 100 miles to the war zones and will not fly over Egypt or Syria until further notice.'

There was a general feeling of disappointment as the meeting broke up into its separate working teams. Daniel Perès went over to Michael and Pete and put on his most encouraging voice.

'Listen, you fellows, don't get disheartened, the photographs you and your team have provided are some of the most valuable items of data Mossad has received this year. We know a great deal more about the Arab posture; I am convinced they will attack within a week. My trouble has been trying to convince the Defence Ministry of my agency's belief that there will be war. Mossad has sent more than 400 reports in a month declaring that war will begin in a matter of days.

'All have been ignored, but nobody can ignore your photographs, your radar maps, your electronic charts. They are reality. I am leaving for Tel Aviv tonight. Thank you, son of Abraham, you've done your job, you have repaid your debt to Israel.'

But Daniel Perès was too late.

17
Yom Kippur

David Berglass folded his prayer book and closed his eyes. With a sigh he leaned back against the sandbag and prepared to snooze. The flak jacket rubbed painfully against his armpits and for a few moments he thought of taking it off, wondering if it was worth risking a bawling-out by his platoon leader. He decided not to, and this saved his life. He'd be relieved in an hour's time at 3pm, but there was always a chance the corporal might surprise him with a spot check.

The heat was oppressive enough to induce a soporific state of mind, accentuated by the blinding glare of the sand. It made prayer difficult and there were many yet to be read on this the holiest day, the Day of Atonement.

The sense of calm after the past week's unsettling news lulled him rapidly to sleep and the prayer book slipped softly to his side, almost falling off his lap. The radio crackled occasionally with cyphered bleeps that undoubtedly meant something to another observation post along the 'line' but thankfully not to him.

He'd been replenished only the day before; food, water, new batteries, postcards from well meaning 'friends of the boys on the Bar Lev' bearing Tel Aviv, Haifa, Eilat and Jerusalem postmarks. His helmet tipped forwards shading his eyes as his heavy breathing tuned up for a full-blown snore. All that disturbed him was a fly on his left wrist, tickling its way up his thick, matted forearm.

It climbed onto the thick silver strap of his watch, and stopped momentarily on the broad polished dome, its brain attracted to the super-high frequency hum of the quartz oscillator, its tiny sucker feet smelling the pools of sweat on the sand-blown optical glass, while its myriad eyes watched the large yellow hand sweep slowly below it until the point covered the Roman number XII.

With a crescendo that rocketed him out of his seat four Sukhoi fighter-bombers cannoned over the lone Israeli and thundered into his patch of Sinai. He was stupefied: it was impossible, not today, not Yom Kippur, for the sake of sanity, not the Holiest Day . . !

A moment later the first bomb struck the base of the fortified bunker, its shock wave slamming him like a rag doll against the sand bag. There was a blistering wave of heat that baked the hair straight off his arm, effectively cooking his exposed skin to a deep red while a hypersonic skewer of steel impacted like a sledgehammer against his flak jacket. David Berglass was a casualty three seconds after the War started, a contorted heap of pain in a junkyard of shattered equipment.

A moment later came the barrage, a fantastic, brain-splitting, body-shaking wall of detonations that tore the entire land to choking smithereens.

His terrified eyes stared transfixed as the very earth itself vaporised into mountains of black clouds rolling across the eastern horizon as far as he could see. Like some nightmare vision of hell, the ground had turned to a tidal wave of fire that swept towards him at the speed of an express train. The second bomb blast swatted him off the wall like a fly, straight through the blast door and into the soft body of his mate, stone-dead already from the first explosion, lungs totally shredded by the shock wave.

One hour and ten minutes later, the first Egyptian commandos following in the wake of the barrage, clattered screaming into the bunker, firing crazily as they went. The scene of destruction was total and they kicked Berglass over onto his face and left him for dead, his staring eyes never flickering for a moment. He was in full catatonic seizure.

For one solid hour, between 2 and 3pm on 6 October 1973, 2,000 Soviet-supplied field guns had fired 3,000 tons of high explosive onto David Berglass and his fellow Israeli soldiers on the Bar Lev Line. Hundreds of Egyptian commandos in rubber dinghies had paddled furiously across the placid canal and scrambled desperately up the 70-foot rampart of sand to annihilate the stunned remnants with grenade, gun and flame-thrower. 240 Soviet Sukhois and Migs, flying in wave after wave, straffed and rocketed anything that bore a resemblance to the enemy and straddled the camouflaged bunkers with tons of high explosive bombs.

David Berglass was the first of thousands to be injured or killed by the most ferocious combat in the recent history of the Middle East.

The Egyptian attack had started brilliantly, from the first moments of H-Hour. In 30 minutes, 8,000 men had crossed the Suez Canal and among them were engineers with high-velocity water pumps that literally washed away the sand barrier creating 60 breaches in the 100-mile bank, excavating 1,500 cubic metres of sand. To enable the armour and infantry to cross, special Russian PMP modular floating bridges were stretched across the Canal whilst 50 motorised rafts ferried construction crews over to build the first anti-aircraft sites and command posts. 60 large Soviet transport helicopters flew commando troops deep into Sinai across the entire Suez frontier straight into the teeth of the Israeli Air Force.

Sadi Al Mahmoud was excited but frightened. Nothing he'd experienced in manoeuvres was like this. He grinned inanely through the meagre port-hole of the helicopter, clutching his part of the Miliutka's firing mechanism, watching the hand signals from his friend Liaquat in the other big Mil, a good 200 feet away. He knew he was making history, the second generation of his family to fight the Israelis. The noise inside the cavernous cabin of the Russian helicopter made it almost impossible to hear a thing so the flight had been a melée of gestures and grimaces as they clattered low across the Canal, one of 60 heliborne commando units leading the huge infantry assault.

He could see Liaquat suddenly turn away from the window, his attention obviously attracted to something beyond the formation to his far side and his helicopter began to bank sharply away.

Then something strange happened, something quite unreal: Sadi watched appalled as the tail folded up like paper and flew straight up into the air, shed like some insect's appendage. The big machine, tailless and tracking bits of cable and scrap, kept on banking more and more steeply. It performed one ghastly roll and shed further pieces.

First the rotor head flew apart, the blades scything through the air like javelins, then a moment later an entire door flew off fluttering down to the desert as out of the gaping hole poured the bodies. Sadi saw three or four, twisting helplessly, smash into the approaching rocks before, mercifully, the dismembered carcass of the machine exploded in one booming inferno, splattering the Sinai with the fresh dead of Egypt.

A moment later, all muscular control lost, Sadi saw the Israeli Phantom thunder past him, its pilot rolling and jinking round for another pass at the lumbering helicopters. His own pilot pushed his nose down sickeningly and careered at a crazy angle towards the desert. At the last brain-numbing moment he pulled hard back and slammed the machine brutally, but intact, onto the sand.

Sadi was pushed, rather than allowed to jump, out of the craft and he fell like a jelly onto his knees. Others streamed past him as he struggled to stand and then he was running, the small metal suitcase banging against his knees. He sprinted desperately after his team, ecstatic at having left the horror of flying behind him and fell flat on his face beside his number two, a good 300 yards from the drop point. Without even stopping to catch his breath he dug into the blistering sand, knowing it was all he had to protect him from Israeli fire. The great shadow of the empty helicopter roared over him, blowing the sand into a stinging blizzard as it turned away, back to the safety of the West Bank.

It never made it. The Phantom's rotary cannon blew it apart like a bag of tissue paper. The fighter shot overhead at all of 50 feet and disappeared towards the east leaving the shattered victim to erupt in one final explosion.

Sadi cursed the Jews with every obscenity he could muster as his trembling fingers helped assemble the pathetic little winged missile on its tiny launch pad before connecting the joystick controller. It was ready in little over a minute, their hours of rehearsal paying dividends as they prepared to wait. They didn't wait for long.

The familiar clanking and moaning of the first tank reached them across the dunes. Sadi lifted his eyes a fraction and saw the fast-approaching columns of churned-up dust. The Israelis were counter-attacking, desperately attempting to destroy the vanguard of Egyptian forces before they broke through their Bar Lev Line. And now it was infantry against tank, as the nineteen-year-old Egyptian selected his target.

Suddenly the ground shook as the Centurions opened fire with fragmentation shells. The clatter of machine-gun bursts grew clearer and clearer as the tanks opened up on the scattered infantry but Sadi lay transfixed, watching the one nearest to him reveal a clear outline. For a moment he gasped as he thought he saw the barrel traverse and apparently lock onto him.

Like an automaton now, he aimed the telescopic sight and pressed the firing button. The Miliutka flashed off, trailing its tiny wires and tracking flare as he gathered the brilliant, dancing pinpoint of light in his sight. Within seconds tank and light coincided, and then it was all over for the Israelis.

The six-pound warhead struck the joint between turret and chassis at nearly 400 miles an hour, the vicious impact and explosion detaching a chunk of metal from the inside of the turret which ricocheted into the equipment and crew before hitting the bagged charge in the loader's arms. The resulting explosion blew the massive turret, complete with the commander, 100 feet into the air. The tank was nothing but a cauldron of melting men and metal.

Sadi screamed with delight, exultant with the taste of victory, and thanked God for granting him the chance of regaining his pride in his people. The Egyptians were back in Sinai.

Shlomit Kovner pulled back hard on the stick, trailing a perfect curving shock wave behind him as he turned towards the remaining helicopters. He'd got two of the bastards and he had enough fuel and ammunition for one more pass before he'd have to return to refuel and re-arm near Bir Gafgafa.

The horizon streamed past his reflector sight as he turned at a painful 6G, the twin afterburners of the Phantom draining his remaining fuel at a prodigious rate. The two funeral pyres swept into view and then came a third, as he saw a tank blow apart below him. He was going too fast to see the cause but he knew it must be Egyptian firing that hit the tank.

A large formation of helicopters approached, swarming like great locusts and hugging the terrain. One settled before he could aim so he chose its mate, about to drop a hundred yards away. The fantastic crescendo of the six-barrelled cannon echoed off the desert and blew the helicopter's nose clean off. Even he, the enemy, winced at the thought of the carnage inside its decapitated fuselage. The big green and brown fighter rocked, then shot up in a climbing turn away from the Canal leaving a swathe of destruction in its wake.

Kovner rolled through a hundred degrees anxious to clear any anti-aircraft fire as his WSO suddenly screamed, 'Missile astern! Break!'

Kovner barrelled round instantly as trained and jinked madly towards the safety of the desert. It was to no avail.

Sadi gazed at the incredible chase as the missile shot seemingly out of the Canal itself, weaving its blistering trail of white smoke as it hunted the Phantom. It must have hit it at twice the fighter's speed, detonating its warhead mere feet below the plane's port wing. The explosion blew the wing clean off leaving the crippled machine a comet of flaming metal. Kovner and his crewman were dead before they disintegrated in the final impact with the Sinai.

Once again Sadi screamed in exhultation, an early witness to the disaster that befell the Israeli Air Force those first hours of Yom Kippur.

Protecting the whole Egyptian effort was the world's most sophisticated missile and gun barrier, providing a fire curtain stretching from 50 feet above the desert up to over 50,000 feet. Every weapon was Soviet-supplied and co-ordinated by Soviet controllers, working with Egyptians, Sadat's 'favourite sons'. Mossad was right, the Egyptians had a brand new missile, SAM 6; the very latest Soviet mobile surface-to-air weapon, mounted in triplicate on PT-76 tank chassis operating in groups of three launcher vehicles. Along with the SAM 6 were a host of SA2s, SA3s and SA7s, together with their accompanying radar.

Into this curtain of missile fire the Israelis sent their Phantoms and Skyhawks to be blown apart above the desert. And soon the Egyptians started to move their tanks.

Michael Allon was still at Jericho's temporary headquarters under the Trudos mountains as the first news flashed across the short channel between Cyprus and the Middle East.

It was bad and looked as if it was going to get worse. Israel was facing disaster. In spite of all the warnings, Jericho had failed, and he had failed, or so he thought. His genuine response to Daniel's letter that night in Pasadena had been a pious platitude. He had turned his back on his homeland despite his proffered loyalty to America, and whilst she was facing her greatest crisis.

General Wheeler had anticipated the outburst before it came and so he let Michael have his say, privately but noisily, in 'The Office':

For ten minutes he listened and then he'd had enough.

'Colonel Allon . . . hold it. Just hold it.'

Michael blinked in surprise at the sudden sharp retort.

'Sir . . . I must go to . . .'

'HOLD IT! That's an order . . .' and it had worked.

Michael clenched his teeth and waited, the frustration boiling up inside him.

'Allon, you're an American officer and you're an American citizen. You are under American command. You are acting emotionally and without due consideration. You are reacting, not thinking, so hold it.'

'Sir . . . I . . .'

'Shut up, Allon, and listen, that's your only privilege in this office.'

Michael kept silent.

'Good. Now hear this. I'm madder than you but I have my orders. You are an instrument of my orders and I of my superiors, the Joint Chiefs and the Commander-in-Chief. You do not have the full picture, neither do I, but mine at least is bigger and clearer and if I've done my job, the Brass in Washington have got it in Panavision and full Dolby sound.

'You've done your job. Now you wait until you're called to do it again. Maybe tomorrow, maybe next week but on no account am I going to lose an experienced, specialised pilot to a firefight that he isn't a party to.'

'But, General, I was born in Israel. . . .' Michael protested with vehemence.

'So were thousands of Americans. Thousands of others were born in Egypt, or Russia, or Europe, or God knows where, but they came here and became American citizens and most of them came here to leave war, oppression and dictatorship behind. Maybe they haven't found the milk and honey, the greener grass, the crock of gold, but one thing's sure, they left behind the pogroms, the secret police, the crazy family feuds.

'They left behind them a world saturated with bitterness and revenge, and you know better than anybody under *this* mountain—an even higher mountain, of bodies. You're in a New World now; my world, stay and behave but if you go, seeking your precious revenge, you'll become an instrument of death, nothing else. You unforgetting Jews, Arabs, Catholics, Protestants, Buddhists or what other fancy name you call yourselves have killed enough . . .'

'I take it you have no religious or moral principles then, General . . .' Michael interrupted, the frustration turning to anger at the older man's smug position. '. . . and what about your own civil war eh, your lunatic Yankees and Southerners, your blacks and whites, your Ku Klux Kan, why don't you preach to them, tell them to be Americans, eh?'

'We're trying, we're learning, Allon, but we've only had 200 years, you've had thousands. Remember, you're the ones who've preached about goddam civilisation, Greeks and Romans and the "enlightened" Minoans eh? As long as you, particularly you Jews and your semitic brothers, the Arabs, are blowing each other up there'll never be anything but hatred, washing around the world, a bloody red ocean of hatred. Just don't pollute my beach Allon.' Wheeler was getting angry too.

'Your beach?' Michael almost sneered. 'Your beach? Your mountain, you mean,' and he swept the room with his hands. 'You're under a mountain in Cyprus now, General. And you talk about Jews and Arabs, what about Americans and Russians? I've been trained to fight Russians by Americans, haven't I? Isn't this why we're arguing under a mountain? So we can survive long enough to blow away one Russian for every American.

'At least we Jews have lived in the Holy Land for thousands of years, we've got a history of reasons for fighting. America and Russia have only been at war since 1945, yet you've created the greatest war game of all. You don't even share the same land, for God's sake.'

'Wrong, Allon, we share the earth. If we go to war we take the world with us, not just a country. That's why the world needs you, not just Israel. As long as you keep flying we have a chance of balancing the aggression of the opposing sides by making both parties accept the futility of war.'

'But it hasn't worked, General, has it?'

And of course Wheeler knew the man was right. In spite of all the Intelligence, the Arabs believed they could still surprise the Israelis and it looked as if their huge gamble would pay off.

'Colonel, the war is a few hours old, we have no way of stopping it immediately but there may be a way in the days to come. Meanwhile I need you to concentrate on one task. Get ready to fly over that bit of sea between this island and Israel because I have a feeling you're going to be pleased you stayed and did your job; and I think Israel will too.'

The steam had gone out of Michael now, he knew he'd touched Wheeler on a very sensitive nerve; the man believed in the role of Intelligence, whereas *he* wanted action. Maybe the General was right. After all, he wasn't the boss for nothing.

'Sir, I apologise for my manners, I felt I had to say what I believed I should do,' and he stood half at attention.

'I understand, I'd have done the same thing if it had been Pennsylvania they were attacking. It's better to let it all out. I need a pilot I can rely on, not some dedicated idealist who could turn nasty on an operation and do something really crazy.' And neither of them knew just how prophetic that remark would be.

'Let's get back to business Colonel,' and Wheeler returned the salute as Michael left.

In the operations centre the news was grim, the huge status board showed advancing red flags deep into Sinai. Suez to the Little Bitter Lake saw the Egyptian 4th and 25th Divisions cross. Between Duweir Suweir and Ismailia north of the Great Bitter Lake, the 21st crossed. North of Ismailia at El Firdan bridge the 23rd Mobile Division crossed and at Kantara the 15th crossed north-east making for Balya and the Mediterranean.

By morning, 500 Egyptian tanks and five Infantry Divisions had crossed the Suez Canal from Suez to Port Said. The Divisions were split up into two Armies, the 2nd and the 3rd, under Major Generals Saad Mamoun and Munim Wassil respectively.

While Israel was being attacked across Suez, the Syrians launched a massive attack on Golan at H-Hour minus ten minutes, also on 6 October. The Syrian army comprised 1,700 Soviet tanks in five Divisions including the latest T62,-115 mm gun models, backed up by over 1,000 guns and three Infantry Divisions. Facing this, Israel had the 7th Armoured Brigade of 100 Centurions and the Barak Brigade with 75 tanks located on the slopes of Mount Hermon. The sole protection the Israelis had was a hastily constructed tank ditch 20 miles long from Hermon south to Rafid. Michael had photographed it three times already.

The Syrians launched a brilliantly timed low-level strafing and rocket attack on the IDF HQ at Nafahk, just as the Israeli commanders attended their orders group. At H-hour, the tanks started rolling up the slopes and simultaneously the crack Syrian 82nd Commando Battalion assaulted and took the important Israeli observation post on Mount Hermon.

The Israelis watched astonished as the huge tank force, accompanied by armoured personnel carriers, ground its way up to the ditch. The first were bridge-layers but the Israeli tanks destroyed all but two with deadly accurate shooting. A desperate Israeli air strike flew into a wall of anti-aircraft fire, and Skyhawks and Phantoms exploded in mid-air until the surviving remnants were ordered to withdraw.

As night fell, the Syrians, using brand-new Soviet night-fighting equipment, maintained the assault with a 15-to-1 superiority in numbers against the twenty-year-old British Centurions. The battle lasted all night, the Israelis firing at point-blank range into the mass of armour. When dawn broke the survivors saw before them the most incredible carnage, literally a countryside of destroyed Syrian tanks and APCs.

A gap had opened at the Rafid-Kudne sector and on came a new wave of 500 Syrian tanks against a handful of Barak Brigade survivors. Again, the Air Force flew into almost certain death as defeat at Golan came nearer for the Israelis.

The Commander of the Barak Brigade felt he was dead already and living in Hell. Only his twenty-year-old

Centurion remained out of 75 tanks under his command the day before, the day ironically named Day of Atonement. He was surrounded in carnage. Dozens of huge Soviet tanks and armoured personnel carriers lay strewn as far as he could see, many burning with lazy colours of black smoke or erupting spasmodically as overheated ammunition exploded.

For hours his boys had held the Syrians and now he was alone with his crew. A new crew this: he'd hopped from tank to tank as each one finally ran out of shells or lurched under the impact of a hit. By some miracle he and three men were alive, the last Israeli soldiers between the attacking Syrian tanks and the undefended flank of northern Israel on the plateau looking over the Sea of Galilee. He knew that once he'd gone, Syria could encircle this entire section and the door into Israel would be opened wide.

His voice was hoarse with the effort of shouting orders over the crash of firing and exploding shells. But he had to keep going. He could hear in the distance behind him the rumbling of the first reinforcements groaning their tortuous way in a long straggling line up the hill from Galilee. He knew the Syrians were also desperate. They'd lost hundreds of tanks, modern T62s with every conceivable device to defeat Israel's famous machines, and now they could see an historic victory in their grasp.

The fire pattern was changing: they were concentrating on him, not receiving any return fire from any other Israeli tanks. His red, bleary eyes saw a giant T62 rumble into a firing position some 200 yards away, its field of fire restricted by the wreckage around it. He shouted and signalled to the men below and waited for the gunner to traverse, but it never happened. His turret remained motionless, pointing in the wrong direction. He thumped the sides in frustration and looked down to gain the man's attention. But it was too late, they were all dead and he hadn't even noticed the shell that had hit them in the din of the last few minutes. He noticed too that his own legs were sticky and bloody and he turned to face the coup de grace. His only fear was that he had not done enough for his country.

A moment later, the Russian shell blew him away across the plateau overlooking Galilee. For the first time a sort of silence reigned as if the Syrians could not believe what had happened, they were looking down on Israel.

But, ten minutes later, the first Israeli reinforcements reached the plateau, guns firing as they climbed, witnesses of the most ferocious tank battle of the day. The Syrian confidence turned to despair as they realised the enemy was back in force and as they watched amazed, the fresh Israeli gunners shot them to pieces as more and more of them pitched onto the plateau. With a hysterical grinding of gears the Syrians went mad. They turned around, reversed or slewed desperately into each other in the scramble to retreat from the avenging Jews. The retreat became a total rout as the Israelis pursued them mercilessly, firing as they went, back into Syria.

However, a separate Syrian assault, further north at the Nafahk crossroads, threatened a Syrian breakthrough. Israel's General Eitan had two tanks left under repair in his workshop at command group headquarters. He and a handful of men prepared to fight to the death as the Syrians roared through the camp fence and aimed at the operations room, where they waited to die. At that instant the first tank of the Israeli 79th Armoured Brigade appeared round the corner of the road, saw what was happening and fired at a distance of a few yards at the first Syrian T62. The result was total panic as the 79th pushed the Syrians out of the camp.

In three days, against continuous attacks by three Syrian tank forces—the 7th, 3rd and Assad Divisions—the Israeli 7th Armoured destroyed 300 tanks and hundreds of armoured vehicles, all in the 'Valley of Tears'. They were finally relieved by a small contingent of tanks hastily assembled by a veteran commander, returning from his honeymoon. While the Israelis stabilised their Syrian front, the Suez front changed dramatically, mainly under the impact of the tiny, lethal, Soviet anti-tank missile Miliutka, accompanied by the familiar RPG-7 rocket bazookas.

The initial Israeli counter-attack, codename 'Dovecote',

was launched in the centre towards the Egyptian 2nd Army in a vain attempt at rescuing the Bar Lev troops. Against Egypt's 500 tanks were Israel's 300, stretched from north to south. By mid-morning on 7 October, less than 100 Israeli tanks were fit for combat, furthermore the IAF could not provide air cover as it was desperately trying to check the Syrian armoured thrust in the north-east of Israel. By evening, the first Israeli tank reservists trickled to the Suez front and a massive counter-attack was planned for the next morning. This attack against the five divisions of Egyptian infantry failed.

The solution for the Israelis came on 9 October when they concentrated on long-range precision sharpshooting, accompanied by armoured infantry to deal with exposed Egyptian infantry. Israeli losses dropped dramatically. Meanwhile, the Egyptians under the cautious General Ahmed Ismail dug in, protected by the massive anti-aircraft umbrella now established along the Eastern bank of Suez through which few Israeli aircraft could fly.

It took the Egyptians four crucial days to launch their major assault towards the Sinai passes and on 14 October, 1,200 Soviet tanks massed in attack formation, roared forwards through their smoke screen, accompanied by artillery and armoured infantry. The Israelis, hull-down on high ground, waited until they were within range and then shot their front line to pieces. Three hundred Egyptian tanks and hundreds of armoured vehicles were destroyed in one day by Israeli 105mm tank guns. At Jericho HQ in Cyprus Michael ran to the operations centre to receive this latest news. The tide of war was changing in favour of Israel. Michael was changing too. For the first time since childhood, he was praying.

During the four crucial days of 10 to 14 October the Syrian front altered completely. The Israeli northern command under Major General Yitzhak Hofi decided to counter-attack before Jordanian and Iraqui reinforcements arrived to support the Syrians. The first task was to use the IAF to destroy the Syrian air defences. At last Michael saw the wisdom of General Wheeler's advice and he began to feel less guilty at not having returned immediately to Israel.

The role of the reconnaissance flights by the IAF and the 'Jericho' team was paying off as the Israelis systematically destroyed the entire Syrian Soviet-designed missile defence system. The key aircraft were Phantoms fitted with 'Shrike' anti-radar missiles and the tiny but powerful Skyhawks flying at 50 feet over the rolling Golan hills with four tons of bombs suspended from their sturdy delta wings.

Then came an event the Israelis dreaded. The Syrians, desperate to retake the initiative, launched Soviet 'Frog' rockets onto Israeli towns in the Jezreel valley. The war was escalating towards direct attacks on civilian populations. The Israeli response was immediate. Precision attacks were made by the IAF on the Syrian Air Force Headquarters and Ministry of Defence buildings in Damascus. Simultaneously the oil facilities at Homs, Latakia and Tartus were bombed into infernos, along with selected power stations. The 'Frogs' abruptly ceased and no further civilian targets were attacked during the war.

Wheeler called in the team for a briefing on 11 October at 10.00hrs and there was no doubt of it: he was a happier man. He told them that the next hour would see a crucial development in the War. Nobody asked him how he knew. Michael had already guessed. It must be Daniel.

The Israeli offensive commenced at 11.00hrs with the basic intention of taking the northern part of the Golan and the strategically located village of Masrath Beit Gan from which Israeli artillery could reach Damascus in one shot. The attack was led by General Eitan's remarkable 7th Armoured Brigade, while further south on the main road to Damascus General Laner's division pushed east towards the Awag River and Damascus. Eitan achieved his objective that evening against massive Syrian artillery and anti-tank attacks. Laner, facing the original Syrian pre-War defensive positions, fought a hand-to-hand battle, tank against bazooka at ranges of a few yards, throughout the night. Israeli parachutists moved in and literally refuelled and serviced the tanks in the midst of the artillery barrages while the exhausted tankers tried to rest.

For the first time the 'Jericho' team in Cyprus picked up hysterical calls to the Soviet Union by Syrian commanders. Panic was developing and the Russians began to fly in complete SAM missile systems in their giant Antonov transports.

As dawn broke on 12 October, General Laner started a wide flanking move south of the Syrian forces and observed crews abandoning their tanks in total panic, retreating towards Damascus, now an exposed city. Then he saw the long-awaited Iraqui reinforcements in the south-east arriving after their thousand-mile road trip, and he prepared a perfect ambush for the brand new Soviet T62s. Unbelievably, the Iraquis stopped in the middle of the prepared spot and 80 tanks were destroyed in the first minutes.

A similar Jordanian attack failed, leaving twenty Centurions burning while a further Iraqui attack left behind 60 T62s and T54s burning or destroyed. In the south of Golan, General Peled fought to within twenty miles of Damascus defeating further Syrian and Jordanian attacks.

On 13 October, the Golan battle had been won by the Israelis, apart from the remaining problem of the Hermon observation post. This was finally taken by the Golani Infantry Brigade and heliported paratroopers, before the final cease-fire. The final count of the Golan front was 1,200 Syrian and 150 Iraqui or Jordanian tanks destroyed for 250 Israeli tanks lost or damaged.

The Israelis were now free to turn all their attention onto the Egyptians. Wheeler called for Michael again on 14 October to tell him that General Sharon had commenced Operation 'Gazelle' at noon. The entire basis of the incredible operation was the evidence produced by Michael and Pete Peabody on the flight that had confirmed the electronic gap between the Egyptian 2nd and 3rd Armies.

The selected crossing point was Deversoir or Duweir Suweir on the northern tip of the Great Bitter Lake. It was the precise place at which Moses, according to tradition, was reported to have crossed from Egypt into Sinai 4,000 years before. To draw the 2nd Army forces north, away from the point, a secondary attack was launched against Ismailia while Sharon's main force of two armoured brigades and a paratroop unit reached the shores of the Great Bitter Lake as darkness fell. One battalion made for an Egyptian bridge over the canal and Sharon pushed more and more armour into position awaiting the special bridging unit to take the tanks.

Suddenly the Egyptians realised that this extraordinary development could cost them the War, for here, in their own administrative area, was an Israeli armoured force. Their reaction was to lay on a massive bombardment of the massed Israeli tanks waiting to cross. The key to protecting the new bridgehead now required Israeli control of the strategic crossroads to the west of the Canal through which the bridging units had to move to reach the bridgehead. At midnight, while the battle raged in the bridgehead area by the Canal, Sharon ordered Paratroop Unit 101 to secure the crossroads.

Thus started the Battle of the Chinese Farm, named after the nearby experimental farm, built in fact by the Japanese before the Six Day War. It cost the Israelis dearly, but by morning 150 Egyptian tanks and hundreds of vehicles lay destroyed and the Egyptians withdrew leaving the road clear for the huge bridge sections to be brought up, albeit under continuous artillery bombardment. The first Israelis to cross the Canal into Egypt were paratroopers in rubber boats, but in two days significant columns of armour had gathered waiting to cross as soon as the bridge was ready.

The Egyptians tried desperately to destroy the bridgehead, but were tenuously held by the Israeli line. An Egyptian column of 80 tanks was totally destroyed in an ambush by General Adan on the eastern shores of the Bitter Lakes.

The bridge comprised huge pontoons each of which was placed at night under continuous Egyptian fire until finally, on the morning of 18 October, the two armoured brigades had crossed the Canal and could roam freely behind the

Egyptian 2nd and 3rd Armies. The 2nd Army Commander, Major-General Mamoun, had a heart attack and the Chief-of-Staff, General Shazli, collapsed with exhaustion and strain. The Israelis lost General Mendler, killed on 14 October.

The final phase of the great War in the Middle East now began as the Israelis on the west bank of the Canal rode rampant, destroying every missile site within twenty miles of the Canal bank, thus clearing the air for the Israeli Air Force. The Israelis split north and south towards Ismailia and Suez respectively, taking the harbour of Adabieh on the Gulf of Suez and the outskirts of Suez City and thereby completing the entrapment of the Egyptian Third Army.

They had reached within 62 miles of Cairo when a totally new development changed the course of the war, and the Jericho team were at the hub of it.

Wheeler was grim-faced as he summoned his team for an emergency briefing. The atmosphere was charged with tension as Michael and his RSO were warned to prepare for an emergency evacuation. There were no preambles.

'Gentlemen, I have been ordered by the Chief-of-Staff to prepare for a direct attack on our facilities here in Cyprus. Satellite evidence has revealed that the Soviet Union has massed airborne troops and marines in the Ukraine and is preparing for an invasion of the Middle East either directly into Israel or on two fronts in support of Egyptian and Syrian forces.

'In view of our position and our mission, there is every possibility that Cyprus will be occupied—or at least the RAF base at Akrotiri. We have advised the British Government, who have placed all Mediterranean forces on a pre-war footing. Soviet commando forces may be prepared to isolate this facility or capture its personnel to prevent us playing a significant part in the War.

'All pilots and crew will standby in full kit and fuelled up until the crisis has passed. These are your flight plans, only to be opened when you are ready to take off, in accordance with maximum alert conditions.'

Wheeler's aide handed out the thick, red plastic envelopes as each crewman signed his receipt.

Within the hour Allon and Peabody were sitting in the air-conditioned van adjacent to the Blackbird. Their destination was the Black Sea, and within minutes they would be airborne and ready to observe any Soviet air and naval movements out of Odessa and provide Israel with adequate warning.

The Russians had suffered the greatest setback of the post-war period. The Arab forces, co-ordinated, trained and equipped almost entirely with the latest Soviet weaponry had been defeated by a tiny nation smaller than the city of Moscow. The Arabs had lost 2,500 Soviet tanks, over 450 aircraft, thousands of armoured vehicles and tens of thousands of troops. Furthermore, at sea the Israeli Navy had fought and won the world's first all-missile naval battle, destroying five ships for no losses to themselves. Israel had lost 2,500 dead, over 100 aircraft and up to 500 tanks.

In Russia, Brezhnev was utterly incensed by the defeat, knowing that the Israelis now possessed a complete selection of the very latest Soviet missiles, aircraft, tanks and other weapons.

In the United States, Nixon responded with direct flights of US Phantoms and Skyhawks, hastily repainted, which flew non-stop from USAF bases in the United States and Europe. Some, collected by Israeli pilots, flew straight into combat, the paint still wet. Giant C5A Galaxy transports flew round the clock, supplying Israel with missiles, bombs and ammunition as both Superpowers tried desperately to influence the outcome of the War, short of direct involvement of their own troops. As the 'Jericho' team heard of Brezhnev's threat, Nixon immediately placed on nuclear alert all US forces throughout the world. The War was on the verge of escalation to a direct confrontation between Israel and Russia as the Soviets grew more and more desperate.

Emergency meetings were held in Moscow whilst Soviet forces started to mobilise in response to the US President's order. US reconnaissance satellites continued to monitor the massive assembly of Soviet paratroop transports in southern Russia and the preparation of troop ships in the Black Sea port of Odessa. United States and Russian troops could be at war within the next 24 hours.

Wheeler slept in cat-naps, maintaining his strength for the real task ahead, ready to move the moment he was ordered. For the Blackbird pilots it was just as difficult. It had proved impossible to sleep in their bulky pressure suits so they'd hung them up ready. As they waited there came the unceasing roar of RAF Phantoms taking off on combat patrol, ready to intercept the first Russian aircraft that might strike at this the most critical base in NATO's southern flank.

The huge, bat-like Vulcans thundered off on long mysterious flights, low over the sea, fully armed with the innocuous fat cylinders that Michael saw being escorted from the remote, camouflaged bomb dumps by armoured patrols. The world's most experienced bomber force would be ready. Sitting there on the very edge of a full-scale war Michael realised that very soon he might no longer be an observer but a combatant and for the first time he wished the Blackbird was armed with defensive weapons, not just sensors.

The tension was almost unbearable as each hour passed with further news of Soviet threats and mobilisation while in Sinai and Golan the real combatants waited, eyeing each other across their gun barrels, sights checked a dozen times. Israel was in a position of complete domination, her artillery within range of Damascus, her tanks surrounding an entire Egyptian army. And she had the greatest weapon of all on her side: time. Time for the Egyptian 3rd Army to die of thirst in the baking wastes of Sinai. The Israelis had cut off their water supply, and now watched through their field glasses and their Phantom-born cameras as the Egyptians' lives evaporated under the blistering sun. Minute by minute men simply stopped living as their bodies dried up and stiffened in the merciless heat, all rational thought baked out of them hours before the end.

Then very gradually the Israeli mood changed from exultation to pity as they saw once proud soldiers, not unlike themselves, melt before their eyes into tattered, crazy rag-bags, stumbling and crawling towards them, speechless with swollen tongues that ballooned from their mouths, speckled with flies. Awkwardly the Jews began walking hesitantly towards their defeated enemy and, one by one, they started to share their precious water.

Within days it was all over, the combatants finally ceased fire and the blue-helmeted troops of the United Nations signalled the water tankers through the Israeli circle of armour at Kilometre 101. The war of Yom Kippur was over. In Odessa the troops disembarked from their landing craft, the big Antonov transports rumbled back to their eyries in the vast landmass of Russia, and Michael Allon slept in a proper bed, naked.

Nixon and Brezhnev came up from their caverns and walked in the fresh air with their wives and families, both pleased they'd ridden through the storm, for the time being at least.

David Berglass never recovered from his first shattering experience of modern war and died in Egyptian captivity, incoherent to the end.

Sadi returned to his village a hero and decided to stay in the army, ready to try again when and if Anwar Sadat called him.

For the pilot of the glistening, silver Mig 25, totally cocooned in its bomb proof shelter at Cairo West airfield those days of October had been a time of profound disillusionment. There he had sat, day after day, in the world's most powerful fighter, armed and fuelled, desperate to hit back at the Israelis, willing the massive blast door to rumble aside to unleash him, him the avenger.

But it had come to nothing. The Russians had played it safe, reeling out one excuse after the other until he had climbed down from his cockpit and burst into the Soviet fighter controller's chamber demanding to be sent on a mission, any mission, so long as he felt he had taken part in the War. But the dour Ukrainian had stonewalled him, even to the extent of disconnecting the essential ground power unit and ordering the aircraft to be guarded by two Soviet marines.

For the Palestinian it was a personal insult and an affront to his people. At the hour of their greatest need his so-called allies had abandoned their commitment and prevented him, their protegé, from using the very weapon that could disrupt the Israeli Air Force. Why couldn't the Russians supply more Migs and Sukkois just as the Americans had flown in Phantoms and Skyhawks? Surely a squadron of Mig 25s could be despatched from the hundreds already in service? For all his entreaties and protestations he received nothing but platitudes and to him they meant only one thing, deceit.

As he sat hunched, alone on the edge of his small metal bunk he began to appreciate the bleakness of his situation. The dream of Palestine had been shattered in a few tumultuous days. From the first giddy heights of the early successes to the dishonourable ceasefire, his emotions had been held in check, as they changed from exultation to despair. All the time he'd waited to be summoned to help wrest victory from defeat, a commando of Palestine, brandishing the deadliest blade of the Soviet Union.

And he thought of the glittering machine sitting there ready to thunder into the skies over Suez, capable of destroying any American aircraft, even the Blackbird, and he had come so near already. A mere squeeze of his thumb could have unleashed a salvo of missiles and brought the extraordinary craft down into the wastes of Sinai. The image of that helmeted face was still vivid in his mind. Like a helpless robot the pilot had watched him and then very deliberately had raised his golden vizor, like a medieval knight, and revealed his face. A face so like his own, probably only a few years older. Obviously he was a highly skilled pilot to have been entrusted with the greatest aircraft of the American inventory.

Shabir had responded to the gesture by raising his own vizor in silent salute to his adversary while his interception cameras had recorded the Blackbird in great clarity for later examination in Russia; no doubt the other crewmember had done exactly the same for his intelligence officers.

It had only been a matter of seconds and then his Russian flight controller's agitated voice had broken the silence and ordered him back, back to Cairo West before anybody tried anything 'silly'. They couldn't afford to provoke the Americans, not then, within hours of their great assault. And Shabir had cursed the voice and flashed his wings in the brilliant sunlight and swooped down from the indigo sky and silver craft to skulk uselessly in his cavernous bunker.

Shabir unrolled his prayer mat and laid it carefully on the bare concrete floor. He knelt to pray and offered his life to God as an instrument in the struggle against Zion, not for the Union of Soviet Socialist Republics but for the people of Palestine. And gradually he became calm again, at peace with himself, resolved now to exploit at the right time any opportunity afforded him by his unique situation, 'Imsh'allah'.

18
Tyuratam

The big black limousines glided down the ribbed concrete ramp to stop in the underground reception block, the only sound being the idling of their engines and the clunk of their heavy doors. Within twelves minutes all the cars had driven up and out of the exit ramp and completed the 90-degree sweep that brought them to the single fenced access road. For a quarter of a mile around the underground facility the ground was levelled and white with snow, totally exposed to the multi-spectral sensors that guarded the KGB's holy of holies, the Central Planning Unit, the brain of the body Soviet.

Each delegate was processed through a special security room where he was required to change into a single one-piece zipped tracksuit, placing all his clothes in a grey polythene container which was sealed until he had been cleared to dress again. It took an hour to process all of them, but it was a necessary security measure to prevent the smuggling of 'foreign' devices into the facility.

As they sat, naked, waiting for their tracksuits, each was required to slip on a combined breathing mask and plastic body vest like a 'Mae West', which plugged into a biomedical recorder, identical to the ones used by their own cosmonauts. This provided the only certain total-body correlation with their own unique record in the data bank and avoided all the ridiculously unreliable fingerprint and voice-recording tests of the past. Once dressed in the 'delegate suit', as it was known, they were escorted individually down a 200-foot lift shaft by two KGB guards, specifically empowered to immobilise them in the event of any suspicious behaviour. 'Stun, don't think' was the guards' primary instruction.

The delegates entered the conference chamber in silence and were escorted to their allotted seats. No discussion was permitted until the Chairman had entered. In fifteen minutes the 100-seat conference chamber was half filled and the doors closed. The soft green colour scheme and colour-matched chairs were selected to relieve those delegates who might suffer from claustrophobia. The raised stage was backed by a single stretch screen in front and to each side of which were placed two lecterns with built-in overhead projectors, reading lights, cue controls and microphones.

The Chairman, wearing a black tracksuit, entered and stood at the lectern. He scanned the audience for a moment then softly addressed them.

'Gentlemen, this is an emergency session of the third Joint Planning Unit Conference, convened to assess the findings of the War Analysis Group under the late Lieutenant-General Yeliskeiv's successor, General Bodkin.'

General Mendeleiv asked for Bodkin to open the conference. The tall thin man stepped briskly up to his lectern.

'Chairman General Mendeleiv, Delegates. As Chairman of the WAG I will first summarise our findings and then identify our recommendations before we enter into detailed analysis sessions, with your permission.

'The Soviet Union has suffered a defeat such as never experienced since the Patriotic War! In spite of the most complex propaganda and disinformation campaign ever mounted since the British Double X Committee's concealment of the Invasion Plans for Europe and their protection of the Ultra team who read the Nazi High Command cyphers throughout the War, we were defeated. In spite of a surprise attack on an enemy literally at prayer, our weapons, our tactics, our strategy were overcome.

'We can only ignore the lessons of the October War at the

risk of being defeated in a conventional war against NATO. We have lost our most advanced missiles, radar and communications equipment to Israel, who in turn—we can be certain—will trade them with the USA and NATO for guarantees of security and political support. We may, therefore, have sown the seeds for defeat in the event of a nuclear war.

'The Israeli Defence Forces in a period of ten days destroyed a force as great as the whole of NATO Central Forces. How? That is the question my committee asked of every battlefield commander, of every KGB, GRU or military officer attached to the Arab forces.

'How did obsolete twenty-year-old British tanks defeat brand-new T62s, Stalin Tanks and T54s? How did the IAF neutralise the most comprehensive missile and gun network ever assembled in war?

'How did the Israelis fight on two separate fronts against the best-equipped forces outside the Soviet Union and the United States?

'How did they do all of this with a loss of 2,500 killed, to them a disastrous waste of human life, to us a minute fraction of acceptable losses in a single battle?

'If we can find the answers then the Soviet Union could "conventionally" fight every army in the world including the United States, NATO, China, France, South Africa, simultaneously, and defeat them in ten days!

'Chairman and Delegates, we have a task ahead of us that will take us to 1979, assuming we can maintain our control of Arab policy-making. Meanwhile we must maintain support of the Palestinian liberation groups, and other Communist-supplied groups in West Germany, Japan, Northern Ireland, South America and Africa. Simultaneously, we must stall, stall, stall the SALT II agreements and establish total nuclear superiority over the United States. Finally, before we enter the detail analysis session let us consider the Chairman's plan for focussing world attention on the Palestinian struggle—a plan which, if I may say so, is the cleverest single propaganda exercise my committee has ever considered. Thank you Chairman General Mendeleiv, Delegates.'

And Russia's leading Middle East military expert stepped down to polite acknowledgement from the delegates.

The conference finished fourteen weary hours later as dawn was breaking in the east. The same procession of black cars drove in funereal silence up the black freshly swept ribbon of asphalt, swung into the circle and coasted silently into the ground. Each one emerged at precisely spaced moments from the concealed lobby, accelerating up the salted exit ramp before turning into the circle and out along the access road.

Two minutes after the last one disappeared there came the whine of a turbine helicopter which settled its dull grey body on the snow over the concealed entrance. A perfect circle of snow like an Eskimo's fishing hole, three feet in diameter, lifted backwards and from it emerged a man in a black track-suit who then disappeared into the helicopter. In a flurry of snowflakes it lifted off as the hatch closed, invisible to curious eyes. The helicopter, a Mil Mi-8, banked away to Domodedovo, its anti-collision beacons flashing into the whiteness. In minutes it had disappeared on its 55-mile flight to catch the SOVAF transport flight to Baikonur. Its passenger was General Mendeleiv, Head of the Central Planning Unit of the KGB.

Shabir Al Timimi stood in the small grey soundproof room trying to establish which way was east. After a few seconds he laid out his pilot's scarf, his makeshift prayer mat and commenced his prayers. The door opened a foot then closed quietly again. As soon as the Palestinian had finished he stood up and opened the door to admit Mendeleiv.

'Good day Colonel, my apologies for the interruption.' Mendeleiv said.

'Not at all, General. I'm sorry you had to wait.'

'Please sit down, Colonel Al Timimi. Here will be fine. Your escorting officer Colonel Moskalenko tells me the flight was a revelation. What did you do, fly inverted all the way?' The General allowed himself a flicker of a grin.

'No, it was a normal transit flight, General.'

'Well, Moskalenko has asked me to arrange for you to join

his squadron if we can spare you. That's high praise indeed.'

'I'm grateful sir, but I only know one way to fly the 25, the way Mikoyan Guyerevich designed it,' and the Palestinian meant every word.

'I'm afraid Moskalenko will be disappointed. But I doubt if you'll fly the 25 much, ever again.' Mendeleiv saw the Palestinian's eyes turn slowly towards him, a growing look of puzzlement appearing on his dark polished features.

'No, Colonel, your craft will be very different. Let me assure you it requires even more careful handling.'

Mendeleiv sat down to one side of Al Timimi and rested his forearms gently on the table.

'It will be the New Year in four hours, Colonel; I believe that 1974 will be your special year, for tomorrow you will be given the most respected job the Soviet Union can offer a pilot. You have been selected to train as a cosmonaut.'

Shabir was speechless with surprise. Never in his wildest imaginings had he believed that he would be anything more than a first-class pilot groomed to assume the task of building a Palestinian Air Force. Not even his late and trusted 'adviser' Lieutenant-General Yeliskeiv had talked of anything but training him for the job of becoming first Chief of Staff for an independent Palestinian Air Force.

Not once had he or the Soviets assumed that the outcome of the October War would be anything but the destruction of Israel and the creation of the Peoples Palestinian Republic, with Jerusalem its capital city. It would be comparable in many ways with Cuba under Fidel Castro. For two years Al Timimi and 116 other Palestinian Arabs had attended a special course designed to groom them to take over on 1 November 1973 as heads of the new Palestinian government.

The KGB printing presses had prepared five million identity cards for all residents of the PPR, each of whom would be classified as Palestinian Communist, Palestinian National and Palestinian Jew. A team of 1,200 KGB officers, male and female, had undergone a six-month training course in basic Arabic ready to interrogate every resident of the state. 300 had also learnt Hebrew to a basic standard adequate for carrying out searches, arrests and initial interrogations.

The same KGB team that co-ordinated the Soviet administration of Czechoslovakia after its invasion by Soviet troops were appointed to mastermind the smooth transition from Israeli surrender to the creation of the PPR. A complete air-transportable communications headquarters was sitting in the fuselages of a squadron of Antonov An 22 transports near Odessa ready to fly in to Tel Aviv airport and establish total control of all TV, radio and telephone services.

Two camps had been built in Syria under KGB administration for holding 'high-profile' Jewish personalities such as political leaders, businessmen, scientists and artists. They were specially designed for controlled propaganda press conferences and so forth to reassure the world media and particularly the United States. A third one, known only to a special team of selected KGB men was called 'The Temple'. It covered 2,000 acres in northern Siberia, hidden from US satellite reconnaissance by camouflage netting resembling fir trees.

Shabir himself had been unknowingly working with the same squadron of Foxbats which would be 'invited' by the PPR's new Government to 'protect' the new state from 'aggressive Imperialist excursions'.

'Well, aren't you pleased Colonel, or perhaps you don't feel too well?'

Mendeleiv was genuinely concerned at the sweat that broke out on the Palestinian's face.

'I beg your pardon, General, I am very confused by this news. Please, I am not ungrateful, just simply confused.'

'That's understandable, Colonel, you've had to change your planning totally since the cease-fire, as we all have. Would you like some refreshment? You may be catching a chill you know, it's twenty degrees of frost today.' The General started to relax. 'God, these Arabs are bloody sensitive,' he thought, his impatience under firm control for the moment.

'General Mendeleiv, do I understand correctly that, in spite of the shame of my people's defeat, in spite of the loss of even larger areas of Golan and the Canal's west bank, in spite of the loss to the Soviet Government you are asking me to become a cosmonaut, to fly spacecraft? Russian spacecraft?'

'Exactly, Colonel.'

Shabir closed his eyes tightly feeling the emotion well up inside him.

'Imsh-allah, Imsh-allah . . .,' he murmured quietly to himself.

On 1 January 1974, Shabir Al Timimi became the first Arab, and almost the first non-Russian, to begin the outstanding course in space-flight training that the Soviet Government provides at its various facilities in Moscow and Baikonur Cosmodrome. To be selected as a cosmonaut was to achieve the pinnacle of one's military or scientific career, a guarantee of acceptance among the highest echelons of the Communist Party, attendance on VIP platforms during the May Day parades, free transport, 'luxury' goods, excellent accommodation in Star Town or Stellar Village, but above all, on completion of one's flight, the award of Hero of the Soviet Union. But every cosmonaut earned his reward ten times over.

Shabir Al Timimi, already a superb jet fighter pilot with excellent academic qualifications, commenced his training on 1 January 1974 with an introductory briefing on the cosmodrome. His guide was Lieutenant-General Vladimir A. Shimatov, Chief of the Soviet Space Flight Training Centre.

The two men were introduced to each other by General Mendeleiv, accompanied by Colonel Moskalenko, in the State Visitors reception room at the Tyuratam Launch Complex. Shimatov was immediately warm and friendly towards the Palestinian.

'Colonel Al Timimi, it is a great pleasure to meet you after all I have heard from General Mendeleiv. It seems you are considered rather a star pupil. Your record at the Zukhovsky Air Academy is excellent and your subsequent operational flying quite exceptional. Even I, an old man of 40, am not allowed to fly the Mig 25!' He turned his handsome intelligent face to the General with a grin that showed off his perfect set of teeth. He brushed his untidy brown hair off his narrow face characteristically and looked Al Timimi up and down, smiling still.

'We flyers will have a lot to talk about, Colonel, I'm sure we won't want to keep the General waiting here.' Shimatov stared at the KGB man who ignored the offer, addressing Colonel Moskalenko across Shimatov's chest instead.

'Moskalenko, before I finish here today would you kindly return General Shimatov's file to me. Sorry, General, you were saying?'

Shimatov and Mendeleiv were obviously ill at ease with each other.

The party moved away, Shimatov leading with the young Palestinian, followed by Mendeleiv and Moskalenko a few steps behind. They walked across the lobby to another more functional room with 50 seats in five rows. A small raised platform with a sliding display unit were its only other furniture. The party of three sat awkwardly two rows back as Shimatov stepped onto the platform and slid open the display panel.

'Colonel Al Timimi, this is a map of Tyuratam launch complex.' He paused, turning back to the board. 'Oh no, my mistake, this is Cape Kennedy, Florida, much nicer climate, so sorry.' Shabir grinned at the joke and Moskalenko almost did. Mendeleiv certainly did not. Shimatov pulled down another chart and there was the plan of the world's first space centre.

'Tyuratam is located here, 45.6 degrees north, 63.4 degrees east.' He pointed to a small inset map of the Soviet Union.

'As you can see, we are east of the northern end of the Aral Sea—lots of good fishing, by the way—and due north of the Arabian Gulf, just for you of course, thought you'd be interested, Colonel,' said Shimatov with a twinkle in his eye.

'We are linked by road and rail north-west to Moscow via Novakozalinsk while Tashkent is south-east down the Syr-Dar Ya River. Our home town is Tyuratam itself, here on the river, less than half an hour's drive, lovely for a picnic in the summer I'm told.

'By the way, nobody moves in or out of this zone without permission from General V.F. Tolubko, Commander of the Strategic Rocket Forces. The entire area for a radius of 250 miles is monitored with multi-spectral sensors, is it not, General?' Without waiting for a reply Shimatov continued.

'We are here in building seventeen in the Central Administration Unit, the CAU. Nobody moves out of CAU without a further security check. As you can see, the main launch complex or MLC is to our east. Don't be fooled by the map, the entire complex is 45 miles long! Due south, twelve miles, is our support staging area or SSA by the main road and rail lines. Finally, we have fuel depots and water reservoirs out to the west end. Missile launches are monitored out here 30 miles to the north-east. The town of Baikonur lies 140 miles behind the monitoring point.

'What you see, Colonel, is the largest space facility in the world. It was from here on 12 April 1961 that Yuri Gagarin, the world's first spaceman, was launched in the Vostok spacecraft on the top of our first ICBM launcher.

'Gagarin, like you, was a good pilot, but even he was damn scared when he was waiting for the lift-off. You see, we'd launched the first Sputnik, the first-ever earth satellite, here on 4 October 1957, using the same launcher. Korolev, our chief designer, was worried sick about risking Gagarin's life. Isn't it ironic that they should both die within a few years of each other? Poor old Yuri, he had it made you know, could go anywhere, but what does he do? Pisses about in a Mig 15 and kills himself. What a waste. But I'm digressing. Let's see the next pretty picture.'

Shimatov stretched up again and pulled down a diagram outlining the basic design of the Soviet space launchers and their manned spacecraft. Shabir leaned forward, his interest aroused because he suddenly realised that this was no abstract diagram, but the very machinery on which he would one day, God willing, be launched into space.

He felt a curious lightness about him, finding it hard to control his thumping heart, his hands started to go clammy and he forced himself back into his chair, trying to match Shimatov's relaxed manner. Both Mendeleiv and Moskalenko watched him out of the corners of their eyes, curious to see his response to the presentation.

'The entire approach to successful spaceflight in the twentieth century is based on the brilliant thinking of one man, Konstantin Tsiolkovsky. He was born exactly 100 years before the first satellite was placed in orbit. These rockets you see before you are based on his thinking. You see, he came from Kaluga, near the Yachenka river. Just an ordinary schoolteacher, but what a brain! Thank goodness his notebooks were preserved.

'In 1883, he realised that according to Newton's Third Law of Motion a rocket would work in the vacuum of space because the exhaust gases coming out through a hole would cause a reaction inside the chamber and push the chamber away from the gases, in the opposite direction. Clever, eh!

'Didn't stop there though. Designed his first rocket, like a tadpole, in 1903, the same year the Wright Brothers were building flying bicycles. What's more his fuel was liquid oxygen, necessary for combustion in space, and liquid hydrogen. Whoever told you the capitalists invented the future? I won't bore you with all his inventions. Suffice it to say that he proposed liquid-fuelled spaceships, conical nozzles, gyroscopes, control valves, exhaust vanes for steering, gimballed nozzles, self-cooling motors and—most important of all—the "Step" principle.

'In other words, all modern rockets are based on the fundamental work of a Russian schoolteacher! But he didn't stop at basic rockets; no, he calculated the velocity necessary to escape earth's gravity and the orbital velocity whereby satellites travel at a speed that exactly balances the centrifugal force slinging them out from the earth and the centripetal reaction, pulling them in.

'Colonel Al Timimi, you will be flying on Tsiolkovsky's brainwaves!'

Shabir was beginning to relax again—here was a man who had flown twice in space before and returned. He felt his confidence growing.

'Finally, to finish with our friend Konstantin, he conceived of pressure cabins, spacesuits, airlocks, umbilical tethers, closed-loop biological life-support systems, hydroponics, space stations and most important of all, aerodynamic control of re-entry into the atmosphere at 18,000 miles an hour.

'These rockets here, Colonel Al Timimi, are the brainchild of the late, great Sergei Pavlovich Korolev, a close and dear friend who died in January 1966. He started working with Friedrich Sander and in 1931 he led the CGIJP, the Central Group for Investigation of Jet Propulsion. They launched our first liquid-fuelled rocket in August 1933. Would you believe it, Sergei designed the RDI rocket motor in 1943 and we still use its developed versions today in 1974.

'The "nameless one", Stalin, loved rockets you know; he made Sergei head of the bureau for long-range rockets in 1947. Sergei improved German V2s and fired them from Kapustin Yar on the Volga. It's still an important launch site, you know. Korolev scared the Americans stupid in 1957 when he rolled out the T1, they talked of blowing up Russia with hydrogen bombs, can you believe it? You have to understand, Colonel Al Timimi: the Americans get hysterical if they see that somebody else can build better weapons than they can. They still believe we don't have electric toasters or colour television or washing machines and all of us work in tank factories. I know, I've been to America: Washington, New York, Cape Kennedy, Houston. They kept coming up to me and asking if I was in the KGB,' and Shimatov looked directly at Mendeleiv and laughed.

'Were you old enough to remember Cuba in 1962?' Shimatov enquired of the Palestinian, forgetting that Shabir was fighting Israeli troops at that time.

'Maybe not, but I tell you, if those Americans had decided to attack us then, POW! no more Russia, eh, General?' They both knew, Shimatov and Mendeleiv, that it had been a knife-edge situation. Krushchev was sacked because they thought he'd gone too close, the rockets weren't sufficiently reliable to guarantee surprise destruction of the USA, and they had no effective way to defend themselves against the US SAC bombers.

'Poor old Nikita, that second "unperson", eh, General?'

'He loved visiting us down here, always wanted to fire off a satellite launcher himself. We were terrified he'd even fumble that.

'So, let's get down to our rockets. This is the Type A that launched Sputnik, with its central body and four parallel boosters. All we did was fit another stage on top of the centre or fiddle with various bits and this old fellow has launched all the manned spacecraft; Vostok, Voskhod and Soyuz; one, two and three men each; the Sputniks, Luna, Mars and Venus probes. Oh, it also carried our test hydrogen bombs.

'Incredible, eh! This old steamer, still going strong nearly twenty years later. And think of Sergei Korolev's brilliance. He didn't design dozens of different engines like the Americans are always doing. No, he just designed one, the RD107, which he arranged in groups of four to give 225,000 pounds of thrust per group. He then put four groups around a central group and so he had 1,125,000 pounds of thrust, enough to lift the Soyuz spacecraft off the pad outside.

'Do you know, I was in Paris in 1967 at the 27th Salon de l'Aeronautique et de l'Espace when Yuri got dressed up in his Air Force best and signed autographs. We lifted a complete booster, on trolleys and on a short section of track onto the showground, then we lifted it up by the crane on to the transporter-erector. Can you imagine the faces on those Western "experts" when they saw twenty motors and twelve vernier motors at the base of the launcher? I'll never forget it. Were you there, General?'

'No, I was in Egypt, General, fighting the Israelis.'

Mendeleiv's expression was rock steady as he quietly folded his arms.

'Anyway I know where I stayed, Colonel. Here at Tyuratam, because I was busy with the design engineers of the late Sergei Korolev's team building the next launcher. The Type D, which lifts the Salyut Space Station into orbit while you, Colonel, fly in the Soyuz on the nose of the Type A. This is the Type D or Proton launcher. It has six strap-on boosters—that's two more than Type A—a two-stage central core giving it *three* times the thrust of Type A. Back in '65 to '66 we fired three Proton satellites into orbit and each one weighed over twelve tons. Imagine that. The rocket motor is a beauty. It's very high energy, smooth and reliable. Like a good woman, eh?

'I think that we've covered more than enough for this morning, Colonel, so how about some refreshment and then let's go and see the rockets being built? If we're lucky we'll see an actual launch tomorrow!' He led the now-dazed Palestinian on his first visit to a spacecraft factory.

Coffee was a mixed affair, Shimatov and Al Timimi absorbed in their joint love of flying whilst Moskalenko and Mendeleiv sat, a table away, talking of other matters. As in all of Mendeleiv's work, humour assumed a very low priority.

'Moskalenko, you have now seen our rising star and you have studied his file. You will provide me with a weekly report on his progress, contacts, relationships. You will keep a daily diary of his movements. If you see anything that suggests a failing, a weakness, apart from his Muslim convictions, then report to me by phone immediately. Do you understand?'

'Yes, sir, it is very clear what I have to do.'

'Good. You will be relieved every other weekend by a replacement and I will have others introduced at my discretion. You will not be informed of their identity.'

'Yes, sir, I understand.'

'Finally, I want Shimatov's file today and I will have him watched also. Do not interfere in his work—he is outstanding at his job, but politically adventurous.'

'Yes, sir, I'll bring his file to your room before supper if that's convenient to you, General.'

'Good, make sure you do. Now let's join the happy pair and see the other sights Shimatov promises so seductively.'

The two men rose and were followed by Al Timimi and the expansive Shimatov, who led them, as before, to the waiting Zil for the journey to the Main Assembly Building, the MAB. As the four of them were driven by the KGB chauffeur through the three separate security checks it began to dawn on Shabir Al Timimi that for the first time he was at the heart of Soviet power. All around him were massive anonymous buildings whose eventual product was the most complicated family of machines ever built. Manned spacecraft, satellites, space stations and God knows what else.

'General Shimatov, do you assemble nuclear weapons here?'

There was complete silence for half a minute before Mendeleiv intercepted.

'Colonel, you are here to man spacecraft and I know you will be successful. The Soviet Union has many responsibilities including the protection of the Palestinian people. We must do whatever is necessary to ensure your security. But the answer to your question is: no.

'We have signed an agreement with the Americans not to put nuclear weapons in orbit around the Earth. You yourself know that the Mig 25 is almost a spacecraft in itself, so why should we place nuclear weapons further out of reach where we cannot guarantee to control their use.' Shimatov silently breathed a sigh of relief at the factual reply given by his colleague.

Then why are there Radiation Warning signs on two of the buildings we just passed?' Shabir retorted.

'Oh, that's quite correct, Colonel.' Shimatov interjected, 'Those buildings are used in the assembly of satellites using nuclear-powered generators or isotopes. They are a very common type in the Cosmos series. The Americans, British and French use similar radioactive units to generate electrical power for satellites deprived of adequate solar power. I tell you what, we'll have a look at one later. Now, we're almost there, gentlemen. The second door please, Captain.' And the Zil slid to a silent halt by a white-painted door, set in a white frame—good for security illumination at night. Shimatov slid their security passes through the one-way flap and waited. The TV camera above them transmitted their images to the Security Officer and the door lock released electronically after a silent 30 seconds.

'One at a time please,' said Shimatov, stepping over the bulkhead.

Each man went through a security chamber and then joined up with the building's mobile security escort. The 'All Clear' sign flashed overhead as they passed the X ray scanner into the huge vaulted lobby of the world's first spacecraft factory. Shimatov was in his element.

'This is where we carry out final assembly of the central cone with its spacecraft. We can handle both the Type D and Type A launchers.'

They walked together through the light grey painted building, its sides reaching to 60 feet and its floor spanned by a heavy steel truss roof with parallel crane runs. Set into the floor were railway lines which guided the trolleys on which the vehicles were assembled horizontally. The entire layout was full of launchers in varying stages of assembly.

'That one there with the white nose shroud, Colonel, is a Soyuz, the kind you'll fly in, and behind it on the line is its back-up. We build them in batches of two in case of a launch failure or hitch.'

Shabir watched as the assembly technicians in their white 'clean' suits and elasticated caps worked quietly on various gantries around the giant assembly of pale green cylinders and tapering cones. They walked to the tail and looked up at the sparkling bank of twenty polished, dark grey nozzles, the RD108s, that would soon be roaring with the force of over a million pounds of thrust.

'The flight vehicle for tomorrow's launch is already on the

pad being fuelled. We'll see it later.'

Then they saw the huge Type D with its six conical strap-on boosters arranged hexagonally around the long central core units. Attached to its nose was a glistening space station of the Salyut kind, its details partially obscured by the gigantic protective polythene bag enveloping its spotless surface. It was waiting to be wrapped in a massive rigid plastic shroud that protected it on its one and only journey through the atmosphere into the silence of space.

'We Russians make the world's largest contraceptives, eh?' Shimatov laughed at his own joke.

'When is that one going up, General?' Shabir pointed at the phallic nose.

'The Salyut? Oh, about six weeks yet, if they're on time. Never flown in the Salyut myself, just Voskhod and Soyuz.'

'What was it like?' Shabir asked.

'Soyuz was beautifully smooth, no problems, child's play, promise you. They made me a hero for going to sleep in space. Still can't believe it. Voskhod was different though. Very cramped, noisy re-entry and quite warm. Still, it worked. Only poor old Vladimir got it on Soyuz One.'

'What happened . . .?' Shabir enquired.

'Lots of things, Colonel. Sticky thrusters, the altitude gyros played up, bad orbital insertion, you name it, but the worst thing was that he knew as he orbited that the parachute casing had been damaged.

'He had to come down early too. I was in the Control Centre and heard him talking as he re-entered. Then he operated the parachutes and sure enough the lines were all twisted up or severed. Imagine falling out of space. He talked and cried and talked and cried. So did we all until it was over. He hit the ground at well over a thousand miles an hour. Nothing left to bury. Marvellous man. I still think of him. Still, he never felt a thing at the end. Now, let's look at a Soyuz, shall we?'

They walked between two rockets towards a massive steel half-ring supported on a trolley like the ones used for the launchers, but smaller, about 35 feet long. Suspended within the ring, across its diameter, was an ungainly assembly of geometric solids mounted one in front of the other—as if someone had just removed the skewer from a giant kebab.

'Let's walk up to the working platform, shall we? After you, Colonel.' The four men negotiated their way on to the metal deck that ran along the axis of the assembly line. Two suited technicians made way for them and stopped work for a few minutes.

'Hello Viktor, Pavel. I'm sorry to interrupt your work but I'd like to introduce you to my friends.' And they shook hands respectfully then excused themselves for ten minutes.

'The assembly is lying on its side obviously. Here on the end, my right, is the attachment ring which bolts onto the upper stage of the central core of the launcher.

'You see it is flared and is in fact a drum containing our main orbital engine with its fuel and oxidant spheres. This is the Service Module. It also contains the guidance computers to make sure you are going in the right direction when it detaches itself from the launcher and enters orbit.

'Next we have the Re-entry Capsule, the same diameter as the drum, about two and a half metres, it is convex on its base and then tapers away very gradually forwards until it becomes the hemispherical nose.

'This capsule is your "cockpit" if you like, Colonel. Here, you and two other cosmonauts will sit during take-off and re-entry. There are three couches inside arranged across the base so that you have your back to the launcher and the ground when you take-off from the pad, outside here. This ensures that the acceleration, which is about four to five G maximum, is spread evenly over your backs and legs. I can assure you it's much more comfortable than combat manoeuvring in a fighter.

'So, when you are in orbit, sitting in your cockpit with your service module behind you, where do you work? Right here in this sphere. This is your Orbital Section which you enter through the hatch at the top of your cockpit. Straight ahead of you, in fact. The Orbital Section contains your experimental equipment and two men can work reasonably comfortably here. Three at a squeeze.

'So there it is. One, two, three—Service Module, Re-entry Capsule, Orbital Module.

'The complete Soyuz package, but for one more very important assembly. On each side of the service module you have two identical "wings". These are the solar panels which are unfolded in orbit to catch as much sunlight as possible. They are covered in tiny silicon squares which convert sunlight directly into electricity. Therefore, your solar panels should always face the sun to give you electrical power for your experiments and equipment. OK?

'So there you are in orbit in your Soyuz spacecraft but like the best pilots you would like to know how to get back down safely. Well, remember your cockpit is specially designed so that it alone will re-enter the earth's atmosphere. First you jettison your orbital section, the sphere, using a spring release, then you are left with your own capsule and service module. You then jettison your service module leaving you riding along happily in your re-entry capsule.

'You turn the capsule around to present a good strong back to the atmosphere below you and fall backwards in a long trajectory. Here it can get bumpy because you try to skid off the atmosphere, losing energy through friction and as a result you start being dragged in by the earth's gravity, so you re-enter on a ballistic trajectory.

'Have you visited South America by the way?'

The abrupt question took Shabir off-guard.

'Uh, no, General . . .'

'Pity because you'll miss it again when you return in Soyuz. You will fly over South America, across the Atlantic, Africa, the Middle East and the Caucasus mountains. You will usually land about 300 kilometres West of Tselinograd, in Kazakhstan. This last bit requires your parachutes to work. It's very smooth and a few feet before you hit the ground these small braking rockets on your backside fire and set you down as if you were sitting on a pillow. For a few minutes, if you're lucky, it's all peaceful until the helicopters land, damn noisy things, and then comes the most dangerous part of the entire mission. Flying in the helicopter or being trampled by stupid journalists from Novosti Press.

'By the way, you will be given a traditional Russian gift for a traveller, a loaf of bread and a bag of salt. Then it's back to Kalinin control centre—or Moscow if it's politically important, eh, General?' and Shimatov raised his eyebrows towards Mendeleiv.

'In your case, Colonel Al Timimi, I dread to think what stunts they'll line up for you. I got to travel all over the world, I ate and screwed myself stupid before they gave me this job I tell you.

'Now, any further brilliant questions, Colonel, or shall we go and have something to eat while the General and his friend plan your future?'

The tall Russian brushed back his hair again and put a hand on Shabir's shoulder before leading him along the huge assembly hall. Shabir was embarrassed with Shimatov's manner but felt it was better to play a neutral role in what was obviously a situation pregnant with negative possibilities.

'General Shimatov, how long will it take me to achieve flight status? Do you have any idea?'

'Yes, about five years.'

Shabir stopped in his tracks, much to the surprise of the following pair.

'Five years to fly that Soyuz?' He was incredulous, pointing at the silent spacecraft.

'Yes. If you're lucky, it could be as little as three years or less, but you are a special pupil. Normally a Soviet pilot with your flying background could do it in three to four years comfortably but I anticipate you will be treated as a guinea pig. They will save you for the appropriate time. Walk on, please.' They continued their stroll.

'Who do you mean by they, General?'

'Your advisors, Colonel: the General and his friend. You see, I'm an ex-PVO Strany flyer, on Mig 21s mainly. I'm a Lieutenant-General in the Soviet Air Force, not a member of the Committee for State Security, the KGB, not me.

I'm not a political character.'

The Palestinian had noticed the estrangement between KGB men and the other military servicemen and pilots he had worked with in the Middle East and in the Soviet Union, although he knew that every military unit had its overt and covert KGB officers, reporting on potential defectors, spies or any evidence of political revolt. He was now entirely used to it. It was a natural element of Soviet military life but he never expected to see it in the manned space programme. Certainly not at Tyuratam.

'I know what you're thinking, Colonel. It took me a long time to get used to it but I have never really accepted it. Seeing General Mendeleiv and Colonel Moskalenko reminded me that the KGB must have its own plan for you. Mine is simply to make you into a safe, reliable cosmonaut and I will do everything I can to assist you, especialy now I have read your Air Force file. But the file I'd like to get hold of is the KGB's own report file. Did you know, Colonel, every human being in the Soviet Union is in a data bank. And do you know who controls it? The KGB.

'Now I'm no dissident, although I'm not a member of the Communist Party, I, like the vast majority of Russians, do not want every aspect of our life monitored by the Party. Don't get me wrong now, I'm as patriotic as the next man. But I have a job to do and I don't like amateurs, busybodies or KGB people interfering in my own work. They're incompetent, I find. Although the good General behind us is probably one of the cleverest men in the business, he is still not a flyer or a scientist or an engineer, but one thing I do know, when you get that medal they give you for flying these things, he'll be right next to you when you receive it. Also, a friendly word of advice, pilot to pilot, eh? Watch Moskalenko. He'll get friendly but he'll be reporting back every week to Mendeleiv. That's his job, bless him.

'Oh, you've probably been meaning to ask me one very important question all the time, eh? . . . what does a man do to get himself a good woman round here, eh?' and Shimatov roared with laughter while Shabir grinned from ear to ear and looked away towards the next spacecraft.

That night General Mendeleiv did not appear for supper in the visitors' building but left a message for Shabir through Colonel Moskalenko wishing him good luck on his new career and promising to keep in touch. The meal was a relaxed, jovial affair at which the three men were joined by another Soyuz crew under training, Alexei Gretchko, Valery Romankoy and Georgei Kovalyenov. Gretchko and Kovalyenov were in their early thirties, both ex-Mig 25 pilots, whilst Romankoy was a thirty-year-old scientist-engineer from Lvov with limited flying experience, but sufficient to confirm his ability to adapt to the course.

By midnight, Shabir was shown to his room in the visitors' compound and fell fast asleep almost as soon as his head touched the pillow but not before he heard faintly through the wall the sound of somebody talking, possibly on a telephone. He had noticed also that his room had no phone . . .

He brought his knee up with a sudden jerk and shot out a chopping left hand blow that missed Moskalenko's surprised face by inches.

'Oh, pardon. Sorry, Colonel, sorry.' Shabir woke out of his dream, confused and embarrassed at his reflex. Moskalenko relaxed.

'My fault, Colonel Al Timimi, I was just touching your shoulder to wake you up.' The man looked embarrassed.

'I sleep deeply, Colonel. I must have been dreaming. Did I hurt you?'

'No, never touched me, but I'm glad I wasn't three inches closer.' He laughed weakly.

The car took them out the ten miles to the monitoring station set against the flat bleak snowscape of the Central Asian plateau. It was 22 degrees below freezing but there was no snow and the wind was steady at eleven knots from the north-west. Good launch conditions.

The car drove into a heated garage which connected with the buildings themselves. The three men climbed up four floors and emerged on the Control level looking out through huge, triple-glazed, electrically heated observation windows. The view was spectacularly bleak.

They stood two miles away from the rocket. It was a Type A-2 launcher, a vast towering green missile with four tapering boosters, like legs, sprouting from the central core. About 80 feet up there was a bright orange band while above this the core was again green. On top sat the 32-foot white protective nose cone swelling out like a phallus. A battery of tiny escape rockets mounted on a short stubby mast projected from the cone.

'The launch is spectacular, Colonel. We fire one about once every week, sometimes more, sometimes less.'

'What satellite is going up, General?'

'That's an unmanned Cosmos reconnaissance satellite. It's based on the Soyuz vehicle essentially but highly modified to carry automatic cameras and sensors.'

'How long will it be up for?'

'Oh, that will be a short time only. I believe a week or so.'

'Why so short a time, General, isn't that a waste?'

'No, Colonel, we're launching it into a low orbit over the Middle East. We're checking the Israeli positions in Sinai and Golan to make sure they don't cheat the ceasefire terms.'

'How good is your photography, General?'

'Good enough Colonel, good enough.'

'Could you pick out my plane when I was at Cairo West?'

'Oh yes. I read about that, very good flying and if I may say so, very lucky too.'

'Yes, the American pilot was making his third trip up the Canal and never tried evasive manoeuvres, otherwise I'd have been in trouble for lack of fuel.'

'I wish we had some of those Lockheed planes. Why the Americans built so few I will never know.'

'Very strange I agree, General. Maybe we could persuade them to loan us one of their Blackbirds in exchange for a Mig 25.'

An hour later they were still chatting when the flight controller told them to watch the launch. All three men were given binoculars which they focused on the missile. The four massive steel service arms had folded flat, leaving the rocket poised on its four smaller hinged support arms.

Liquid oxygen boiled off from the vent pipe like clouds of steam and then suddenly they saw a flicker of blue flame followed two seconds later by a belching cloud of brilliant orange as the motors built up to full thrust. Slowly at first, then with increasing speed the rocket left the pad. The noise hit them a second later, a deep thundering tremor that shook the building, changing to a crackling roar as the rocket climbed steadily into the sky on a tongue of solid flame. Clouds of smoke and steam shot out horizontally from the pad gradually enveloping the entire launch area.

The rocket started to arc over slowly on its launch trajectory. After what seemed like half a minute Shabir watched the impressive sight of main booster separation, the four pointed cones blasting away like flaming petals to fall into the far distant landscape. The central core carried on firing, its tail only now visible, a disappearing brilliant flame in the clear blue sky over Tyuratam. The noise, like distant thunder, rumbled on for several minutes.

Shabir felt a strange mixture of elation and fear flowing through his body. Here was a totally different experience to flying. There was no way of controlling the machine until you were in orbit but then to look down on the entire earth, and on to the sun and stars.

Gradually the significance of this day, 2 January 1974, dawned on him. He, the boy from a nameless refugee camp, sole survivor of his family, was going to become the first Arab to fly in space.

'Imsh'allah, Imsh'allah,' he murmured to himself. It is God's will.

'General, would you please excuse me for a few minutes. My prayers, you know?'

'Oh, what, your prayers, oh yes, of course.' The Russian was embarrassed. He had completely forgotten that the man was a devout Muslim, that he believed in a deity in spite of his scientific education. The other controllers turned with curiosity to watch the dark man in his Air Force uniform step out of the Control Room into the staircase lobby.

Nobody spoke as they heard his fading steps. Then two or three of them walked quickly over to the rear observation window and watched the bottom exit door. In a minute it opened and out walked the Palestinian. He walked through the snow until he was at least a hundred yards from the building whilst the other Russians who were not immediately involved in the launch gathered curiously at the window. He slowly removed his jacket in spite of the bitter cold and lay it, as he would a prayer mat, directly towards the East, to Mecca. He took out his book and commenced reciting passages from the Koran. Then he went down on his knees and finally touched the mat with his forehead, his low chanting blown away by the wind.

19
Jericho II

'I must say, I'm puzzled, do you think the guy dropped his jacket and was looking for something in the snow?'

'Don't know, almost looks as if he was praying or doing calisthenics or something.'

'Any facial shots?'

'No, just the back of his head.'

The photograph was in positive form, mounted on one of the massive light tables used at the National Photographic Interpretation Centre in Washington DC. Captain Jonathan Bixby, the Officer of the Day, leant over the diminutive shoulders of Lieutenant Harvey Conroy, a newly trained Photo Interpretation Officer.

'Well, it's an anomaly and should be reported in the Events File.'

'Very good, sir, do you want this copy?'

'Yes, slip it in the file with the time and date.'

'Yes, sir.'

An hour later it was in the hands of Colonel David Greenberg, Deputy Head of the Unit and being studied also by Bixby and four other officers.

'TYURATAM, 11.14 HOURS LOCAL, 2 JANUARY

Source : Big Bird No 6.

Report reads : Anomalous human activity, single male adjacent to monitoring building.

Event coincided with successful launch of a Cosmos reconnaissance satellite.

Analysis : No Firm Conclusions.

'He's praying. That's his mat. That's his book,' Greenberg said.

'He's a Mohammedan?' Bixby asked in surprise.

'He's wearing Soviet Air Force Uniform and he's just observed a Cosmos launch.'

'He's very special, I think,' said Bixby.

'Any enhancements?' Greenberg asked.

Greenberg was noted for his cryptic style of speech, speed of analysis and difficult manners. He had an IQ of 155 and ignored anything irrelevant to his passion in life, the microscopic examination of the Soviet Union. He was 52 years old and looked 60, his heavily creased face thrust out of a large head of smooth grey hair that he combed sideways across his emerging scalp and let hang limply over the top of his ears. And his ears like his nose were highly developed sensors. They were big, well-structured and stood out. All the better to hear you, he used to say.

The computer-processed 'enhancements' as they were called were direct developments of the first systems developed from the Lunar Orbiter spacecraft of the 1960s.

They were electronically 'cleaned' images taken from the photograph. The process enabled minute details to emerge, beating the laws of conventional optical photography by an order of magnitude.

'OK, lets have a stage one enlargement, Bixby.'

They watched as the image enlarged. Bixby steering two control wheels to keep the selected point at the centre of the screen. Nobody spoke.

'Hold it there. Go to stage two.' Greenberg said.

And once again the image dissolved until all of them could clearly see the prone figure on what must have been a jacket or coat in the snow of Central Asia. The figure was that of a man kneeling and obviously praying. By his right hand lay a book. The snow looked about a foot deep where he'd chosen his point of devotion.

'Bixby, measure him, give me an estimate of weight and then send all data to General Wheeler today. I want this man compared against all known Arab pilots in our data bank. Send a copy to Colonel Daniel Perès at Mossad Headquarters by personal courier through London. He was the Israeli head of the "Jericho" team during the Yom Kippur War. Contact Colonel Michael Allon through General Sharpe at Beale Air Force Base and ask him to see me as soon as possible, priority. Then get me the "Jericho" file, this guy might just be on it. Finally I want everything on the movements of a certain KGB General, Igor Mendeleiv. I want to know where he was when this photograph was taken. Check with Langley but meanwhile I want all shots of KGB main offices brought to me covering the period up to two weeks before this anomaly.

'You did well Bixby, good judgement. You may have opened up something new here.

'Now, Lieutenant Conroy, I want you to set up the Bird for intensive close-look of the residential and recreational blocks at Tyuratam, maybe the guy skis or throws snowballs but I want his face. I've got a feeling about this one.'

Greenberg had to wait a week for Michael to be available. He was at Shermya in the Aleutians working with the Aerospace Defence Command on the calibration of the latest 'Cobra Dane' missile warning radar, and that had the very highest priority.

'Colonel Allon, Shalom. Good to see you. I understand you had to come a long way.' Greenberg proffered a seat by the screen.

'Yes, sir, about 5,000 miles,' Michael replied.

'My, when did you leave?'

'This morning, Alaska time.'

'Wow, the Blackbird sure beats the Eastern shuttle . . . Now, let's not waste any more of your time. Take a look at this photograph.'

The stage two image of the man appeared.

'He's praying,' Michael said.

'Sure?'

'Positive, he's using a coat or something as a prayer mat.

Oh . . . and there's his book. Where was it taken, over Damascus?'

'Tyuratam.'

'Jesus!'

'No, he's a Mohammedan. An Arab pilot, a Lieutenant-Colonel in the Soviet Air Force, no less, praying outside the launch control building at the Soviet's most important missile test facility. What's more he's just witnessed the launch of a Cosmos reconnaissance satellite. They only let selected Russians do that—normally. This boy is somebody special. But that isn't all. Next.'

Bixby switched to another photograph, one that Michael was completely familiar with because he had taken it.

'That's a mug shot at 100,000 feet, check?'

'Check.'

'That aircraft, a Mig 25R, took off from Cairo West and intercepted you on 2 October last year, correct?'

'Correct.'

'OK. Next please, Bixby.' Again the screen changed.

'This is a Big Bird photograph taken at 80 miles over Cairo West a few days before that incident. Notice the two Foxbats being towed out of their shelters. The time is 11.15 in the morning. Now this was a puzzler before you arrived. You see the corner of the dispersal hut there?' Greenberg pointed to a half-shaded area to one corner of the photograph.

'There's a guy there in flying overalls and he's praying. Both our subjects were facing east.'

Michael looked hard and could see the bent posture of the pilot.

'Now let's see the next shot.' The image was fantastically unreal 'chemical' red-and-orange picture with a white circle in the centre.

'This is an infra-red shot from a Big Bird of the KGB's Central Planning Unit about 50 miles out of Moscow. Next.'

The same image was now transformed by a half circle of white where it had been black before.

'That is a procession of limousines believe it or not,

entering the CPU. The brain centre of the KGB. We keep that place on "alarm" surveillance as we call it. Any change in the heat pattern is picked up by our satellite and triggers a photograph.'

The next photograph showed the line of limousines.

'Now take a look at this one. Next.'

A helicopter had landed alongside a clear, black hole that had suddenly appeared in the snow. Then followed a sequence of shots of a man emerging from the hole, looking straight up at the camera.

'Very lucky, that one, Colonel. It could have been night and overcast but it was clear and daylight. You are looking at the Head of the KGB Central Planning Unit, General Mendeleiv.

'Now this one is very cool. He's the guy you go to if you want something done. His particular zone is the Middle East and he is the only man out in Egypt who would recommend an Arab to fly a Foxbat. Only he could do that and even then it would have to go to Brezhnev. Follow my thinking?'

'Yes, I do,' Michael replied quietly, genuinely fascinated by the bizarre story unfolding before him.

'Next shot, Bixby.' It was the clear face of a young man about Michael's age, flat on his back, laughing, while a uniformed figure leaned over with what looked like a snow-ball in his hand. Michael felt he had seen the face before.

'Isn't he the same guy I photographed in the Foxbat?'

'Exactly.'

Captain Bixby pressed a switch on an adjacent projector. The two faces were similar.

'Hey, they look the same to me,' Michael pointed.

'And me,' replied Greenberg.

'Now, one of our people at Domodedovo logged Mendeleiv's helicopter at the airfield and saw him embark on a flight—we guess to Tyuratam—that day.

'I believe the young Arab pilot is a protegé of Mendeleiv's and we should establish exactly what he's doing at Tyuratam. We're always carrying out identification and tracking exercises, as we call them, of important selected people who turn up on our satellite data. This guy's no exception. Our fellows have been briefed to simply keep tabs on him, albeit at eighty miles up, see where he goes if possible, log his movements, he's a very important Arab. Finally, we believe we know his name, don't we Daniel?'

Greenberg turned to face the man standing quietly to one side of, and behind, Michael. For the second time Michael was surprised to see his uncle.

'Not again, I don't believe it! I thought you were back in Tel Aviv.'

'I was until yesterday. I got in this morning too. I came about the same distance as you, Michael.' The two shook hands warmly.

'Tell me his name, Daniel.' Michael waited impatiently.

'He is Shabir Al Timimi.'

'Where from?'

'Jerusalem. He's a Palestinian, an ex-PLO fighter, a very remarkable young man—like you, if I may say so,' Daniel Perès replied.

'How do you know this?'

'One of our people, a girl, fought with him in Golan. She gave us a lot of information. He was being groomed by the local GRU man, a Colonel Yeliskeiv, who died during the Yom Kippur War. She recognised the satellite picture and she's pretty sure about the Foxbat air-to-air shot also.'

'It's incredible. What's he doing in Tyuratam do you think?'

'I believe he's going to be used in the Soviet space programme and, as Mendeleiv is almost certainly involved, he'll have a very special job to do one day.' Daniel was confident of his and Greenberg's analysis.

'What sort of job?' Michael asked.

'I think he'll be trained as a cosmonaut.'

'Why? Surely it's a big risk for the Russians to take?'

'Possibly, but imagine the political bonus, especially after Yom Kippur: they're desperate to maintain a hold on the Arabs. This will do it. It's a clever idea, if it's true.'

'What are you going to do about it, Uncle? Do you have any plans?'

'No. That's my honest answer.'

'Gentlemen, Colonel Allon, Daniel, let's not plan anything until we have much more data. Now, I propose the three of us submit a joint report to General Wheeler, Chief of US Air Force Intelligence and see if we can't get some form of instruction backed by his authority. OK?'

'Fine by me,' Michael replied.

'And me, David,' said Daniel Perès.

'Good. Let's go, then. Thank you, Bixby. Conroy, could you fix these gentlemen up with some coffee please. None for me, just a glass of water.'

That same evening the three men completed and signed a report entitled:

SHABIR AL TIMIMI

INVESTIGATION OF A POTENTIAL PALESTINIAN COSMONAUT

David Greenberg typed it himself and placed it in his security safe. The next morning it was sent by courier to General Wheeler while the three men started to plan a joint US-Israeli intelligence operation. Two days later they received a call from General Wheeler requesting they meet him at Stanford University the following day.

On 1 February 1974, Wheeler ordered the reassembly of the Jericho team members,—Jericho II as he called it—to organise a long term assessment of the implications of their report in political and security terms. The National Reconnaissance Office was requested to put Shabir Al Timimi on the 'Wanted List' as it was colloquially known, or the Strategic Personnel List as it was officially described. The Photo Interpretation Officers were circulated prints of the enlargements and told to keep looking. Mendeleiv had been on the list ever since it opened in 1961, but his file was still too thin for Wheeler's comfort.

Mossad had other plans. Daniel Perès flew back to Tel Aviv and arranged a meeting which was attended by 'Aliah', their girl agent who knew more than anybody what Shabir

Al Timimi was capable of, she had told the Head of Mossad, Ephraim Zuckerman, and nobody else. Aliah was asked her opinion first.

'Gentlemen, I never met a more intelligent, or dedicated fighter in Golan. He has a brain and a spirit. He will do something extraordinary, given adequate resources. I believe that the Russians do not fully comprehend his motives. He is not one to be controlled by the KGB but he exercises great self-control. If he is the man in the pictures, and I believe that is the case, then we can either wait and see or take action before he becomes inaccessible.'

'Daniel?' It was Zuckerman speaking.

'I agree with you, Aliah. If I was Mendeleiv then I would use him very carefully, conserving him until the time was right. But I ask myself, what can one man do that is so important? All right, he's a political pawn, a good propaganda tool but there are easier ways. No, I think Mendeleiv must be planning to exploit his skill as a cosmonaut when he's trained.'

'How long will it take to train him?' Zuckerman asked.

'At least three years, but Mendeleiv will wait ten years if necessary. Remember we know from our other agents that Mendeleiv is reported to have established some kind of training school for political leaders of countries under Soviet domination or subject to Soviet influence. He is without doubt a puppet-master. He just moves his fingers and things happen a long way down the strings. He has a remarkable sense of timing. I wish I'd killed him when I had the chance once in Alexandria. He and Yeliskeiv were walking into his office at the port, completely oblivious to their surroundings, when both of them stepped in front of my car without looking. I should have accelerated instead of braking. It would have saved a lot of trouble but I respected old Yeliskeiv. By the way, what happened to him, anybody know?'

'Yes, he was killed by one of our tanks in Golan. I suppose he was over-confident.' Aliah was thinking of the engagement and how she found Yeliskeiv. She had been brought in specially to identify any dead Russians for Military Intelligence.

Yeliskeiv was sitting bolt upright in a T62, propped up by the armoured hatch covers. The tank had been hit by an Israeli 105mm gun firing a discarding Sabot. The shell had struck the joint between the turret and the body of the tank, leaving nothing but a bloody stew inside the charred vehicle. Yeliskeiv had his lower torso clean blown away from the waist down. As she clambered off the turret it had slid into the mess below. She hated tanks more than any other weapon. Nobody who passed this striking red-haired young woman in the street would have guessed she had driven Centurions, T62s and Shermans as well as being a marksman with Israeli Uzi and Russian AK47 automatic weapons.

'Well, what are we going to do about our Palestinian friend?' the Deputy asked. 'Do we kill him or watch him, Daniel?'

'Watch him, I think, keep him under surveillance. He might lead us somewhere interesting or to people we should know. Remember, if he is important then the people he meets must be important.'

'I agree,' said Aliah, unhappy to condemn the gifted Palestinian into the hands of the 'hit team'. Her years with the PLF had made her respectful of her enemy but still unwavering in her determination to fight for her people's survival.

'Good. Then, Daniel, I will confirm this action to the Prime Minister and you will maintain constant liaison with the Americans. Please keep me informed on a monthly basis, one page is enough. We'll meet again in a year. OK?

'OK.'

'By the way, what shall we call the file?'

'Jihad.' Daniel smiled ironically. 'I think that's what Mendeleiv wants.'

And he was right.

20
Stellar Village

In the Sholkovo region, north-east of Moscow, was a small, hidden village called Zoyozdrui Gorodok, or 'Stellar Village', where Shabir Al Timimi was sent to train as a cosmonaut. This tiny hamlet, the home of many of the Soviet space crews, was isolated from other rural communities by distance, geography and a battalion of KGB security troops. 'Village' was not the right description as far as Shabir was concerned. To him it was yet another 'camp'.

Here were housed, in separate buildings, the main simulators and trainers for flying the Soyuz spacecraft and the Salyut space station, the Soviet's primary vehicles for manned space exploration.

Al Timimi was accompanied everywhere—discreetly—by either Moskalenko or one of his colleagues, all of them pilots. Soon he relaxed and deliberately avoided reflecting on the fact that he was under surveillance. Shimatov had warned him at Tyuratam and now Shimatov was here, accessible and unchanged. Shabir knew that any time he felt he needed someone to talk to then Shimatov's door was open.

Many of the younger cosmonauts (there were 30 in his group that spring of 1974) shared Shabir's affection for their Chief of Cosmonaut Training. He was a pilot first and last, dedicated to the well-being and morale of his protégés, particularly Shabir. Every Soviet-manned space flight had been commanded by a serving military officer and Shabir was part of that military element in the course. Shimatov had never considered any alternative approach. When Shabir's fellow cosmonauts learned he was a Palestinian they were at first amazed, then sceptical. He sometimes heard in the early weeks and months the odd snide comment, and tried to ignore it when it happened. Gradually, the comments grew less obvious until they vanished completely. The reason was quite simple. He was the best in his group.

He excelled in almost every aspect of his training. After spending eight minutes in the sickening, revolving centrifuge, strapped in the tiny capsule and turning in every direction, he could stabilise his craft, using the thruster controls, more quickly than any previous trainee. His ability to withstand high positive and negative G forces exceeded all but one of his fellow cosmonauts. His experience as a Foxbat pilot placed him ahead of most in his tolerance to oxygen deprivation or pressurisation failure. His dexterity within the simulator was likened by the instructor to that of a concert pianist.

Shimatov had once commented quietly to Moskalenko: 'He's got very smooth reactions. He looks as if he's playing the thing.'

But it was his exceptional results in his theoretical papers that won him the highly contested seat at the Red Square Military Parade as an official representative of the Soviet cosmonaut delegation. 7 November 1975 was a memorable day for millions of Soviet citizens as they watched yet again the most awesome display of weaponry ever paraded in one city—in history.

As usual, it rained, and the front seat Shabir had been allotted was wet and cold. The moisture spread through his buttocks, soaking his perfectly tailored dress uniform and forced him to keep shifting his weight from one cheek to the other. It didn't matter though: the fact he was sitting was a privilege and the fact he was there, in Moscow's Red Square, was little short of remarkable.

Shabir Al Timimi had arrived, of that he had no doubt. Only people of special value to the Soviet hierarchy were provided with a ringside view of the greatest show on earth. Like everybody else in the audience he had felt the excitement building up during the past days and weeks. The briefings, the inspections, the travel arrangements, all had been thoroughly planned by an army of military staff dedicated to the task of presenting an image of power tempered with the olive branch of peace. A cast of thousands had rehearsed continuously for weeks and as Shabir swayed deliberately from left to right he knew he was about to witness a memorable event.

'Excuse me, sir, but you're sitting on my order paper.' It was a woman's voice. Shabir ignored it.

'Excuse me, sir, may I ask you to sway once more to the left.' There it was again, soft, unhurried, reasonable. Shabir turned, expecting to see some wife of one of the officers peering out below the inevitable fur hat, watering eyes and red nose just visible above a tightly wrapped knitted scarf. He was wrong. Completely wrong.

The face couldn't have been more than twenty years of age. It wore an Air Force officer's hat and emerged from a full dress uniform, almost identical to his own. It was a very pretty face. Shabir blinked, colouring slightly, surprised at his own reaction, embarrassed at realising his discomfort had been noticed.

'Oh . . . sorry,' and he raised himself up, touching the peak of his braided hat, his eyes still fixed on the girl's.

'Thank you, uh . . . Colonel, I'm sorry to disturb you . . . .,' she replied and a smile flickered across her face as she retrieved her damp programme. Shabir stammered on

'. . . Um . . . please, would you care for my papers. They are quite dry, and I've spoiled yours, I can see that.'

'No, that's kind of you to offer, mine will be quite alright.' She straightened up, glancing down at him once more, punctuating her reply with a gentle nod before looking away at the approaching formations.

Shabir stared briefly, then turned to follow her gaze. Someone touched his sleeve. It was Shimatov, arriving at last to take his seat next to him.

'Al Timimi, thanks for keeping my seat warm.' His nudge pushed Shabir onto the cold, wet adjacent seat.

Shabir winced as he sat down in acute discomfort. Shimatov grinned, then turned to look above Shabir's shoulder.

'Ah, General Kurkotkin, good to see you,' and the ebullient Shimatov had reached behind Shabir to shake hands with a long-remembered friend from Cadet School days.

'Damn cold, eh, but always worth the wait.' The two older men grinned at each other. Shabir felt slightly awkward under the weight of shaking hands across his shoulder.

'General, I'd like to introduce one of my chaps,' and Shimatov touched Shabir again on the arm. Shabir turned round and stood awkwardly in the cramped seating as he saluted the General.

'Colonel Al Timimi, General. At your orders.'

'Colonel, I'm pleased to meet one of the favoured sons at last.' Their handshake was firm and short. 'May I introduce a favoured 'daughter'. Eh, Shimatov?' The distinguished grey-haired officer turned to the girl at his side. 'This is Captain Bykovsky . . . General Shimatov and Colonel Alt . . . Al . . . I'm sorry, what was the name again, Colonel?' And Shabir shook her hand before directing his reply, to her.

'Colonel Al Timimi,' he said.

'Captain Bykovsky, sir,' she replied, her eyes glittering in the pale November light. Their exchange of looks was interrupted as Shimatov offered to exchange seats with the girl, anxious to talk again of old times with his good friend, Alex.

Shabir extended a helping hand as Captain Bykovsky stepped down to Shabir's seat which he hastily covered with his programme. He noticed the pilot's emblem on her shoulder flash.

'I see you are a pilot, Captain,' Shabir said.

'Not yet I'm afraid Colonel. I have flown the Mig 15 trainer but not solo. I hope to complete my course at the unit flying school in about two months.' Her voice was soft like honey. She didn't give him a chance to stammer again.

'Are you really a cosmonaut, Colonel, forgive me but you

look too young?' She smiled and nervously placed one gloved hand behind her back obviously impressed with his 'cosmonaut' badge.

'No, I'm still training. It will be a long time yet, I think, before they fire me into space.'

'What did you fly beforehand?'

'Oh, various types. You know how it is.'

She was suddenly afraid she had asked too much and that this was embarrassing for him. Military Security was second nature to them all.

'Sorry, I've done it again. I didn't mean to pry. Tell me how you like Moscow. Is this your home?'

'No, I studied here at the University but my home is further south.' Her face lit up with interest.

'You aren't from Georgia are you? You're dark like a Georgian.'

'No, I come from south of Georgia,' he replied.

She frowned then looked puzzled. 'How far south can you get, Colonel?'

'As far as Palestine. I was born in Jerusalem.'

Her hand went up to her face and hovered over her lips. 'Oh!' she exclaimed.

'Yes, Oh! is the right expression. What is a Palestinian doing in Moscow, you are thinking, eh?' And she gently nodded her head before breaking into a smile. He liked her eyes, they were a soft grey, like pearls.

He continued. 'I'm here for May Day, like you. I'm here for the celebrations.' He returned the smile, all thoughts of the parade rapidly disappearing from his mind.

'Please . . . say something in Arabic for me, Colonel, would you?' Her hand almost touched him, its small gloved fingers were an inch from his elbow. Almost without thinking he replied, in Arabic:

'Your eyes are like pearls.'

'Oh! Say it again.' She gave a little squeal of delight.

'Your eyes are like pearls,' he repeated.

'What does that mean, please?' she enquired.

He felt slightly embarrassed at his own boldness.

'Your eyes are like pearls,' he replied, meaning every word.

'Oh!' She flushed with embarrassment, both hands covering her face, her eyes shut tight.

'I did not mean to appear rude, Captain. Please, what is your name, your first name?' he asked. He wanted to hold those little hands away from her face so that he could see her expression.

'Valentina, Colonel.' And she let her hands drop and looked away to the rapidly filling stands.

'Valentina . . . Valentina Bykovsky, it's a good name,' he said.

'It was my mother's, also.' She turned towards him, her head slightly lowered. 'Look Colonel, I'm sorry for appearing so silly, please don't worry about me, I'm sure you'd like to join General Shimatov and talk about your flying. I'm quite happy to listen, really,' and she looked up again at him and her eyelids flickered as he looked at her. Her lips were now held very slightly apart. She was the most lovely girl he had ever met.

'Captain Valentina Bykovsky, I would rather talk to you about the weather than to General Shimatov about spacecraft.'

And she looked at him steadily now and her hands started to curl up and she wanted to take off his hat and touch his beautiful dark face. He was without doubt one of the most attractive men she had ever met. The two of them would have happily looked at each other for much longer had they not been interrupted by the sudden sound of the loudspeakers announcing the arrival of Brezhnev and other leaders, on the main podium. Over 100,000 guests stood to attention as the rulers of the largest country on earth took their places for the forthcoming salute.

In spite of his ideal position on the main military stand the Palestinian would remember little of the incredible arsenal that thundered past him. He felt distracted, unable to concentrate his attention on the spectacle. There, in front of him, passed every kind of weapon imaginable. First came a formation of the huge SS-18 ballistic missiles, each of whose eight nuclear warheads could explode with a force equivalent to two million tons of TNT. Behind them he recognised the SS-N-6, like a giant green phallus lying dormant on its twelve-wheeled articulated transporter. Operationally, it stood vertically in the bellies of 'Yankee' class nuclear submarines patrolling the distant American coastline.

Each type of formation emitted its own characteristic rumble depending on its size, weight and number of wheels or tracks. There came the high-pitched whine of a host of surface-to-air missiles that Shabir recognised as the familiar V-750-K, the type which had blown Gary Powers out of the sky of Sverdlovsk in 1960 and were still killing Americans over Vietnam, fifteen years later.

Behind them came the deadly SA-6, in triplicate salvoes on PT-76 chassis, which had killed many young Israeli pilots in 1973, followed by the huge SA-5, powerful enough to reach a Blackbird if it flew over Russia, and annihilate it with a single nuclear warhead. Soon there appeared the compact, low-altitude SA-9 missiles that Shabir had seen film of, being tested against targets flying a mere 200 feet above the ground.

There in front of the young Palestinian passed the most powerful weapons ever built. Not in ones or twos but in rows and rows that had taken days to marshal and manoeuvre so that the world would know that the Soviet Union could exercise its power with absolute precision. And he knew that all he saw that day was a mere sample of one-third of the total output of the Soviet Union. He felt it was remarkable that he, Shabir Al Timimi, was being entrusted with its most valuable product, the pinnacle of all its technology, the Soyuz spacecraft. And he felt very proud that he was there, a trusted guest of the most determined government on earth, friend of the Palestinian people.

Had October 1973 gone the way they had planned he knew that he would have been standing there as a leader of his country's air force. But it would come right one day, Imsh'allah, and meanwhile they had encouraged him to greater things, to the ultimate test of a pilot, to fly in space. Shabir felt his whole body tingling, almost singing with satisfaction at all the sensations he was experiencing that cold November day. He had felt similar exultation before but nothing as strongly as this. It wasn't the spectacle however, not the parade. It was the girl.

'Valentina Bykovsky,' he breathed the words almost silently into the frosty air. 'Valentina.'

He turned his head slowly, slightly to the left and caught her glancing up towards him. They both smiled for a flickering moment, faced forwards again and stared without looking, as a swarm of tanks clattered across the huge square. And as the time passed he found himself looking not at the trucks, the soldiers, the rows of smiling gymnasts, but towards the darkening sky over Moscow, and he wished more and more he could be back at home, under the sun in Jerusalem.

'I'm exhausted, all that standing. How do you feel Colonel?' she asked in the officers' mess afterwards.

'Tired. It's a fantastic sight, isn't it?' he said.

'Yes, I think this was the best, though.'

'It was for me, most certainly the most memorable.' He felt he could not talk much more, just look at her beautiful face and he wanted to cup her chin in his hand, very gently, and pull her towards him and kiss her softly.

'When do you return to your training, Colonel?' she asked, trying to sound as casual as possible.

'In two days. I have a four day pass. And you?' He prayed she would be there tomorrow.

'I'm here all the time, my office is near the river,' she said, and Shabir knew he had to act now or the opportunity might be lost.

'May I ask you to dinner tonight, Captain?' He felt hot and weak, dreading a rebuttal.

She felt her reply was too quick, a reflex almost. 'I'd like that very much Colonel Al Timimi. Tomorrow night, though.' And she looked at him and felt like screaming 'kiss me, please, kiss me,' but forced a smile instead. She felt she would fall over soon, her legs were trembling with excitement. 'I'm rather tired after all that's happened today.' He felt a mixture of disappointment and frustration at the postponement.

'May I show you to your room meanwhile, Captain?' Shabir kept looking at her, his eyes boring into hers.

'Thank you, that would be nice,' she replied and lowered her eyes. They left Shimatov getting more and more happy—drunk, just as expected—and walked over to the staircase of the Military Hotel.

'You won't be able to come all the way I'm afraid, Colonel. There is a Major on duty.' Valentina warned him at the bottom of the stairs.

'Let's see what we can do, eh?' he replied not hesitating but walking ahead. She caught him up, her hands clammy, her breathing shallow with excitement. The Major was not there. She had obviously got bored and joined the crowd downstairs for a quick drink or a chat with friends. The corridor was very wide and so were the doors. They had no proper locks. There were four beds in Valentina's room. It was about twenty feet square and looked very crowded.

'We're a bit tight in here, Colonel. I'm sorry, you'll have to sit on the bed.' And she turned away from him to check that there was a bed tidy, but he could not stop himself any longer.

Shabir stepped forwards and touched her shoulder very gently, turning her round to face him. She did not resist, she could not, she was numb. He took the peak of her cap and gently lifted it off. Her hair was auburn and pinned like a bun, and he touched the side away from him and pulled her head very slowly towards his face. He kissed her dry, trembling lips and they were soft like delicate paper, so he wet them very slightly with his tongue, and he kissed her again as he dropped the hat on the bed and pulled her body close against him. She closed her eyes and lifted her hands behind him and held him to herself for a long, long minute of time.

He moved his face away and saw that her eyes were glistening. He kissed her again, firmer, and held her more tightly, wanting to absorb her completely in himself. He raised his hand behind her and stroked her hair, very slowly. The silver pin came out easily and her hair fell in little waves onto her shoulders. She was exquisite. She looked at his dark sensitive face and traced its high cheekbones and long, fine nose, his dark brown eyes with their heavy lids that gave him an air of sensuality.

'Valentina . . . Valentina, Valentina . . .' His words were hardly audible, 'Valentina Bykovsky, you are the most beautiful girl I have ever seen.' He kissed her again and she could feel the passion rising in her body as she pushed his tongue down with her own and licked his soft mouth and squeezed her lips hard against his, parting them, wanting to grow into the very body of this strange, beautiful man. The two of them hardly spoke for several minutes, absorbing each other's presence by touch and scent and soft, gentle sounds. It was Valentina who said it first.

'Whoever you are, you are so beautiful. I feel so marvellous. I wanted to touch you and hold you from the first minute of meeting you. That parade was far too long and you were much too close.'

Her face was soft and gentle as a child's with beautiful pearl-grey eyes framed by rings of long auburn lashes sparkling with brimming tears. Her skin was like that of a bird's egg he had once seen, nearly transparent, like bone china smoothing over her round high cheekbones. Her chin was a perfect thing to hold and tilt up to kiss, and he kissed it. Her nose was pretty and very gently lifted at the tip, with delicate nostrils set over her parted lips.

'Valentina, you are so lovely, so lovely.' He held her to him and rocked her very gently, and he forgot the time and the place.

They stood like that for several minutes and then Shabir said, 'Valentina, may I see you tomorrow?'

'Yes.'

'Here?'

'No, Shabir, my flat is nearby. I live with my father and brother but my brother is on parade duty tomorrow and

Papa is very quiet. Meet me here and I'll take you over. When can you come?' She smiled with joy at the thought of being with him in the privacy of her home.

'Dawn.' He smiled and she laughed gently, her eyes sparkling and her hair cascading back over her shoulders.

'Silly, after breakfast, eh?' she said, pressing her cheek against his chest.

'Eight o'clock.' And he had no thoughts of breakfast. He wouldn't sleep, not now.

'Oh, Shabir, yes, why not eight o'clock? Now, you must go or I'll be confined to barracks and I'd have to get out to see you, no matter what.'

'Valentina, lovely Russian girl.' He hugged her closer. 'Valentina Bykovsky, kiss me.' It was difficult to stop, for both of them.

The following day she was there at the top of the marble steps to the old pre-revolutionary building. She had changed out of her uniform. Shabir caught his breath at the sight of her. He slowed down as he approached. They were both early but she had been there for half an hour already, unable to stay at home, wishing for everything to start again. Shabir walked slowly now up the stone steps and Valentina started to walk down hesitantly on slim, black, high-heeled boots that brought her eyes level with his as she halted one step above him. Under her beautiful chin nestled a pearl-grey sealskin collar and she wore a little black sealskin hat not quite covering her hair which again she had pinned up in a bun.

She wore no gloves: she wanted to touch this man and feel his skin through her fingertips. He spoke first, 'Valentina, you look wonderful.' He felt shy saying it, hoping that the feeling of the previous night had not just been something to do with the parade.

'I love you, Shabir Al Timimi.' She had no doubt this was true.

They turned and made their way towards the river, Shabir unable to touch her, being in his uniform, but both brushed arms and ignored everything around them until they arrived at Valentina's apartment block. Shabir looked up at the honey-coloured rendering that covered the concrete structure to its full ten storeys. Here was a wealthy country indeed, he had often thought, that could afford large apartment blocks like these for so many of its citizens.

They walked up to the third floor through the perfectly clean entrance lobby, and arrived at the long balcony that served all the apartments on that floor. The fourth door on the left had a number seven set high above the centreline and under it a metal tab with the name 'Bykovsky' stamped on it.

'Shabir, this is my home, you are welcome here always,' she said before opening the door.

The apartment was small, just four rooms: one for her with space for a single bed, a wardrobe and a folding bed; one which her father and brother shared; a living-dining room with combined kitchen; and a tiny bathroom off this. Shabir was impressed. He knew from his own time as a student at the University that Valentina's family, all of whom were members of the military services, must be well regarded to be given such generous accommodation. He wished he had a family he could introduce her to, at home.

'Shabir, are your family still in Jerusalem?' she asked, watching him scanning the rooms.

'No, Valentina, my father died when I was a baby, my mother died when I was a boy.' The memory didn't hurt any more, it had long been exorcised by the determination to right the wrong.

'Oh, I'm sorry.' She felt silly not to have used her common sense.

'It's a long time ago now. A lot has happened. Did you lose your mother too?'

'Yes, she died of cancer two years ago. Papa misses her very much. I do too.' And she held his hands firmly now.

'Where is your father, Valentina?'

'He is out visiting his friends at the parade barracks. They'll be talking about old times. He'll be quite tipsy when he gets back home.' She paused and looked up at Shabir. 'I hope he stays the night there. He said he might visit my brother's barracks.'

Shabir pulled her urgently to him and they kissed passionately knowing that there was very little time before he would have to go, a day at the most. Then she broke away, taking his hand and led him to her bedroom. He closed the door behind him and rested against it, his heart pounding in his chest, his lips dry with anticipation. He felt that excitement course through him.

Valentina stood in front of the bed and removed her hat, placing it on the little table. Then she started to undo her collar and the black coat opened. She looked down at herself then up at Shabir who slowly lifted the coat off her shoulders. She wore a dark grey woollen dress that buttoned down to her waist. He undid the four buttons feeling her trembling and breathing more urgently now. She closed her eyes and murmured his name. He lifted the dress as she raised her arms and she wore a simple white bra that held her soft pointed breasts. She had a beautiful figure and he slowly slid the cream waist slip down over her hips to the floor.

She wore no stockings just a pair of small cream panties and the knee-length boots. He pushed her very gently onto the bed and she started to moan as he undid her bra. Her breasts stood out like perfect taut cones, her nipples stiff with excitement.

She put both arms round him and drew his lips hard against hers and they kissed with passion. He undid his uniform jacket and belt, looking at her exquisite body as he did so. He unbuttoned his shirt and pulled it off his shoulders, then took off his boots, trapping each heel under his toes. Valentina gazed back at him as she lay aquiescent, aching for him to touch her again. And then he was naked. His trousers slipped off with his pants and he stood slim and sinewy and brown.

He started to stiffen and came down on top of her and slid her panties down and off each boot then cupped her firmly between her thighs and she started to moan more loudly now and dug into his back, aching, then screaming with love as he slid himself firmly into her tight warm body. They both cried with ecstasy at the moment of consummation and the tears wet their cheeks as they loved each other with increasing abandonment and adventure. And when they lay still, entwined, exhausted, they never dared to ask each other of their pasts.

Igor Bykovsky was too happily drunk to get home that night, in fact he never even made it to his son's barracks, but fell asleep alongside an old army friend, just like in the days during the War. It was the greatest gift he could have given his daughter Valentina, the gift of time.

As Shabir left the next day it began to snow and he walked away silently through the white silence of a Moscow dawning, the tears hanging cold on his face. He had fallen in love, of that he had no doubt.

'Moskalenko, what's happened to the man, is he ill?' Shimatov's voice was very different to the one his young cosmonauts would know.

'No, sir, his medical reports are excellent. He's in perfect physical shape,' the KGB man replied nervously, feeling his career at stake that morning of December, a month after the Red Square Parade.

'Have you kept him under observation?'

'Yes sir, continuously,' Moskalenko replied.

'And what is he doing with his time?'

'The same as before sir. He trains a great deal, more than anybody else in his group.'

'Why are all his results declining?'

'I don't know sir. He does spend more time alone, reading and writing letters,' the Colonel answered.

'But surely being in love with this Captain Bykovsky isn't affecting him physically?' protested Shimatov.

'The last thing I want, Moskalenko, is to see my plan affected by a mere Captain, and a girl at that. Give me her file tomorrow. Go now and watch the Palestinian. Keep giving me his letters as usual.'

Shimatov was angrier than he had felt for a long time and

ignored Moskalenko's salute. After 25 years he was getting tired of the act of always having to appear the confidante, the good guy, the fellow flyer. He pressed a buzzer and the other door opened.

'You called, General.'

'Yes Mendeleiv, sit down and listen. We have a difficult, delicate job to do and it concerns that precocious Arab and that Captain Bykovsky he met in Moscow.'

Mendeleiv always listened hard to his Commanding Officer.

A week later Shabir ran to Shimatov's private apartment. He was flushed, sweating and highly agitated as Shimatov opened the door to his continuous knocking.

'Hey, Shabir, my friend, you look as if you've been chased by a wolf! What's up?' He gave the man a warm smile, stepping back to allow him in.

'General, forgive me, but I had to see you.' Shabir looked totally distraught. He had no tie, no jacket. He must be freezing, Shimatov thought.

'Why, is there anything wrong? What have you done now, crashed the simulator again?' The sarcasm was not lost on the Palestinian.

'No, I've done nothing wrong this week, sir, but I may well do so tomorrow.' He was panting and very distressed, clenching two pieces of paper in his hand.

'Come in, sit in your chair and tell me about your problem.' Shimatov showed him the vacant seat.

'Thank you, General.' Shabir sat down on the edge of his favourite chair, a carved pine rocker with two big embroidered cushions, typical of Shimatov's individuality, his gesture at officialdom. Shabir continued, his eyes red from lack of sleep.

'General, I received this letter yesterday from Valentina. You know, I told you how much I wanted to marry her and you explained that this would be possible after I have completed my course.' He held the letter up to his friend.

'Yes, I know, Shabir.'

'But today she has written to me, and she has changed her mind. She says she is leaving Moscow. I don't understand, we love each other, I know we do. I must see her, talk to her. Something strange is happening. Please, may I have leave to go to Moscow, General?'

'Let me see the letter, if you don't mind Colonel?'

'Yes, sir. I'm sorry if this embarrasses you.' Shabir replied.

'Not at all, the welfare of my cosmonauts is the most important thing in my work. Have I not proved that with that fox Mendeleiv, eh?' And Shimatov stretched out to read the letter he had forced Valentina Bykovsky to write. He read silently for what he judged was an appropriate time then handed it back to the Palestinian. He shrugged his shoulders and clenched and unclenched his fingers.

'Colonel . . . Shabir, I am very sorry. It sounds quite final to me.'

Shabir was even more distressed. His voice became pleading.

'But it can't be. She loves me. I love her. She's never talked about this Naval Officer Borodov before, never. How can she say she is going to Odessa? She couldn't even get a pass in time. It's all wrong, I know it.'

'Shabir, please understand this . . . now, it's difficult to say this . . . it will hurt but I know you rely on the truth and so I'll give it to you. I have received a confidential report from Captain Bykovsky's commanding officer, you know, the man I met at the Military Parade? I wondered whether to tell you, warn you of its contents, but I hoped you would not suffer so much.'

Shabir felt a wave of nausea sweep through him and he went rigid before his whole body started to tremble. Shimatov continued.

'I don't want to go into details but I assure you, it is better that you don't see Bykov . . . I mean Valentina again. For your own peace of mind.'

Shimatov looked over the top of his steepled fingers like a wise old bird.

'Please, General, tell me. I'm not afraid of the truth but I cannot stand this air of mystery about Valentina. Will her father not permit her to marry an Arab, is that it?' Shabir asked, his voice near breaking point.

'No, no, Shabir, we Russians practise no racial discrimination, you know, unlike the United States or Britain.' He shrugged his shoulders. 'No, it has nothing to do with her father or the fact you are an Arab. It is, I'm afraid, another man. This Borodov.'

And Shabir almost felt like retching. Shimatov continued.

'He's a Naval officer on a Krupny-class destroyer in the Black Sea Fleet. It's been going on some time now, over a year. You happened to come in at . . . let us say . . . a convenient moment. Captain Bykovsky is an excellent officer but, shall we say, easy-going. It's simple, Shabir. She's already pregnant.'

Shimatov reached out for a cigarette on his desk. Shabir closed his eyes tight to fight the tears. He sat back in his chair clenching his hands and crushed the paper, still in his fingers. He opened his eyes to the ceiling and Shimatov could see the glistening eyelashes. Shabir's voice was a monotone.

'General, I must resign. I cannot work properly. Please, let me go home.' As he spoke he knew there was no home to go to, there was nobody. Jerusalem was as remote as another planet. And the tears trembled on the unblinking eyelashes.

Even Shimatov began to feel sorry for the poor man. But he knew he was doing the right thing, he had to maintain the lie. The girl would be alright after a bit. She would be transferred to Odessa by the end of the week and nothing the Palestinian could do would ever find her again. She would find somebody to look after her, and the baby when it came. Now, when would that be. Nine months after 7 November. Eight months time. The summer of 1976, when Shabir would be 29.

Shimatov stepped over to the desolate man and touched his shoulder then turned and opened the solitary filing cabinet. He took out the precious bottle of Bells Export whisky and placed it in Shabir's lap. He laid both of the man's hands on it and said quietly.

'Shabir, my friend, go back to your room, drink some of this, get drunk if you wish. You might as well start forgetting her . . . now.'

Eventually, like an automaton, Shabir stood up, his eyes staring lifelessly ahead and stumbled out of the door and into the snow. Shimatov watched him disappear towards the cosmonauts' quarters, then ordered a guard to be posted outside his door, just in case he heard anything other than tears and drunken mumblings during the night.

Sitting on the edge of his bed, all Shabir could see was her face, through a film of tears. He could not accept that somebody who had loved him, even though it had been a matter of so little time, who had written so lovingly every day for a long month, should suddenly change completely.

He looked at the neat pile of letters and knew almost every word by heart. She was the first girl he had ever been in love with, the first one to break through that invisible barrier he had erected to protect his innermost feelings. Only two women had got that close and they were dead—his beloved mother and his ever-remembered cousin Leia. He picked up Valentina's photograph, aching to touch the face that smiled shyly, self-consciously, at some imaginary point in the unknown photographer's studio. As the tears welled in his eyes he croaked out a prayer for her to be with him—smiling, saying again, 'I love you, whoever you are, Shabir Al Timimi, I love you.'

The tears fell onto the bottle and the prayer changed to a mocking curse at his fate. There had been many girls on his course at University. He remembered how some had wanted him. Three or four had succeeded. One in particular had become very close. Ludmilla had been tall, red-haired, and passionate to the point of embarrassment. Then he'd found out from a Cuban friend that she was KGB, and had done the rounds already, looking for CIA 'plants'. Then he had vowed that Russian women were for treating like Western girls, as objects for his own convenience and satisfaction. And through the years his sexuality had been primitive, urgent, selfish. He'd demanded everything he had imagined, and got it. There were no more surprises, or so he thought.

And then, out of nowhere, there was Valentina, and the barrier had crumbled with every new word she uttered. She had given him everything and she had told him, 'Shabir, I love you.' And she had made him into a man for the first time in his life.

He broke the seal on the bottle and threw the cap onto the floor. He put the neck onto his lower lip, opened his mouth and poured the liquid down his open throat. It swilled messily over his chin and ran down his neck, his throat distended like a man savouring cool water after a great thirst.

For the first time in his life Shabir drank alcohol, an entire bottle of it, neat.

21
Foxhunter

The next day Shimatov met with Mendeleiv. He ordered him to report to him outside the security fence at the next village of Kolchik. They went to the cosmonauts' favourite meeting place, the local collective social hall, and sat around the fire while the superintendent ensured that they were well-fed and given plenty to drink. They talked for three hours, feeling more and more relaxed under the effect of the alcohol. Mendeleiv was delighted to see his boss so pleased that his plan was back on the rails. He knew the Palestinian had nowhere to go and would simply concentrate on his work. He was almost right.

When they left, the superintendent—a veteran of the Stalingrad campaign—cleared up their glasses. He took his time, reflecting deeply on what he had just heard. He finished washing up and started talking to himself, almost as if rehearsing a speech. He was noted for it. Everybody in the area knew he was a bit strange—'the War, you know'. Nobody thought it odd to see him wandering, quietly smoking his pipe, out in the snow, day or night, winter or summer.

'There goes old Polkova again, he'll get lost in the snow one day, you'll see,' they used to say.

Dimitry Polkova put on his warmest coat and hat and double-layer gloves, still murmuring to himself, and laboriously took out the empty crates in which the vegetables came in from the collective. He walked into the yard and arranged them in a curiously haphazard pile that took him a chilling half hour. Then he went back indoors and spent a quiet evening alone listening to his radio.

Three days later it dawned clear and bright. Thank god, he thought, and he dressed again, this time in his thickest boots, put his pipe in his mouth and walked out into the snow to the largest field on the collective. He walked for twenty minutes until he arrived at the centre of the field. He looked at his watch then all round him at the trees and hedges in the distance. He looked up at the sky, due south, and started to speak with exaggerated movements of his lips, like a slightly deranged old veteran.

Dimitry Polkova spoke perfect silent Hebrew for twelve, neck-craning minutes at the Big Bird satellite's ultra-high-resolution TV camera as it passed in total silence 90 miles above him.

Its 96-degree orbit, almost due north-south, took it over the spinning earth below. Dimitry knew he had been lucky. Every three days it passed over this spot, its orbit exactly synchronised with the sun so that each time it passed a given location every object it photographed presented an identical length of shadow. If anything moved, then its shadow would change. Dimitry was being televised, his specially arranged crates were the signal to warn the people in Washington that he had urgent information which had to be transmitted to the Hebrew lip-reader, David Greenberg. It was news of the utmost importance.

He was certain now that he had found the identity of the real head of the KGB Space Planning Group. It was Vladimir Shimatov, Chief of Cosmonaut Training, always the friendly, helpful, human Russian at international conferences. The man the American astronauts got on best with, the man many women in different parts of the world enjoyed meeting, day or night. Mendeleiv was only his deputy, the one who herded everybody towards Shimatov without them ever realising. Mendeleiv was the sheepdog, Shimatov the shepherd.

In Washington, the watching Jericho team could not

believe their good fortune as Greenberg translated. Suddenly, previously unrelated events started to fall into a logical sequence. Vladimir Shimatov had a file in the data bank no thicker than any low-grade Soviet military officer. A man with an excellent record as a purely military pilot who, through his natural charm and winning ways, was in charge of all cosmonauts. He had led them ever since the days of Voskhod and the early Soyuz spacecraft. Since 1964, this man had been the controlling influence possibly on the Soviet Space Programme, and he was KGB totally, although his entire service record put him in the Soviet Air Force. David Greenberg sent a top priority signal to General Wheeler asking him in for an urgent meeting, and the very next day they met alone at 'The Office'.

Greenberg did not falter in his report to Wheeler.

'General, I believe yesterday's report from our man near Stellar Village is fundamental. It appears that Vladimir Shimatov, Chief of Cosmonaut Training, is the closest equivalent in Russia to yourself. We can fill that vacant space on your wall.' Greenberg pointed to the gaping 'hole'.

'We think he is the top policy-maker for space activities in the Soviet Union. There may well be a committee, but if there is, he's the chairman. We also believe that he and Mendeleiv are chief and deputy, with Mendeleiv playing the role as Chief of the Central Planning Unit while Shimatov walks in among the delegates finding out their true responses, becoming their confidante, the good guy against the familiar tedious bureaucracy of the KGB.

'Now, assuming this is true, then for fifteen years, while we've concentrated our attention on people like Mendeleiv, Korolev, Tsiolkovsky, Gluchko and others, we've accepted Shimatov as the clown, a thoroughly competent one, yes, but not the star attraction.

'Let's assume that Shimatov is the brain, then. Let's check back on everywhere he's been since 1961 or before, and let's concentrate particularly on where he goes from now on.

'In the case of this Palestinian, our man is absolutely certain that he is about to be moved. He's come to the end of the normal training course so if we follow him we'll know what Shimatov has in mind.

'We know already that Shimatov has destroyed the Palestinian's genuine love affair with a Captain Valentina Bykovsky. Shimatov needs the Arab badly. He's invested as much time and effort in him as they did for Kim Philby and he, I know you will remember, became Head of the Soviet Section of the British Secret Service while being an officer of the KGB.

'I have organised a new programme for the computers at Langley and our offices. It will correlate all stored information previously rejected on Shimatov's movements and contacts.'

Within an hour the first print-out appeared.

Wheeler looked at it for a minute then handed it to Greenberg. The hunt was on.

22
Race

The move did Shabir some good. Being back at Tyuratam helped him. There was a great sense of urgency there. Every week there was a launch of one satellite or another. It had never occurred to him before that the satellites played such an important role in his life.

But the reality was there around him, as rocket after rocket rolled along the railway lines to the launch area. Each one was a brilliant manufacturing achievement of engineering design and workmanship. There were many workers at Tyuratam who had been building rockets or satellites for twenty years, who talked of past achievements, nights of celebration. There was one man Shabir liked to listen to in particular: Vladimir Nagy, a metallurgist who had been at Tyuratam since 1957. He looked like a monkey. There had been the first night of all when Korolev, the Chief Designer, had not slept for days except for a brief doze on his camp bed. On 4 October, at dawn, he had gone out to the pad with just a few of his closest colleagues to make a last check of the launcher. Nagy remembered seeing him, a tiny figure by his machine, looking up at it silently.

'. . . And then, when it was time to fire, a bugler had sounded his trumpet, there were no klaxons or sophisticated alarms installed yet. And it had gone like a dream, Sputnik 1, the first object ever put in space by mankind . . .

'The greatest day of all was when Gagarin made his flight in 1961. The day was cold and bright and Yuri looked nervous—who wouldn't be—and he went up in the lift and climbed into the capsule. Vostok 1 was a steel ball, weighted at its base where the re-entry heat would be greatest.

'Gagarin sat in an ejector seat in a cylinder which spanned the diameter of the sphere. He only had a tiny glass porthole at his feet to look out of. It was as small as a coffin in there. He knew that if the rocket failed at launch he could eject, so long as it was high enough above the ground.

'But once he was in orbit he had to sit there, sealed in, praying the retro rockets would fire correctly and then that the heat of re-entry did not incinerate him. Oh, yes, Yuri was the bravest.'

Shabir wanted to ask about Valentina Tereschkova, the first woman in space, but could not bring himself to say the name Valentina again, it hurt too much. So he asked Nagy about their feelings when the Americans landed on the moon in July 1969.

'Bad time that was, bad time, Colonel. The only day I saw General Shimatov really angry. I never realised he had such a hatred of the Americans, not after all his trips abroad and all the American women he screwed. No, this place was like a slave camp, they drafted people from all over Russia, you know, to try to beat the Americans.

'In August 1968, after Komarov had died in Soyuz 1, they tried to launch Soyuz 3 to dock with Cosmos 238 to test the orbital rendezvous system, but the Soyuz was faulty. I worked on it myself. When we tried it in October, again manned, it still did not dock. But the spacecraft that was to take three men round the moon in March 1969, that went well. We called it Zond and sent it, unmanned, round the moon. It landed back successfully in Kuzahkolan in November. That was Zond 6. We even had the special launcher ready for the manned lunar flight. Its prototype flew in November also. All we Russians needed to do to be first round the moon was complete a practice crew transfer in orbit.

'Then we heard the Americans were going to send Apollo 8 around the moon on Christmas Day. Shimatov was incensed, he screamed at all of us to work 24 hours a day. Nobody believed the Americans would risk three men on the first flight of a brand new rocket, and Saturn 5 was the biggest by far.

'We even prepared a D-1-E launcher on 8 December for two cosmonauts to travel around the moon in a Zond but it was faulty, never ignited. Thank goodness. We fired it all right on 4 January and it blew up on the pad, luckily unmanned.

'Then came Apollo 8 and we all hoped it would fail, that something would go wrong. We were that close. But it didn't. The bloody thing went perfectly and that American, Frank Borman, read from the Bible and it was over for us then.

'We still tried to catch up though, to beat them to the actual landing but the launcher gave a hell of a lot of trouble and it was too late.'

'What did you do the night they landed on the moon?' Shabir had asked.

'I heard it on the radio officially, but they were monitoring the TV broadcast here, sound only of course, and I listened with a lot of other guys to Armstrong's landing. Believe it or not, a lot of us were pleased it was over then, and we could get back to a more sensible pace. A lot of the chaps cried that night out of frustration, disappointment, who knows what. We'd lost. In spite of all they tell you about the Americans, they did land first. They can't be all that bad, can they?'

'I don't know, I've never met one.' Shabir said.

'No, you're pulling my leg, Colonel!' Nagy's monkey face expressed disbelief.

'No, I'm not. The closest I got was over Suez once when I intercepted one of their spy planes. I remember the pilot's face very clearly; you know, he looked a bit like me. I felt then: what am I doing up here intercepting an American aircraft? I should have been shooting at Israelis.'

'Didn't you?' Nagy was even more surprised at this information.

'No, I was only allowed to fly reconnaissance versions of

the Mig 25 but I did a little combat flying in Vietnam.'

'Really?' and the engineer's face broke into a proud grin.

'Yes, but don't say I told you,' Shabir warned him.

'Did you hit anything?' Nagy asked, rearranging his expression. He was an enthusiastic listener, as well as a talker.

'Only once. I was lucky I suppose. We'd just received an experimental radar jammer and it was fitted to my aircraft, a Mig 21 and the whole aircraft was loaded with equipment, just to show the Vietnamese pilots what a Mig could carry . . .'

'What happened?' The little man was quite excited now.

'Well, it was pure luck. I'd just taken off from this strip—it was very well camouflaged—when I literally flew onto the tail of a Phantom that was flying over at that moment. He was heading south, probably after a raid, and I just fired as he came into the sights.'

'Did he crash?' Nagy was absolutely fascinated.

'Yes, the crew bailed out also. Incredible reflexes that pilot must have had. I flew over him, I think he survived, but I couldn't risk being hit by a wingman or running out of fuel. It was a long way back. Migs have lousy endurance.'

'Tell me, have you heard about Belenko, Colonel?' Nagy winked at him conspiratorially.

'No, who's Belenko?' Shabir enquired.

'That criminal who flew a Mig 25 over to Japan two months ago.'

'What?' Shabir was astonished, 'Belenko flew a 25 to Japan? How? Why?' Nagy was now delighted at his superior intelligence data.

'Defected, flew from Vladivostock or somewhere. One of the Novosti Press men told me when they came over with those French scientists last week. The Americans bribed him, 100 million dollars they paid.'

'For a Mig 25, ridiculous.' Shabir immediately felt the story might be mere fabrication.

Nagy was not going to concede his position though. 'It's not you know. The Americans are scared of them. You should know that, you flew them, didn't you?' Shabir shrugged.

'But the Americans have got many good aircraft.'

'Maybe, but they want to be able to beat the Mig when it comes to it.' Nagy was positive.

'I suppose so,' Shabir replied, happy to change the subject.

'Still, all that will be obsolete when you fly the new stuff, eh, Colonel?'

'No, Nagy, Soyuz is a spacecraft, no good for air-to-air combat or bombing.' Shabir was surprised at his ignorance especially after twenty years at the world's largest space complex.

'I don't mean a new Mig Colonel, I mean there'll be no more fighters, or bombers for that matter. Not after the beams.'

'The what?' Shabir was puzzled and curious now.

'The beams. The new ones from Semipalatinsk.'

'Oh, those.' And Shabir surprised himself with the deliberate lie, curious to find out what the metallurgist was talking about, 'Are they performing alright?' he asked.

'I should say so, Colonel. I had to make up different metal samples for them to test on the intercept flights. Went clean through steel, nickel, titanium, niobium, you name it.' Nagy's voice had dropped to a conspiratorial whisper.

'Good. The intercepts did well too, did they?' Shabir desperately maintained the pretence of prior knowledge.

'Fantastic! Destroyed about a dozen Cosmos targets. The interceptor works like a dream.' Nagy was in his element, his eyes darting about the canteen.

'Have they cured the rendezvous problem yet?' Shabir put on a coolly detached air.

'No trouble at all now! They can fire the launcher at any inclination from O degrees to 65 degrees. That covers all the American satellites except the polar orbiting ones. They'll all be covered from next year.' Nagy was pleased to be able to share his little secrets with a cosmonaut.

'Are the beams controllable now? I heard they were

wobbling a bit.' Shabir's mind raced ahead trying to establish whether Nagy was referring to laser beams or something else.

'Totally controllable, on the ground-to-space beams that is. They'll try the space-fired ones next month.' Nagy's confidence was growing.

Shabir tried to hide the strange fascination he felt as the extraordinary story unfolded. Nagy continued:

'Beautiful sight it is, you know, Colonel. When I was up at Semipalatinsk last month I saw a night test. It was incredible. A solid beam of blue-white light, generated by the air being ionised. It changes colour in space to green, something to do with electron excitation. Amazing to think that space is actually full of electrons and neutrons and rays and so on.'

'Yes, it's beautiful to see the sky turn from blue to deep indigo at very high altitude.' Shabir felt a contribution from him was needed to keep Nagy going.

'Now, that's where you're lucky, Colonel, only Mig 25s give you that sort of view. Or space itself, of course.'

'Have you worked on the beam satellites yet yourself?' Shabir asked, idly adding more sugar to his coffee.

'Oh yes, but only on the ground tests. Worked on the trigger you know, they couldn't make it rigid enough so they asked me to have a try, thought a practical fellow might solve it for them.'

'It's difficult mounting those units, then?'

'Very.' Shabir decided on the friendly approach. 'Look Vladimir, you probably don't now this but I'm an aerospace physicist by training. I studied at Moscow State, if I can help you sort out any problems I'd be pleased to. It'll keep my brain exercised a bit more but let's just keep it between ourselves, eh? I don't normally get involved in another department but if you can help me, then I'm pleased to help you.' Shabir smiled and placed his hand on Nagy's forearm gently, as one friend to another. It worked.

'Well, that's very nice of you, Colonel, maybe we can solve it together. It will be a surprise to my section leader, I tell you, he'll be pleased if I can fix it for him. He's under enormous pressure now it's near to flight status.'

The two men went to their separate quarters that night. Nagy was asleep within a minute of placing his head on his pillow. The light in Shabir's room was still on when dawn broke. A plan was forming in his mind seemingly without conscious effort. As he stared at the ceiling, Nagy's words repeated themselves like some damaged recording disc:

'. . . they'll try the space-fired ones next month . . . a solid beam of blue-white light . . . went clean through steel, nickel, titanium, niobium, you name it.' It was like science fiction. It was too obvious, too simple. They'd worried about it at University, death rays, beams, lasers, blasters, comic-strip stuff. Every child had imagined them but they were for the future, the distant extraterrestrial cosmic future, generations ahead, long after Soyuz and Salyut and Cosmos were historic names in the archives in Moscow. Not now, not today, not when the world was still divided, not before a world socialist order, no. Maybe in thirty or forty years . . . when Palestine was liberated from the Jews—maybe then.

Nagy was a fool, he talked too much . . . or—maybe he was like Ludmilla, a plant, a KGB plant sent to stir up rumours and find out who said what to whom . . . who were the talkers. He would have to be careful, nobody would have to know, he would have to do it alone, without help—a secret. Nobody could be trusted—ever.

He turned to the photograph, placed as always on his bedside table and felt a sudden shiver run down him. Something was going to happen . . . he was never going to trust again, never waste time on individuals, certainly not Russians . . . no, he would *use* Russians . . . he would choose his time and place. Never again would he have to endure the shame of being prevented from avenging his people. He would be a commando again, he would fight the Zionists on their own ground. He would give them the future, ahead of time.

'Liar,' he muttered, and reaching out he picked up the metal frame and tore off the back to reveal the letter. Valentina's last letter, carefully folded and now, open. He tore it up into pieces. He opened the small cupboard door and pulled out the pile of letters. He tore them up, one by one, and they formed a pile on his bed that fluttered onto the floor. The photograph he crushed in his fist, a tight ball that bounced off the wall.

'Russians, lying infidels.'

He closed his eyes, then slowly a smile broke across his face; he'd just remembered, tomorrow would be his birthday.

'. . . and I bet nobody remembers,' he mumbled aloud.

Shimatov smiled as he read the short telex.

'Olga never forgets, does she?' He turned to grin at Mendeleiv.

'Never, sir. After all, you invented her.' Shimatov nodded.

'Yes, she's been a good 'wife', never forgets a thing, totally reliable, and still under 30, eh? Well, let's give our Palestinian friend a party, a surprise. I bet you he thinks we've forgotten.'

The horseplay started early in the evening, with each man forced to don a complete cosmonaut's suit including the dummy EVA backpack before embarking on a crazy obstacle course through great piles of canteen furniture whilst being pelted with every scrap of stale food the cooks had been forced to hand over. The Duty Officer had walked straight into it on receiving complaints from two security patrols and had walked straight out again, but not before he'd caught a crotchful of chocolate ice cream.

Shabir enjoyed it hugely. He had been quite wrong. He felt a great affection for Shimatov, at least *he* was straight, the man had actually remembered. He was touched.

He sat watching the last man emerge from a makeshift 'Salyut' constructed out of tables, chairs, trolleys and other assorted items, and pretend to float off into space, the once pristine white-and-silver spacesuit a palette for every colourful daub of food in the canteen. The 'cosmonaut' disappeared under the table, clutching an empty bottle of whisky. At that moment Shimatov interrupted his thoughts.

'Cosmonauts of the Gagarin Training School, please charge your glasses and join me in celebrating the 30th birthday of our good friend Colonel Shabir Al Timimi, from Jerusalem.'

And they all stood up, all 32 of them and together cried out, 'Shabir Al Timimi!'

It was a great moment in Shabir's life. He felt very moved by the depth of their affection. He stood up to reply. Shimatov, beaming now and slightly flushed, embraced him, kissed him on both cheeks and said:

'Shabir, now comes the final test in the programme, keeping upright for at least one minute.' He sat down, laughing uproariously.

Gradually the others quietened down. There was the odd wisecrack 'Up the Palestinians' and from Moskalenko, apeing the American flight controllers, 'You have lift off, Shabir.' The laughter subsided as Shabir banged his spoon on the table cloth, pretending to frown menacingly.

'Friends, fellow cosmonauts, General, thank you for your friendship and for this completely surprise party. At last I know why they keep files on all of us. It's to make sure we don't forget our birthdays.' This was greeted by a barrage of hoots and laughter from the guests. Shimatov winced.

'. . . I certainly forgot mine. May I say that I have never enjoyed a birthday so much in my life and I have never felt so at home as I do among you all.' Further clapping broke out.

'. . . I am not a speech-maker. I am a pilot. I do not flatter myself that I am a cosmonaut until I make my first successful flight. I hope that I have justified your faith in me, an Arab, a Palestinian. The Soviet Union has given me the greatest support and encouragement an individual could ever have wanted. This great Republic has taken me to its bosom and has entrusted me with its most sophisticated machinery.

'The Soviet Union has supported my people in their struggle for their homeland. I am as old as that support. I have pledged my life and the skills which you have taught me to winning back my dignity and my home.

'Meanwhile, this is my home and you, all of you, are my family, my brothers. Most of all, you, General Shimatov', said Shabir, turning towards his host, 'have been like a father to me, and since my mother was killed, Russia has been my mother.'

The guests were quieter now, they recognised the change in mood. Here was the Palestinian in him coming to the surface, and after all the years in Russia.

'I hope that when my time comes to fly then I will do it well and that it will benefit the Soviet Union and the People of Palestine and the world will recognise that the Arabs, the greatest astronomers of ancient history, have a role to play in the exploration of the infinite space around them.

'Finally, I have never spoken of my personal religious beliefs to any of you before. You have never prevented me from praying to God. I know you have thought it curious that I, a man who lives at the forefront of the future, a scientist by training and now shortly to be a cosmonaut, should have non-scientific beliefs. It is not a burden to me. I am grateful for your tolerance because we of the faith of Islam are basically a tolerant people. I have no animosity towards any particular race, religion or non-religion. I believe my life is shaped by my Creator. Imsh'allah, as we say. It Is God's Will. I do not hate Jews for being Jewish, after all the Jews and Arabs are both Semitic people. We are closer than neighbours but like a family, and the worst arguments are within the home between the members of that family. The worst wars are between people of the same country, I know that, I saw it in Vietnam. My struggle is against those who killed my parents, my sister, for those who took my home, Jerusalem.

'So good Russian friends, I join in celebrating my birthday, not as an excuse for my own enjoyment but as a celebration of the 30 years of support the Russians have given to the Palestinians.'

Everybody stood up and with one voice toasted: 'The

Russians and the Palestinians.' The canteen was a terrible mess.

The next day Shimatov asked Shabir to report to him at Building No 8, the main training hall. Moskalenko came too to show Shabir the way and clear him with the security guards. As they emerged from the security lobby Shabir saw that the rest of the building was in complete darkness except for a tiny emergency light near them, under which stood the familiar figure of General Shimatov.

'OK, Moskalenko, you may wait in the lobby. Turn off this light after I have entered the main hall.'

Shimatov opened a door beside him and ushered the Palestinian through. It was even darker the other side but felt cooler and his footsteps echoed around him. Shimatov followed, closing the heavy metal door behind him before flicking a bank of switches. Shabir turned and looked into a room that must have been about 80 feet high and 200 feet square. Standing in the centre was the most beautiful sculpture he had ever seen.

He gazed awestruck as each of the arc lights blossomed into life, illuminating one section after the other, until the whole extraordinary assembly shimmered in a golden glow. Neither of the two men spoke, they were like priests before an idol of the future that stood isolated and awful in the centre of the chamber.

Shabir, still in his pure white 'clean room' outfit, walked silently around it absorbing the visual power of the thing. It took him some seconds to appreciate its structure. It was not symmetrical. It comprised a series of elongated hexagonal cylinders each of different length, about three feet across, packed together in a bundle. One in particular soared a good 50 feet above its support table, whilst the others varied in length from 30 to fifteen feet. Around the central cluster were randomly grouped polyhedrons, like enormous gemstones, multi-faceted and reflecting the powerful arc lights in brilliant flashes as Shabir walked around them.

Projecting at various angles from the polyhedrons and the hexagonal cylinders were fronds, shallow dishes and tapering cones—the machine's sensors—while sailing out from a point one third of the machine's height from the ground were two vast multi-segmented wings, covered in electric-blue glass cells like the wings of a butterfly but edged in beautifully machined golden frames. Each one of the segments was maintained in a wave pattern by an array of extended pantographs which obviously enabled both wings to fold back towards the central core.

Finally, girding the hexagonal cluster at its junction with the wings, were three symmetrically arranged golden cubes about three feet square, one being slightly larger than the other two. The entire assembly sat on a lattice ring, the same diameter as a Soyuz spacecraft.

'It's magnificent General, quite exquisite. What does it do?'

'Colonel, you are one of the first people not directly involved in the programme to view our latest achievement in space technology. Let me explain its function, very basically. You will have plenty of time to understand it in the next few months.'

They stood close to the central cluster now. Shabir silently gazing at the machine towering over him.

'This, we believe, is the ultimate weapon of the future. It is a charged particle device that focuses a concentrated beam of energy at any target, at a range of infinity, with an energy density greater than at the centre of a hydrogen bomb. The maximum temperature it reaches is ten million degrees centigrade, at a range that could be ten million miles.'

Shabir was astounded: Nagy had been telling the truth. Shimatov continued.

'It is important for you to understand its particular significance. During the past 60 years we have seen the epic struggle of the Marxist-Socialist doctrine against the forces of Capitalism, Imperialism and Revisionism. This struggle has been led by the Soviet Union, the Mother of Socialism, your Mother as you so elegantly described her yesterday.

'Since October 1917, over 50 million Soviet people have died in that struggle. We fought the Tsarists and the

Mensheviks in spite of intervention by Imperialist British and American troops. We won only at a massive cost to Russian lives.

'We fought the evil of Fascism, again at a huge cost in Russian lives, far greater than that suffered by all the other Allies collectively, and we won.

'Since the end of the Patriotic War, Russians have hardly ever fought in the 200 subsequent wars and battles to overthrow the Capitalist order because instead of giving our lives we have acted as the arsenal for the Liberation armies around the world, in the same way as America was the arsenal for Britain before Pearl Harbour.

'In 1945, the Americans exploded the first atomic bomb. We followed in 1949 having received essential details, including their actual drawings and fission material, through the courage of a number of our Jewish agents ironically enough, such as David Greenglass who worked in Los Alamos.

'In 1953, we exploded a hydrogen bomb only nine months after the Americans' first test at Eniwetok Isle in the Pacific. Since then we have devoted one third of our total energy and resources to neutralising the nuclear and conventional power of the United States and NATO.

'We have now achieved strategic superiority over the West and the Chinese Maoist-Revisionists are totally surrounded by our missiles, powerless to survive a nuclear strike.

'The world is in a strategic balance at last, except for one thing. The Liberation armies are still fighting and still being resisted by reactionary forces backed by American and NATO Imperialism.

'You know, Colonel, as I do, that the struggle against Israel suffered a mortal blow in October 1973 when, let us face the truth, we were defeated—Arabs and Russians together, by Israel supported by the United States. What is more, the initiative by the turncoat Sadat may well achieve its objectives and Israel and Egypt may sign a peace treaty. There is even talk that Sadat and Begin will receive the Nobel Peace Prize next year.

'We are doing everything in our power to destroy the initiative and I believe we will succeed. Sadat will find the Israelis more and more intransigent while you Palestinians launch more and more raids against them. Soon we will have a way of breaking that deadlock, of pushing on with the struggle for liberation, and the key is here, above you.

'This weapon is totally irresistible. There is no conceivable way that the United States could defeat it and their scientists know that. We are at least twenty years ahead of them in its development and it is ironic to think that they could have had it themselves from their own allies, the British, by 1960. In 1951 Klaus Fuchs, their greatest nuclear physicist, had his own charged-particle-beam project, called Zeta, cancelled. That is why Fuchs defected to us from Britain.

'Now you may argue that the Americans will attack us with nuclear weapons in order to prevent this weapon's development. That we have considered. But since we now have a superior nuclear and conventional force they will never take the risk of starting a full scale nuclear war, especially if American lives and property are affected.

'The beauty of this device is that it is not referred to in any International Agreement or Treaty so the Americans cannot mount a political campaign against its development. All they are left with is the certainty that we, the Soviet Union, have it and will be capable of using it exactly as we wish, while avoiding a nuclear war.'

'But how does it help the Palestinian struggle?' Shabir asked, slightly confused with the vast amount of new information he was having to absorb.

'Because it is the most perfectly designed weapon for conventional wars. It is so accurate that you could destroy a single selected aircraft in a formation or the entire formation, by the simple turning of an energy focussing device. And there is no fallout: it is not a nuclear weapon.

'Shabir, we are going to entrust to you the most powerful gun in history. A gun with the power of a hydrogen bomb, the precision of a laser beam and a range of infinity.'

'General Shimatov, one final question. Where do I fire it and when?'

Shimatov looked at him steadily for a few moments before replying:

'From orbit, over Jerusalem, in 1982.'

23
Pasadena

Michael drove his 'Esprit' carefully out onto the driveway from the road and parked in the shade of the carport. He noticed as he slid out of the low reclined seat that a cab was parked on the other side of the road and was reflected in the integral wing mirror. He glanced over, while locking his car, but the sun reflected off the cab's windows making it impossible to see who was inside it. He felt he was being watched but went into the house, closing the door, glancing again at the cab. He made for the kitchen and poured himself a Pimms with plenty of ice, then walked through to the pool, undoing his shirt as he went.

Michael had just settled down to read the *Los Angeles Times*, left there by John Cohen, when he heard the door chime ring just once.

'Shit.' He folded the thick paper and tossed it down on the grass, but held onto the Pimms, feeling it cool and wet in his hand. He went through the empty house to the hall and opened the door. She was by herself.

'Hello Colonel, I finally took up your offer, do you mind?' It was Diana Koh, the nurse he had met wayback in Vietnam.

'Well, well, Sister Koh, this is a pleasant surprise. Please come in, are you by yourself?'

'Yes Colonel, I am. Thank you.'

Michael saw the cab driver smiling up at him from the far side of the road, obviously making sure the lady was alright.

Diana turned and waved, smiling, and the cabby waved back, then slowly drove off.

She looked even better than Michael had remembered. She wore a pure white dress with a slim gold belt and matching sling-back shoes on tall heels that showed off her legs to perfection. Her hair was black, long, past her shoulders and looked as if it had just emerged from the salon. It had. Her face was beautiful, completely devoid of make-up and her skin was that warm-honey colour he had admired so much in the ward.

'Here, let me take that,' he said. She had a small suitcase by her feet and she carried a rather overfilled white shoulder bag.

'Oh, thank you Colonel, if I could just leave it in the hall. I won't take up too much of your day. Did you get my call?'

'No, Miss Koh, I've been out some time. I expect Mr Cohen took it. Please go through there and you'll see the pool ahead of you. There are plenty of chairs.'

She hesitated, then walked quietly through the lounge and out to the pool. Michael took her case into the study, then glanced at the message pad by the phone. Sure enough there was a note in John's scrawl:

'Miss Koh phoned, sounds delicious. Met you in 'Nam, wants to call in about noon. I said fine. OK? John.'

And for Michael it was most definitely OK.

They sat by the pool, she drinking a Coke, he sipping his Pimms while she told him her story.

Two days before Saigon was abandoned by the Americans she managed to get a lift on a 'Huey', which lifted her out of her hospital that was about to be occupied by the Vietcong.

After a series of misadventures she finally made it to the City. She joined the thousands of panic-stricken South Vietnamese around the American Embassy, desperate to get out before the Communists took complete control. At the gate she gave up in despair as she saw the Marine Guards fighting off their terrified allies. She was standing, numb, still wearing her nurse's outfit when a car screamed in towards the gates. It was a group of helicopter pilots returning to fly out Embassy personnel.

As the gates swung to let it through one of the car doors opened and she felt herself being grabbed, then dragged into the vehicle which roared through, its door still open and her only halfway inside. The car pulled up inside the compound and she suddenly recognised the face of the man who had dragged her in. It was one of the pilots she had nursed near the DMZ and by a miracle he had recognised her, appreciated her plight and saved her from abandonment.

She had then been airlifted out in the same pilot's helicopter and deposited on the deck of the US carrier being used for evacuating selected personnel. The rest was a series of flights, first to Hawaii and then to California where she had been interned at the refugee camp hastily established for those South Vietnamese who had made it out. She had been at the camp ever since while various officials interviewed her, obtained corroboration of her identity and work in Vietnam and finally had issued her with a temporary visa while the politicians in Washington considered her future and that of the few others who had escaped.

She had lost Michael's address in the desperate evacuation but one of the pilots who had corroborated her story remembered Michael's Commanding Officer who had reluctantly furnished him with Michael's Pasadena address, believing the fellow pilot wanted to meet up with him again.

'And that's how I found you, Colonel. I am leaving next week to stay with some distant relatives in San Francisco and I wanted very much to see you before I left. I am not here to beg for charity. I have a nursing job ready for me but it may be some time before I am back in the Los Angeles area.' Michael's brain was racing, it was being powered by a very strong sense of expectation. 'Diana—may I call you that? —it was always Sister Koh wasn't it? I can't tell you how delighted I am to see you again, safe and obviously well in control of your life, as usual.'

'Thank you Colonel.' She said, lowering her eyes slightly.

'Mike, please.' He asked her.

'Mike, then.' and she looked up at him, her lips glistening wetly from the Coke.

And they touched glasses and they each felt very good inside, as if something was happening.

'Diana, when did you say you were leaving for San Francisco?'

'In a week from today. They sound very good people.' She smiled.

'Are you staying nearby?' His mind was formulating a plan now.

'Not too far, I am at a hostel near the Airport.' She felt as if she was reading a script.

'Pity.' He frowned, inspecting his glass.

'Why?' She looked puzzled.

'Shame to leave a good empty room. Still, they'll find somebody to fill it no doubt.' He maintained the look of concern.

'I don't understand. Please . . .?' Her voice was slightly nervous, a pitch high.

'Diana. After what you've been through and I've been through, there is no way I'm going to let you spend the next week in a hostel near one of the busiest airports in the world.'

'But it's fine, Mike, it's very clean and . . .'

'Nope, this time I'm giving the orders. You're my patient, OK? I prescribe one more Coke, then a meal out at my club before you meet the Cohen team who I am utterly certain will lock you in one of their two vacant bedrooms for a week.' and he caught her glass before it spilt all over her beautiful white dress. He could not catch her tears though and they fell in tiny drops onto her lap.

'Hey, the Cohens aren't that awful.' He wanted to kiss away the tears.

'Oh, Mike, that's so nice. I hardly know you. Why are you all so kind. Why?' She gave another little sob while rummaging in her bag for a handkerchief.

'Diana, you gave me a week of your time in your country, let me give you a week of my time in mine.' He took the glass out of her hand and gave her his handkerchief.

The Cohens were delighted with their guest, Sheila clucking round her all the time telling her to eat more protein, not to go downtown at night and never to walk anywhere before checking with her or Michael. John winked his way through every meal, totally captivated by Diana's charm and gracious manners. Once, out by the pool as Diana prepared to dive in for a swim (which she did perfectly every time), John turned his gaze to Michael and just whispered one sentence:

'You won't get the ceremony, but I promise to come to the Registry Office, instead.' Michael smiled back at John then looked at Diana, now swimming at the far end of the pool.

The day before Diana was due to leave for San Francisco they drove out to the hills above Pasadena to look out at the view over the Los Angeles valley. Diana was very quiet, strain showing in her face, avoiding Michael's eyes and staring out at the valley, apparently unaffected by the grandeur of it all. Michael stood quietly, not saying anything, reminded suddenly by the silent falling of a meteorite of the night John Cohen showed him Daniel Perès' letter. He turned to Diana and he said quietly:

'Diana, I love you. I don't want you to leave me here, alone in Pasadena.'

She stared at him and he saw her lips part slightly, very slowly and then the tears came into her eyes. For the first time Michael placed his hands on each side of her beautiful wet face and kissed her tenderly on her soft lips.

The telegram sent to San Francisco read quite simply:

'FORGIVE CHANGE IN CIRCUMSTANCES STOP MAY I VISIT NEXT MONTH WITH MY HUSBAND STOP LOVE DIANA.'

And they did.

24
Shuttle

'You look like a cat who's got the cream! Congratulations Michael, good to see you respectable at last and good to see you, Pete. Looks as if you're getting plenty of cream too. Gus, this is Colonel Allon and Pete Peabody, the men I've been telling you about.' General Wheeler beamed with pleasure as he introduced one of his oldest and most respected friends to his two protégés.

'Just to balance the books here, gentlemen, you'll hear a lot more about Mr Lancaster as well. He's Director of Astronaut Training at Johnson Space Center in Houston.

'Now relax, make yourselves comfortable and enjoy the film. Briefing and questions will follow. OK, Linghorn, let's go. This will take about six minutes.'

The four men sat back in their individual armchairs and viewed the small screen of the briefing cinema. After a few seconds of experimenting Linghorn got the focus right and the images became crystal clear.

The first few frames showed what was obviously a large delta-winged aircraft being towed out of a hangar into brilliant sunshine. The vehicle looked as if it was a model as its entire upper surfaces were painted in a dull semi-matt white giving it the appearance of being unfinished, awaiting a final polish.

Its fuselage had flat vertical sides and a rounded back like a giant railway wagon, only larger, much larger. The nose tapered from this massive body to a rounded, pointed grey cone set a long way ahead. What were obviously cockpit windows were set high and far back along the nose, blending smoothly into the fuselage. The tail end had two large curved blisters emerging above the shoulders of the 'box car' between which rose a swept fin and rudder. The entire fuselage was almost flat underneath, its smooth belly blending into the double-swept thick delta wing. The leading edges of the outer part of the stubby delta were grey while all the lower surfaces of the blended wing-body configuration were a deep black sheen which covered the lower nose like a bluebeard.

The next film then showed the entire vehicle supported on a three-point rig growing from the back of an unpainted 747 airliner. The extraordinary aerodynamic duo took off and everybody recognised Edwards Air Base.

A chase plane sequence focused on a view of the combination in flight, before their eyes realised that the giant white vehicle was very slowly separating, almost imperceptibly, from the back of the 747.

The following tail-chase shot revealed three grey cones in a triangular pattern emerging from the flat tail-end of the fuselage in a cluster, they were obviously rocket nozzles. Soon the party recognised Edwards' long runway 04 below them but the vehicle was pointing down at a very steep approach attitude, far steeper than any aircraft Michael had ever seen.

Finally, there was a magnificent shot from a camera mounted in the under-carriage bay below the wing as the runway surface rushed upwards at a speed that even worried a Blackbird pilot. The twin nosewheels touched down smoothly ahead of the camera and the last shot showed the vehicle, now stationary, surrounded by people who were dwarfed by its heavy proportions. The lights came on as the screen went blank.

'OK, gentlemen, that's just a quick shot of the Orbiter during the Approach and Landing Tests, completed in October 1978. One question, Mike, do you want to fly it?'

'General, I can't wait.' Michael beamed with pleasure,

sitting back into his chair and stretching his legs, 'Looks like a hot ship though. That final approach was very steep, General. Is that normal?'

'Don't ask me, ask Gus here, he's flown it, not me. Tell them about it, Gus.'

'OK, Adam. I'll stand up for this, makes it easier. Lights please, Captain Linghorn.' Gus Lancaster was a lean six-footer, a near-bald, highly polished head tanned to a light metallic bronze, sat on a long neck which emerged from a wide-shouldered loosely fitting cream jacket. He wore a pale blue shirt and blending blue-and-grey check trousers.

Known as 'Lanky' to his team and always 'Gus' to his old college lecturer, he and General Wheeler were reckoned to have as much God-given computer power as the whole of IBM Federal Systems Division.

Gus Lancaster, like Adam Wheeler fifteen years before him, had been a star pupil of Stanford and RAND. Both had come out way ahead of their year. Lancaster chose aero-dynamics and mechanical engineering while Wheeler preferred the then novel subjects of nuclear physics and electronics. Both were accomplished musicians, Wheeler playing the cello and the other flute. The main difference was that Wheeler could not fly, while Lancaster could fly anything with wings and an engine. Lancaster had in fact flown the Shuttle Orbiter, without engines.

'Gentlemen, the Space Shuttle Orbiter which you have just seen on the short film I brought with me is familiar to you all. Millions of people throughout the United States and around the world have seen the ALT, the Approach and Landing Tests on TV and I should say 90 percent believe the Space Shuttle is nothing but a Boeing 747 Jumbo Jet which launches this big white bird off its back, somehow getting it into space. This is totally wrong as I'm sure you also know.

'The Orbiter which you saw there was built by Rockwell International at Downey, California, finally assembled at Palmdale and then tested at Edwards or, as it's now called, Dryden Flight Research Center.

'All you've seen is the way we place the Orbiter at a

22,000-foot altitude in order to see how it behaves on the very last leg of its flight.

'It's rather like filming a racing car as it stops at the pits. I understand from General Wheeler that he hopes that you, Colonel Allon, and you, Colonel Peabody, have the right qualifications to begin full-time training to become Space Shuttle pilots—notice the term 'pilots', not 'astronauts'. Rockwell, as prime contractor to NASA, have built the vehicle as a true aircraft and spacecraft. Some people call it the world's first spaceship and here I would entirely concur.

'A ship, to me, is a benign vehicle that suggests size, safety and long distance travel around the world, whilst performing a useful function. This is exactly what the Shuttle does. But one round-the-world trip takes it 88 minutes. So let's start today with explaining its function.

'This system will enable the United States to place satellites in orbit at a considerable cost-saving over throw-away rockets. It will carry very big satellites: up to 30 tons, almost 60 feet long and up to fifteen feet in diameter; that's the size of its cargo bay, covered by two huge carbon-carbon doors in its back.

'Then it can return with a damaged satellite using a giant mechanical arm, 60 feet long, which it keeps safely stowed along one side of the bay when it's not using it.

'All the best arms have a hand and so does the Shuttle. It's a large, articulated, electronically controlled 'claw', made by Spar Aerospace up in Canada. It's very sophisticated as it has to have not only strength but also very delicate precision controls because when it places a satellite in orbit, it does just that. It holds the satellite in its claw having removed it from the bay, then places it at a given position appropriate to the satellite's function.

'If it's the Space Telescope, for example, then it points it towards a selected group of stars, leaves it be, and the Telescope's own attitude system does the rest while the arm folds into the cargo bay and the Shuttle Orbiter moves away.

'However, if a satellite goes wrong then that same arm,

known properly as the Remote Manipulator System, can pick the sick fellow out of orbit and tuck it away in the cargo bay before it flies back to Earth for proper servicing. In other words it acts as a breakdown vehicle in space. When you realise that there are over 10,000 satellites and major particles of space junk in orbit you know that the Shuttle is going to be very busy. It's as if we built a freeway and twenty years later sent a bunch of mechanics along in a truck for the first time. Now that has got to be good business.

'I don't want to step on General Wheeler's ground but nobody but a fool would ignore the other possibilities of the arm, the claw and its body—the vehicle you saw in the film —the Orbiter.'

Michael wanted to know more about its performance both as an aircraft and a spacecraft:

'What is the launch configuration, Mr Lancaster, should we expect high G-loads?'

'No, Colonel, the Orbiter is launched vertically from either NASA's Kennedy Space Center or the Air Force's Vandenberg Air Force Base. The maximum vertical acceleration is 3G, no bother to a Phantom pilot. Same for landing.

'The vehicle comprises the winged Orbiter which you just saw on the film and if you all concentrate on this model here I'll tell you how it gets into Earth orbit, the only freeway it's designed to travel on. This is no inter-planetary vehicle, that's why it's called the Orbiter. Now you may well ask, "How do you get this big Orbiter, which is 122 feet long, 78 feet wide and 56 feet high, into space?" Well the Orbiter has to travel at 17,500 miles per hour to stay up there and to give it that velocity you fire it up from a vertical position. Now you use two big SRBs, Solid Rocket Boosters, to help and these sit under the Orbiter, not attached to the wing but to this huge pointed cylinder here, called the External Tank. The Tank is suspended along the centreline of the Orbiter, below the wing, and on each side of the Tank are mounted the SRBs. The Space Shuttle is in fact a System, the Space Shuttle Transportation System as it's called by us at NASA.

You've only seen the film of the Orbiter.'

'How big is the system, Mr Lancaster?' Michael asked.

'Well the Orbiter, as I said, is 122 feet long. The Tank is 154 feet long and 27½ feet in diameter, while each of the SRBs is nearly 150 feet long and over 12 feet in diameter.

'The whole system stands 184 feet high on its tail, so it's a big brother.'

'What thrust does it need to get it into orbit?' Wheeler asked, beginning to appreciate the size of the system.

'At lift-off, the two SRBs fire simultaneously with the Orbiter's three main engines giving a total of 6.5 million pounds as against a 747's typical 0.16 million pounds. That's a huge amount of power, sufficient to lift the system which weighs in at 4.5 million pounds.'

'That must be one hell of a noise,' Wheeler added.

'Sure is, it'll kill a man at a mile or more. Literally shake his insides to jelly.' Lancaster replied, then continued his description.

'Now, you two fellows are sitting in the nose about 150 feet up, facing straight up at the sky when the ignition sequence starts. You'll feel the roar of the noise below you, you're safe at the centre of the noise hurricane, and slowly you go, still not seeing a thing but the blue Florida sky over your head.

'The acceleration is never more than 3G, so as to make our delicate satellites easy to build, but at 62 seconds after lift-off you're at 37,100 feet. Two minutes after lift-off you're at 27 miles, higher than Blackbird, and travelling at 3,111 miles an hour.

'At that instant you've used all the solid fuel filling your SRBs and they're then fired off the sides of the Tank, still supplying you with fuel for your remaining three main engines.

'The SRBs look beautiful from the ground as they move away, one each side, because you're travelling half way upside down with your heads pointing more and more towards Earth as the vehicle follows a ballistic trajectory.'

'What happens to the SRBs. Are they destroyed?' Peabody enquired.

'No, we recover them on big parachutes from the Atlantic, tow them back using a tug, wash 'em out and refill them for more flights.'

'Sounds remarkably economical,' Wheeler acknowledged.

'Essential part of the Shuttle's concept, Adam, economics. Anyway, where were we? Oh, yes, you've had SRB separation and still you have power from your three main engines.

'They keep firing until the big Tank is empty of liquid hydrogen and oxygen. That happens at 69 miles and eight minutes from launch. You're two per cent under orbital speed and so you jettison the Tank, which is above you since you are on your back now and the Tank sails away.'

'Is that recovered also?' Peabody asked.

'No, that two per cent factor means it will fall back to the Ocean, big splash, no more tank,' Lancaster replied.

'Seems a waste,' Michael commented. 'Couldn't you recover it?'

'No, the recovery equipment would be excessively heavy and costly but we do have plans to use Tanks later in the Program, in orbit.' Lancaster paused.

'So there you are gentlemen, you are in your Orbiter, you fire your three main engines to gain that missing two per cent and you are then true astronauts.'

'How high will we fly?'

'Well, like an aircraft, it depends on your cargo or payload weight. Now if you're carrying a 65,000-pound satellite you would fly at 100 miles altitude in a due east or 0-degree inclination orbit, making use of the rotational speed of the earth at the Equator.

'The more you change the direction of the launch from 0-degree, to a north-south or 90-degree inclination, then the more fuel you need. It's like either travelling on the level or climbing up a hill.'

'Gus, I'd just like to come in here,' General Wheeler interrupted. 'I think it's a good time to point out that we're interested mainly in the 55-degree orbit, right?'

'Yes, Adam, that's correct,' Lancaster replied. 'You

fellows are going to find yourselves flying more between 55-degree and 90-degree orbits more often than not.'

'Why's that?' Peabody asked.

'Because the Russians do. Their launch sites favour those orbits.'

'Can we leave that aspect for a moment, Gus, and just tell the Colonels what weight they can carry?' Wheeler said.

'Right, we call the 55-degree a Type II mission, the 0-degree launch a Type I. You can carry 25,000 pounds as high as 270 nautical miles on a Type II. Bear in mind there's yet a third mission, Type III, which is the polar orbit mission where you can carry 32,000 pounds to 100 miles, but then you have to take off from Vandenberg in California.'

'Why's that?' Peabody asked again.

'It's a safety consideration, Colonel. Makes sure that if you drop anything at launch it'll land in the Pacific not the East Coast or somewhere busy if you had taken off from Florida.'

'I understand that we'll be travelling at orbital speed, how fast is that again, and for how long?' Michael enquired.

'That's 17,500 miles per hour to the first question and seven to ten days, normally, to the second.'

'What's our landing speed, Mr Lancaster?' Michael asked.

'To arrive safely back on earth you first decelerate the Orbiter using your main engines after rotating before facing forward again. You keep the nose at a very precise angle riding down through the atmosphere.

'Now, let's assume you're passing through 400,000 feet height, then by the time you're at 150,000 feet you've decelerated from orbital speed to about 1,000 miles per hour. You've travelled 4,800 miles and that's nearly twice the width of the Atlantic.'

'Can we land anywhere from that point?'

'No; you could move left or right of your return trajectory up to 1,000 miles from that arrival point in the sky.'

'How do I put her down?' Michael asked again.

'Well remember you have no jet engines or rocket power

after leaving orbit, so you're gliding all the way like a very expensive brick, but you do have energy. I believe you fellows are more experienced than most pilots in energy management through flying the Blackbird, when you come down to refuel using an "energy ramp".'

'Correct. Ten out of ten.' Peabody interjected.

'Well, you have an excess of energy all the time in the Orbiter so at 70,000 feet you are below Mach 1.5 and about ten miles from the runway. You approach at between 18-degrees and 28-degrees nose down, bleeding off energy by controlled turning. Finally you ride from 10,000 feet down to 200 feet using a microwave controlling beam linked to your control electronics. At 200 feet you're nose up and your descent path is an easy three to six degrees before touch-down.'

'How fast do we touchdown, Mr Lancaster?' Michael asked.

'If you're heavy, 220 knots. Light, 190 knots, and you'll stop in 9,000 to 11,000 feet although we've done it in 5,700 feet.'

The General stood up at this point and motioned to Lancaster that he wanted to say a few words.

'Gus, thank you for the introduction. I'd like a break here to give you both a chance to absorb that data. That's strictly flyer's talk and you men have got to be patient with a guy like me.

'What I want to discuss next is applications. What do we want you gentlemen to do with the Space Shuttle once you're properly trained?'

25
CBR

A third of the world away four other people were trying to come to terms with the future.

Ephraim Zuckerman, Head of Mossad, Daniel Perès and Shimon Yariv, and 'Aliah' as she was known only to her controllers.

'Are you absolutely certain about your source, Daniel, there is no doubt whatsoever?'

'No doubt, sir, David Greenberg is our best man in the United States.'

Zuckerman picked up the photograph of Dimitry Polkova mouthing Hebrew at the Big Bird's invisible camera.

'And the file, this story of Shimatov's deception of the Palestinian Al Timimi, that has been corroborated?'

'Yes, sir,' Daniel replied, 'when Polkova recorded Shimatov and Mendeleiv, Shimatov said he'd invented the name of the naval officer but just to make sure had checked there was a Krupny-class destroyer of the same name.'

'What about the girl, Valentina Bykovsky? Did we find out if she had the baby?' Zuckerman asked, wanting to be certain of the facts.

'Yes, our girl in Odessa checked with every maternity home in the city and sure enough, she found the record of ex-Captain Valentina Bykovsky having given birth to a male child on 2 August 1976. The girl was then discharged and given a restricted movement pass confining her to Odessa.'

'Do we know what she looks like?' Yariv asked.

'Yes, here is her photograph. Our girl took it when she was walking with the baby near one of the public beaches this summer.

'She is very beautiful, I can understand why the Palestinian was so upset. Tell me does he know that he is the father?' Zuckerman looked hard at the photograph.

'No, he eventually accepted Shimatov's story.'

Daniel was wondering what direction all this questioning was taking them. Zuckerman turned to 'Aliah'.

'Can you do it?'

'I will try, sir. The girl in Odessa is very good.'

'Thank you Aliah, report only to me. It takes absolute priority over any of your other jobs. Any complications, tell me, nobody else.'

'Yes, sir.'

'Good luck,' and she left the office. Zuckerman turned back to Yariv and Perès.

'Right, that's taken care of the mother and child. Now, what's the father up to?'

Daniel drew out more photographs from his brief-case.

'These were taken a week ago at night with infra-red and synthetic aperture radar from Big Bird 7 over Tyuratam. This is the track of the rocket from the assembly building to the launch pad at night. Here is a print-out from British Royal Aircraft Establishment of its orbit and inclination.

'Here is the second rocket fired from Tyuratam the following night. The satellite from the second rocket docked automatically with the first satellite already in orbit.

'The two linked satellites then started to change height and orbital inclination. According to these transmission signals recorded by Big Bird's ELINT sub-satellite that David Greenberg has access to, they're electronic satellites.

'Now, this third picture is the key to our discovery. This is a Big Bird 7 photograph.'

Daniel placed the print on the table very deliberately.

'But it's pure white, there's nothing there!' Zuckerman exclaimed.

'Exactly,' Daniel replied.

'Exactly what?' his Chief asked, puzzled.

'Sir, that double satellite destroyed Big Bird's camera.'

'How? It's not possible, surely?' Zuckerman asked with incredulity.

'Big Bird photographed itself being attacked.'

'Good God, explain it.' Zuckerman demanded.

'Imagine you are watching an assailant approach you, he aims a gun, shoots you and blinds you permanently, do you remember his face even though you are blind? Of course, it is stored in your memory. Now Big Bird does not have just one pair of eyes but four, even five 'eyes'. The radar eye and the infra-red eye recorded the passage of the Soviet satellite directly below it whilst the infra-red eye recorded a direct hit with a certain frequency of radiation. It recorded being shot, in other words.'

'By what, a laser beam?' Zuckerman guessed.

'No, something much more powerful.'

'Such as?' Zuckerman enquired, worried now.

'A beam of ultra-high energy, a charged particle beam.'

'Like the tests at Semipalatinsk?' Yariv interrupted.

'Yes, we believe this is a photograph of the first satellite in the world actually capable of firing a charged particle beam.' Daniel said with conviction.

'How powerful is it?'

'Not very, not even enough to kill you. It'll give you a form of radiation sickness and possible genetic damage, but not fatal.' Yariv replied.

'What are you worried about then? If it's so weak, what is the danger?' Zuckerman asked.

'We're not sure.' Perès took over, 'but since we've been monitoring the American surveillance of Semipalatinsk the chaps at the Weizmann Institute in Jerusalem have built a theoretical model of the Soviet charged particle beam. What is ruining my sleep is something our chaps told me yesterday and which is the reason for my asking for this emergency meeting, sir.'

'What's worrying you, Daniel?' his Chief asked.

'The Institute people have discovered that, theoretically,

a small beam can act as a trigger for a larger one, in just the same way as an atomic bomb triggers a hydrogen bomb a thousand or a million times more powerful. They call it a Catalytic Beam Response, or CBR for short.'

Zuckerman sat back from the table, and quietly placed both hands on either side of his grey hair.

'Why were we cursed with our own genius for inventing cleverer ways to kill each other?' he asked nobody in particular.

Without lifting his head he continued in a quiet, resigned voice, 'Do you think the Russians know what their beam can do?'

'Yes, sir.' Daniel replied without hesitation.

'Why do you say yes?'

'Because they have just done it, sir.'

'Where?' Yariv was also surprised at Perès' answer.

'At Semipalatinsk, yesterday. Greenberg signalled me. It appears that an American 'Elint' satellite picked up the largest electrical flare ever recorded over the Soviet Union. The flare was generated at the same frequency as the Weizmann boys predicted the CBR would work. It did, and the Russians now have the most powerful gun, literally, in the Universe.'

'That's excessive talk, Perès.' Zuckerman objected.

'No, sir, the beam is at the theoretical limit of energy efficiency. There is literally no more efficient device for concentrating or transmitting energy. It is simply the ultimate weapon sir.'

Zuckerman suddenly stood up and addressed Yariv.

'Yariv, I want all the papers, the photographs, the recordings, every single calculation, I want every scientist, everybody who knows part or all of this information rounded up immediately!'

Zuckerman knew exactly what was at stake.

'Use any pretext, traffic violation, drunkenness, complaints from the neighbours, anything, but assemble them at the Weizmann Institute today and have the place guarded now.

'I will talk with the Prime Minister and the Chief of Police, the Chief of the IDF and the Head of the Institute.

'Warn David Greenberg to standby to break his cover. It is a price we'll have to pay to protect the State. Now, Yariv, report to me immediately it is done. I will be at the Knesset. Daniel, tell me everything you and Greenberg have discovered from the Americans. Come with me.'

For the rest of the day some of the brightest brains in Israel suddenly found themselves questioned about a host of imaginary offences. By dusk 48 angry Israelis were being restrained by police in the main canteens of the Weizmann Institute, brought there in a convoy of police cars and vans.

Zuckerman arrived at 8pm, grim and determined. He carried a bulging briefcase with him. Complaints started as soon as he climbed first onto a chair then a canteen table. But his sheer presence gradually calmed them into a muttering assembly. He wasted little time on preliminaries.

'Thank you for your co-operation.' More abuses were hurled, he ignored them. 'The safety of Israel may depend on you all co-operating with me and the State, from this moment.' People started to quieten down.

'All of you have been involved in the investigation of the Russian Charged Particle Beam.

'I have received information today that your predictions of a CBR have been confirmed by the Russians at Semipalatinsk. Only they actually fired a real beam!'

There was a stunned silence.

'Now, I have other information regarding two individuals who are responsible for directing Soviet space activities on the military front. It is important for you to know about them. I know the minds of these men better than any of my staff, but one man in particular presents the greatest threat to our State and possibly to the non-Communist world.

'Remember this name and remember it well. He is the enemy, his name is Vladimir Shimatov. And he is the KGB Head of military aspects of the Soviet Space Programme.

'He is brilliant, ruthless and totally dedicated to fight all enemies of the Soviet Union at whatever the cost. He is a man without normal controls. He is a fanatic and today he knows he has achieved the fanatic's ultimate ambition, he controls the ultimate weapon.

'Now you people created it theoretically, so your job from this hour on is to create a means of destroying it. "Uncreating" it if you like.

'The greatest evil of this weapon is the very knowledge of its feasibility. You must convince the Russians totally that it is not practical. That it can be easily defeated. Because once they know, and the Americans know and everybody else knows the real truth, then nothing, nothing will stop its development. And we will be faced with a situation that will make nuclear war look like a tea party.

'You have the total support of the Government and the leaders of the main opposition parties in this, all of whom are sworn to absolute secrecy on pain of incarceration for life. All of you are required to retain your knowledge forever as a State secret, do you understand?'

The group said nothing, every single one of them was in mild shock. One girl started to cry and one or two men had to steady themselves against a table or chair, but within an hour every one of them was thinking as hard as he or she had ever thought at that famous institute of learning.

Zuckerman had left Shimon Yariv to act as his liaison officer at the Institute, impressing upon him the need to erect a security barrier around the team which would not break down even under the most extreme pressure of outside events. But Yariv clearly did not appear to be convinced of the necessity of such extreme action.

'What I want you to do, Yariv, is to create an environment which will gradually isolate them from their normal routine. They must structure their lives around this one task, nothing must interfere with their thoughts. Talk to the Institute's welfare officer and draw up a chart of every team member together with his domestic background including such things as his home address, family, children's schools, bank, sponsor, whoever or whatever makes up the core of his world. Make sure no one has financial worries, arrange for food supplies, set up a leisure room, a music room, a library, within the Institute. My friend, we have to build from nothing the equivalent of the Los Alamos laboratories and we must work fast.'

'But why shouldn't we tell the Americans of our plans? Only they have the resources we might need,' Yariv protested, concerned for the first time at Zuckerman's extraordinary proposal.

'We will tell the Americans. I will do it myself in about a week's time, but we cannot entrust the survival of our State to them. We have seen their withdrawal from Vietnam and Taiwan. In each case their only realistic choice, we cannot allow the Russians to force them into making another 'realistic choice'.

'Also, I cannot believe the Americans will risk getting involved in a stand-off against the Russians over Israel. I know Nixon alerted their nuclear forces in October 1973 but in the past six years or more the Russians have overtaken them in nuclear capability. No, we cannot rely on the Americans.

'Remember the lesson of the Second World War, when Britain was literally the last country prepared to fight the Nazis, where were the Americans then? It was the young men of Britain and her Commonwealth who saved the world from Fascism in 1940 during the Battle of Britain. The original Commander of the Israeli Air Force was one of those Few, as Churchill called them.

'Roosevelt fought a long battle in Congress to bring America in on the side of Britain from 1939 to Pearl Harbour, three years after the War started. It finally took Japanese bombs and dead sailors to bring America into the War. But now the Arabs own significant shareholdings in General Motors, IBM, Ford, Pan Am, Boeing, every one of the Fortune 500 Companies as they call them. They can strangle America by cutting her oil supplies or quadrupling the price again. For the first time since Independence the United States economy can be controlled by a people sitting on the other side of the earth.

'Yariv, I know Shimatov, I now know he has a weapon which, with Soviet Government support, will be in space, I guarantee, within two years. He is not going to lose the first opportunity to use it, because he has a man to do the job now, the Palestinian.'

Zuckerman looked Yariv in the face, seeing the man's lack of understanding while his own frustration mounted with every sentence.

'Sir, please, what job are you talking about? We haven't any job identified yet,' Yariv asked.

'Yariv, think. Shimatov, a super weapon, a space satellite, a dedicated trained Palestinian cosmonaut. For God's sake, man, is it not obvious to you?'

'No, sir, these are separate, individual events. We don't know that they are tied together.' Now Yariv was angry too at Zuckerman's hasty analysis of the situation.

'Yariv, I believe Shimatov is training that Palestinian to use that beam and he will become his automaton. Now what do the Palestinians seek more than anything?' Zuckerman asked.

Shimon Yariv thought briefly then said, quietly now: 'The destruction of Israel?'

'What does the Soviet Union seek more than any area in the world, even more than Europe?'

'The Middle East, sir, we know that from the analysis of Yom Kippur,' Yariv acknowledged.

'And who is their greatest enemy in the Middle East?'

'Israel.'

'Now, do you understand the logic of these 'unrelated events' as you call them? They are part of a Shimatov plan. Somehow, we don't know exactly how yet, he will use that Palestinian to destroy Israel. He is so clever that with one letter he has already deluded the Palestinian, bright as he is, and now the Palestinian will become his tool, I promise you.'

'How long have we got, Chief?' Yariv asked.

'I guess two years at the most.' Zuckerman was tired of the argument, thinking how easy it must be for a man like Shimatov to achieve his own objectives once given the power he obviously possessed, without arguing with fools.

'Couldn't we kill Shimatov or the Palestinian?' Yariv felt suddenly that the situation could be controlled conventionally.

'Yes, that is exactly what I considered, but I fear even their deaths would be a mere postponement of the beam work at Semipalatinsk.'

'Couldn't we destroy Semipalatinsk?' Yariv asked.

'We considered that at the Knesset this afternoon but I fear it is impossible without a nuclear strike as most of the facilities are built, like our own nuclear headquarters, to withstand a limited nuclear strike,' Zuckerman replied.

'How much do we know about Semipalatinsk, Chief?'

Both of them were much calmer now as they began to absorb the problem.

'General Wheeler, Chief of US Air Force Intelligence, we now know from David Greenberg, raided it about two years ago. It was all clandestine of course. They recovered a vast quantity of papers proving that this beam research was as large as the whole of the Soviet nuclear programme. The Russians have spent over 200 billion dollars on it in twenty years. The entire Apollo programme only cost 24 billion dollars. That's how important it is to the Russians.'

'What can they do with this charged particle beam?' Yariv was now becoming fascinated with the task.

'Daniel Perès says that nobody knows for sure but it appears theoretically possible to focus the beam from the ground and aim it at passing bombers or missiles. It creates a field of particles with sufficient energy to disturb the molecular structure and even electron shells of the atoms of the target.

'In other words metal fails catastrophically and concentrated uranium, plutonium and similar nuclear materials are rendered ineffective. That is the theory. What we intend to do is find out what were the results of the first CBR tests. That is our next immediate task and why I must go to the United States.

'Now may I suggest you do what I asked, confine your job

to the security of the Institute. Report to me every week starting from next Sunday, understand?' Zuckerman was now impatient to leave.

'Yes, sir. One thing, Chief?'

'What's that?'

'Thank you for explaining the problem. I promise you I will give my life, if it means saving Israel.' Yariv was quite serious.

'Shimon Yariv, fine and worthy sentiments. Just keep alive for Israel's sake, please.' Zuckerman patted him on the shoulder and walked down the famous steps to his bullet-proof car, still amazed at the eagerness of people to die.

The next morning he met with the Prime Minister, the Chief of the Israeli Defence Forces, the Head of Military Intelligence and Chief of the Air Force, Yigal Beer, for their second emergency meeting of the week.

26
Rebecca

There were no preliminaries.

Prime Minister Rebecca Limpel had become the second woman to lead Israel since the creation of the State. She was a complete contrast to the much-lamented Golda Meir. At 52, she was young to have reached the top of the most vociferous democracy in the world. She could shout louder than any of her male cabinet colleagues, but rarely did so, now that she had achieved her primary ambition.

She had come from England directly to Israel only twenty years before, making her way up the political ladder by sheer brilliant oratory and with an excellent business head which she used to earn herself a fortune as a leading exporter of citrus fruits. She had sold out everything to do just one thing as she said, namely to pull the country by its hair into a new 'realistic posture' regarding an Arab-Israeli settlement. She was like a breath of fresh air blowing into the dug-outs. She travelled extensively, talked as often as she could to the world's press and had announced at a press conference in Washington that she would go to bed with every Arab leader in the Middle East if it meant that afterwards she could talk face-to-face, sensibly about co-existence.

None of the Arabs had accepted, although most would have welcomed the opportunity, for Rebecca Limpel was a handsome woman. She was blonde with a good figure and she used her assets subtly to get her way. She would not tolerate the extreme postures of past Israeli leaders. She was determined that as God had spared her and her family from the Holocaust, she would do everything to spare the world from the final Holocaust which she believed was the logical conclusion to the Arab-Israeli conflict and its abundance of masculine aggression.

She spoke from a certain academic base having been a biologist at Cambridge and a lecturer in anthropology. It was in fact her doctoral thesis on Male Aggression in Primitive Societies that led her to identify a way of changing society. She married her college tutor when she had completed her doctorate and bore him three children, two boys and a girl. She never let the press near them or her husband.

This handsome blonde simply opened the meeting with—

'Zuckerman, what have you done since yesterday?'

He told the three of them as briefly and succinctly as possible all that had happened. The news was greeted in silence. When he had finished she turned to the Chief of the IDF, General Mordechai Landau and said to the small, burly, black-haired man,

'Now let's hear your news, General.'

Landau was noted for his pipe, which he kept in his mouth continuously, except when attending the Prime Minister. At 56, he had seen a lot of wars.

'Prime Minister, gentlemen. I feel you ought to be brought up to date with the very latest war game analysis entitled 'Response Posture in the Event of a Catastrophic Attack on Israel'. Having heard Ephraim's news I believe we must evaluate the possibility of an attack by this weapon, presumably mounted from a satellite, and its implications.

'First, we have always struck back at every blow inflicted on our State. Even a small shelling has been followed up by the Air Force with an air strike. This "controlled response" posture, as we call it, has carried on since 1948, 30 years. If we apply it to the new situation then what will happen?

'Assuming the beam weapon is fired by a Palestinian at Israel it is no different to a Soviet-trained Palestinian firing a shell or mortar from Lebanon or Syria. We might therefore choose to attack a Palestinian base in one of those countries. We can't attack space itself.

'However, we don't know the scale of damage a beam like this can achieve. So I propose we hope for success through Ephraim's efforts and if not then we destroy an appropriate target on Arab soil.

'Assuming the weapon might damage a building and kill, say twenty people, then we should destroy a guerilla camp and hopefully a hundred guerillas, to put it crudely.' Landau clasped his hands in front of him on the polished table, wishing he could smoke.

'What if the beam is used on a wider area?' the Prime Minister asked.

'Then we expand our target area accordingly,' Landau replied unhesitatingly.

'And what if the effect is similar to a nuclear weapon?' she asked sharply.

'Then we carry out a massive conventional air strike, am I not right Yigal?' Landau turned to Yigal Beer, the tall austere Air Force chief.

'Yes, that would be planned procedure.' Beer sniffed slightly through his broken nose, the result of surviving a take-off accident twenty years ago in an old British Meteor. His soft brown hair and pale face made him look like a college lecturer, not a first-class fighter pilot, capable of teaching any of his instructors how to instruct.

'Any comments, Uri?' the Prime Minister asked her favourite advisor.

'Not yet,' he replied.

Uri Hamelech played it cautiously after taking over the remains of Israeli Military Intelligence a few years after the findings of the Agranat Commission of Inquiry into the Yom Kippur War. Then his branch was severely criticised for its failure to heed Mossad warnings. He had no intention of ignoring the signs and portents.

'Can any of you tell me what would happen if the Soviets launched a nuclear war using Palestinian soldiers. Have you played that War Game yet?' Rebecca Limpel asked.

'Yes, we call it a Palestinian Nuclear Incursion,' Landau replied confidently.

'What do you plan to do?'

'It again depends on the scale of damage, its location and the type of weapons used, Prime Minister.'

'Supposing a Palestinian fired a tactical nuclear artillery rocket such as a 'Frog' from Syria onto a kibbutz, killing 200 kibbutzniks. What would you do?' The Prime Minister knew her Soviet weapons list well. Landau was impressed.

'We'd launch a heavy conventional air strike on a Syrian town,' Landau replied.

'And if they did it again?'

'We'd bomb out one section of Damascus.'

'No nuclear response?'

This question was always an embarrassment at the full Israeli War Cabinet meetings. It was no less so now.

'No,' Landau replied hesitantly.

'No? You have the weapons, I know that. Beer showed me the stockpile list.'

'We will do everything to avoid a nuclear conflict. Israel is simply too small to survive a sizeable nuclear war, even a tactical one, unless it is confined to Sinai, the Negev or Golan—unpopulated areas mainly.'

Rebecca Limpel sat back and thought to herself: 'It's like a thesis exercise, it's so unreal and yet we have to imagine it.' She made her decision.

'Gentlemen, I want you to tell me within the next week what exactly you would do or be capable of doing if Israel is attacked by the equivalent of a nuclear bomb in one of its cities, be it launched by Palestinians, Syrians, Lebanese or whoever. The weapon will be Soviet-made, of that you can be certain!

'Thank you, meet me here next week, at the same time. Zuckerman, I want to speak to you so don't leave yet. In fact come home for lunch.'

She rose, followed by Zuckerman.

'Beauty before age' he thought as he followed her out.

27
Tanks

Michael floated weightless in his full EVA suit, a good 40 feet above the 'Arm' as the crews called it. He was attempting to release the satellite from the locked Claw because unless he did so then he and his crew were doomed.

The satellite had already deployed its solar panels but a series of electrical failures had left it gripped in the Claw, preventing the Arm from being stowed back in the cargo bay prior to re-entry.

He knew he had at least two choices. One, he could cut off the Claw using his metal cutter, thereby releasing the satellite, albeit with Claw attached like the remnant of some galactic monster. Two, he could cut off the entire Arm at its joint, or, three, he could ask Houston for advice before attempting either course of action.

'Houston, this is Allon, do you copy, over?'

'Roger, Allon, we copy you, over,' Flight Director replied.

'Houston, this is Allon. We appear to have a locked RMS Claw here preventing deployment of the payload. All electrical tests show a power failure in the Claw only. Please advise procedure, over.'

'Roger, Allon, we copy you. We will set up a simulation now with the contractors and attempt to help you, over.'

'Roger, Houston, I will ask Peabody to run another deployment test after I've moved away to a safe position, over.'

'Roger, Allon, we copy your proposal. Good thinking.'

Two hours later, as Michael emerged from the Orbiter Neutral Buoyancy Trainer, a giant water tank at the Johnson Space Center in Houston, he was pleased to be told by Gus Lancaster that he and Peabody had done a good job.

'You didn't assume a disaster and you remembered you were part of a team, essential characteristics for all safe Extra-Vehicular Activity. In fact that simulation identified a way of solving an actual foul up of the Claw. Spar Aerospace are going to fit it with a quick manual release to enable it to be opened to free the payload and save the mission.'

For Michael Allon this was a typical training task on the route that would lead him into space. The Shuttle training course for him to become a pilot required him to spend 1,800 hours learning to handle the incredible machine in water tanks, simulators, mock-ups and classrooms during an intensive two-year period.

The most important simulator was a large box on hydraulic arms that gave the box six degrees of freedom in motion including pitching, yawing and rolling in opposite directions. Inside the box, accessible by steel ladders, was a perfect replica of the forward and aft flight deck of the Shuttle Orbiter.

Here, Michael in the left seat and Pete in the right had arranged before them the most advanced instrument panel ever designed. From his commander's seat Michael could control the world's first true spaceship. The flight deck was a uniform mid-grey with crisp pale grey edging to its panels, dominated by three centrally placed rectangular television screens or CRT displays, which in turn were mounted below the horizontal glare shield underneath the six polygonal 'windows'. The view was surprisingly good, similar to a 747 but less cramped.

CRT displays 1, 2 and 3 were the primary means of informing the crew of the Orbiter's performance for they were linked to the quintuple redundant flight control system with its incredible bank of computers. On either side of the CRT panel was the pilots' flight display on which were duplicated the primary spaceflight instruments consisting of the central attitude indicator—a black-and-white floating ball indicating the Orbiter's position relative to an artificial horizon, essential when the horizon is not twenty miles away but 2,000 miles away and the ground is up to 600 miles below.

On either side of the AI (attitude indicator) were mounted vertical strip indicators showing acceleration forces. Directly below the AI was the compass with two digital displays showing distances in miles. To the left and right respectively below, Michael could read off his airspeed in the atmosphere during the landing phase and on the right was his altimeter giving his altitude.

Directly in front of his seat was the dark grey control grip mounted on the control column which was covered by a pale grey corrugated sleeve. Large pedals controlled the rudder 100 feet behind him while on either side of the flight deck, and on the roof, were further banks of switches. Right in the middle below the CRT panel was a box, like a giant car control console, into which were recessed the communications switches and which both pilots could reach.

What surprised Michael was the clarity and simplicity of the flight deck, the direct result of an enormous amount of thought and the latest electronic display technology.

Behind the pilots' seats was a further seven feet of space before the rear bulkhead of the entire crew compartment. Set into this bulkhead, facing directly aft into the cavernous cargo bay, were two windows arranged at eye level for two standing crew members. From there, two men could operate the Arm and Claw using a centrally mounted control column set at elbow height which emerged from the cargo bay instrument panel. By simply looking upwards the same two men also had a perfect view through the two overhead windows.

The Orbiter Flight Deck enabled the crew to look forwards through the windscreen to land; backwards into the cargo bay to control the Arm and Claw, the RMS; and finally vertically upwards, relative to the flight deck floor, to observe satellites or EVA activities or more often than not, the panorama of the earth if the Orbiter was floating on its back.

Michael and Pete never failed to be impressed with the highly realistic effects of spaceflight which were created for them in their training simulators. The Singer Link Shuttle Mission Simulator or SMS became more familiar to them than their own homes. As they 'flew' in orbit or down to a landing at Kennedy Space Center or Vandenberg Air Force Base, they saw projected in front of them computer-generated visual effects of the world outside.

They could see the sun rise above the earth's horizon, the moon, the stars, the layers of cloud, all with these images being reinforced with complete audio backing from the thunder of launch to the hum of the electronics in orbit. As they came in to land they experienced the buffeting of re-entry, the steep approach to the runway and finally touch-down itself. The secret of spaceflight, they knew, was safety achieved by thorough training.

When standing and viewing into the cargo bay they could operate the RMS exactly as if it were in space, unstowing its articulated Arm and delicately placing its Claw on the appropriate point on the satellite's structure. The SMS was only one of several simulators they trained on at Houston.

The flight deck of the real Orbiter sat above the mid-deck, accessible via a connecting ladder in its port side. Down on the mid-deck was a space seven feet high tapering in plan from fifteen feet wide at the rear bulkhead to about eleven feet at the front. Here were the Orbiter's living quarters and the air-lock which connected aft to the cargo bay for EVA missions.

Together, the flight deck and mid-deck, mounted in one sealed, pressurised capsule, sat in the nose of the Orbiter airframe ahead of the cargo bay with its huge 60-foot-long doors. The Orbiter would carry Michael and Pete on the flight deck in the Shuttle Pilots' seats while behind them were two more stowable seats for the single Mission Specialist and a Payload specialist. Up to three more Payload Specialists could sit, again on folding seats, below on the mid-deck. They would work on a three shift program as on a ship. In case of an emergency, such as the rescue of a three-man Soyuz crew from a Soviet spacecraft, then there were three more folding seats available giving a maximum number of ten seats. Down in the mid-deck the crew stowed their equipment, ate their meals from a special food service module and used the vacuum-operated waste management unit, screened off for privacy behind the main circular access hatch by the connecting ladder.

The different phases of Shuttle flight were reproduced in the appropriate simulator. The main SMS could be rotated to the vertical to simulate the effects of a launch, including the noise and vibration and the view of the sky ahead as it changed from blue to black. All non-dynamic use of the crew capsule was carried out in the 'Orbiter 1G Trainer', an exact replica of the entire capsule, but without the audio-visual effects.

For operating the Arm and the Claw, Michael and Pete had to master the RMS Task Trainer where they learned to remove from the Bay helium-filled models of the different satellites they might encounter, or literally pick them out of space like floating electronic plums.

For Michael, the most interesting part of the training came when he had to learn how to land the vehicle from space, and to do it he had to fly a real aircraft first.

'Colonel, you're now well into your 1,800-hour space-flight orientation course but you've got a further 1,400 hours of flying to do as well.'

Gus Lancaster sat on Michael's right at the controls of the highly developed Grumman Gulfstream twin-engined executive jet.

'This aircraft has been specially modified to recreate the impression of landing the Orbiter so it's been bugged to approach steeply and land fast in the same way as the Shuttle. We've seen you on the SMS so let's get even closer to reality and see you fly this bird like a good Shuttle pilot should.'

It was uncanny, Lancaster thought after the flight, the Jewish boy was very good, just as Adam Wheeler had said. He might well become the best he had ever trained.

28
Beer

'Well, gentleman, the week is up. What do you have to tell me?' Rebecca Limpel was her usual cryptic self, looking better than ever, Landau thought, as he prepared to deliver his report, the pipe sat uncomfortably stuffed in his jacket pocket.

'Prime Minister, this report is of necessity brief but it has involved a great deal of thinking owing to the seriousness of the position we might well find ourselves in by 1980 or 1981. You asked us to say what we would do in the event of a nuclear bomb landing in one of our cities. No matter what the nationality of the soldier who dropped it, we were to assume it was Soviet-made.'

'Correct,' the Prime Minister replied looking straight at Landau.

'We would destroy a Soviet town of the same size,' Landau replied firmly. All eyes were on his.

'Why?'

'Nuclear war is totally different to conventional war. A country who uses it is saying that they will go to any lengths to destroy another. In other words, they are beyond compromise.

'The only country which makes nuclear weapons that are likely to be exploded on Israel is the Soviet Union.

'We must treat the attack as a Nuclear Strike by Russia,' Landau concluded.

'What form would our response take?' she asked.

'We would launch a single aircraft with a bomb of equivalent power on a one-way mission to Russia.'

'Why one-way?' she asked, puzzled now.

'We have few tanker aircraft. Russia is a long way and one aircraft is less vulnerable statistically than a flight of four say, which would then have to carry four bombs. Russia could retaliate with four more bombs.'

'What if the pilot is killed before bombing the target?' Limpel asked more concerned now.

'The bomb will explode anyhow as proof of our ability. There will be no safety device switched on over Russia.' Landau replied.

'Who will fly the aircraft?' she asked looking out of the window at Jerusalem's blue sky as she said it.

'We have 256 volunteers.'

Beer interrupted quietly: 'But I will fly it myself. I created the mission, therefore I accept responsibility.'

Rebecca Limpel tried to conceal the catch in her voice.

'How will you escape . . . once you've dropped the bomb?'

'I will attempt to fly out of Russia, if I don't make it I will go down with the aircraft. I've already practised it once before.' And he rubbed his broken nose, smiling at the memory. 'It is over very quickly, Madam.'

'What aircraft will you use?' she asked.

'The F-15 Eagle.'

'Why not the Phantom?'

'The F-15 is better, far better, and I will be carrying the long-range tanks. I may even make it home again.' Beer replied.

Turning to Zuckerman she asked: 'How will the Russians respond?'

'With surprise, no doubt! They know we have airborne nuclear weapons and the aircraft to deliver them. They will be shocked, angered and vengeful but I think they will not proceed further.' Zuckerman firmly believed this.

There was silence in the room for at least two minutes as Rebecca Limpel rose and walked to the window. The others watched her, knowing that this was not a moment to interrupt her thoughts. She had final responsibility and authority in extreme situations such as these.

She stopped, her figure outlined hazily against the glare of the noon sun, facing towards the 'City of Peace'. She could see due east across President's Park over Nahlat Ahim to the Jaffa Gate of Old Jerusalem. Beyond it stood the holiest land on earth for Jew, Christian and Arab. For some extraordinary reason, she thought, that tiny patch of barren earth was the focus of religion for up to a billion human beings. If this Palestinian existed and was not just a figment of somebody's imagination, then she knew that it would not be Israel that he would destroy. Before that he would start at the place of his birth, Jerusalem.

When Ephraim Zuckerman had followed her out of the committee room the previous week he had brought with him the files on Shimatov and Al Timimi.

'I leave Shimatov to you Mr Zuckerman. Leave me with Al Timimi when you go. Now, please join my family and me for some lunch. I've heard that you are not eating too well since Judith died,' she had said as they walked to her car. Zuckerman was touched that she should remember his wife's death three months before.

'Thank you, Prime Minister, it would be a pleasure to sit down with a "family" again.'

And it was. Ephraim enjoyed himself more than he had for many years. Here was the most revered, feared, abused, acclaimed woman in Israel behaving like a mother, serving her husband and clucking over her youngest, Golda, a girl of eight named after Rebecca's own heroine and predecessor. Rebecca had said to Ephraim as he left after a blessed hour free of work:

'Mr Zuckerman, I will send a car for you every Tuesday at twelve o'clock to bring you here for lunch. Jonathan and I would consider it a privilege if you would consider visiting us any time you wish, free from work of course.' And she had smiled and shook his hand once, firmly. He had not said anything just nodded and smiled back. He could not trust his voice.

Rebecca Limpel had then read Shabir Al Timimi's file at night while her husband slept alongside her in their king-size double bed—her idea, not his.

'Well, gentlemen, what would happen if he attacked Jerusalem . . . or should I say if the Soviets attacked Jerusalem?'

Beer replied for them all.

'I would bomb Leningrad.' His voice was flat, almost matter of fact. There was silence for several seconds, all eyes focused on the woman's face.

Rebecca closed her eyes tight and had an image of death: cindering, writhing death over acres and acres of people and trees and animals and houses and cars and offices as if a giant wall of flame had enveloped the city. And then the flames disappeared and all that was left was utter stillness. She thought of the images of Hiroshima and Nagasaki; of the bomb tests, familiar to the world through repetitive, strident news bulletins; of clever programmes and seminars and conferences and exercises; and—always holding the shining weapons—the smart, disciplined young men acknowledging the cheering crowds. The military bands, the hurrahs and cries and calls; the tramping feet and slapping salutes, of ranks of rifles and the grinding, clanking tanks and suddenly instant total utter irrevocable eternal Death.

Rebecca herself had seen a city bombed by remote control, for she had been a child in London on 15 June 1944 when the German 65th Army Corps had launched more than 200 flying bombs across the Channel towards that sprawling target.

'No, there must be another way. Can't we destroy the weapon before it does any damage?' she asked.

'Only with a Nuclear Strike, Prime Minister,' Landau replied.

She turned towards them and returned to her seat.

'Gentlemen, we cannot countenance a nuclear attack on defenceless civilians. If Israel ever did then she would have forfeited her right to exist. Surely there must be another way.' Her knuckles pressed whitely against the polished table top.

'Madam,' Ephraim Zuckerman interjected, 'we Jews lost six million dead in the Holocaust, we have been persecuted for more than 2,000 years, we now have a State—Israel; we are but 30 years old, as old as that Palestinian. We must defend ourselves. Nobody is contemplating anything but an eye for an eye, the Russians understand that language.' Zuckerman was convinced. 'Besides, we've been through these scenarios time and again.'

She knew he was right, the Cabinet had deliberated regularly on the options for nuclear response.

'Then tell them, Mr Zuckerman, that if they contemplate an attack on Jerusalem or any Israeli city with this beam weapon then we will respond in kind, but for God's sake tell them before they make the mistake. Let them know that we know.'

Landau recognised her tactics immediately.

'Prime Minister, if we tell the Soviets then they will exert enormous worldwide pressure to get us to destroy our nuclear weapons and then we will be utterly defenceless against a nuclear attack. Bluffing will not work.'

She realised immediately she had been wrong to assume Landau's concurrence. Her tone of voice was more sombre, she placed her hands flat on the table, and her wedding ring caught Landau's eye. She seemed resigned. He waited.

'General, if you have seen through my bluff then I'm sure the Russians will, you're quite right.' She turned to the rest, leaving Landau surprised at her candour. 'Please. I want us to create a scheme which will render the Beam ineffective but without resort to nuclear weapons.'

She clasped her hands together.

'Only if there is a major loss of life, involving several thousand Israelis, and a series of nuclear explosions, only then must we countenance a nuclear response. But one thing must be done: the Russians must be warned, clearly, that we know their plans. Please prepare an appropriate plan for us to consider next month, General Landau.

'Meanwhile I want you all to support Ephraim Zuckerman's work at the Institute while he is away in the United States.'

There were raised eyebrows at this new item of information regarding Zuckerman's travel plans. Beer asked: 'What trip is Zuckerman making?'

'He is going to tell the Americans everything we know. We must work with them on the problem but we also cannot rely on them. Mr Zuckerman will be taking Daniel Perès who was leader of the Jericho team working with their General Adam Wheeler, Chief of US Air Force Intelligence, and boss of our own Mossad agent in the US.'

29
Snap

Wheeler was very worried. He had not met Ephraim Zuckerman before but he had great confidence in Daniel Perès, so he addressed him first.

'Daniel, let me get this straight. You are saying that David Greenberg at the National Photographic office is an agent of Mossad, the Israeli Intelligence Service. And that he has been supplying Israel with data and photographs of Soviet developments taken by US reconnaissance satellites. Am I correct?' Wheeler stared hard at the table as he spoke.

'Yes, General. I regret to inform you that your man is also our man. The Government of Israel assures you that no information that he has passed on to us has ever been used against the United States but solely to ensure the survival of the State of Israel.' Daniel looked straight at Wheeler, noting the man's solemn expression. Wheeler looked up at Zuckerman then at Perès, before saying:

'But why are you telling me? You've blown your most important agent in the United States. His information is priceless. It's cost us over ten billion dollars to mount the reconnaissance effort but it's saved us ten times that in avoiding developing weapons to counter non-existent threats. That information has probably saved Israel, so why blow your cover?' Wheeler appeared perplexed.

'Because, General, Mr Zuckerman believes it is essential for us to establish total trust and integrity to overcome the crisis ahead as it could drag the US into a confrontation with the Soviets, Daniel replied. Wheeler turned to the older Israeli.

'Mr Zuckerman, I understand you are Daniel's Chief. Let me tell you, he's the best. We worked together on Jericho I and II. I hope we'll keep it that way. Now I'm trying to put these crazy bits of data together in some sort of order.' Wheeler sounded resigned now.

'Tell me about your crisis before I start on David Greenberg's case.' Wheeler sat back, inviting the man in the baggy suit and open shirt to reply.

Zuckerman spoke for twenty minutes. He'd rehearsed his speech a dozen times in his head. He knew it needed the skill of a diplomat—and the truth—to maintain the trust of the Americans.

When he had finished Wheeler had not interrupted once. A blue haze floated around him, the pipe aroma was strong but not unpleasant. Wheeler sat back and said quietly, 'David, please come in.'

Both Zuckerman and Perès were taken by surprise now as their top US agent came in confidently, a slight grin creasing his face. He sat down next to Wheeler, completely relaxed. The General continued:

'Mr Zuckerman, thank you for the data and a most eloquent analysis of a complex and critical situation. Because of your honesty I will now level with you . . . I have known for seventeen years that David Greenberg was a Mossad man!'

Zuckerman and Perès both sat upright, the statement had come as a total surprise. Wheeler matched Greenberg grin for grin before saying:

'Let me explain some background information. When I was first given this job as Chief of Intelligence for the US Air Force I started with a manhunt. I scoured the country for the best men in their fields. I found David here and I had him trained at the "Photographic Office" as we call it. But I assumed that if he was the best Jewish photo analyst around, then Mossad must have known it also.

Every item of data he supplied to Israel I knew about. My

staff knew about it. It was a decision I made based on my own analysis of the Soviet threat. I won't dwell on it much longer. Suffice it to say that when I heard that you, Mr Zuckerman, were coming to the US, I felt that it was time I relieved David Greenberg of the pressure. So I told him of my knowledge this morning. Which is why he wears that stupid grin on his face,' Wheeler beamed.

Zuckerman burst out laughing, then Perès started, until all four of them recognised the irony of the situation.

Bixby rushed in anxiously. 'I heard shouting. Any trouble, General?'

But Wheeler waved him away saying, 'Captain, I just beat the Mossad at their own game.' Bixby looked perplexed. Wheeler stood up and circled the table.

'Gentlemen, I accept your findings and I want time to assess your proposed responses. Meanwhile, I believe we have a solution that will avoid a catastrophe. It needs the Jericho team again, Daniel. I assume Mr Zuckerman knows all about them, eh?'

'Yes, General, he's fully briefed,' Daniel replied.

'Good. Well, my friends, what we've got to do is work out a way of nullifying that beam satellite if it does in fact endanger Israel, or Jerusalem in particular.

'Also, bear in mind this fact. The United States Government has no intention of allowing the Soviet Union to hold a gun to its head. Even if that gun is the fastest and most powerful gun on earth.

'Do you know how we are going to do it?' he asked.

They didn't. So he told them.

30
Zhukov

Shimatov was jubilant, the latest test had been a total success. The Test Beam at Semipalatinsk had now succeeded in vaporising a brand-new T72 tank at a range of 24 miles in fifty nanoseconds. The tank weighed in at 40 tons. In a few millionths of a second it had vanished in a cloud of glowing gas that saturated the target zone, two miles under Semipalatinsk in Central Asia.

The test had finally confirmed that the beam could now be precisely controlled to transmit a given density of charged particles for a given density of target. Any excess of charge affected anything in the path of the beam behind the target and vaporised the appropriate mass of matter. The scientists at Semipalatinsk called it the Proportional Charge Effect. It was very significant, for by turning a density control and focusing the beam automatically, using a laser rangefinder, the operator could tune the beam to match the target.

As Shimatov flew back to Tyuratam he felt more excited than at any time since Gagarin's flight way back in 1961.

He was approaching the achievement of his sole objective in life. The control of a weapon with which he could break the nuclear stalemate between the Soviet Union and the United States. With this beam he knew the Soviet Union possessed a weapon of exquisite discretion. From its unassailable platform in space it could cover the entire earth, ranging free to do its Government's bidding.

The tests now confirmed it could be controlled by one man

in orbit who could track, range and lock onto his selected target, be it a man, a tank, an aircraft or a missile. Then, by throwing three trigger switches, he could arm, charge and fire the beam having already focused the beam spread—from half a metre to several metres in diameter. It had perfect accuracy!

Shimatov thought of the tests he had witnessed, including the cadaver that vaporised in a pink mist, the section of submarine hull twenty feet below the surface of a salt water tank—everything had disappeared in a ball of metallic steam. He had seen sections of one-metre-thick reinforced concrete 'pop' into a flinty sand that took ten hours to cool down—the crew had even brought in an obsolete Mig 21 and fired a half-metre beam at it along the 22-mile steel-lined tunnel. The light metal had vaporised so completely that the entire mirrored glass target sphere in which it sat had received a further coating of aluminium oxide over its surface. 'Zhukov' worked very, very well.

The big Mil M-I8 helicopter whined to a halt as Shimatov walked to his black Zil. He smiled at Mendeleiv and climbed in beside him. Tyuratam was always windy, he thought.

'Mendeleiv, Zhukov works. It's perfect. We'll have the flight model ready for launch by 1980. It's beautiful, quite beautiful.'

Mendeleiv was delighted with his boss's enthusiasm and the two drove straight over to meet the men they'd selected to operate it. The three men stood to attention as Shimatov and Mendeleiv appeared in the Simulator Building. The crews were always pleased to see Shimatov but disliked Mendeleiv's presence. After all, Shimatov was the flyer, Mendeleiv one of those 'KGBastards' as they sometimes called them. Always probing around, checking up on you. Shimatov led off as usual.

'Well, Soyuz Team 47, I hear you've completed all launch, rendezvous and docking tests both with Salyut and Zhukov, and you, Colonel Al Timimi, have carried out a successful simulated operation of the Zhukov trigger.'

'Yes sir, Instructor Kerensky has given us full flight

clearance,' Shabir replied with pride. Their 2,500 hours of training was almost at an end.

'Excellent, cosmonauts. Congratulations.'

Then with a sardonic grin Shimatov added: 'I'm sure General Mendeleiv here is pleased also.'

Mendeleiv concurred, distant as usual. He started his speech.

'Cosmonauts, you have done well, congratulations. But remember your task is only now beginning. When you leave Colonel Al Timimi in the Salyut, from which he will operate the Zhukov, you must ensure that you return to earth as soon as possible. There must be no Soviet cosmonaut anywhere near Zhukov when Al Timimi is firing it. The political repercussions would be complicated. Good luck and my congratulations to you, General, on your excellent direction of the training programme. I must leave you now. Goodbye and I will see you at the launch in twelve weeks time.' Mendeleiv left and everybody relaxed, Shimatov took over.

'Marvellous my friends, he's very impressed, and I have excellent news for you. You can forget that mock-up of Zhukov. The real one will be here next week!'

31
Orbiter 102

For Michael it had to be one of the most memorable days of his life. He had at last, after 3,218 hours of instruction, been awarded the coveted certificate of clearance to fly the Space Shuttle and, only the morning before, Diana had said to him at the hospital in Houston:

'Darling, he's just like nobody I know.'

And Michael had not laughed, just gazed in awe at his infant son David, named after the long dead tractor boy who had pulled him out of the furrows of the potato field in Golan. Michael gazed at the tiny, helpless, pink person who lay silent and sleeping, wrapped in a bundle of whiteness and cradled in his arms. He wrote to Liza that night, enclosing the Polaroid photos with the letter. He felt very good about life and now he had a son there was even more of a future to build.

The following week the Allon family, the Cohens and most of the Jericho team were at Kennedy Space Center to watch the launch of the very first Space Shuttle. Little David had arrived just in time.

Orbiter 102 sat on the pad at launch complex 39A, and piloting it were Michael's two good friends, John Young and Bob Crippen. He wished he had been in on the Shuttle as early as them so as to have the chance of actually being the first into orbit, but at least he would be among the first Shuttle pilots during the orbital flight test programme.

The white spacecraft looked massive and clumsy as it sat

on its tail, the Orbiter soaring over 120 feet above the huge grey mobile platform while the immense External Tank, weighing over one and a half million pounds, reached 184 feet high, full to the brim with the most violently explosive fuel of liquid hydrogen and oxygen.

On the other side of the ET the two Solid Rocket Boosters looked like giant legs supporting the tank while the whole assembly appeared to balance on the tip of the Orbiter's sloping tail fin. The atmosphere was electric: American men were going back into space after five long years. As they watched, along with over half a billion television viewers around the world, the Jericho team witnessed the start of a new era in space travel and the first flight of the successor to Blackbird.

In silence, three columns of solid flame flooded out of the Orbiter's three main engines before the noise travelled the three miles to the viewing stands. It was a crackling, thunderous, quaking sound that shook the spectators and flooded their senses. Michael felt a shiver run down his spine and then everybody started to clap as the boosters poured out two massive pillars of flame, generating enormous clouds of steam from the cooling ducts under the pad. Then the cheering started and Michael found himself shouting at the sheer grandeur of the scene as Orbiter 102, the world's first spaceship, slowly lifted off into the Florida sky.

The glistening white assembly rose faster and faster on a huge cascade of flame and the noise intensified as the source rose above the absorbent marshes of the Cape. Now it was deafening, almost painful, and it went on and on as the Space Shuttle headed towards SRB separation in two minutes time. Up and up it soared as people cheered and screamed and clapped.

Michael realised his cheeks were wet and Diana gazed in awe and fright, clutching her infant, thinking that soon it would be just her and little David in the stand praying while Michael rode in that giant, frightening machine.

Michael looked at his father's watch that he had worn ever since Liza had visited him in California and for a moment felt a pang of sadness at the thought that his dead parents had been robbed of the knowledge that their own son would one day go into space. Then he looked up and saw through the telescope they had mounted for the Shuttle crews to watch the launch, the disappearing spaceship, clear white against the deepening blue. Dead on time he saw the booster separating from each side of the Orbiter as it slowly offered more of its tail to the observers, now 27 miles below.

Within another minute it was all too far away and Michael looked back at the towering cloud of steam engulfing the empty pad while the noise still rumbled in the sky. He turned towards Diana and seeing the look of fear behind her eyes, he put both arms round her and his child saying softly into her long black hair:

'Baby, it'll be alright. I promise it'll be alright.' But all Diana could see was an image of a giant fireball bursting across the sky.

32
Jericho III

'It's definitely arrived, look, there on the visual image. We plotted the same truck leaving Semipalatinsk two days before. We caught it along the Northern shore of Lake Balkhash and now we see it entering the Assembly Building.' Greenberg was becoming excited.

'Any SAR imagery?' Wheeler asked, hoping the synthetic aperture radar might have revealed the shape of the satellite concealed by the truck's bodywork.

'Yes, it's here,' Daniel interjected.

'That's good, very good.' Wheeler admired the clear outline of the satellite revealed by the radar's reflected beams, like an X-ray picture taken at 100 miles.

'Any infra-red?' Wheeler asked, always anxious for corroboration.

'Yes, and this one is the final piece of the jigsaw,' Greenberg said pointing to a white spot on the third photograph.

'That's the emission characteristic similar to a protected nuclear isotope or a nuclear device. As the Weizmann people assumed, it must have a nuclear fusion generator coupled with a cryogenic cooling system. That's shown in the long black lines and plates, areas of extreme coolness. It's a brilliant piece of work, quite outstanding. I'd give anything to see it in reality.'

'We will, David, we will, I'm afraid to say. My, she's a big baby, isn't she?'

'We scaled her to 48 feet long and 10 feet wide but I guarantee they'll fit her with solar panels at Tyuratam. She's fairly big by Soviet standards but not larger than our own Big Birds.' Greenberg continued.

'The next major event for us to photograph will be a few days before the actual launch, they'll need the big D-I-H Proton booster, same as they use for Salyut. And remember, they'll need two further launchers as well as another D-I-H to launch the Salyut space station. Finally, they'll need a third smaller Soyuz launcher to lift the guy up there. It's going to get very busy at Tyuratam.'

'How's our crew doing, Gus?' Wheeler turned to Lancaster, who was enthralled by the entire operation.

'Well, Adam, I think you sent me the best apple in the store there. That Colonel Allon is some pilot. The best I've seen in nearly twenty years of working with astronauts. He's got the coolness of an Armstrong, the brilliance of an Aldrin and the character of a Borman. Yes he's ready to go. His buddy Peabody is the ideal partner, utterly reliable and good-natured. David Brown, the Mission Specialist, is going to do more for astronauts than John Shaft ever did for detectives. He's outstanding on the Arm, better than Allon or Peabody and that's his job. The three of them will match any three Russians, Arabs, Chinese or what have you, any day of the week.' Lancaster was confident.

'Not just any day of the week, Gus. On THE day, remember that.' Wheeler said.

'How's the vehicle progressing, Bill?' Wheeler turned to Bill Kennedy, the man in charge of the preparation of Orbiter 102 from the contractors Rockwell International.

'She's going fine, General. She'll be ready in three days now. She's made nine flights already with very few problems. She's got the modified Claw as you requested and the retaining jig you asked for. That's worked fine in the tests and those guys of yours, Mr Lancaster, know exactly how to use it. Yes, I'm pretty confident, sir.'

'Well done, Bill. Tell your people at Downey and Palmdale that they've done an outstanding job under considerable pressure. We'll make sure we take care of your baby.' Wheeler turned to Jerome Mancini, the NASA co-ordinator:

'Everything ready at Houston, Jerome, your guys in position to control the show?'

'Sure thing, Adam, just tell us when. This one's got to be a sell-out. We're running a series of readiness tests now with the TDRSS satellites. We can guarantee you worldwide real-time satellite communications. You'll get voice, telemetry and TV coverage right there at Omaha, including launch and landing. We've got eight Baker Nunn camera teams around the world ready to record their observations and we're fully integrated into NORAD's Space Tracking service. Your fellows won't be able to scratch their fannies without us recording it a dozen ways.'

Jerome Mancini was an excessively thin, highly intelligent, communications 'nut', as he readily admitted, who felt his greatest achievement had been the filming of the birth of all six of his children. He'd donated a video copy that was much appreciated by the Houston Maternity Hospital for use in pre-natal classes.

Bill Kennedy, on the other hand, was a short stocky man in his forties, looking much like Wheeler but with less hair. They could almost have been brothers. He was one of the finest engineers produced in Minnesota and ran Orbiter 102 like a watch, with infinite care and attention to detail. He was very proud of his company's achievement and never let an opportunity go by without making that fact known. He had even jokingly suggested that Rockwell paint a big sign on the side of NASA's Boeing 747 during the ALT tests, pointing up at the white Orbiter 101 Enterprise and saying: 'This Boeing Will Shortly Be Dropped By The Rockwell Space Shuttle'.

Wheeler appreciated enthusiasm and he needed it more now than on any special operation he had ever undertaken because only he and the Jericho III team, as it was now called, knew that the future of a city, a state or even the world would depend on every member of the team carrying out his job perfectly. Wheeler looked at his digital watch and said:

'Gentlemen, I think we may be in business within 14 days from now. So let's take up our positions. I will be at Omaha, along with Daniel Perès, to act as liaison man with Ephraim Zuckerman, who will remain in Israel as part of the Government's War Cabinet. Bill, you'll stay at Downey to stand by to solve any special engineering problems that might develop during the flight. Gus, you'll be at the Cape for 102's launch and then return to Houston to be with Jerome during the flight. I think you'll all be pleased to know that I have briefed the Chiefs of Staff of all Services, the NSA and the CIA.

'NASA, Rockwell and Jericho III will liaise solely through me with the Pentagon and the White House. Here are your organisation and communication charts, with your code names, call signs and security clearances to use on secure Defence lines.

'Each of you will be responsible for his own organisation and will contact me using a mobile communications set that will be manned and maintained by my own technicians, so there'll be no foul-ups. My guys are standing outside the door right now already assigned to each one of you. Dave Greenberg will feed me with all sensor data from satellites, U2s, ELINT, vessels, monitoring stations and agents-in-place. He will co-ordinate with SAMSO—the Space and Missile Systems Organisation—and Aerospace Defence Command so that I will be at the hub of the data network around the world. If any of you guys need a decision or an opinion you come to me. Never hesitate. I will get clearance myself from the Chiefs of Staff and when necessary the Commander-in-Chief himself.'

Wheeler was in his organisational element now, reminding Daniel Perès of a Merlin preparing his magic spells for the final conflict with the Necromancer. Wheeler continued.

'Finally, you should all know that I flew yesterday to see the President personally at the White House. He is now fully briefed, as are the Secretaries of State for all services and Defence.

'President Stockman spent twelve hours discussing the situation and, believe me, this is not the first he's heard about it. He has now spoken to our Ambassadors for the UN, the Soviet Union and Israel. NATO has been briefed through the Supreme Allied Commander in Europe and all US military commands have been placed on alert. We know the Soviets will monitor this and that's exactly what we intend. When Brezhnev assembled his troops to invade Israel in October 1973 after the Egyptian 3rd Army was surrounded, President Nixon alerted US forces throughout the world. He only slipped up in not telling NATO too much, so the Europeans got cross and rightly so. This time there will be no foul-up. Nixon's response worked and we hope the Russians will behave the same way this time.

'The President asked me to assure you all that he has no intention of having a gun, no matter how powerful, held to his head by any Russian—let alone any Palestinian. He firmly believes that there is a peaceful solution to the Arab-Israeli conflict but the enormous military, economic and propaganda resources of the Soviet Union, under the direction of the KGB, have been designed to achieve one goal—namely a State of War in the Middle East, which the Soviets could then exploit eventually to control the oil. The President is tired of it as he believes the Russians are the protagonists, so from now on, gentlemen, the United States Government is going to concentrate its efforts on exposing the KGB and its agents whilst creating a climate of conciliation between Arabs and Jews.

'Our job is to neutralise that rogue Palestinian and his Beam satellite before he starts a major war.' Wheeler turned to Daniel Perès and said quietly:

'Daniel, you and your people have every right to question the word of the US Government after recent events in the world. I assure you that we know we made mistakes and I believe that with President Stockman we have a leader who will set us back on the right course. He is acutely aware of the weakness of our strategic position being so dependent on imported energy and capitalised by politically sensitive rulers.

'I know you Israelis fear the leverage of these Arab rulers because of their control of oil and you have every good reason to do so but things are changing. Within the next twenty years he aims to put this country back on a self-sufficient basis, through nuclear power and solar energy, including solar-powered satellites.'

Wheeler turned back to the others who listened quietly to the man's discourse.

'At the same time, he intends to resolve conflicts by peaceful negotiations and that means he has to reduce the power of the KGB severely. The President knows Russia fairly well, gentlemen, from having visited it as a young businessman many times. He's been to Moscow, Leningrad, Vladivostock and even Odessa, selling agricultural machinery back in the early sixties, when trading was really tough. So he speaks Russian fairly well. He's also visited Cairo, Damascus and Beirut, before it was destroyed, as well as Jerusalem and Tel Aviv.

'All of this information, gentlemen, he's asked me to tell you because he wants you to be confident that all your efforts have one goal—peace in the Middle East and a rekindling of our self-respect as American citizens.

'He's going to keep personal tight control on our overall posture and he'll be flying in the E4B Command Post from Andrews Air Force Base when necessary. As you all know the E4B is a very special version of the Boeing 747. In fact it's the most expensive aircraft ever made. It's fitted out for the Commander-in-Chief to command all US and NATO forces throughout the world. It's got a full conference room for all Chiefs of Staff together with their coding and communications facilities. It has a satellite-tracking antenna in its back so it is fully integrated into the Defence Communications Satellite network. President Stockman can maintain direct voice and television contact with the men in Orbiter 102 if they are required to fly and, believe me, the President will be in a position to make immediate and direct contact all the time with the Soviet President now that the 'Hot Line' is satellite-powered. I assure you, gentlemen, that the Russians cannot make a significant move in the game without us knowing about it, and they will know that.

'The President will not communicate with the Soviet leader until a certain stage has been reached. He has no intention of being forced to show his hand until it is absolutely essential, so the first moves will be directly between Israel and the Soviets if, as we suspect, Israel is the target.

'History is too full of major conflicts started by reckless single-minded individuals totally dedicated to avenge their own particular grievances. Many, many times battles and major wars have started with a single outrageous act. The First World War started when a bomb killed the Archduke Ferdinand in a carriage in Sarajevo. The Third World War could have started when John Kennedy was assassinated, believe me a lot of people in the CIA and the Pentagon thought, and still do, that the KGB was behind that one. Back in 1963 the US could have blown the Soviet Union off the map, but at a significant loss to our own population.

'Incredible as it may sound, when my team completed the first accurate satellite survey of the entire Soviet Union between 1961 and 1965 using the Discoverer, Samos and Midas programmes, we found that virtually all major Soviet cities, towns, harbours, railway depots, you name it, were an average of fifteen miles away from the position shown on official Soviet maps. And that's a fact! Imagine if we'd gone to war with Russia as a panic response after Kennedy's death, using their maps, our bombs and missiles would have landed fifteen miles off target. Even with a big weapon you cannot destroy a strategic target if you're that far away.

'So we will act during this emergency firstly with accurate data, secondly with thoughtful planning, thirdly with adequate secure communications, and fourthly using minimum force. Is that clear, gentlemen, do you have any questions? Daniel?'

'Only one. It isn't even a question, but I wish you'd just made that speech to my Prime Minister. You're her kind of man.' said Daniel with genuine admiration.

'Well Daniel, I just did. She's watching us all on that camera.' and Wheeler pointed to the TV surveillance camera covering the conference room.

'I thought we ought to start the job together, right now. Say hello to your Prime Minister, Daniel. I already did two hours ago when my boys made the hook-up.' Wheeler beamed. It was obviously a pleasure to work with the Israelis. Rebecca Limpel's face appeared on the TV monitor screen beside the conference table. She was smiling and said to Daniel:

'Shalom, Mr Perès, we are all together now. I have the War Cabinet here with me and of course Mr Zuckerman, your Chief. We have complete confidence in you and the Jericho team. I have spoken personally to President Stockman earlier today, whom I have met on two occasions previously. Once in Washington last year during my official visit and once many years ago in London during a quite unofficial visit,' and she smiled, obviously enjoying her reputation as the femme fatale of world politics. 'You have nothing to fear in this situation, Daniel, but fear itself. Just do your job as you always have. Good luck. Shalom.' She was gone, never one to waste words or time. Daniel Perès watched the blank screen for a few seconds before turning to General Wheeler.

'General, with a leader like that and a President such as you Americans have, we must succeed.'

33
Apartment 21

The pregnant woman waddled in obvious discomfort up the entrance steps of the apartment block clutching her heavily loaded shopping bag in one hand while she steadied herself with the other. The young policeman, fresh from cadet school, hurried to her aid, anxious to feel he had done his 'bit' for the day. Her face smiled through the heavy woollen headscarf that framed her brown curls and she thanked him at the top of the steps for carrying the bag.

'Only another month, thank goodness.'

She panted as she took the bag. He even gave her a little salute as she walked into the lobby. Suddenly he remembered he had not asked her name or who she was visiting. But it was too late now. She had already closed the lift doors behind her. Within minutes he had forgotten to worry about the little slip in his duties.

The lift rocked noisily upwards until it reached the fifth floor and Tanya Ludmilla stepped on to the landing, closing the doors quietly behind her. She looked around before she spotted the number 21 on the door and knocked twice. She could hear noises and then the door opened and she looked at the face she felt she knew so well.

'Bykovsky, please, Valentina Bykovsky?' she enquired.

'Yes?' The voice came from the most beautiful face she could remember. She was even lovelier than her photographs but that was not surprising considering they were so fuzzy and out of focus.

'Valentina, my name is Tanya Ludmilla from the Odessa Maternity Clinic.'

'Oh yes, can I help you?' Valentina recognised the name of the place very well. She had been an ex-patient.

'I wonder if I could ask a favour of you?' Tanya winced at her own discomfort.

'Yes, please come in, you look tired. How long is it?'

'Just another month,' Tanya replied as she walked into the tiny apartment, smiling her appreciation.

'There, is that comfortable?' Valentina spoke with concern as she showed her visitor to the sofa.

'Perfect. I'm sorry to disturb you, Valentina Bykovsky.'

'That's alright. I was just putting my child to sleep,' She wiped her hands on a towel over a chair.

'How is he?' Tanya asked.

'He's fine, but . . . I don't remember meeting you at the Clinic. Forgive me, my memory isn't too good,' Valentina replied.

'No, Valentina, we didn't meet at the Clinic or ever before, but I feel I know you so well.' Tanya meant every word. Valentina looked puzzled and sat on the chair opposite, leaning to avoid the towel, clasping her hands together.

'I'm sorry, I don't understand. Was it a friend we both know?' she asked.

'Yes, in a way, but tell me first, is your son asleep?' Tanya asked, lifting her eyebrows as she did so.

'Yes, he's very good, no trouble at all.'

'I'm sure he is.' She paused, then said, 'Valentina, this will come as a shock to you. I am a friend of Shabir Al Timimi, the father of your son, Nicholas.'

And Valentina went cold all over and sat up rigid in the chair, her heart racing as she felt the blood storm into her face, then she felt giddy and weak. She stretched out a hand, but Tanya caught it in time and held her before moving her crumpling body onto the small sofa. Then the tears came welling up out of her lovely eyes and she covered her face with her hands and started to sob as Tanya bent down to cradle her in her arms.

Tanya Ludmilla left the next day, her eyes red with emotion and fatigue, totally drained of nervous energy after the longest night of her life. The young policeman watched her go, waddling slowly down the street towards the harbour at Odessa, there on the Black Sea, home of the Soviet Black Sea Fleet.

He looked at her slowly diminishing figure then smiled to himself, returning quickly to his dreams of one day making the most important arrest of the year.

34
Tablet One

Yigal Beer said one phrase into the phone at his underground headquarters:

'Tablet One.' Then he stood up and walked out of his chamber on the route to his plane.

At last the news had come through on the red cypher machine, confirmed three times and in three different ways, all of which required an electronic inter-lock for final proof of authenticity. The Russians were moving the first D-I-H launcher onto the pad at Tyuratam complete with its shrouded satellite. Big Bird proved it. It was time to get ready.

As Beer walked, already partly dressed in flying kit, his Deputy, Eli Hamodai, calmly prepared to take command at the Control Centre when required, having received Beer's call. It was standard procedure that at least six senior officers were sufficiently trained to assume Command of the Air Force in case of death or incapacity. Beer took seven minutes to kit up fully at the Ready Room, then stepped into the air-conditioned van that would carry him to his aircraft. The armoured van travelled a mile away to the shelter and drove straight into an opening in the armoured steel blast doors.

Inside, protected from anything but a direct hit, waited the world's best combat aircraft. The McDonnell Douglas F15 Eagle. The plane that now ensured that no Foxbats dared to fly over Israel because this lethal weapon was designed to blow them out of the sky, at any altitude. The aircraft sat in its dirty grey camouflage, fully fuelled and armed. As Tablet One was the first stage of deployment agreed by the Emergency War Cabinet, it would test the ability of the IAF to disperse in readiness for a nuclear war.

Tablet was the best kept secret of Israel's nuclear capability. It was also known as 'Total Nuclear Response' and unofficially as the 'Armageddon Posture'.

As Beer walked round his aircraft he checked the surfaces, ensuring that nobody had forgotten—they never had yet—to secure the many inspection panels, safety devices and most important of all, the single streamlined 'nuclear device' as it was called, slung under the centreline of the aircraft's wide belly.

The Eagle had sufficient power from its twin Pratt & Whitney F100 turbofans to reach 100,000 feet in less than four minutes from brake release. Once there, its normal armament of four Sparrow air-to-air missiles mounted in two rows along the bottom edges of its twin air intakes could snap up or down under the guidance of its incredible Westinghouse radar. Its further complement of four Sidewinders and the massive 20mm M61 rotary cannon ensured its survival against all known aircraft.

Beer looked up at the big shoulder-mounted delta wing with its swept-back tips, checking the leading edge was undamaged. Back at its tail he walked behind the twin jet pipes with their corrugated black nozzles, noting the tall vertical fins carried on opposite sides of the engines.

He checked the tailplane leading edges with their 'dog tooth' projection and then approached the device. It looked unimpressive, a simple white cylinder with a pointed nose cone and a conical tapering tail with long sharply swept tailfins. It had no distinguishing marks saying 'Israel' or 'Dimona' or 'to Russia with love'. It was a neutral object, twelve feet long and two feet in diameter, suspended from his aircraft.

Beer checked the safety shackles and approached the ladder. He climbed up, checked the ejector seat safety flags and then, gripping the single canopy frame arch, settled into the aircraft. The view always pleased him for, after flying Phantoms, the F15's single seat emerged a good three feet above the base of the tear-drop-shaped canopy.

Within minutes he was ready to move out. He signalled his ground crew and closed the canopy over his white bone dome accompanied by the gentle hum of electrics. The long tapering nose of the Eagle pointed at the massive roller-mounted blast door. A brilliant crack of light appeared to his left, widening gradually until eventually, stretched across his view, was the panorama of the airfield. With a whine that grew to a roar IAF F15 Eagle under the Command of Yigal Beer taxied menacingly out into the Middle East sun.

It stood on its brakes as the huge engines roared into an ear-bursting crescendo of noise, and then started its take-off run. The combined afterburning thrust of the engines exceeded its actual loaded weight of 49,000 pounds, giving it tremendous acceleration, for within 900 feet it was off, its nose-wheel folding forwards while the main undercarriage snapped into the air-intake fairings.

Beer pulled his plane back so that its twin tails cleared the desert runway and scorched over the airfield boundary at 200 feet before banking steeply to the left and turning through 180-degress. As he approached his intended bearing of due south he flicked back, wings now dead level, with the ground disappearing below at almost 700 miles an hour. He headed straight for the Negev Desert.

At eight airfields in Sinai, Golan, Galilee, Tel Aviv and Eilat, a further 47 Eagles, Phantoms and Kfirs roared off to their lairs in near-perfect synchronisation. They were the members of the super-secret Nokum squadron, the 'Revenge' force of the State of Israel in its ultimate crisis.

As Beer flew south to Negev he thought of the day Nokum was born, just an idea of a young Air Force pilot. It was back in 1957 and he had been leading a flight of three Mystère fighter-bombers over Golan. They were attacking a Syrian artillery position that had shelled one of the kibbutzes. He even remembered the name, Kibbutz Ramta. Yigal had gone in first followed by his younger brother, Moshe, warning him as always to keep close and not to try anything stupid.

As they approached the target they had seen another Mystère returning from a raid on Syria, and obviously lost. They had intercepted it, waggling their wings to warn it as they turned on either side of it through 180-degrees to fly alongside. The pilot was from another squadron and not too sure of his position. They had signalled for him to follow them for the fun, his cannon and fuel tanks coming in useful, they thought. Down they had dived before separating for a 360-degrees cross-over attack.

Yigal remembered seeing the startled face of a little boy peering out from the kibbutz shelter as he screamed overhead, very low, before pulling up for a second run. He saw for a moment Moshe's aircraft below him on its bombing run. He had two 250-pound bombs that smacked straight into the target area with enormous bangs. Then the visitor had come in a few seconds later and he was not carrying fuel but napalm, and it just spewed all over the position.

Yigal had then come in on a strafing run to make sure of the target's destruction, flying straight through the smoke before banking for the return flight to base. As he looked over his shoulder he saw Moshe and the visitor screaming in, also to strafe, but then he broke into a sweat as he saw Moshe do a crazy victory climb, directly over the blazing target.

'No, Moshe, no!' Yigal screamed down the throat mike but it was too late and the Syrian cannon shells blew off his brother's port wing, opening the tanks.

'Get out Moshe, eject, eject!' He had screamed and was relieved to see his brother's seat fire straight out, cleanly, from the climbing, dying aircraft. Yigal cheered as he saw the parachute open and he pulled over hard, desperately flying towards him where he could fly a protective circle once his brother touched down safely. The erupting plane blew up some distance away and then Yigal felt a cold sickness flood over him. Moshe was falling into the fire of his own bombs and the napalm.

Yigal powered towards the second burst of cannon fire, joined by the visitor, but there was nothing they could do and he distinctly saw his brother steer deliberately into the fire rather than be captured by the Syrians. It was all over in seconds, the canopy caught alight and Moshe fell silently, tumbling a thousand feet to the inferno on the ground.

That night Yigal had talked to his commanding officer about forming an élite squadron to avenge the death of his brother. The 'old man', as they thought of him, understood the young pilot's feelings but gave him advice he had always remembered.

'Yigal Beer, you are no good to Israel dead. Keep alive, use your mind. Plan for Israel, not for yourself or even your family. Israel is now yourself and your family. Consider its enemies and vow that Israel, not you, will be avenged if she is destroyed by them.'

Beer was now close to his landing strip in the Negev. Not a runway or a strip of desert salt, but a perfectly ordinary road, indistinguishable from any other, threading its way across the barren land broken by its outcrops of ancient rocks and caves.

Beer did not circle, that was strictly forbidden, but simply placed his aircraft down firmly on the road, having memorised its location from many familiarisation flights. He stopped with airbrake fully deployed above his aircraft's spine, the braking parachute, painted black for camouflage, streaming, and the Eagle came to a halt 500 feet from a particularly large cluster of rocks partly overgrown with desert scrub.

Suddenly the 'brush' moved aside off the face of the rock to reveal a large cave. Without hesitating he taxied straight into the blackness, leaving sufficient space to swing round inside in a half circle where he stopped, facing the entrance. Within seconds the bushes and desert plants slid back to conceal the opening and Beer was sitting in his 'Muara', his cave. Nokum and Muara were Beer's own ideas that he had planned for many years while he was promoted rapidly up the ladder of command of the world's toughest Air Force.

Among the IAF's few hundred aircraft were dispersed Nokum pilots, their planes discreetly adapted to carry the nuclear devices that Israel built at Dimona in the Northern Negev Desert.

Tablet was the posture that Israel had decided to adopt as its final answer to Soviet aggression. In the event of nuclear war being launched by the Soviet Union on Israel's four million population all the Weizmann Institute's studies showed categorically that 90 per cent of Israelis would die. The State of Israel would be destroyed.

Having lost six million Jews in the Holocaust, Israel was determined that never again would she rely on any state for ultimate protection. Tablet assured the destruction of ten Russians for every Israeli because 48 nuclear devices were targeted to destroy or immobilise Moscow, Leningrad, Odessa and Minsk whilst a second contingency plan would destroy Damascus, Baghdad, Tripoli or any other Arab capital city from which the attack might originate. For a tiny nation that had destroyed the equivalent of the entire NATO front-line forces using conventional weapons in 1973, Israel knew better than anybody how to fly through Soviet defences and win.

As Beer waited for his engines to run down and the steps to be extended, he thought of the black tarmac of the road. That had been Zuckerman's idea, to act as a heat absorbing surface, making it difficult for Russian infra-red sensors to track the Nokum aircraft as they slipped into their Muaras.

Within five minutes, Yigal Beer was sitting 200 feet below his aircraft in his Dispersed Command Post receiving the results of Tablet One. It had all worked smoothly without any hitches. All 48 aircraft were now ready and being refuelled. He picked up the red phone and said simply:

'Tablet Two. Stand by.' Israel was now ready to fight a nuclear war with the Soviet Union.

35

Soyuz 47

Shabir watched on his TV monitor the launch pad at Tyuratam, just as he had that day five years back, only this time it was not a Cosmos reconnaissance satellite going up on a Soyuz launcher, but Zhukov, protected from the Russian winter under its white metal and glass-fibre shroud on top of the huge D-1-H launcher.

Even from two miles distance it looked big with its six cylindrical first-stage boosters clustered round the central core. The whole rocket was shaped like a magnum of champagne but with a long neck and an even longer cork. It was a military green as usual, including the third stage sitting on the core.

Above this sat the orbital insertion stage below Zhukov itself. The whole assembly exceeded 200 feet in height and when the wind blew it actually swayed a perceptible two centimetres at the top.

And then as Shabir adjusted the TV picture the launcher ignited. A huge cloud of flame and steam shot out like a dragon's breath from the pad, the service arms lay folded back and were totally enveloped when the vehicle started to rise. Slowly, but with gathering momentum, the world's most sophisticated weapon of war was lifted into the skies of Central Asia. It was a vivid experience as the most powerful rocket in the Soviet Union thundered away arcing slowly towards its orbit 100 miles above the earth and inclined at 55-degrees to the Equator.

The launch was a total success as signals from the vast Soviet tracking network and the rocket itself confirmed in succession: booster separation, central core burn-out and separation, third-stage separation, and finally the news Shabir and his cosmonaut friends had waited years to hear: 'Orbital insertion completed successfully.'

The three of them cheered, in spite of the cramped conditions of the Soyuz capsule and their full space suits, knowing they were one step closer to their mission.

The next 90 minutes were totally taken up with their own pre-flight inspection as Shabir Al Timimi, Boris Tsiolkovsky and Valentin Karpov prepared themselves to follow in four and a half hours time, after the launch of the second D-I-H carrying Salyut 7, their own space station with which they would dock their Soyuz spacecraft.

As they waited Vladimir Shimatov was having the fight of his life with the President of the Soviet Union, to prevent him from cancelling their flight.

'General Shimatov, I have not cancelled the flight of Zhukov 1 or of Salyut 7, but I must consider changing the crew of Soyuz 47.

'The Foreign Minister of Israel has declared in the United Nations General Assembly in New York within the past hour that the Soviet Union has prepared a super weapon which it is launching today into earth orbit, and which orbit passes over Israel. He has asked for an emergency meeting of the Security Council. Needless to say, the Arab nations and our other friends have vetoed this. We ourselves have exercised our veto and promised to veto any moves in the Security Council.

'Do you understand what has happened? You've been found out. As the Americans say, Shimatov, you've been blown.'

'But, sir, this could all be a bluff, there is no way the Israelis know enough about Zhukov to convince the United Nations, and even if they did, who would care. The Americans? Never, not nowadays. Things have changed since Vietnam, sir. They are falling over backwards to avoid offending us. Who but a maniac would rely on SALT talks, but the Americans do. Sir, we are winning, the Soviet Union is winning, we have achieved nuclear superiority. Now the Americans can spend the next 35 years wondering if we will drop a bomb on *them*!' Shimatov was controlling his frustration just enough to avoid offending the only individual more powerful than he in the Soviet Union.

'Shimatov, tell me, how did the Israelis discover Zhukov? You and Mendeleiv told me and the rest of the CPSU that your security was perfect. How, how did the Israelis find out?' The President was coldly furious now at the enormous coup the Israelis had pulled.

'Through American Big Birds, nothing else. They don't have anything but photographs and rumours. The Israelis are bluffing them,' Shimatov replied with absolute conviction.

'Can you assure me and the CPSU of that?' the President asked.

'Yes sir, nobody could have penetrated our security, nobody.' Shimatov sat back in his chair placing his hands on his knees and looking hard at his Chief. The President sat back himself and thought for a few minutes before saying:

'Shimatov, I want your assurance in writing, now. In return you may launch your crew, including the Palestinian. Call the Israeli bluff, let's draw them out. Carry on while I instruct the Foreign Minister.'

An aide appeared, summoned by a silent signal and the Soviet President said one sentence to him. Within a minute a wedge of white stationery appeared on a tray of seals and fountain pens.

After Shimatov signed the declaration dictated by his leader, he rose stiffly and left. Once outside he ran for his car and made straight for Dzerzhinsky Square, headquarters of the KGB, the infamous 'Centre'. He arrived at his office via a separate building that acted as a 'filter' for agents wishing to conceal their identity. He walked briskly into the communications room and ordered the TV cameras to be switched on.

Shabir and his colleagues were delighted to suddenly see the face of their Chief on the monitor. He wished them good luck as he would now be leaving for Semipalatinsk immediately by helicopter and military jet. They cheered him enthusiastically before his face disappeared, replaced by the view of the second D-1-H, ready to chase the unmanned Zhukov in orbit.

Again the launch was a total success and seven minutes later the last step before their own launch had been successfully completed. The Salyut space station was now in correct orbit and ready to receive them in the silence of space in three hours time.

36
Stand-off

General Wheeler was very, very worried. The diplomatic approach had failed and monitoring showed conclusively that a second giant Proton launcher had just left Tyuratam and now NORAD tracking confirmed its satellite in close orbit with the previous payload, thought to be the Beam satellite. What was more, NORAD's high-resolution ground-based TV cameras and worldwide Baker Nunn cameras were able to photograph the two satellites clearly enough to reveal their shapes. The first had deployed larger solar-cell wings and was a mere twenty miles ahead of the second, the familiar Salyut-type craft. All that the Russians needed to do now was to launch what was almost certainly a Soyuz, and the three basic components would be ready for action.

Wheeler found the easiest way to imagine them was that Soyuz was the gunfighter, the Salyut was his holster and the Beam satellite was his gun. He knew he would either have to destroy the gunfighter or the gun. . .but maybe there still was another way. He picked up the phone and called Bill Kennedy down at the Cape.

'Everything alright Bill? Is 102 still ready?'

'Sure is, General, ready when you are. We're rolling her out right now. The boys are in the crew room kitting out.' Bill sounded as positive as ever. He turned to Daniel Perès and said:

'Well, Daniel, it looks as if we've got to go.'

Daniel nodded as he sat silently watching the bank of TV monitors and electronic displays arranged specially for the Jericho team at Omaha. He, like Yigal Beer, was deep underground, he in Cheyenne Mountain while Yigal was under the Negev.

'I'm going to call Ephraim Zuckerman in Jerusalem at Mossad HQ,' Daniel said, his brain racing to keep ahead of events.

Zuckerman's picture appeared brilliantly clear on the monitor after Daniel had pressed his 'Comkeyboard', linking the Jericho team to the incredible worldwide US Defence Communications Satellite System, all at the touch of eight orange buttons.

'Ephraim. The Russians wouldn't play, as you will know from the Foreign Minister's report. They have launched a Salyut, we believe, very close to the Beam satellite. We've got probably less than one hour until they launch the Palestinian in a Soyuz. What is the next move in the game?'

'Press 83771422,' Ephraim replied.

Daniel was puzzled but pushed the buttons and they glowed into life.

'83771422 is ready, oh. . .!'

The handsome face of Rebecca Limpel was framed by the screen.

'Shalom, Daniel Perès. Mr Zuckerman and I are in separate locations now. He is underground at Mossad HQ whilst I and the War Cabinet are underground near the Knesset. Ridiculous, isn't it? Now, I've listened to your last conversation and spoken to the Foreign Minister. It seems that General Landau was right. The Russians believe we are bluffing. Tragically for all of us they are wrong. We have decided to adopt our second step.'

'Tablet Two is standing-by as required. We are not mobilising fully but have alerted all troops in the usual way. What we have decided is that Ephraim Zuckerman will speak on the telephone directly to General Mendeleiv at the KGB Headquarters. We believe they will put us through. We'll keep our knowledge of Shimatov's role under our hats until we need it to surprise them at the time of our choosing.

'Zuckerman will simply tell Mendeleiv that Israel is aware of the identity of one of their cosmonauts, that he is Shabir Al Timimi, and that we have kept surveillance on him in Russia and throughout his military career. Maybe that will shock them into taking him off the crew. They'll never risk a Russian cosmonaut firing that Beam on an Israeli target. It's not their way at all. Do you have any comments? Time is pressing.' Her face gazed steadily at the camera.

'No comments, Prime Minister, I fully concur. General Wheeler?' Daniel turned to Wheeler, both of them framed in the overhead camera's lens.

'No comments, Madam, excellent proposal. We're standing by just the same if the US is needed.'

But Ephraim Zuckerman could not speak to General Mendeleiv at KGB Headquarters in time for he was with his chief Valdimir Shimatov in a Mil Mi8 helicopter, flying towards Domodedovo airport to catch the military jet to Semipalatinsk, birthplace of Zhukov. Shimatov grinned to himself, knowing at last that his plans were coming to fruition. He relished the name Zhukov, the greatest Russian General of the Second World War, the man who painstakingly marshalled enormous forces until he was ready to annihilate the Fascist enemy with massive lightning thrusts.

'Revenge is sweet,' he thought. After all the years of play-acting he was going to emerge as the most influential military strategist since Zhukov himself for he, Vladimir Shimatov, was the world's first Space General. The ideas flashed through his mind for he knew that once he controlled the 'High Ground' of Space he could truly control the earth itself. His thoughts were interrupted by a noisy crackling message on his headphones.

'General Shimatov, this is Centre Control, Tromsky speaking, we have received a call from Israel. I repeat, Israel!'

Shimatov could not believe his ears. He looked at the pilot who also looked amazed, allowing the helicopter to wallow briefly.

'Did you say Israel as in Palestine?' Shimatov asked, his voice drowned by the noise of the turbines overhead.

'Yes, General, Israel as in Palestine. It was their chief of Mossad, Ephraim Zuckerman.' The voice said slowly.

'Is this a stupid joke, Tromsky, because if it is. . .'

'No sir, this is genuine. Five minutes ago, he left his number, would you believe it?'

Shimatov's mouth opened even wider, never had he in his wildest dreams expected a telephone call from his greatest enemy, the Chief of Israeli Intelligence.

'I'll ring him when I get to Semipalatinsk, not before, I don't want a telephone patch-up to this aircraft on any account.'

'Understood, sir, I'll await your next instruction.'

'Correct, do that.'

And Shimatov gazed, still bewildered at the disappearing suburbs of Moscow, 3,000 feet below him. Mendeleiv never said a word. He was too bewildered at the change of events. The big helicopter landed gently in a flurry of snow and within minutes Shimatov had taken off for the largest underground research facility in the world.

The big Tu20 Badger bomber thundered into the sky heading south-east for Central Asia. It, like the E4B Airborne Command Post, was fully fitted out as a communications and control aircraft for the use of senior military commanders in time of war. Shimatov and Mendeleiv sat quietly with four aides discussing the developing situation. After a few minutes, Shimatov left them and wandered into the quieter sleeping quarters to give himself a chance to think. Semipalatinsk was the best place to be during the next crucial hours and days. There he felt completely at home.

Like the Central Planning Unit outside Moscow and many, many similar establishments in the West, Semipalatinsk grew deep roots into the protective earth, turning its back on nuclear blast, radiant heat, firestorms, hypersonic winds and invisible deadly radiation that would come in the War it had been built to wage: Armageddon, Total Nuclear War.

After an hour and a half the Tu20 made a perfect landing at the special airfield at Semipalatinsk and once again Shimatov boarded a waiting Mil, its blades spinning up the moment the door closed. Within five minutes it hovered to a halt by a single massive block of concrete containing one armoured door, through which Shimatov's party entered. Deep into the labyrinth the silent group rode in their high-speed shock-absorbent lift until they arrived at the Control Centre from which even the End of the World could be observed in reasonable comfort.

As they entered, Shimatov saw the giant monitor screen, similar to the one at Kalinin Control Centre. There in the middle was the Soyuz launcher, ready to go. There were now three minutes left and Shimatov waved away the prepared telephone while the caller, Ephraim Zuckerman, waited anxiously for the Russian to speak.

The minutes ticked by and suddenly it was all too late for the Israeli. The Soyuz launcher, girdled by its four tapering boosters lit up perfectly as it invariably did, and with a roar of flame rose slowly off the third pad at Tyuratam. As its image disappeared from view, Shimatov raised the yellow telephone with slow deliberation to his ear and said:

'*Ephraim Zuckerman, I presume.*'

37
Erebus

Shabir sat on the left-hand couch with Karpov in the centre and Tsiolkovsky on the right. For Shabir and Tsiolkovsky it was their first flight. For Karpov, a veteran cosmonaut of the Soyuz programme, his third.

He, as Flight Commander, and with the rank of full Colonel in the Air Force, maintained the tradition Shimatov had set, that all manned flights would be commanded by serving Soviet military officers.

'One minute to booster separation, over.'

'We copy, one minute to booster sep.,' Karpov replied.

The three of them tensed as they waited for the noise of separation. The acceleration approached 5G as the rocket gathered momentum, its fuel load decreasing rapidly at several tons per minute.

'Booster separation, Kalinin, over.' They all felt the clunk and high-pitched roar of the boosters as they fired off like giant metallic petals from the central core above which they rode. Shabir saw the angle of sunlight changing outside the capsule as the big rocket arced over gradually in its controlled trajectory.

'First-stage separation in eight minutes,' Karpov announced drily.

When it came, Shabir felt the growing silence as the rocket left most of the atmosphere behind it. There was a clunk, then a flash of hot blue gas around them as the central core slowly fell behind them towards its impact point in Central

Asia. For several seconds there was total silence before the final motor fired. They felt their bodies gain weight for a few seconds only for the sensation to disappear completely and Shabir Al Timimi was the very first Arab in space.

He quietly murmured a prayer of thanksgiving and turned his weightless head towards Valentin Karpov, shaking him by the hand before reaching across to Boris and touching his gloved fingers. Karpov unclipped his visor, slid it right back into his hood and said:

'That was the best yet, Shabir, the very best.' Smiling with great satisfaction.

Shabir and Boris also unclipped their visors before letting out a long breath of relief after the tension of the launch. A voice came on the speaker bringing a flowery greeting to the cosmonauts of Soyuz 47 and congratulating Shabir Al Timimi on his historic achievement. There was a burst of military music, first the Soviet anthem and then the March of the Freedom Fighters, recorded specially by the KGB's radio monitoring service in Damascus several months before. Karpov turned to Shabir.

'Well my friend, let's see if you can fly this baby in space as well as you did in the simulator. Shabir, you're a Soyuz pilot, so let's see you earn your pay. Somewhere ahead of you are the two most expensive satellites I've ever chased, so go find them.' Karpov beamed with pleasure knowing that with Shabir he had the finest pilot he had ever seen.

As Soyuz 47 commenced orbital rendezvous with its first target, Salyut 7, Vladimir Shimatov was literally wetting his pants. Mendeleiv, standing in front of his boss, saw the blood literally drain from his face. He could not believe it at first. He rushed for a chair before Shimatov collapsed. Never had he seen him so deathly pale.

Shimatov never said a word in reply to the distant caller, incredulous at how much the Mossad chief knew of his plan. It was almost as if the man had been living in his head for twenty years. The Jews knew everything. They knew the Palestinian, they knew his name, where he was born, when members of his family died. They knew how long he had been training and what he was training for.

His mind reeled, it was a catastrophe, never before had any of his operations been uncovered. But the timing! The Palestinian was in orbit and so were the Salyut and Zhukov vehicles. It was too much. Shimatov slammed down the phone and stormed into the conference room waving away the startled Mendeleiv and his aides. He needed time to think.

Within a few hours Soyuz 47 would dock with Salyut 7 and the Palestinian would transfer to the Salyut, leaving the two Russian cosmonauts to return immediately to Kazhakstan in their Soyuz craft. Then the Palestinian would be ready to dock with Zhukov whilst the Soviet Union could marshal its massive propaganda power against Israel and demand their own solution to the Middle East conflict.

Shimatov thought of all the planning and effort that was at risk. Shabir had been trained to live in orbit in Salyut for more than a hundred days, replenished from Tyuratam by automatic Progress spacecraft, already used highly successfully to refuel and reprovision Salyut 6.

While Salyut 7 and Zhukov flew in formation around the earth there were to be huge KGB-inspired demonstrations in every Arab capital city orchestrated to push their Governments in one direction, namely the forced disarmament of Israel and the declaration of the Palestinian People's Republic. He thought of how his colleagues at the 'Centre' had rehearsed it nine years before when on 1 November 1973 they had fully believed that Jerusalem would become the new capital city of the Republic.

And now with literally hours to go, what greater, more inspiring symbol of Soviet-Arab unity could there be to avenge the defeat of Yom Kippur than this incredible achievement—a Palestinian cosmonaut in space? And that was only the first stage. The next would be the charged particle beam. If Israel responded with military mobilisation and prepared to fight the Arabs again, then the Palestinian would dock with Zhukov, train the beam on a single Israeli tank and vaporise it as awful proof of the power the Arabs now possessed.

The demonstration would be so awe-inspiring, the clamour of Arab ululation so overwhelming that the United States would be confused and panic-stricken, exactly as it had been when the war they had been fighting for ten years collapsed in one cataclysmic week and Saigon had fallen to the Communist forces.

Shimatov was absolutely certain that America would never dare to meet the Soviet people face-to-face in nuclear confrontation, overwhelmed as they were with Soviet weaponry. Not ever for the sake of Israel, that growing thorn in its gross, overfed flesh. No, it would not risk war, nor would it risk a 50 per cent cut in its energy supplies. How many Americans would be prepared to give up their air conditioning, their heated swimming pools, their gross automobiles, their very profligacy, for a tiny minority of argumentative, demanding, precocious Jews in a barren land half a world away? Shimatov began to feel confidence flooding back into him after the shock of the Israelis' knowledge.

And then, when the Israelis found the phones dead as they begged America for guns and missiles and aircraft fuel, what then? The Israelis would fight, no doubt of that, but for how long? And if they ever dared to move—there, high above them and totally untouchable, would be the most powerful weapon in the world, aimed, armed and fired by their most implacable enemy, a Palestinian.

Shimatov slammed his fist into his open palm for now he felt utter determination. Russia could afford to go to war with Israel. He himself would confront Ephraim Zuckerman, the man he had just listened to, and then he would do to him what the Fascists had failed to do in the Great Patriotic War, he would see him dead.

Shimatov spun on his heels and stormed back into the Central Control room, his anger and determination cowering his subordinates. He addressed his deputy first.

'Mendeleiv, the operation will go ahead. I have seen the President and he has authorised the launch. Unless I receive contrary instructions from him personally the full propaganda campaign will start the moment Al Timimi has taken command of Salyut 7 and Karpov and Tsiolkovsky have landed back at Kazahkstan. Now order Soyuz 47 to dock with Salyut 7 without delay. Understood?'

'Yes sir.' Mendeleiv almost ran to confirm the instruction to the Flight Director at Kalinin Control Centre while Shimatov collared the next man.

'Moskalenko, is everybody ready at the Press Conference?'

'Yes sir,' he replied.

'Right, the conference will open now. Tell Boris Masursky to start. We are ten minutes behind the schedule. Go!' Moskalenko definitely *did* run for the phone that linked him with the International Press Conference supervised by 'Big Boris', the man who had lost a hand at Stalingrad. He was delighted to be the first to tell him that at last the press conference was for real, not another practice run. Moskalenko heard Boris's deep growling voice answer the direct line at Kalinin Control Centre and said one word to him:

'Erebus.'

Neither man knew that Shimatov had chosen it from the name of the winged horse that flew the prophet Mohammed to Heaven from the site of the Dome of the Rock, in Old Jerusalem.

38
Kalinin

Kulikov never finished the sentence. The place broke up into cheers and hoots as the Arab journalists went wild with delight. Several of them hugged their colleagues as the impact of what they had heard sunk in. One of them, a particularly devout Muslim, removed his shawl, placed it in front of him towards what he guessed was east and went down on his knees to pray, the tears forming little damp patches on his scarf. Others started to follow, creating little gaps in the crowd, leaving bewildered, embarrassed Western journalists trying respectfully to make room for them.

The man from *l'Humanité* cheered until he was hoarse, realising at last why his trip to Tyuratam to cover the launch of the French X-ray satellite had been postponed at such short notice. James Holloman of the *Washington Post* never said a thing, his boss at Langley had briefed him three hours before. Holloman was CIA. Frank Munger of the BBC said: 'Good Lord, what a bloody story.' He then proceeded to fight his way, apologising profusely, towards the podium where he could be closer to the microphones and hopefully have some questions answered. The journalist from *Le Figaro* missed the whole thing. He was in bed with a maid at his hotel, a KGB junior officer, a friend covered for him instead.

Over a billion people viewed the press conference. The world's TV companies had been specially primed 24 hours before by KGB broadcasting experts who worked for Tass,

Novosti Press, *Pravda* and hundreds of other media outlets infiltrated or established by the Centre. There was hardly a country in the world which did not receive coverage and every major Arab city and town suddenly found scores of large TV sets made available in their town squares, courtesy of the local Soviet Embassy, who in turn were supplied exclusively by the KGB. There was never a propaganda impact as good as the flight of Soyuz 47.

Literally millions of posters showing the face of Shabir Al Timimi flooded the world as every KGB printing press available churned them out the way they had when Gagarin had become the world's first spaceman. Within hours of the press conference a third of the world's population could recognise the name and face of Shabir Al Timimi and below every portrait was the same legend:

'Cosmonaut Shabir Al Timimi from Jerusalem, Palestine.'

Across one corner were the words:

'The Union of Soviet Socialist Republics honours the bravery of our Palestinian friends in their struggle against the Israeli aggressor.'

The KGB factories had produced millions of replicas, souvenirs, posters and badges. They even provided a special recording of his voice made during training which was featured on one side of the disc whilst the other side recorded the marching song of the Palestine Liberation Organisation. Within the day, streets, squares, buildings, even an airport had been renamed in his honour.

The Soviet switchboards in their major embassies were flooded with calls of congratulations and thanks for giving back to the Arabs the dignity they felt they had lost after successive defeats by Israel.

The rulers of the Islamic world, from Saudi Arabia to Yemen, from Morocco to Syria poured out their thanks to the Soviet Union. The Saudis created an Al Timimi Trust of a billion dollars by nightfall, after checking from their contacts with other Arab states that the Palestinian was definitely a devout Muslim. The Trust only operated in Riyadh.

Even the Pope sent a telegram of good wishes to the Soviet

Premier, expressing the hope that the flight was an example of peaceful co-operation. Being a Pole, he immediately suspected the Soviet motivation.

The United States Government and Israel never said a thing. Their answer to the huge campaign was silence, while the Jericho team prepared its answer.

39
OV-102

On the pad of Complex 39A, Orbiter 102 prepared to make its tenth and most testing flight into space. Lying on his back in the crew-capsule, 120 feet above the base was the other boy from Jerusalem, Colonel Michael Allon of the United States Air Force, Commander and Senior Pilot of NASA's Space Shuttle. On his right lay Colonel Peter Peabody, USAF, also Space Shuttle Pilot, while behind them reclined Colonel David Browne, USAF Mission Specialist.

For these men there were no photographs, no propaganda campaign, a few cheers from close friends and the normal complement of journalists and visitors to what was announced as a routine Shuttle Flight by NASA's press office 'to test new cargo handling systems'.

Their vehicle contained no weapons of any kind. Each man had been searched and filmed during the process to ensure he had nothing on him that could be construed as a weapon, strictly in accordance with NASA's declared policy on the Space Shuttle System. President Stockman had insisted, as did Rebecca Limpel, knowing Michael was an ex-Israeli, that this would be done. General Wheeler had fully concurred.

The three men lay there knowing OV-102 was now ready to go. The only argument they had had was what their call sign should be prior to the flight as it was traditional for all NASA astronauts to select their own flight symbol, subject to NASA's final approval. Michael had rejected Pete's suggestion of 'Icarus' because, as he had pointed out, he had no intention of having his wings fall off. Dave Browne, the Negro Mission Specialist, had suggested 'Claws' because of the articulated metal hand, on the suggestion of his eldest son, an avid movie freak.

All three had finally agreed on 'Rocky' because the Orbiter had a big, friendly feel about him. 'Like a happy truck driver,' Michael had said, 'with his big cargo bay and his black beard below his jutting chin.' Bill Kennedy at Rockwell International had almost swooned with delight at the word association, humming to himself, 'Rocky from Rockwell, Rocky from Rockwell.'

It was a beautiful day at Cape Kennedy made particularly memorable for the visitors by the sight of the Space Shuttle out on the Pad. Among them were Michael's wife and baby son David. Diana stood alongside Dave Browne's wife Virginia and Pete Peabody's wife Martha. Two Peabody kids were racing Virginia's little girl around the three women while the adults tried to make easy conversation. It was difficult for them all as each knew from the past month's highly intensive training programme that this flight was out of the ordinary, if a Shuttle flight could ever be thought of as anything but out of the ordinary. Virginia was the calmest of the three. She had total confidence in her husband's glowing assessment of his two colleagues. She had the additional advantage of knowing her husband had already flown in the Shuttle once before, also as Mission Specialist, during the Orbital Flight Test program on the fourth of the six flights. He had, however, landed back at the first Shuttle landing site, Dryden Flight Research Center in California, and so this would be the first time he would be returning to Kennedy Space Center after a Shuttle mission. Gus Lancaster had specially selected Dave Browne because of his excellent performance on the RMS system when he had practiced for the cancelled Skylab recovery attempt. His performance in the RMS Task Trainer with the new cargo pallet had fully vindicated his choice.

As she waited two miles away at the press stand, attended

by NASA officials, Diana suddenly heard an excited cheering about a hundred feet to her left. She glanced to see a couple waving their arms about in obvious delight over something they must have heard on the small transistor radio pressed to their ears. The man abruptly shouted in an unfamiliar language, which could easily have been Arabic. Diana could not understand a word he was saying, neither could the people near to him. He was too excited. It fell to his companion, a very attractive young American journalist to pass the news to their curious neighbours.

Diana felt her spine begin to tingle and she instinctively leaned over towards David, blissfully asleep in his folding pushchair. And then the news spread and she felt sick and suddenly had to steady herself against the pushchair. She slowly sank to her knees almost in a faint as Virginia and Martha rushed to prevent her from falling.

'What's the matter, honey?' said Virginia, completely bewildered by Diana's sudden collapse. 'Here, you shouldn't be out in this hot sun with so little food in you. I told you, the waiting's the worst part of it.' Diana sat on the grass, with Martha holding her up.

A NASA official ran over with a handful of ice from somebody's picnic box and asked Diana if it would help to cool her head. She nodded, looking quite strained and obviously unwell, but as they fussed round her they soon understood why she'd fainted. The newsflash was grim. Virginia crossed herself and Martha looked towards the Orbiter and whispered:

'Oh, my God, I knew there was something going on.'

They all knew now why their husbands were waiting there on Pad 39A. The Russians had launched a Palestinian into space, just half an hour before. That was the only explanation for the extraordinary additional work their three men had been doing for the past month.

Diana was terrified. Just those two words—'Russians' and 'Palestinians'—were enough for her mind to start making connections. Her husband Michael was a Jew from Israel, his parents had been killed by a Russian landmine planted by Palestinians. Now, half an hour earlier than the launch time planned for him to fly the Space Shuttle, a Palestinian commando, trained by the Russians, was in orbit. There could be only one purpose. Michael and the Palestinian must be planning to meet somewhere in orbit around the earth. But why? Michael was an American Jew, no longer an Israeli. Why did they use her husband, could not they ask somebody else? Was Michael going to fight the Palestinian in space?

Diana reached for her handbag and took out the little present he had left for the child as a memento of his first flight. She undid the gold paper and saw the little card on top of the single box:

'Just a symbol that I am with you both always, even above the earth. Love, Michael.'

It was his father's wristwatch. He had had it specially cleaned and repaired, and now it read the correct time. Its glass was clear and unbroken. She turned it over and inscribed on the back were the words:

'The past is over. We will build a bright future together, you and I, for our time is come.'

At that moment she turned, as the noise reached her. Orbiter 102 had started its main engines. Diana grabbed little David from the pushchair and held him close to her, the watch dangling from her wrist. They both looked towards the noise. The three main engines thundered to full thrust followed by the ignition of the two huge motors of the boosters. The vibration shook the earth between them and flooded their senses like a solid wave, as very slowly the Space Shuttle lifted off into the sky.

Diana glanced down to see if David was frightened but his tiny hands had clasped his grandfather's watch and he gurgled with pleasure, basking unafraid in the noise around him. His mother looked back, blinking through the tears, praying as never before in her life for the safe-keeping of the man she loved so dearly. It was a spectacular sight as the five motors roared and crackled, slowly accelerating the heavy vehicle towards its unknown destination in space.

40
Rocky

'Houston, this is Rocky, all systems normal, over.'

'Roger, we copy you, Rocky, they look fine down here, over.'

Michael felt very relaxed as the six million pounds of thrust of the five motors pushed him straight up into the sky.

'Houston, this is Rocky. One minute 57 secs to SRB separation, over.'

'We copy you, Rocky, you're fine for SRB, over.'

'Accelerating through 1,000 miles per hour now, over.'

'Rocky, you're looking good, all motors are nominal.'

'Houston, SRB sep. in twelve seconds, over.'

'Rocky, you're go for SRB at twelve seconds, over.'

'Houston, SRB sep. in five seconds, four, three, two, one . . .'

Michael felt the tremor as the big boosters separated from the external tank that stretched way ahead of the Orbiter just below his angle of vision. He looked over to his left at the truly spectacular sight of the left-hand booster roaring away on the thrust of its sixteen small separation motors. Pete Peabody was watching the right-hand booster as the two 150-foot monsters, each twelve feet in diameter, flew away travelling alongside the Orbiter at more than 3,000 miles an hour, while it thundered out of the atmosphere.

As OV-102 accelerated the two empty boosters reached the peak of their ballistic trajectory before starting the long fall to the Atlantic Ocean, now more than 30 miles below.

Michael imagined the flight of the SRBs as they fell faster and faster until the nose fairings would be automatically jettisoned allowing the drogue, then the main parachutes, to deploy, eventually dropping them with a huge but harmless splash onto the surface of the ocean, where they would be recovered by the tugs.

'Houston, RTLS approaching in two minutes, over.'

'Roger, Rocky, you look fine, all systems nominal, speed 13,000 miles an hour, over.'

Later: 'That's RTLS behind us, Houston, we're fine.'

Everybody was relieved. RTLS stood for 'Return to Launch Site' an emergency flight routine in the event of the failure of one of the Orbiter's main engines. It required a minimum altitude of 58 nautical miles before Michael would have had to turn back towards the Cape, jettison the huge heavy external tank in the ocean below and land back on KSC's Runway 33 about 20 minutes after lift-off. Nobody liked the idea of RTLS.

'Main engine cut off at 69 miles, over.'

There was sudden silence as the three Rocketdyne SSMEs cut.

'Roger, Rocky, you are go for ET sep., over.'

And eight minutes after lift-off, in total silence, Michael Allon could look straight ahead at the breathtaking edge of the earth directly above him. The Shuttle was upside down, flying almost parallel with the earth's surface.

'Houston, ET sep., now!'

And there was nothing but a slight vibration through the Orbiter as it separated from the huge, empty external tank as they travelled at 17,500 miles an hour.

Another hurdle had been passed: AOA—'Abort Once Around'—the emergency flight routine where, if the Shuttle had had problems it would fly a semi-ballistic trajectory once around the earth, just grazing orbit before landing back at the Cape after 90 minutes.

'Rocky, you are go for OMS-1, ignition in nine minutes, over.'

'Roger, Houston, let's go, OMS-1, ignition now.'

And for the first time the two smaller Aerojet Orbital Manoeuvring System engines fired, giving the small velocity increment for orbital insertion. The now-unencumbered Orbiter was in its element and within a matter of minutes OV-102, complete with Michael Allon, Pete Peabody and Dave Browne, was truly in orbit, 100 miles above the Earth. The feeling for Michael was almost indescribable, he was truly in space.

Two men from Jerusalem, 'the City of Peace', had arrived in space within an hour of each other.

'OK, Pete, Dave, let's check our orbit with Houston and Norad and see just how well we've done.' But before they even started a new voice cut in on their headsets.

'Rocky, this is Jericho III here, congratulations. You guys are right on the button, we have you on Norad tracking at 65-degrees west, Long Island is below you.'

It was amazing to think that in less than ten minutes they had travelled from the Cape to New York and would cross to England in 15 minutes while the Earth revolved below them. Their 55-degree orbit matched that of the Soviet spacecraft, who normally flew at 67 degrees but on this occasion were being confined like them to cover all the world south of the line that passed through the southern edge of Hudson Bay in Canada, Edinburgh in Scotland, Moscow in the Soviet Union, the northernmost tip of Japan, the Aleutians, and Vancouver in Canada. Their southernmost limit reached the line that joined Cape Horn, the edge of the Arctic Ocean, south of New Zealand and across the vast expanse of the Pacific back to the Cape again.

Michael looked ahead, the earth still above him, dazzled with the beauty of the scene. As they carried out their checks of the communications facilities the crew of OV-102 coasted silently 100 miles above the Atlantic. They passed directly over the spot where another young man, Charles Lindbergh had crossed only 53 years before, less than a man's lifetime, as he set course for his long solo flight across the grey ocean. In fifteen minutes, in the absolute comfort of weightlessness and the benign silence of space they covered the same route that had taken him over twenty hours of flying in the *Spirit of St Louis*.

Michael turned to Pete whilst signalling a thumbs-up to Dave Browne, remembering another even earlier feat of airmanship.

'Hey Dave, are you any relation to a Mr Arthur Whitton Brown?' Michael asked.

There was a moment's silence.

'No, Mike, don't think I've met him, was he from Illinois too?'

'No,' Mike smiled, 'he was from England. Back in 1919 he and another Englishman called Alcock were the first people to fly the Atlantic.'

'No kidding!' interjected Pete Peabody, 'Well, I never.'

'Yep, they flew from St Johns, Newfoundland to Ireland in a Vickers Vimy, a First World War bomber. Some brave guys, eh?'

'Incredible,' Dave replied. 'Here's us riding this great big Cadillac while those fellows risked their lives in a bundle of canvas and wire.'

'They sure did,' Mike replied. 'Not like us,' he almost added before checking himself.

'Here come the British Isles, that's Northern Ireland and beyond it is Britain. Any of you fellas been there?' Mike asked, looking out for the first signs of Europe. Then suddenly he remembered, and it made him feel rather strange.

'Hey, we're over Manchester nearly. That's where my parents met, Manchester University.'

Ninety seconds later they crossed into Europe.

'We'll fly over Frankfurt and in five minutes we cross Odessa then the Black Sea.' Pete said.

'OK, let's run through our circularisation status, we've got ten minutes,' Mike reminded them.

'Rocky, this is Houston, you are go for circularisation in nine minutes 52 seconds, over.'

'Roger, Houston, we copy, Circ. in nine 52, over.'

'Rocky, special message from Daniel Perès at Jericho

Control for Colonel Michael Allon, message reads: "In five minutes you will be almost directly overhead Kibbutz Ramta. Mazeltov from all of us, Mike, over." ' He smiled, grateful for Daniel's message and thought of his home as an orphan, with Liza, near Mount Hermon. Never could he have imagined then that he would fly over his home in a spaceship only 25 years later.

At 31 minutes 30 seconds from lift-off, as they passed directly over Bahrain in the Persian Gulf, they began to manoeuvre under the power of the OMS engines. Several seconds later they stopped firing and Houston confirmed they were now in the correct circular orbit as Orbiter OV-102 slipped into the dark side of the earth, where a new experience awaited them.

All of them, including Dave Browne, who had seen it before, were spellbound by the beauty of black, infinite space. Michael gazed in awe at the panoply of stars ahead of them, never could he have believed that space would be so beautiful. Everywhere he looked were millions of solid points of light that never flickered or dimmed, undistorted by the blanketing atmosphere of the earth.

'Ana ad Hoshiya: O Lord, save us,' he whispered into his microphone. For the first time he felt deeply moved by the majesty of the universe. He knew well that no astronaut had ever returned from a space flight without his thoughts or beliefs altered irrevocably in some way. He experienced a sensation of peace with conflicting emotions of joy and sadness, almost a sense of nostalgia, a feeling that he had been this way before.

Below them appeared the Indian Ocean as they started their 23-minute period of darkness before they emerged into dawn at a point fifteen degrees north of the Antarctic continent. It was time to concentrate on the purpose of the mission.

'Houston, this is Rocky, we request a link-up with Jericho at Omaha over.'

'Roger, Rocky, we copy your request and switching now, over and out.'

'Jericho, this is Rocky, do you read me, over.'

'Rocky, this is Jericho, we read you, strength five, go ahead, over.'

'Jericho, Dave Browne will now prepare the RMS ready for door opening. I will remain in my EVA suit until successful completion of the mission, over.'

'Roger, Rocky, we copy you, here is the latest status on the situation. These communications lines are completely secure, we are on directional antennae throughout with full electronic encypherment, so you may speak in clear, over.'

'Roger, Jericho, that's a big help, tell us the news.'

'Rocky. Item one. The Soyuz craft is approaching Salyut 7. It should dock in ten minutes according to our tracking. We have it on our TV and Baker Nunns. They're only 100 feet apart. They've got a good flyer there. Item two. Shimatov broke contact with Zuckerman after he flew to Semipalatinsk. That means Shimatov will probably accelerate his plans, whatever they may be. Item three. President Stockman will speak to the Soviet President in 30 minutes, after Soyuz has docked with Salyut in a final attempt to avoid Jericho having to take action. Item four. You are now authorised to search for Salyut 7. Norad will give you your flight data which Houston will pass into your computers. Message ends. Over.'

'Roger, Jericho. We copy, give us the rendezvous data and we'll find that spacecraft, over.'

'Roger, Rocky, here comes the data you need, over.'

And within ten minutes Orbiter OV-102 had stored in its incredible brain all the information from Norad tracking to enable it to hunt for Salyut 7.

41
Soyuz-Salyut

Shabir steered the Soyuz spacecraft towards the empty, waiting Salyut, the last few feet using manual controls. Although Soyuz and Salyut had extremely efficient fully automatic rendezvous and docking radar with externally mounted TV cameras to guide the vehicles, all cosmonauts were encouraged to dock manually to test their skill and judgement.

The Salyut glinted in the sun like a big complicated modern sculpture more than 30 feet long and covered with docking ports, observation windows, sensor modules, antennae and two big solar wings. Shabir saw the white target cone ahead of his TV cameras and steadily crept towards the space station. Fifteen seconds later there was a clunk and the Soyuz trembled.

'Soft dock,' he said to Karpov and Tsiolkovsky.

A moment later there was a hard thump and he announced: 'Hard dock.'

The main docking ring had gripped the Salyut rigidly to the Soyuz.

'Beautiful, Shabir, absolutely perfect docking, congratulations,' Karpov beamed at the skilful Palestinian, while Tsiolkovsky gave an imitation hand-clap.

'Kalinin, this is Soyuz 47, we have completed our docking successfully, over.'

'Roger, Soyuz, we copy your docking, well done, that was fast work. Prepare to enter Salyut, we will have some new data in 30 minutes, over.'

'Roger, Kalinin, we understand. It will take us an hour to prepare our transfer to Salyut, over.'

'Roger, Soyuz, over and out.'

Shabir felt an immense elation; all the training had been worth it for this one experience. He had carried out what he knew was a very smooth, fast rendezvous and docking without a single hitch. He would not let Shimatov down. Karpov turned to him and said:

'Shabir, why don't you let me accompany Boris while you stay here in Soyuz. You have a rest and I'll help him check Salyut. Just relax and let me do some work for a change. We'll get out of these suits now we're in orbit, the job will be much easier.'

'Fine, Commander, it's a shame you won't be staying up with me in Salyut. Next time, we'll see if we can, eh?' He smiled at the friendly Karpov.

42
Détente

'Mr President, this is President Stockman, good day to you, sir. I'm sure you know why I'm calling from the White House on the Direct Line. Your Ambassador at the United Nations received a note from our Ambassador a matter of three hours ago regarding the serious allegation made yesterday by the Israeli Ambassador to the UN.' Stockman paused, his blue grey eyes scanning the notes he had prepared in consultation with his aides.

'I am fully aware of that allegation, President Stockman, but of course it is without foundation. It is a typical gesture of the Israeli Government to placate their Zionist elements and camouflage their aggressive intentions towards their Arab neighbours.'

Alexei Beriev appeared confident of his position, but Stockman replied steadily, his Russian still very good after many years away from the Soviet Union—linguistics was his favourite hobby.

'Sir, I do not intend to argue with you regarding the Soviet Union's attitude towards Israel unless there is direct confrontation between yourselves and the Israelis, whom we are solemnly pledged to protect, as ratified at the United Nations on three occasions. What I say is that my Government is cognisant of a most dangerous development in weapons of warfare. Specifically the charged particle beam weapon launched from Tyuratam earlier today. . .'

The Russian interrupted immediately.

'President Stockman, we know you fly satellites over us but you cannot bluff us into believing you can prove this tissue of lies supplied to you by the Israeli provocateurs.'

Stockman continued, unconvinced by the Russian's aggressive manner.

'Sir, our Ambassador to the United Nations is on his way to the Secretariat building in New York with a complete set of photographs, taken in several wave-lengths, of the satellite as it moved from its assembly point at Semipalatinsk to Tyuratam.

'He also has photographs of the launcher, the launch itself and then of the satellite in orbit. They are clear enough to show its configuration. The technical means at our disposal are very comprehensive and fully allowed for under the SALT agreements.'

The Russian was silent for a few moments before Stockman continued.

'Furthermore, our Ambassador has a detailed photographic file on the man you sent up today. This file proves conclusively that the Soviet Union trained, supported, then retrained one Shabir Al Timimi, first as a Palestinian commando, then as a fighter pilot and finally as a cosmonaut.'

Stockman did not have to wait for the Soviet reply.

'President Stockman, of those facts we are proud and have told the world that also,' the Russian replied with growing assurance.

'Yes, Mr President, but there is more to it than that. We have proof that your Director of Cosmonaut Training, General Shimatov, is not what he claims to be but is in fact a senior General of your KGB and has been directly responsible for the preparation of the charged particle beam satellite and of the training of Shabir Al Timimi in the use of that satellite.'

The Russian protested.

'Rubbish, rubbish, you have no proof. This is typical of your Administration, President Stockman, anxious to maintain your voting power in Congress. . .'

Stockman replied:

'Mr President, in my country the people can kick me out, as they did Richard Nixon, if they don't believe I'm the right man for the job. Yes, I am anxious to maintain my Administration because I am determined to resist any further threats to peace in this world created by men like Shimatov. I have no argument with the Soviet people, having visited your country many times and made warm friends with Soviet citizens, as you well know. But as long as you permit people like Shimatov to shape your foreign policy I will do everything in my power as President of this great nation, to resist his force which I believe is a danger to world peace.'

The Russian replied with a steady, firm voice:

'President Stockman, I am the leader of the Soviet Union, and as President of the Communist Party I will decide with the CPSU and the Politburo what men I will choose to employ to carry out Soviet policy.'

'That I accept, sir, so long as no one individual has the power by virtue of modern weaponry to cause a nuclear war. Shimatov and the beam are together a destabilising factor in world peace. With the Palestinian anything could happen that you and your Government might not be able to control. We believe that to be an unacceptable position. Unless the Soviet Union does something positive to prevent the meeting of the Palestinian and that beam satellite then I must say now that I have authorised our own agencies to prevent the use of that beam by that Palestinian. Do you understand, Mr President?'

'President Stockman, this is preposterous, I will not have your Government interfere with Soviet satellites. I will call an emergency meeting of the Cabinet, the CPSU and the Politburo and we will give you our answer.'

'Thank you Mr President, I will await your call,' and Stockman put the phone down looking around at the concerned faces of his Chiefs of Staff and Secretaries of the Armed Forces.

'Gentlemen, we've got to stop that Palestinian from using that satellite.'

The Soviet President put the phone down and turned towards the waiting War Committee.

'Gentlemen, we've got to change this mission. It's getting out of control. On no account can we lose face and the propaganda momentum but we must not let the Palestinian near that beam satellite. It is not worth the risk to our overall strategy. The Americans, as I suspected, know far too much. We will still be in an enormously powerful position without firing a shot.

'Now tell them in Soyuz 47 that they are only clear to dock with Salyut 7, not with Zhukov. Do it immediately. Then get me Shimatov, I want him controlled also. We're being outmanoeuvred by the Americans because of an appalling lack of security on our part.

'I want a full investigation now of how they got their information. I thought after Belenko and the Mig 25 we had tightened up but no, our most secret projects are going to be discussed in one hour at the United Nations. What is this nation coming to?'

He was very angry indeed.

43
Solo

Shabir was stunned. He could not believe it. There was the message again.

'Soyuz 47 this is Kalinin Control. Zhukov docking is cancelled, repeat, Zhukov docking is cancelled. Is that you, Karpov?'

Shabir thought quickly before replying.

'This is Karpov,' he said, imitating the Russian Commander's voice. He could see Karpov at least twenty feet away in the airlock and Boris was already in Salyut, both out of communications.

'Karpov, is the Palestinian with you, over?'

'No, he's in Salyut with Boris, over.'

'Good, we have bad news for you, you must not allow him anywhere near Zhukov: do not dock, understood, over.'

'Yes, Kalinin, what's up? Over.'

'Orders of the President. Stay in Salyut with the Palestinian for three days, we will prepare a new flight plan and bring you back, over.'

'Kalinin, this is Karpov, what's the problem with the Palestinian, over?'

'Karpov, we can't afford the risk of an escalation, the Americans and Israelis know everything about Zhukov and Shabir. They threaten direct intervention.'

'Kalinin, what is our distance from Zhukov, so that I will avoid it, over.'

'It's only 30 miles directly ahead of you, it's within rendezvous radar range, over.'

'Is it armed, is it live, over?'

'Yes, it will certainly work, but we'll try it on another flight when the fuss has died down, over.'

'Kalinin, thank you, I understand everything now, over and out.'

'Roger, Soyuz. We'll contact you in an hour, over and out.'

'You may try,' Shabir thought, 'but you'll get a nasty shock.'

With careful, deliberate movements Shabir Al Timimi zipped up his suit and went through the checks to prepare himself for EVA, the condition where he could survive, floating in the vacuum and utter coldness of space. Within five minutes his suit was fully pressurised, and he set up a series of switches on the spacecraft before relaxing, floating gently in his harness. He thought for a moment then reached out for the empty suits discarded by his two colleagues while they worked in the comfort of the pressurised assembly.

Picking up both suits in his ungloved hands he fumbled around until he had the back of Karpov's suit facing him. With great care, so as not to puncture his own suit, he slit through the layers along a seam and then repeated this for Tsiolkovsky's suit using the folding knife from the maintenance locker below the seat. Having done that he lay the two suits back in their previous positions, released his harness and called the two Russians on the intercom.

'Vladimir, Boris, you have to return to Soyuz, something's come up.'

Within half a minute, both men floated back into the reentry capsule of Soyuz asking what the problem was.

'Kalinin have a warning light on their telemetry for the docking tunnel hatch. We'll have to put on our suits while we run a pressure test.'

'Shit,' said Tsiolkovsky, 'I was almost finished. Everything will be just fine for you, Shabir, you could live like a Tsar for a year in there. Wish I was staying.' And the two

Russian cosmonauts closed the docking hatch thereby isolating the Salyut and Soyuz from each other. They zipped up their suits, locked their visors and plugged in to the pressurisation connectors.

'Funny,' Karpov said, 'gauge must be wrong. I'm getting a pressure loss in my suit.'

'Mine, too,' said Tsiolkovsky, 'must be a switch fault, they've never done this before.' They watched as Shabir, still plugged in to the suit pressurisation loop, floated over them towards the emergency dump valves.

'I'll just check the valves are closed.' He said.

Neither felt any alarm. Shabir always knew what he was doing and they both looked up at him as he opened the valves, letting the pressurised atmosphere of the Soyuz jet straight out into space.

Before the Russians could do anything to stop this insane act, their blood boiled! They were both dead in less than a second. The gas, previously dissolved in their blood under the near atmospheric pressure of the capsule, was suddenly allowed to expand as the air exhausted through the dump valves. Both were blue in a minute. The Palestinian looked at their dead faces, then closed the valves and floated gently back to his seat.

With calm efficiency Shabir stabilised the now slowly tumbling assembly, caused by the air jetting through the dump valves, before smoothly undocking Soyuz and withdrawing a matter of three feet from the Salyut. He undid his harness and floated over the bodies to the docking hatch. Within a minute it was unlatched and he pulled the hatch cover inwards, stowing it securely on its mountings. He looked out through the metre-wide opening into the utter blackness of space until, by leaning out, he could see Salyut just above him. He had committed Man's first murder in space.

Shabir unclipped Karpov's harness and manoeuvred the blue-faced, staring corpse into the hatch opening. In one smooth glide, Vladimir Karpov sailed out of the Soyuz, his body instantly frozen, harder than concrete in the utter coldness of space. Boris Tsiolkovsky came next but just as Shabir threw him, the reaction of his throw caused the Soyuz to start rolling gently, according to the predictions of his famous namesake from Kaluga and the even more famous Isaac Newton. Tsiolkovsky's body floated out, spinning silently on its centre of gravity straight towards one of Salyut's antennae which it struck, wedging itself firmly between the space station and the antennae array.

Shabir never noticed the event for he was even more concerned about correcting the tumbling Soyuz craft. With measured movements he closed the hatch firmly then floated back to his seat and clipped up his harness. Within minutes he had repressurised the Soyuz and within half an hour of opening the valves he was firmly docked again with Salyut.

He waited for a few moments to collect his thoughts then checked his position relative to the earth below. He was at an odd angle so he fired the thrusters very gently to orientate himself, then undid his harness again and opened the hatch after checking that all pressure zones between Soyuz and Salyut were again in equilibrium.

Shabir floated up the tunnel and just as his late colleagues had predicted found Salyut to be in excellent order, warm, well lit and cavernous after the cramped Soyuz. He kicked out straight for the flight control switches, effectively isolating Salyut from the ground controllers at Kalinin, who could normally control the vehicle's orbit by switching its engines on or off.

Without waiting to rest, the Palestinian checked his gyro compass against the star compass, then identified his orbital path using the navigation computer. It took him only a few minutes to manoeuvre the large vehicle into the correct position, just as he had been taught at Tyuratam, for the operation of the rendezvous radar. Then, very gently, he fired the orbital propulsion motor and started to move.

He turned on Salyut 7's own ranging radar and watched the screen. Instantly it was there. A mere 22 miles ahead was the weapon he now sought more than any other to avenge the dignity of the Palestinian people. It took 32 minutes to catch up with Zhukov, but it was worth everything that he had suffered in his life to be within a few feet of the device.

Looking at the Docking TV monitor he recognised immediately that breathtaking machine he had been shown at Tyuratam by General Shimatov over two years before. Of course that one had been the normal engineering mock-up but it hardly differed from this beautiful object slowly filling the screen. Yes, there they were the hexagonal cylinders, the solar wings, the control boxes, the fusion core, absolute technical perfection, floating like a piece of silver sculpture, against the velvet blackness of space. It was almost as if it lay on a bed of stars, matching them glint for glint a hundred miles above the waiting earth.

Very slowly Shabir approached the weapon and docked. He was now in control of one of the largest spacecraft ever assembled, comprising Soyuz 47, Zhukov and Salyut 7. He manoeuvred it slowly round using minute jets from the thrusters and stopped it with its pilot's observation window pointed due east, its 'barrel' aiming straight down at the earth. He rose out of his seat and floated level with the 'floor' in an approximation of a kneeling position before offering his life to God for the sake of the people of Palestine and in eternal memory of his dead family. His final prayer was for the only woman he had ever loved, Valentina Bykovsky.

Then he turned towards the panel marked 'Zhukov Control System' and started to bring the dormant device to life.

It took little over half an hour to run through the checklist.

44
Sis

Deep underground in Semipalatinsk, General Shimatov was closer to panic than at any time in his life. In front of him ranged the data display panels at the Control Centre, linked to Kalinin Control and telling him an unbelievable story—most of the displays were blank! All communications with the crew had ceased. For over an hour now Soyuz 47 had remained silent. The last conversation had been with Karpov and since then no further messages had passed between the crew and Kalinin. All attempts to contact them had been met with silence. What was more disturbing was the telemetry records of the cosmonauts' biomedical condition. The flight surgeon at Kalinin had reported with a breaking voice that two of the cosmonauts' body charts indicated one thing conclusively: 'Life Termination'. The alarm sign flashed on and off continuously at his position in the second row of the Mission Control room.

'There is either a double electrical failure or both men must be presumed dead,' he had said with his head buried in his hands, barely able to talk.

With growing alarm the Flight Controller at Kalinin had checked and found that two emergency dump valves had opened inexplicably—Soyuz's pressure charts recorded a catastrophic loss in the craft's pressurisation! Then, to throw further confusion into the Flight Control team, there was the sudden isolation of Soyuz from the ground by the flicking of a selected series of switches in Salyut, the pattern following that of 'Isolation in Orbit' when a craft may be abandoned for a long period and not completely powered. This enabled it to be re-used when required; the cosmonauts called it the 'Hibernation Program' and practised it in case they had to wait a long time before rescue after a possible accident in space. To confuse the controls even more, there had come the extraordinary undocking from Salyut followed by redocking ten minutes later.

But throughout all these inexplicable events one set of signals had remained clear and constant, the biomedical telemetry from Shabir Al Timimi. Shimatov ordered a comparison of the Palestinian's heart beat at the times of pressure release, undocking through redocking. There was a distinct correlation between heightened pulse rate and those extraordinary events. Shimatov's mind was fast coming to the conclusion that the Palestinian was the sole man alive in Soyuz 47. A grim premonition came to him and he asked to speak to the Flight Controller at Kalinin.

'Cherensky, this is Shimatov again, did you speak to Karpov last?' he asked.

'Yes, General.' Cherensky replied.

'What about?' Shimatov snapped.

'I told him about the change in the Mission, sir, and not to tell the Palestinian.' Cherensky replied defensively.

'How do you know you spoke to Karpov?' Shimatov asked.

'He said he was Karpov. I recognised his voice and in any case we timed our call to coincide with the period when according to the flight plan Al Timimi would be in Salyut.'

'How do you know it wasn't the Palestinian imitating Karpov?' Shimatov demanded angrily.

'Because he said he was Karpov, and his voice, you know . . .'

'Cherensky, I think you just gave that Palestinian a reason to kill Karpov and Tsiolkovsky. Congratulations, you stupid bastard.'

'But General, why . . . why would he kill his fellow cosmonauts?'

'Because he is a single-minded dedicated fighter who saw the greatest achievement of his life, the defeat of Israel, postponed for yet another time. If you now check with the tracking ships I think you'll soon see Salyut 7 moving towards Zhukov because he wants that weapon more now than ever before. Establish your best surveillance radar on those spacecraft, get photographs, record everything. And Cherensky, nobody is allowed to move out of the building on my orders,' said Shimatov.

'But General Shimatov, General Mendeleiv will have to give authorisation,' Cherensky protested.

'Don't worry Cherensky, I'll order him myself.' Shimatov slammed the phone down hard enough to attract even more attention to his growing anger. He turned to his Deputy.

'Mendeleiv, throw a cordon round Kalinin now, nobody's to move, understood? When this flight is over, arrest the entire control crew, particularly Cherensky, understood?'

'Yes sir, I'll organise it right away.'

Shimatov picked up the direct line to Tyuratam, not to his normal offices but to a very special isolated unit based some miles from the main Assembly facilities.

'SIS, this is General Shimatov, give me General Dobrodolsky, this is urgent.'

A minute later he was through.

'General, we have an emergency situation with the Soyuz-Salyut combination. It may be necessary to destroy the vehicles . . . Yes, I know it sounds mad, but I assure you it may be the sanest thing we do today. I will telex you to confirm this order before linking you with the President for final authority. Don't ask questions, just listen, time is running out.

'First, what is your state of readiness?. . .Good, I want that bomb up there alongside that Salyut within three orbits, understood?

'Second, what warhead have you fitted?. . .Excellent, I don't want anything left up there for the Americans to photograph later. This must look like an accident, understood? Report immediately you are ready to launch. Now, move!'

Shimatov felt that at last he was establishing control again. The story he would give the world's press began to unfold in his head. 'A tragic accident. A martyr to the Palestinian people. A monument alongside Gagarin's for all three of them in Moscow.' Yes, a dead martyr is far more inspiring than a live hero, he thought. The phone from Kalinin rang. He picked it up. It was Cherensky sounding very agitated.

'General Shimatov, Soyuz and Salyut have docked with Zhukov, sir, it's incredible, it can't be happening.'

'But it has, hasn't it, Cherensky? Keep tracking and listening. Tell me do you have any remote-detonation explosives on Soyuz or Salyut?'

'No, sir.' Cherensky sounded apologetic.

'Can you control their engines?' Shimatov was desperate to take command of Soyuz again.

'Yes, sir, but . . .'

'But what?' Shimatov snapped.

'Whoever is flying Salyut has isolated her power control system from our ground signals. The man must be mad.' Cherensky was completely baffled.

'No, Cherensky, he is certainly not that, in fact he is saner than any of us down here. Have you any idea how long he could survive up there?'

'General, that's what is bothering me. He could live up there for months. Untouchable.'

'No, again, Cherensky, nowhere is a single man untouchable. Use your head and come up with a solution fast.'

And Shimatov replaced the receiver, more deliberately this time.

He turned to Zhukov's project engineer, a small round man of 50 in shirt-sleeves.

'Gherman, can you isolate Zhukov electronically from Salyut 7 to prevent it being operated without your authority?'

'Yes, sir.' And he positively beamed, delighted to be the harbinger of good news at last. Gherman was always smiling, he was a very fine technician, a doyen of the space programme. He continued:

'Yes, General, we've found a procedure that will at least prevent the beam being fired from the Control System panel in Salyut. The weapon is useless without your co-operation.' For the first time Shimatov breathed a sigh of relief. He almost became his other self again as he patted Gherman on the back. At last he would retrieve control of the situation.

'So, Gherman, there is nothing the Palestinian can do . . . You know I might even decide to let him rot in space until he went mad, a fitting sentence for a murderer. Yes, incarceration in the most perfect cell ever built, a hundred miles from earth, no escape whatever!'

Another call came from Tyuratam. It was Dobrodolsky, also sounding very pleased with himself:

'General Shimatov? I'm pleased to say the SIS launcher and warhead will be on the pad in one hour and we could intercept Salyut 7 in two hours from now.'

'That's the second bit of good news I've had today, well done, Dobrodolsky, keep it moving until the President calls.' Shimatov was a happier man. At last he had a choice of sentence that he could pass on the murderer. He picked up the phone to the Soviet President in conference with the War Cabinet.

'Mr President, sir, this is Shimatov, . . .'

Considering what he told his incredulous leader, he thought his reaction was very sound. He was to destroy Salyut 7, Zhukov, Soyuz and all, as soon as it was physically possible. The President would call Dobrodolsky himself to give authorisation.

45
Hide-and-Seek

'Rocky, this is Jericho, we've got new data for you, over.'

'Roger, Jericho, standing by, over.'

'Rocky. Item one, we've observed Salyut dock with the beam satellite. We photographed it five minutes ago. Item two. Our monitoring of their telemetry indicates a possible change in their situation in orbit. We've had a call from the Withering Group to say they believe two cosmonauts may have died. Repeat, two. They are still monitoring signals from one. It could be the Palestinian's still in control and can now use the beam. Do not approach, I repeat, do not approach, use the curvature of the earth itself to keep out of the beam's path. You must not get closer than five thousand miles, do you understand, or the beam could destroy you. Once there, start creeping up until we tell you to stop.'

'Roger, Jericho, understood, we'll stabilise at this distance from the target. Tell those boys at Withering that they scooped us again, over.'

'Roger, Rocky, we'll observe your OMS firing and pass on your message. Take great care, over'

Michael grinned with admiration at the famous class of English schoolboys who under their Science Master, Gordon Derry, at the small town of Withering had established a remarkable reputation for analysing Soviet spaceflights. Their equipment was a selected collection of home-made second-hand receivers but because of their years of dedicated guidance under Derry they had been the first to announce the newest Russian launch site at Plesetsk, at 62.9 degrees north, 40.1 degrees east. They had analysed the Soviet signals and tracked them by radio fixes. Now it looked as if they had done it again.

'OK, fellas, let's fire the OMS and maintain relative position,' Michael said.

Within a few seconds they had manoeuvred the Orbiter to face tail first, then fired their OMS rockets to match the tracked speed of the Soviet satellites, although they were still 5,000 miles away.

'Rocky, this is Houston, that's just fine. Standby for Jericho, over.'

'Rocky, this is Jericho, we have new data. The story has broken from England. The *Withering Chronicle* or some such paper scooped it. Within an hour or so the world will know what's happening, over.'

'Understood, Jericho, this thing's hotting up. Any news on the Palestinian, over?'

'Negative, Rocky. We're still tracking and Zuckerman's trying something in Jerusalem but I don't know what it is yet, over.'

'Roger, Jericho, I guarantee we're the first human beings to use the planet Earth as a shield, over.'

46
Scoop

Virginia Kay did not want to spend half a day at a boys' school attending lessons. Her editor had insisted however, as he had promised a friend, one of the Board of Governors, that he would do a small feature on their work for the local *Withering Chronicle*. Virginia, at 22, pretty and interestingly dressed, arrived an hour late and profusely apologised to the Headmaster for being delayed by a 'story'.

Unconvinced by the excuse, the man who listened to absentees every day with disbelief introduced her to Gordon Derry, who was about to take his own weekly science class. Derry, a 'young' 40-year-old with horn-rimmed glasses, overhung by a mass of wavy red hair, did not appear the kind of man who made the news, even in the *Withering Chronicle*. Reluctantly Virginia took a seat to one side of the class after experiencing 26 pairs of pubescent eyes ogling her tight corduroy trousers and even tighter beige cashmere. She wrapped her long open woollen sweater firmly around her as she took out her notebook. All she could think of at that moment was that men were definitely getting younger every day.

Derry opened the class with a request for those boys who had been on listening watch during the previous week to tell the class of their findings. Virginia never understood a word but what she did find interesting was Derry's growing interest in the boys' work. Within half an hour Derry stopped the class abruptly and turned to her. It was a pleasant experience, she was very pretty.

'Miss Kay, I think we may have a story for you.' He smiled mischievously and adjusted his glasses before addressing the blackboard.

'It appears, boys, that we have a double loss of signal from bio-telemetry and retained signal strength from one crew member. Furthermore, we see the characteristic signal pattern of a power-down procedure. We also note a signal pattern between those two events similar to that recorded on the tragic Soyuz 6 flight when three cosmonauts died.' Derry flourished symbols over the board. Virginia was suddenly very interested and copied everything verbatim from that last phrase '. . . when three cosmonauts died'.

'We also have a series of subsequent signals from Kalinin but no response from Soyuz or Salyut. A little later we have the characteristic switch-on signal for the operation of rendezvous radar which lasted several minutes before shutdown. Finally we have silence from Soyuz but a flurry of unanswered signals from Kalinin. Does anybody wish to hypothesise—Carter?'

The brightest and ugliest boy in the class stood up awkwardly, snagging his jacket on the desk lid and just catching his glasses as he rose and said:

'Sir, could that overall pattern indicate life termination for two and life sufficiency for one, who then isolates himself from Kalinin before entering Salyut and eventually docking with Cosmos 1238?'

'I fully concur, Carter, anybody else?' Derry said.

'Yes sir.' It was Wilmot, who contrasted with Carter like Laurel and Hardy. They were in fact so nicknamed.

'Cosmos 1238 emitted rare signal characteristics solely featured previously in launches associated with SIS flights. Cosmos 1238 could be a target.'

'Possible but unlikely, Wilmot, targets usually leave from Plesetsk' . . . and so it had gone on.

When the class finished Virginia asked Derry what, in a few words, he thought was happening.

'Miss Kay, I think we have a space disaster on our hands!

Two cosmonauts died in Soyuz 47, a third survived and transferred to Salyut.

'He then piloted Salyut to dock with Cosmos 1238. Remember, the Palestinian cosmonaut was in Soyuz 47 and Cosmos 1238 was in a matching orbit as if it might be a target for Salyut 7.'

'Anything else?' Virginia asked, now brimming with anticipation.

'Yes—very strange this. The NASA Space Shuttle Flight 10 was launched earlier today, on identical track to the Russian satellites. It started to catch up but appears now to have stabilised at a distance of 5,000 miles.'

'Do you think there's a connection?' She asked writing furiously.

'Could be. If there are problems with the Russian spacecraft the Americans can rescue the survivor and take him back in the Space Shuttle. The two countries signed a reciprocal Rescue Agreement in April 1979,' Derry replied.

'Then why are the Americans holding back, surely they ought to get closer?' She asked, absolutely fascinated now.

'That's the mystery, you'd only hold back if there was a danger to one or both spacecraft.' Derry reasoned.

'But why 5,000 miles, that's a huge distance. Isn't the Earth 24,000 miles in diameter?' She asked.

'Yes, let's see what that means. It's too far for a nuclear device to damage the Shuttle.'

'Why a nuclear device? Do you mean a bomb?'

'We don't know what Cosmos 1238 is, as is the case with almost all Soviet satellites. Whatever it is might be lethal at 5,000 miles.' Derry grimaced and rubbed his strong chin.

'Nothing could be that dangerous, surely?' She argued.

Derry stopped, picked up a piece of chalk and drew an arc across the board. He looked at it, then rubbed it out before walking quickly over to the big globe in the corner. He blew the dust off and placed a ruler on its surface.

'Miss Kay this ruler represents the thickness of the orbit of those spacecraft, this is the separation distance between the two craft. Watch my finger move that distance.

'I can't see it now.' She said, confused.

'Exactly. The American may be *hiding* from the Russian!' He said with a triumphant grin.

The evening papers had it first on a syndication basis, complete with a photograph of Derry and the intrepid Miss Kay. Both looked as if they had just got married.

The headlines emphasised various aspects:

FIRST SPACE DEATHS *Daily Express*

TWO COSMONAUTS DEAD *Sun*

IS PALESTINIAN ALIVE? *Daily Mirror*

US TO RESCUE COSMONAUT SURVIVOR? *Guardian*

The US press picked it up in various editions. Jim Holloman's *Washington Post* did best with a feature article showing the various spacecraft selected from the files. There was no reference to Cosmos 1238. His editor was amazed at the speed of Holloman's despatch from Moscow and the depth of his research in a matter of hours. It was almost as if he had had it prepared beforehand. He had.

'Just good contacts,' he had said when the editor had called him.

When Virginia Kay's editor called her at home it was to get an entirely different angle on the subject.

'Virginia, this is Bob Hoskins again, I want you to drop everything you're doing and get down to Heathrow first thing in the morning with enough clothes to last you a week. Take your passport and pick up your ticket and travellers' cheques. OK?'

'Where am I going, Bob? I was due to go to talk to Derry again tomorrow,' she replied.

'He's going with you. We persuaded his school it would be a good thing for the next term's course. You're going to Washington on Concorde, nail the NASA press people, call Doland on 2394 now—they're five hours behind us—and arrange an interview. There's a new story there, I know it. Then fly down to Houston to the Johnson Space Center, see their PR officer, and finally get to Kennedy Space Center for that Shuttle landing. Take Harry with you, I've already briefed him. Get lots of shots of yourself with Derry and the Shuttle pilots when they return. Clear?'

'I think so. Can I call you later to check?'

'Anytime, but get that Concorde: Go to the British Airways Concorde departure lounge. You've still got a valid US Visa haven't you since that Laker story?' Hoskins checked.

'Yes, its indefinite. I'll be OK,' she assured him.

'Best of luck Virginia, call me every two hours, no matter what, and use your American Express, I'll make sure you're covered. OK?'

'Fine, and thanks. Bye.'

'Just get the story first, Virginia, you're on your way now, use the break. Make it the best ever. Bye.' And she was left holding the phone, her hair still covered in shampoo.

It took a major combined effort by Tass and Novosti Press to handle the clamour of concerned calls from the Arab press and to withstand the probing of the thousands of freelance reporters sent to hunt for the story.

The NASA press office in Washington was suddenly inundated with calls and within hours FBI men were sealing off the families of the Shuttle Flight 10 crew from the barrage of press and TV reporters.

It took an astute Israeli journalist working at the UN building in New York less than a day to connect his country's ambassador's statement at the UN. He changed the story a third time and at last the press started to get close to the truth. To avoid possible censorship in Israel, he sold the story to the *Washington Post* as they had been the first with the news in the US.

The headline read: THE HUNTING OF SALYUT 7.

There followed a highly informed article describing Shuttle Flight OV-102, a typical Soyuz-Salyut spacecraft, and a postulation on the mystery Cosmos satellite launched first from Tyuratam, or as they called it, Baikonur Cosmodrome. Jim Holloman had prepared that information in fact two days before. He pretended to assemble it as a wire despatch from Moscow, once more delighting his editor.

47

SS9

At Jericho headquarters, deep in Cheyenne mountain, General Wheeler, David Greenberg and Daniel Perès stared at the Big Bird photograph. There was no doubt about it. A fourth Soviet launcher was out on the pad and this one was different, it was an SS9 'Scarp', the largest military missile in the Soviet armoury.

'Daniel, I think you better tell Mossad that we've identified an SS9 on the pad and I'll bet you it's a Mod 5 version. Tell them to expect an interception of the beam weapon. The Russians are running scared.' Wheeler said.

'What's a Mod 5?' Daniel asked.

'It's the fifth modification of the SS9. This missile normally carries a 25 Megaton warhead to hit our Titan and Minuteman bases—that's Mod 2—but we've photographed the SS9 at Tyuratam intercepting their own 'target' satellites launched by SS5 missiles from Plesetsk in the Leningrad Military District. The Russians have a special SIS or Satellite Interceptor Force, armed with Mod 5 SS9s and based at Tyuratam. They fire the big one into an elliptical orbit carefully computed to approach a target satellite very closely, in fact within yards! It can even manoeuvre closer if necessary under ground control. Then the warhead explodes, destroying the satellite. The Russians have demonstrated it many times, it's a proven weapon.'

Wheeler put the photograph down on the table and

stared vacantly at the far wall as he tried to understand its implications for the Shuttle crew.

'What warhead does it carry?' Daniel asked.

'It'll be nuclear or fragmentation, could even be carrying a beam itself. Jesus, this thing is getting out of hand. I'm going to call the President and tell him that there's an outside chance the Russians could be aiming at the Shuttle!'

There was complete silence from the others. Wheeler picked up the red phone which the President's aide answered. There was a 'click' then President Stockman was on the line. It took Wheeler only two minutes to précis the situation. A further three minutes passed then Wheeler put down the phone, looking grim.

'Gentlemen, the President is ordering a first stage alert for all US and NATO forces in case of the Soviets' attempting to destroy the Shuttle.'

At that moment an alarm sign flashed and they all turned to view the TV monitor. A computer-generated image appeared of the Globe divided into projection lines. Then a white line suddenly encircled the globe in a green ellipse.

Another line emerged in red on the same inclination but tracing a perfect circle, below them the 'earth' spun slowly. A moment later a series of times, dates and co-ordinates wrote themselves onto the screen followed by a single flashing number beneath.

Wheeler grimaced.

'Gentlemen, the Soviets have launched an SS9 within the past ten minutes. That's the trajectory prediction right there from Norad tracking. It will intercept the Salyut, not the Shuttle, unless it changes orbit. The Russians are going to blow up their own spacecraft, I guess. It must be the Palestinian who's now flying the entire assembly. What the hell is he up to? He must have gotten out of control. Daniel, tell Mossad now. By the way, gentlemen, in accordance with agreed procedure, the President is travelling to Andrews Air Force Base where he will be aboard the E4B Command Post within the hour. We're up the next rung of the ladder.' Wheeler looked very concerned.

'How long is the ladder, General?' Daniel asked.

'Very short, about four rungs and you step out into the abyss.'

48
Trigger

Shabir was furious. Zhukov had been switched off from the ground. The panel told him everything: 'Power Status—Zero'. After all this, all the years of training, of fighting, flying, after murdering Karpov and Tsiolkovsky, nothing! He had a gun without any ammunition. He could not even pull the trigger . . . the trigger . . . *the trigger*! And suddenly he let out a cry of exhaltation. There was still a chance, of course, the trigger! The Palestinian shot out of his seat, banging his head on a hatch cover, but he kept smiling as he steadied himself.

'Calm down, calm down, you're not defeated yet.'

He nudged himself over to the maintenance locker, desperately trying to remember where the equipment would be stowed. The door opened silently and he looked in. Underneath an elastic net were those items which were always useful on a long trip. Knives, screw drivers, wrenches, a welding unit and most important of all for him, four rolls of woven nylon tape. Always handy if you want to tether components together during EVA, or repairs. A thousand and one uses, in fact.

Shabir removed the tapes, putting two in each pocket and zipping them in securely along with two sharp folding knives, their plastic joints specially designed to operate smoothly in space where normal grease would freeze. He then prepared himself for EVA plugging his suit into the umbilical, and floated over to the unused airlock, the other already having Soyuz docked into it. It was already pressurised so he opened it easily, floated in, then closed the inner hatch behind him. He plugged in the umbilical ensuring him of full environmental support during EVA, and checked his suit pressure. He then released the pressure dump valve until the gauge read 'Total Vacuum'. Carefully he raised the locking lever and swung the external hatch inwards until it was secured in the 'Open' position.

For the second time in a few hours he looked out into space. Without further preliminaries he placed both gloved hands on the circular rim and hauled himself out cleanly until he floated about a foot away where he looked up through his visor and gasped.

The scene was quite breathtaking. He was looking straight up at the Pacific Ocean. As far as his slowly-turning head could see was a curving sheet of dazzling blue ocean. A fantastic distance below him were spirals and eddies of white mist. He could see streams of feathering cirro-stratus and nimbo-stratus thousands of miles long. To the north was a mass of whiteness, as if a giant had stirred the clouds. It was a typhoon on the limit of the disappearing side of the planet. He thought he recognised Japan and its islands. He was 100 miles above the Western Pacific travelling at 18,000 miles an hour. All he could hear was the sound of his own breathing and the thumping of his heart.

He could feel the tension on the umbilical and for a moment felt terror at the thought of it coming undone, leaving him totally helpless in orbit, and he suddenly remembered the two men he had pushed into oblivion a few hours before. He knew he had murdered, and he knew he would never see men again. He started to pray. He was only an instrument of God, a soldier of Palestine.

Shabir pulled himself towards the Salyut and as he closed with it he recognised the special EVA hand-holds along its length. He turned, placed his floating belly against the polished metal of the craft and made his way hand-over-hand towards Zhukov. He started to sweat, his heart racing with the stress, pausing for a moment to tilt his head back.

Zhukov looked even more spectacular in the absolute clarity of space, every detail stood out far more dramatically than on earth, particularly the electric-blue solar panels looking as fragile as gossamer. And there along its axis he recognised the object he needed desperately to reach.

Slowly he crept over the docking ring and along the hexagonal columns, until he reached the box. It was the larger one of the three arranged around the junction of the solar panels and the columns. Carefully he floated the last few inches and with thumping heart brought his gloved hands forward on each side of the box, running his gloves along its base. He felt the two catches and, closing his eyes, the sweat misting his inner visor, he pulled the thermal protection cover towards him. The reaction to his movement pushed him away from the weapon and frantically he shot a hand out to grasp the adjacent box, and held on.

The covering panel he had unclipped spun lazily away over his shoulder revealing the very key to his mission. In three separate cavities sat three large switches, their ends specially ribbed to give grip.

Above these was the legend in Russian: 'POWER—ARMED—FIRE. For Manual Testing Only.'

Shabir grinned and wanted to shout with joy to the world below. He stared at the three switches not believing his luck but now utterly convinced of the sanctity of his mission. It had been the chance encounter with Nagy the metallurgist at Tyuratam that had given him the knowledge of the three switches.

He unzipped a pocket, took out a blue nylon tape and carefully pulled it from its dispenser. It took him five minutes to feed out about fifteen metres of tape, then he looped the nearest end around the large 'Power' switch and tied it securely. He left the extended part floating and repeated the exercise twice more, one tape for each function: Blue for 'Power', White for 'Arm', Red for 'Fire'.

He gathered the short ends, still on their dispensers, and fed them over the high frequency antennae, thereby obtaining the necessary leverage to pull the switches in opposite directions, knowing the weapon discharged in a few seconds before having to re-charge. He gathered the three floating ends in his hand and looped them over a pressure probe, bringing their ends together in a bundle with the ends already looped around the antennae. Carefully he pulled each gathered bunch together and knew then that he could power, arm and fire the weapon at a distance by pulling the 'Trigger' tapes in the correct sequence. Similarly he could reverse the switches whilst the weapon charged itself. Nagy had said quite clearly that the device could be fired using the manually operated triggers. Those casual conversations with the disgruntled Ukrainian, who had complained about the problems they had had during ground testing at Semipalatinsk, were now paying off.

Shabir very carefully worked back towards the Salyut EVA hatch, gently guiding the tapes along his route until he reached the airlock entrance. Almost breathing a sigh of relief he floated in, still holding the tapes and clasped them all together in one hand. Then he released the pressure valve for Salyut and within a few minutes he noted the 'Total Vacuum' sign come on, indicating that the spacecraft had lost pressure, enabling him, in his EVA suit, to unlock the inner hatch and enter Salyut, still guiding the tapes gently in his hand.

He floated towards the Salyut navigation panel and took up a stable position, using the safety harness provided. He pressed a series of keys, then looked up at the circular screen in front of him, its face covered by a transparent graticule, like a compass with a gun-sight superimposed. Closing his eyes and with the press of a single isolated switch, he opened the protective shutter of the Salyut primary sensor, the giant East German-made optical surveillance telescope.

The sunlight reflected from Earth would have blinded him but for his precautionary action and he slowly opened his eyes, letting them adjust to the brilliant light that streamed out of the telescope.

It was set to 'Low Magnification' without the 'Tracking Mode' switched on and he saw the incredible sight of

Newfoundland racing by below him. He switched to 'Track' as a selected point reached the centre of the graticule, commanding the telescope to automatically track the object below for a good fifteen seconds before it had passed out of the field of view at a ground speed of eighteen thousand miles an hour. He switched to 'Mid-Mag' and now he could see clouds very clearly racing out of view. He held at this and as he turned to the rendezvous radar scanner he almost jumped in shock and disbelief.

There, clearly visible on the radar screen was a 'Target' only ten miles away, closing from behind at 60 miles an hour. It would reach him in ten minutes. Frantically he grasped the manoeuvring side stick controller, then turned the spacecraft quickly to orientate the 'telescope' towards the unknown intruder. As he spun, he first saw a vast sweep of land before the earth's horizon appeared. The tracking radar gave him his bearing and orientation in an instant and he fed this to the telescope tracking system, and there it was, an unmistakably man-made object, lit by the sun like a brilliant tiny jewel. Shabir gathered the floating ends of coloured tape and selected the two white ends. He switched the telescope to 'High-Mag' and there in front of him was the image of a Soyuz vehicle, but without the familiar paddles!

After a moment's thought he suddenly remembered what it was—a Cosmos Destroyer Satellite. No doubt about it. Everybody at Tyuratam had seen one launched at one time or another, but Shabir never dreamed that one day he would be its target.

Praying that the trigger tapes would work he pulled the blue pair until one extended further than the other. A light suddenly appeared on the 'Zhukov Control System' panel. He ignored it, gathered the two white tape ends and pulled them in the same way, a second light appeared, this time flashing every half second. He looked through the telescope and was horrified to see that the bomb had almost filled the screen. He switched to 'Low Mag' and there it was again only five miles away and dead centre as he gathered the two red tape ends. With sweat pouring off his face and his heart beating crazily in his chest he pulled the red tapes!

The effect was quite extraordinary. The whole telescope screen turned a brilliant fluorescent green and he immediately switched the protective shutter over the lens, hoping it was undamaged. He waited five seconds then pulled the other red tape back, thereby switching off the 'FIRE' trigger. He opened the shutter. All he could see was a cloud of silver gas expanding rapidly from a central point in space.

He could not believe it. The beam had worked. In spite of the effort of the Soviet Union, he, single-handed, had destroyed a nuclear bomb in orbit, and was still alive. God was on his side. 'Imsh'allah.'

He looked down at his gloved hands, at the brightly coloured tapes and prepared them carefully again, pulling them in sequence until Zhukov was powered and armed, and only then of course did he remember why the lights had flashed. They recorded the positions of the three trigger switches.

49
First Rung

Shimatov, Cherensky, Dobrodolsky, Mendeleiv and more than a thousand Soviet witnesses simply could not believe what had happened. The Palestinian had made Zhukov work and then destroyed the Destroyer.

The Soviet President saw it all on his TV monitors hooked up to Kalinin, Tyuratam and Semipalatinsk. He sat watching it in absolute silence for at least a minute, before stretching out a hand and picking up the yellow phone always at his side. There were the usual clicks and hums for a minute as President Stockman was located before his voice answered again in Russian. Beriev silently thanked Stockman for saving him the frustration of going through an interpreter.

'This is the President speaking,' he said.

'Is that you, Alexei?' Stockman asked, his voice clear and steady.

'Yes, Mr President, it is I and I'm sure you know why I'm calling.'

'Yes, Alexei, we saw it too through Norad. Grim, is it not?'

'It is. Very, very grim. We must work to solve it together, James. It is beyond our individual control.'

'Alexei, do you have any idea what he will do next with that infernal beam?'

'No, James, I do not, but I will find out everything Shimatov planned. Never again will he be given executive power in this State.'

'Alexei, I think we do know what he will do next. And so does Israel . . . He will destroy Jerusalem.' There was a few moments silence from Moscow.

'James, can you organise an airlift, an evacuation of the city? The Soviet Union will offer to assist in flying out civilians.'

'Alexei, you cannot evacuate a city in half an hour. The panic will cause congestion and more people will die. The Israelis have their own plans, though.'

'What are they, James? We should know.'

'Alexei, your own KGB trained and armed that Palestinian. He has, I assume, killed your two cosmonauts, if the papers are to be believed. He is a fanatic but the Soviet Union is responsible. Israel will take whatever action she has planned. I have pressed for restraint but that becomes difficult when your country's heart and soul is destroyed.'

'In that case, James, the Soviet Union must prepare to defend itself against an Israeli response.'

'Alexei, I ask you on behalf of the peace of the world not to attack Israel. You know we are pledged to defend that State, and we will. I am speaking to you from my Airborne Command Post. I have placed our forces and NATO on worldwide alert and ordered dispersal of our bombers, fighters and submarines. We will not stand by and see Israel destroyed.'

'James, I will confer with my Cabinet and call you back. Goodbye, only for now, I hope.'

50
Suzy Q

Jack Hilliard loved boats. They were the only way he could get away from his family who bored the pants off him, his office who were always ringing him at awkward times, and his wife who could not tolerate his drinking.

Jack lay on the foredeck of his 40-foot *Suzy Q* clutching his flask of iced bourbon and gazing absently at the Caribbean sky. He hoped he would not catch a fish, he had always bought a few from the marina fishermen as props on his return.

He loved Florida but most of all the Bermuda Triangle. It was the one surefire way of keeping his entire family off the boat. Ever since they had read the books he had had privacy and he toasted the literary fortunehunters who had brought him these rare moments of peace and serenity.

He dozed in an alcoholic haze, the sun heavy on his brain, until he started to dream. He imagined he was alone on his boat in the Bermuda Triangle when out on the blue horizon he saw a thin column of green light suddenly appear from the sky. It started to get brighter as it came closer and soon he could see a circle of mist appear where it dissolved into the ocean. To his surprise it appeared to accelerate straight towards him as if it was an enormous heavenly spotlight but instead of settling on him it swept straight past with a curious humming and hissing. As it crackled and hissed and vanished half a mile past him the most amazing part of the dream was that it cut *Suzy Q* clean in two. As he lay there curious but unafraid he saw the stern float quietly away, to sink silently into the warm flat sea. He even dreamed that he slid slowly off the foredeck to land with a. . .

With a splash that shocked him to sensibility, Jack Hilliard found himself kicking for his life in the sea. He had slid off the *Suzy Q*, and with growing horror he looked and there was the stern, almost gone below the waves. Hilliard thrashed about in panic and with the luck of a drunk grabbed the air bed he had been lying on. It saved his life. Spluttering and kicking he hauled himself onto its warm ribbed surface and gazed at a sight unseen by man. It was as if the finger of God had pointed at the ocean!

The beam was returning. Hilliard screamed as it tracked unerringly towards him, coming to rest a few feet from the air bed. The swell lifted him high enough to be able to see that it drilled a perfect hole in the ocean while jets of steam formed a few feet above the surface, following the circumference of the beam. Then it vanished, as if God had switched it off!

Jack Hilliard was very lucky that day for his next shock came only minutes later as he heard a shattering roar suddenly burst over him. He cowered, convinced of his approaching doom and gibbered incoherently, throwing up Scotch and sea water in his terror. Then out of the corner of his eye he saw with relief that the noise came from a low-flying jet circling his boat. It had Navy markings, thank God. Hilliard did not know it but he had come within feet of becoming the world's first victim of a charged particle beam.

The 'friendly' aircraft was a Viking anti-submarine plane off the carrier *Independence* exercising in the Atlantic. The aircraft's forward-looking infra-red scanner had registered a phenomenal beam of heat energy tracking across the ocean at a fantastic speed. As Commander Steven Lacy followed its track his radar officer observed a single surface 'target', the good ship *Suzy Q*.

Within an hour and a half a completely sober Jack Hilliard was back on shore having been picked up from the ocean by the Coastguard helicopter vectored to the scene by the Viking crew. The humour of the situation did not escape the helicopter crew who listened sympathetically to Hilliard's resolution never to touch a drop again and give up sailing in the Bermuda Triangle.

He repeated to the Coastguard the story of his incredible experience of another Triangle mystery and the UFO that had chased him all over the ocean. Lacy's report meanwhile was flashed to Naval Command Headquarters at Norfolk, Virginia and from there straight to Omaha. In the past 24 hours all US forces had been briefed to report any occurrence involving possible 'beams' to their Headquarters.

51
Texas Wrangler

Zhukov's next victim was also a boat but a great deal bigger than *Suzy Q*.

The *Texas Wrangler* ploughed her 450,000 tons steadily across the Atlantic, 300 miles west of the Bay of Biscay. She was fresh from delivering her cargo of high-quality crude oil to Bantry Bay in Ireland and was now making for Port Harcourt in Nigeria to carry another load to Rotterdam, her virtually empty holds holding large invisible pockets of gas. She was doomed.

Shabir tracked her for thirty seconds using 'High-Mag' to reveal her shape before pulling the red tape. He saw what looked like a thin orange line cross her amidships and a moment later she was enveloped in an expanding ball of flame. The gas, ignited by the heat of the beam cutting through the steel deck like a cigarette end through tissue paper, blew the severed bow and stern apart, spattering the sea in huge lumps of flaming debris. The 35 men on *Texas Wrangler* were the first victims of the charged particle beam.

Shabir only saw a glimpse on the telescope tracker before he had passed out of range, but it was enough to convince him of his ability to identify, track and destroy small or large targets, anywhere beneath his orbit as well as anything that might dare to approach him in space.

The news of *Texas Wrangler's* destruction reached Omaha via the Royal Navy's frigate *Warrior*, on anti-submarine exercises in the area. Her crew had witnessed the explosion, being five miles away on a parallel course. A number of men on deck spotted the incredible sight of the beam looking like a vertical green line joining the sea and the sky together. They watched fascinated as it appeared to track the distant tanker, then it seemed to focus on the ship and moments later it blew up in an enormous explosion. They were horrified by the spectacle of sudden and total destruction in the middle of a calm blue ocean. *Warrior* was the first vessel on the scene, her Captain Oliver Harvey immediately changing course on hearing the 'boom' and making full speed towards the huge column of black smoke billowing out of the oily inferno. Although he had not seen the mysterious beam himself, sufficient numbers of his crew had, so he took the precaution of immediately radioing the description to the Admiralty in London and also to Norfolk, Virginia. His second signal half an hour later confirmed his worst fears. There appeared to be no survivors but he intended to keep searching.

The explosion was so violent that both sections had sunk by the time *Warrior* arrived, leaving no trace of her massive presence except for a junkyard of floating debris amidst a mile-wide sea of flames.

Utterly remote from the scene of devastation, Shabir felt a growing confidence in his ability to select the target of his choice. He sensed that destiny was leading him towards his ultimate goal. He would avenge Palestine.

52
Protégé

As Captain Oliver Harvey RN transmitted his first signal, the assassin unclipped his harness and pirouetted around to face the communications panel directly behind him. He left the tapes neatly bundled together and wrapped one around the manoeuvring control stick.

For a few seconds he composed his thoughts, breathing long controlled breaths before placing his right hand over Salyut's 'Comkeyboard'. Very deliberately he pressed the first power switch and saw the display light up. Then he pressed the 'TV link' button and waited for some seconds as the centrally placed TV monitor warmed up. Outside Salyut, the high-gain antennae suddenly turned on its axis, automatically searching for the strongest signal source, its distant partner one of the huge 75-metre communications dishes around the world on land and sea manned by Soviet technicians.

The monitor gradually cleared and there before him was a perfectly clear picture of an empty chair behind which was a scene of total confusion. People were everywhere, many in full military uniform standing close to the rows of controllers. He had hardly ever seen uniformed people standing in the control trenches but now they dominated the scene. At that moment somebody shouted, then another and a controller broke from his seat and ran towards the empty seat.

Feverishly the man pressed his keyboard and the sound of Kalinin broke the silence in Shabir's visor.

'Salyut 7, Salyut 7, do you read me, over?'
Silence from Shabir.
'Salyut 7, this is Kalinin control, do you read me, over?'
Shabir pressed his 'TV transmit' switch.
'Kalinin control, this is Salyut 7, I hear and see you clearly, over.'
The man looked up, startled, directly at the TV camera and saw the visored face of the Palestinian.
'Salyut 7, please confirm who I am speaking to, over.'
'Kalinin, this is Salyut 7, Shabir Al Timimi commanding, over.'
'Shabir, wait a moment, please, I have to connect you to General Shimatov.'
'Kalinin, make it quick, I have things to do, over.'
There was a series of flashes on the screen then another similar scene appeared on the monitor. A few seconds later a familiar figure could be seen threading his way through the crowded control room. He kept his eyes focused on a point directly below Shabir's picture. He was obviously looking at a TV monitor of the Palestinian. General Shimatov displayed no emotion as he sat down at the communications console before looking up directly at the camera.
'Shabir, is that you?'
'Yes, General, don't you recognise me?'
'It's impossible, the mask gives a reflection, I can't see your face.' Shimatov was telling the truth. For all he could see was the interior of Salyut reflected in the visor like a fish eye lens.
'I assure you it's me, General, I am alone, of course.'
'What happened, Shabir, what are you trying to do?'
'I am simply carrying out my mission as I was trained to do by you, General. Albeit more quickly than we had planned, eh?'
'Shabir, what has happened to your colleagues Karpov and Tsiolkovsky?'
'They are dead.' The voice was steady.
'Why Shabir? Was there an accident?' Shimatov asked, with a note of concern.

'You know there wasn't, General, and you know why.' Shabir replied.

'No, I don't understand. Why did you kill them?'

'You forced me to when you abandoned our plans.'

'Nobody abandoned the plans, we had major problems here, totally out of our control.' Shimatov replied, trying to sound conciliatory.

'You abandoned our mission, you abandoned my people's struggle just as it was beginning to succeed.' Shabir replied.

'Never, Shabir, it was a forced postponement, nothing else. When you return we will prepare an even better solution,' Shimatov replied, gesturing with his hands.

'Never. You will kill me, you just tried to with that satellite bomb.'

'No, you misunderstood, that was an American bomb, why would we wish to destroy you? You are our great friend and fellow cosmonaut.' Shimatov tried to sound convincing.

'I misunderstood nothing, General. Remember, you yourself told me on three occasions that only the Soviet Union had the ability to destroy American satellites any time they wished, or do you forget that?' Shimatov was stumped, he could not deny it, the Palestinian's memory was far too good.

'Shabir, please. I would never have allowed that, I am your friend, but we have extremists here who would rather see you dead than succeed. They will be punished for their action.'

'And what about me, General? Will the Soviet Union try me and sentence me for killing two Russians?' Shabir asked, the irony in his voice. Shimatov put on his softest expression, like a father scolding a dearly loved child.

'The Soviet Union is the great ally of the Palestinian people. We must accept that some of our people will die. Karpov and Tsiolkovsky were accidental victims of a tragic misunderstanding but it will be forgiven and soon forgotten. The Soviet Union is a benevolent state unlike the Western Imperialists.'

'General, nothing you can say to me will change the plan

you conceived and I trained for. Nothing, Imsh'allah.'

'But Shabir . . .' Shimatov's voice suddenly revealed his growing alarm, 'please, trust me, have I ever betrayed your cause? Have I ever lied to you?'

'No, General, I don't believe you have. In fact, I respect and admire you for being almost a father to me. But I am free of the pressures you are under and so I, as your protégé, will succeed for both our sakes.' Shabir sounded very confident.

'Shabir, my friend, please show your respect for me by heeding my advice. Nothing can be achieved at this moment. The Israelis are too well prepared. A Zionist agent discovered our plan by chance. We must simply plan for a new and greater mission, soon, I promise you.'

Shabir ignored Shimatov's plea:

'The Israelis are about to see what you planned and I trained for. Goodbye, General. We will not meet again in this world. I have no fear of dying. My life is nearly over but I will avenge my people. I will destroy Israel myself.'

There was a click and the screen went dead and Shimatov curled his fingers into fists and pounded the table.

'Shabir, don't be a fool, Shabir, don't, don't, don't . . .' but he was already too late.

With a sense of finality Shimatov switched off the TV monitor and walked back to the others.

Shabir watched the blank screen for several seconds, now resigned to his fate. Up here nobody could touch him. He, the sole Arab cosmonaut, would bring down the wrath of God on the Zionists below. He, Shabir Al Timimi, was God's humble instrument, for how else could one human being be invested with so much power, literally within his hands? And he looked down at the tapes.

He turned towards the open hatch through which they threaded their way across the airlock and out along the side of the Salyut to Zhukov. Salyut was very cold now, because of the pressure loss through having to give the tapes an uninterrupted pathway. He knew the end would come much sooner than a few weeks, a couple of days at the most, unless he left the tapes in the airlock and repressurised Salyut. But the cold might well have damaged the interior equipment beyond repair.

He turned and floated the few feet to the Zhukov Control Panel to prepare for his final tasks. Suddenly he froze, for there, clearly on the radar screen, was a 'target'! He kicked desperately towards the screen, overshooting in his haste and taking several vital seconds to steady himself in front of the brilliant white dot moving towards the centre of the screen. He could hardly believe it, but it was there. A huge target, far bulkier than the bomb and approaching at two miles a minute. With feverish movements he set about the task of gathering the target in his sights.

53
Duel

'He's seen us, Mike, he's seen us!' screamed Pete. 'The thing's turning round, for God's sake! Oh, Jesus, we almost made it.' Peabody was getting very scared, sitting, watching the incredible assembly turning slowly, a mere five miles ahead.

'Jericho, this is Rocky. We are four miles away.'

'Rocky, this is Jericho, use the OMS quickly, keep moving, spin the Orbiter, we're watching on the Norad monitors.'

'Jericho, here we go. It was a good idea. Not your fault it didn't work. Over.'

Michael spoke to his crew.

'Dave, Pete, hold on. I'm going to tumble the Orbiter. Check your harnesses, stow everything. . .go!'

And Michael Allon pushed the control column hard over and the huge vehicle, its cargo bay wide open, tumbled suddenly like a dead fish, hurtling towards the Russian at over a hundred miles an hour. The black underbelly and brilliant white upper surface flashed in front of Shabir's 'High Mag' telescope scanner making it difficult for him to aim.

The Palestinian had less than sixty seconds to hit the incredible device before it either collided with him or flew past. With skilful manoeuvring he found it in the centre of the target graticule and pulled the red trigger tape. The sight was fantastic as a phenomenal beam cut across space at the speed of light . . . and struck the Orbiter!

It went straight through two of the three main engine nozzles projecting from the flat tail as they spun across its path. The huge nozzles literally vanished, totally obliterated by the charged particles streaming from Zhukov as the Orbiter careered over its assailant, missing the assembly by a matter of inches.

The Palestinian almost collapsed with shock at the totally unexpected turn of events, unable to recognise what had so nearly struck him. It could have been the new US Space Shuttle.

'Now!' Peabody shouted and Michael pulled back hard on the stick to halt the tumbling spacecraft as they almost struck the Salyut.

Michael flew with all his skill desperately correcting the tumbling motion by using the thrusters. Within less than a minute the crippled Orbiter stabilised tail first, an extraordinary feat of airmanship, still disappearing fast from the Salyut and Michael fired the twin OMS rockets above the tail. Gradually OV-102 came to a halt relative to the Salyut, on the braking force of those motors, then without stopping and with painful slowness it very gradually started on the return run to the assassin, now less than five miles away.

'Dave, Pete, start checking fast what our damage situation is. Pete, you concentrate on the SSMEs. Dave, check the operation of the Arm and the cargo bay doors, while I keep watching the Salyut. The moment I see him start to aim towards us I'll tell you. I think he's too busy right now. I hope he thinks we're finished after that hit.

'I'm going to tumble the Orbiter slowly to make him think we're gonners, but we'll be approaching him gradually as we do so.

'Dave, can you see what damage has been done at the back? Look through the rear observation windows.'

'I don't see much Mike, except a lot of metallic fragments floating away from the tail.' Dave Browne replied. He was standing behind Michael and looking out towards the rear of OV-102 across the gaping blackness of the cargo bay.

'Watch the fin while I operate the rudder and split it for air braking. I want to make sure we can get back and stop.' Michael pushed his left and right boots in opposite directions before operating the airbrake handle that split the rudder along its trailing edge, opening each half 45 degrees into the airflow when landing.

'Looks fine, Mike, full and free, as they say,' Browne replied.

'OK, let's start tumbling while we check our status.'

Gently, Michael prepared to roll the Orbiter into a lazy tumble, easy to correct when necessary. But he had to communicate first because, once tumbling his antennae would not be able to hold alignment with the TDRSS satellite that acted as his space relay to Jericho.

'Jericho III this is Rocky, do you read us, over?'

'Rocky, this is Jericho III, we read you fine. Phew! You had us very worried just then, we were watching on Norad close-up cameras. It was an incredible sight. Tell us your plan. They're carrying out a total damage check on you at Houston, over.'

'Jericho, we appear to be in reasonable shape. I think he only hit the main engine nozzles from what we can see of the tail. We'd be OK for return on that basis. We're going to play possum. We'll give the appearance of being dead, therefore no longer a threat. I'll set us on a very gentle return towards him. He'll never notice it unless he watches his rendezvous radar. Tell Zuckerman to keep him talking while we approach, over.'

'Rocky, we understand and we'll inform Zuckerman immediately. Good luck, over.'

'Roger, Jericho. We're still in business. I'm commencing the tumbling manoeuvre in five seconds. If we don't make it each one of us left some private messages in the crew lockers; we thought it would be a sensible thing to do. Here we go . . .'

And with that last terse message the crew of OV-102

ceased communications with Jericho III. The Norad Baker Nunn cameras watched it enter into a tumbling gyration five miles away from the obviously lethal weapon. The men on the ground held their breath.

54
El Wad

Feverishly, Shabir switched the telescope back to 'Low-Mag' and turned Zhukov to face the earth. The target of his lifetime was less than two minutes away, 100 miles below him. He would have to hope that his assailant was crippled or destroyed or he would miss his chance for at least ninety minutes.

The telescope screen suddenly showed a brilliant patch of golden-red mountainous terrain and the unmistakable Aegean Sea, a dazzling blue mirror below him. In two and a half minutes Palestine would be within his sights and with it his first target, El Wad, the City of Jerusalem and at its heart, the very soul of his enemy, the Wailing Wall of the Temple of the Jews.

A hundred miles below Zhukov, Ephraim Zuckerman rushed into the studios of Israel TV and handed over the small flat box to the waiting technician. He hovered over his precious cargo as the man carefully removed the contents, a single video cassette cartridge. The young man, acoustically isolated from Zuckerman by his headphones, pointed rigorously towards the waiting set. The older man, in his baggy cream suit, anxiously wiping his face under the heat of the brilliant TV lights, waited until he could see that the cassette was in place, all ready to run.

With a click the tape was firmly installed in the Philips video player and Zuckerman walked quickly over to the set. It consisted of a blue curtain backdrop with a single chair, a table with a glass of water and two telephones, one red and one yellow, a microphone and two television monitors.

Zuckerman sat down and opened the black plastic file in front of him, loosened his collar and looked at the single television camera. He waited for the red light to tell him when he was 'on the air', closed his eyes and said a silent prayer. He knew that if his plan succeeded in the next few minutes then he might just be able to save Israel from being forced into a nuclear strike against the Soviet Union.

He thought of his good friend Rabbi Groman with whom he had discussed the steps he proposed to take, having sought his advice regarding the morality of his plan. It was the same Rabbi Groman who had felt spiritually bound to Michael and Liza ever since he had broken the news of their parents' death to them in the Jerusalem schoolyard over twenty years ago. It was the same Rabbi Groman who had returned with Liza to Israel after they had stayed with Michael in California on his return from Vietnam. And it was the same Rabbi Groman who drew his tallis back off his head onto his shoulders and walked slowly out of the tiny synagogue that nestled at the corner of the massive expanse of the Western Wall.

Groman adjusted his eyes to the brilliant sunlight, noting the familiar sound of the prayers of the devout Hassidim who faced and kissed the only remains of the Temple destroyed nearly two thousand years ago by the conquering Romans.

He held in his hand the little folded prayer for Ephraim Zuckerman to be granted the strength and wisdom to defeat the vengeance of the Palestinian in this Holy Land. It was no more than a few steps to the Wall, its warm masonry soaring in massive rectangular blocks of stone over a hundred feet above him and, as he approached, he caught sight of two little Arab children, a boy and a girl, running by across the open paved square. It reminded him for a moment of Michael and Liza, as they had been in Jerusalem and he was still smiling to himself as he slipped the tiny fold of flimsy paper into a crack between two of the ancient stones where it fluttered briefly for a second of time.

At that moment, a further 122 seconds had passed for Shabir Al Timimi when, praying to God for guidance, he switched to 'High-Mag' and there clear as a map was Jerusalem. He had only five seconds to find the Old City as he tracked from north-west to south-east over the familiar sights of the Sanhedria Tombs, the Sheikh Jarrah mosque, the Shechem Gate, entering the Old City walls, missing the Church of the Holy Sepulchre where he switched to 'hold', dead centre of the Western Wall, flanked to the north by the Dome of the Rock and to the east by the El Aqsa Mosque.

'Imsh'allah,' he whispered and pulled the Red trigger tape.

Witnesses in Jerusalem and the surrounding areas saw a beam of brilliant green light joining the heart of the Old City to the sky. Some said it reminded them of 'a fantastic thunderbolt from heaven', 'the finger of God', 'an immense spotlight', 'a miracle', 'the vengeance of the Almighty'—and so it went on. All agreed on its effect. It cauterised the heart of most of the world's most ancient religions.

In his desperation to destroy the Space Shuttle Shabir had unknowingly moved the beam's focusing device. Instead of a fine lance of phenomenal energy Zhukov had emitted an 800 metre wide disc of particle radiation that seared right across the heart of the Old City.

Market stalls burst into flames, people's clothing ignited as they walked. Hair frizzled in moments into black dust. For several excruciating seconds there was utter silence as lifeless mouths gaped for breath. Those at the Western Wall were the worst affected, the density of radiation reaching fantastic levels, sufficient to vaporise bone let alone flesh. The very rocks melted at their surfaces, reverting in millionths of a second to their ancient, igneous state.

Rabbi Groman's shadow was left forever seared into the ancient paving stones along with rows and rows of others. The children he'd seen were but a blur in the pavement. Scientists at the Weizmann Institute later explained the macabre 'shadows of death': 'The intensity of the radiation was inversely proportional to the square of the distance from its centre of origin . . .'

Two hundred and eighteen died by the Wall whilst hundreds survived mere yards away. These were the unlucky ones, blistered caricatures of humanity. Others, further away at the Dome of the Rock and the El Aqsa Mosque were badly scorched. The luckiest pilgrims were those inside, particularly at the Holy Sepulchre, where a service had just started. And the beam's effect on the buildings, the fabric of Jerusalem's Old City, was profoundly visible. Everything turned black! The very air over the surfaces was burnt, covering the entire area in a nightmarish dust of pure carbon.

Ephraim Zuckerman saw the girl in the far corner of the studio drop the telephone, her face white with shock as she fell like a rag to the floor. Another girl rushed over, while Shimon Yariv grabbed the phone. He listened for a few seconds, then turned towards Zuckerman and stretched the handset at full arm's length in front of him shouting:

'The Palestinian's destroyed the Western Wall and part of the Old City. He's killed the lot of them there, he's murdered the worshippers. Do you hear me? He's murdered our people at prayer, Zuckerman. He's destroying us while we sit and wait and do nothing. The man is a fiend . . .' and Shimon Yariv quaked with hatred and anger for all Palestinians.

Zuckerman fought to control his reaction, his face twitching with mounting rage as he understood now what it must be to hate with every fragment of your soul, but this Palestinian was evil beyond belief. It was preposterous. He had selected men and women at prayer, knowing they would be utterly defenceless and then he had exposed them to his horror weapon. It was the worst atrocity since the Holocaust.

Zuckerman reached for the glass, drinking it all down then breathed deeply several times as he tried to control himself so as not to lose sight of his objective. He had to see the plan through to the bitter end and would not allow his emotions to affect his judgement, in spite of all that had happened.

He picked up the red phone line to the War Room. The face of Rebecca Limpel appeared simultaneously on the monitor screen and he said to her, 'Prime Minister, I have just heard a report that the Western Wall has been almost destroyed, together with most of its worshippers. It may be the action of the Palestinian. I request that Tablet Three go into operation, now!' There was rage in his voice.

'Mr Zuckerman, we have received confirmation of the atrocity a few moments ago, there appear to be over a hundred dead. Witnesses report a line of green light between the ground and the sky. It seems as if we are too late. Use the agreed plan—Tablet Three—as you wish. Nokum will start now. I will signal full approval immediately.'

'Thank you, Prime Minister, I will do my best to prevent further escalation. Please prepare to monitor this conversation.'

And General Landau, sitting behind his Prime Minister, picked up a green phone into which he said,

'Tablet Three, Tablet Three, this is Gideon, you are clear to go; repeat you are clear to go.'

55
Nokum 1

The bushes parted slowly as the rock face split into a jagged crack that grew wider and wider, exposing the black mouth of the Muara. For ten seconds there was absolute stillness and then came a cough and a whine steadily growing to an earth-shaking thunder of noise as out into the brilliance of the desert sun slid the long, pointed nose of the F-15. The sunlight stripped it from a black shadowy outline to a yellow-grey camouflage as it nosed out into the desert. The world's most potent combat aircraft swung to its right for 90-degrees then braked to a nose-dipping halt in alignment with the brilliant white centre-line markings of the road that would once more become its own secret runway.

The F100 engines began to spin faster, their roar growing in intensity, booming across the Negev and echoing in the great valley of Machtesh Ramon. The horizontal slab of the twin tailplane moved rapidly up and down, accompanied by a droop in the wing trailing edge as the pilot checked for full and free movement of his control surfaces. Twin spikes of blue flame grew from the tailpipes as the afterburners switched on for a few seconds, the added thrust rocking the entire airframe on its undercarriage until finally the Eagle was unleashed.

With a force that pushed Beer further and further back into his ejector seat, Nokum 1, as it was now referred to, started accelerating fast up the road towards the north and its distant target. With 25 tons of thrust accelerating him along the runway, Yigal Beer kept the nose of his aircraft down until he had used over 1,500 feet of road, the desert streaming past him at well over 100 miles an hour. Then, almost imperceptibly, the Eagle rotated upwards climbing into the hot bumpy air.

He knew he could never complete his mission unless he used his precious fuel carefully and also, in contrast to the previous dispersal flight that had dispatched him to his Muara, he kept his cruising speed down to 500 miles an hour, his multimission radar searching the ground beneath and in front of him for obstacles such as hills and mountains that could destroy him before he could even pull the nose up.

In four minutes, he would have to skirt Dimona, Israel's Nuclear Research Centre in the Negev Desert or he would be automatically intercepted by a barrage of surface-to-air missiles ringing the most valuable target in the State.

He would fly on, passing west of Hebron, and then roar over the land between Beit Shemesh and Jerusalem in a further six minutes. Nablus would appear on his right after another three and a half minutes and then he would thunder over the Jezreel Valley crossing Nazareth seventeen and a half minutes after take-off. He would bank right onto a heading of 5 degrees, hugging the mountains and valleys of northern Israel, until five minutes later, he would cross into Lebanon at Metulla, north of Kiryat Shmona, directly over the Trans-Arabian Pipeline. From then on he would have his electronic countermeasures switched on whilst crossing Lebanon. He would then cross Turkey, a country armed ironically with the same types of Phantom that many of his own IAF pilots flew.

Yigal Beer was confident that there was no aircraft yet built that could out-fight the F-15 in combat but he was still vulnerable to natural obstacles and mechanical failures, or perhaps Soviet surface-to-air missiles and radar-directed cannon. But that threat he would not have to face for at least an hour. From the moment of receiving Landau's call, he would not speak again to Israel for fear of being monitored. All he could do now was listen out for transmissions to his aircraft from the War Room via the electronic code machine at his side.

56
TV

Shabir was absolutely ecstatic. Although he could not see the extent of the damage to the Wailing Wall he knew from observing the exploding tanker beforehand that the beam had phenomenal energy. He turned towards the radar screen to check on his mystery target over five miles away, tumbling out of control.

'Whoever you are, fellow cosmonauts, it was a brave but foolish attempt. Now, shall I deliver the coup de grace?' But before he could do so a green light started to flash on the communication panel behind him. He saw it reflected in his radar screen and turned to see that it was a 'receiving' signal on the high-gain antennae. Somebody wanted to communicate with him.

'Why not?' he thought to himself. 'They can do nothing to change things now. I will tell them exactly what I intend to do for my people.'

Shabir floated over to the panel and switched on his 'TV link' button, again aiming the directional antennae on Salyut to point automatically towards the transmitting source on the ground.

The monitor screen flashed in brilliance before it settled down to show the drawn face of a grey haired man looking directly at him. The man must have been about 60 or more but it was difficult to tell his nationality. He had piercing dark eyes bridged below bushy white eyebrows matching his hair. He wore no glasses but Shabir noted the marks on his nose. His face was lined by the folds of his skin, stretched over prominent high cheekbones. His lips were thin, framing a small mouth above a dimpled chin. He looked like a scholar with his long grey hair falling over one eye. The man said nothing, just waited.

The two men looked at each other for several seconds like duellists appraising each other for the slightest evidence of fear or weakness. For Ephraim Zuckerman the task was particularly difficult because the pressurised helmet glass reflected the interior lights of the Salyut and all he could see were glimpses of dark, deep-set eyes above a long, firm nose. The outline of the visor made it difficult to see much more. Shabir opened the confrontation.

It was now eight minutes since he had beamed the Wall; in 80 minutes time he would be within range of his next target, having orbited the planet once. He spoke Arabic.

'This is Shabir Al Timimi, citizen of Palestine and commander of Salyut 7. Who are you and what is your reason for communicating?' Zuckerman was immensely relieved that the man might talk. He replied, also in perfect Arabic:

'Sir, my name is Ephraim Zuckerman, citizen of Israel, and I am Head of Israeli Intelligence. I wish to discuss your action today and give you new and very important information before you destroy your own people, over.'

'My action is not for discussion, it is a fact which you Israelis must live with as we have had to live for over 30 years with the fact of your occupation of our homeland.'

'Shabir Al Timimi, I am prepared to argue and fight with you for the rest of my life and I am sure you are also willing to fight for your beliefs. The State of Israel was created as a result of a majority vote in its favour at the United Nations in 1947. The past 35 years have been a struggle for a tiny but utterly important area of land by your people and my people. I see only two solutions, life or death. No one side can win. Do you accept that?'

'No, Zuckerman, my people will fight to the death as I know your people will, but we will be victorious, no matter how long it takes, because God is on our side.'

'Al Timimi, that may have been the outcome before the advent of nuclear weapons and that device you used only minutes ago on Jerusalem, but you are forcing a conflict that will destroy the land and people you are fighting for, as well as our people. There will be no victors, only death and permanent destruction. Your weapon killed many of our people today and many of yours. You have killed many innocent people on the high seas, I have just heard, but it is nothing compared to the power of nuclear weapons which will annihilate the entire population. So we beg of you to stop this pointless killing before all that you believe in vanishes in a nuclear confrontation.'

'Zuckerman, in war we all must accept death for the life of future generations. I accept that many of my people will die, but we Palestinians are spread around the world, outside Palestine, and we will return one day to our homeland.'

'Shabir, you are totally wrong because you have created a spark that has already lit the fuse of Doomsday. You have not acted alone, you have been trained and armed by the Soviet Union. Your action is simply as an instrument of Soviet policy. The struggle you believe you fight for is not between two neighbours, both of whom are of the same Semitic stock, both of whom have occupied the Middle East for more than 5,000 years and both of whom lived more in harmony than either have done with Christians or Communists. No, Shabir, you are nothing but a pawn to be used by the Soviet Union in their game plan to control all mankind according to their own doctrine and no other.'

'Liar, Zuckerman! The Soviet Government has supported our cause with arms and training to create a Palestinian Peoples Republic that they will protect against the expansionist plans of the Capitalist nations. The Soviet Union has been a mother to me and my people.'

'Shabir, I know all about you, about your real mother, your cousin and your father Mohammed, your life in the camps, your struggle for survival. Look. Here is the story of your life in front of me.' Zuckerman picked up the open file as the TV cameraman composed a close up shot of it.

'You see Shabir, we even call you 'Wolf'. You are as familiar to me as a son, a prodigal son, maybe. Your story is one of tragedy and manipulation. Believe me Shabir, you have been totally manipulated, your losses and grievances exploited ruthlessly by a force more evil, more pervading, than any created in history. You are nothing but a puppet of the KGB.'

Zuckerman prayed the Palestinian would be provoked to anger and consequently would want to argue. He was lucky.

'Zuckerman, you lie. You are a lackey of the Americans, of the CIA, of Capitalist companies. I and my Soviet friends have maintained our trust through everything. It is your work with the Americans that has forced me to take the initiative from my guardian and friend General Shimatov, who is a father of cosmonauts, not of the KGB; they are irrelevant to my actions. Now Zuckerman, I will tell you what that action will be. In an hour from now Israel will suffer a blow to its military strength as great as that to its religious beliefs. I will call you in a few minutes.' The screen went dead.

Zuckerman guessed immediately what the Palestinian referred to. It could only be Dimona. The heart of Israel's nuclear programme, isolated from prying eyes, out in the barren heat of the Northern Negev. The production centre for all the weapons carried by the Nokum aircraft. The processing centre for all bought, stolen, usurped and manufactured supplies of nuclear fission and fusion material in Israel. In one hour's time the Palestinian could destroy Dimona by triggering uncontrollable forces that could blow an entire section of desert into molten glass, killing possibly half a million workers, villagers and nomads within the area.

Zuckerman knew that there were at least eight one-megaton thermonuclear weapons awaiting delivery to Nokum aircraft still at Dimona. It was one of his agency's jobs to guard them as well as to carry out clandestine operations to obtain the raw material.

Zuckerman remembered how the Weizmann Institute had carried out regular analyses of the possible hazards if

Dimona were destroyed in a nuclear strike and he knew that the combined effect of the nuclear material that might be triggered by the action of the beam could instantly destroy all life as far away as Beersheva, Arad, and Yeroham. The effect of fallout, dependent on wind conditions, could kill many hundreds of thousands more in Khan Yunis, Gaza, Hebron and even Kafi, Sarak and Tafila in Jordan.

But Zuckerman's fundamental worry was, that according to War Plans approved by the Cabinet, the nuclear destruction of Dimona rendered Israel such a mortal blow that it was assumed that the Arabs, under Soviet pressure, would then attack, possibly with tactical nuclear weapons, whilst the State reeled in confusion. It was an automatic, planned response that a nuclear attack on Israel would be answered instantly by a reprisal against a selected Arab city or military complex, or even an attack on selected targets in the Soviet Union. This was the only way whereby a State, whose citizens comprised four million inhabitants and who had lost over six million of its kind in Europe whilst the world did nothing could hold in check the threats of the Soviet Union and hostile Arab nations.

Zuckerman knew that all his conversations with the Palestinian were being monitored on television by the War Cabinet. Rebecca Limpel, General Landau and the others would now prepare Israel for nuclear war. Furthermore, in ten minutes time Yigal Beer would cross into Turkey and ahead of him would be his target, the great Soviet Naval Base of Odessa in the Black Sea. Beer would destroy Odessa minutes after Dimona was destroyed by the Palestinian unless he was recalled through his electronic coding unit. The single weapon he carried was a one-megaton thermonuclear device designed to explode either at a selected height for an airburst if the pilot could achieve altitude without being shot down, or on impact in the sea or on land.

Rebecca Limpel's video image interrupted Zuckerman's thoughts.

'Ephraim, this is the Prime Minister, Tablet Four is now at standby. We read your thoughts, old friend. General

Landau has ordered the attempted dispersal of the moveable nuclear material and evacuation of all remaining staff into the nuclear shelters. The Army is clearing the roads. Nokum 1 is being ordered to prepare for an attack on the harbour installations only, the weapon will be dropped a mile out to sea. This is a 'Visible Controlled Response'.

'I will now contact President Stockman to tell him of the latest position to see if the Soviets can be restrained from launching an all-out strike against Israel.

'We are alerting the country now.' And as she said so the sirens started. The coded radio messages confirmed to every Israeli soldier that war was imminent.

It would be the third in fifteen years.

57
E4B

At a height of 38,000 feet above the mid-Atlantic Ocean President Stockman sat at the Commander-in-Chief's position in the War Room of the Boeing E4B Command Post. He put down the yellow phone and addressed his Chiefs of Staff.

'Gentlemen, the Prime Minister of Israel has ordered her country to prepare for a major war that may be a prelude to a nuclear conflict. The Palestinian cosmonaut is likely to attack Dimona within 50 minutes using the Soviet beam weapon. I am therefore ordering our forces to go to maximum readiness in case of a Soviet-Israeli conflict developing. Generals, please prepare for a confrontation with the Soviet Union in the case of Israel being destroyed.'

He ordered a telex sent on the hot line to the Soviet Premier rather than make a personal call which he judged lacked emphasis.

His message read:

TO THE PRESIDENT OF THE SOVIET UNION.

YOUR EXCELLENCY,

I, AS PRESIDENT OF THE UNITED STATES, HAVE RECEIVED GRAVE NEWS FROM THE PRIME MINISTER OF ISRAEL THAT A SOVIET CHARGED PARTICLE BEAM WEAPON IN THE FORM OF A SATELLITE AND UNDER THE OPERATION OF A SOVIET-TRAINED PALESTINIAN, SHABIR AL TIMIMI, HAS INFLICTED DEATH

AND DESTRUCTION ON ISRAEL'S MOST HOLY PLACE, NAMELY THE WESTERN WALL OF THE TEMPLE. I AM FURTHER RELIABLY INFORMED THAT THE SAME OPERATOR INTENDS TO STRIKE AGAIN AT ISRAEL, ALMOST CERTAINLY ITS NUCLEAR CENTRE OF DIMONA. I ASK THEREFORE THAT THE SOVIET UNION DO ALL IN ITS POWER TO ATTEMPT TO RESTRAIN ITS PROTEGE, SHABIR AL TIMIMI, AND TO AVOID A DIRECT CONFLICT WITH THE STATE OF ISRAEL EVEN IF THE SOVIET UNION SUFFERS COMPARABLE DAMAGE.

THE UNITED STATES GOVERNMENT WILL NOT TOLERATE A DIRECT STRIKE ON THE STATE OF ISRAEL AND WILL USE ALL NECESSARY FORCES AT ITS DISPOSAL TO REDUCE THE EFFECTIVENESS OF SUCH A STRIKE IN THE UNLIKELY EVENT OF ITS BEING LAUNCHED.

MY COUNTRY'S AMBASSADOR AT THE UNITED NATIONS IS NOW ASKING FOR AN EMERGENCY SESSION OF THE SECURITY COUNCIL TO CONVEY OUR INTENTIONS.

I URGE THE PEOPLE OF YOUR GREAT NATION TO ACT WITH RESTRAINT AND SEARCH FOR PEACE IN THE MIDDLE EAST DURING THE NEXT CRITICAL HOURS AND DAYS.

JAMES STOCKMAN
PRESIDENT OF THE UNITED STATES

Stockman then called Wheeler at Jericho III while the pilot of E4B circled over the Atlantic ready to fly him to any continent on earth. Around the aircraft flew a series of Navy carrier planes providing protection against possible interception while on the ocean below the carrier *Independence* swept the seas for Soviet submarines. One of the pilots was Commander Steven Lacy.

58
The Message

Shabir turned slowly round to the Zhukov Control Panel and immediately saw that the target was a little closer at about four miles away. He turned the telescope and found it, using 'High-Mag'. Yes, it was still tumbling out of control, obviously crippled in some way. Probably the thrusters were out of action and the resultant tumbling slowed it relative to Salyut. He could destroy it completely but he was conscious of time. Dimona would appear within the hour at an oblique angle to his trajectory. He would need to set up the telescope and track accurately to make sure of a hit first time for the next orbit took him further west over Central Africa.

During the next fifteen minutes he checked his orbit and worked out his exact ground track to identify landmarks for he would eventually fly parallel with the Suez Canal and the Red Sea. If he missed this next chance at Dimona he would have to wait for a further nine orbits before he would be within sight. He had to get it right. But again he was interrupted by the flashing light on the communication panel and he floated round, annoyed at the intrusion. It was Zuckerman again.

'Yes, Zuckerman, another plea, another argument?' Shabir asked coldly, enjoying his invulnerable position.

'Yes, Shabir, another plea. This time not from me but certainly somebody more important to you than the Soviet Union or your good friend General Shimatov.'

Zuckerman said quietly.

'You surprise me, Zuckerman, I must say, you keep trying.' Shabir wore a tight, sarcastic grin on his face, shielded by the visor.

The picture on the TV monitor changed and he immediately recognised her unforgettable face.

'Shabir, Shabir, this is Valentina, darling, Valentina Bykovsky. I love you, my darling. I always have, please listen as I talk to you. This could be our last chance to find peace together. I am at Odessa, near the Black Sea and here with me is our son, Nicholas.'

Shabir looked disbelieving at the tiny beautiful boy, his hair dark and long, curling over his high forehead and a pair of wide brown eyes. The child looked perplexed as he stood very shakily against his mother. Valentina looked as if she had been crying but she was even more beautiful than his memory had recalled. His tears started to flow, forming a wet patch on his chin where they collected against his visor. He was speechless.

'Shabir, darling, this is our son. You are his father. There never was anybody but you my love. General Vladimir Shimatov has lied to you for many years. He is, I know now, a General of the KGB. He forced me to write my last letter to you. He had already dictated it and threatened to take our son from me as soon as he was born. He moved me to Odessa and has prevented me from leaving the city or he will hurt our child. I have tried desperately to tell you the truth and now my chance has come.

'Nicholas and I want you to know that we are your family. Never again need you search for the family you lost in Palestine. The place of your birth is nothing but a tiny patch of land on the planet. Too many millions of people have died for a place they all called home. This earth belongs to nobody, no government, no race, no religion. It is itself only a tiny speck of dust in space. It is everybody's and nobody's home. I know from your work as a cosmonaut that you were being trained for journeying around the earth, so you know that when you are up there you see only a beautiful blue planet, not man-made frontiers or borders, only the land and sea and clouds.

'Please, I beg of you, do not destroy other families like ours. We are all the same under the sun, we are people of Earth. I am a Russian and you are a Palestinian, we came together in love and the product of that was our son, Nicholas. Once you were like him, Shabir, you know what it is like to lose a father so I beg of you, stop whatever revenge you plan now. The only winner is death itself.

'You men are so ready to die for your country and your people and you will sacrifice us your women and children for what you believe is right.'

Valentina was crying now, her voice trembling with emotion. Shabir saw her clutch their son closer to her as she went on.

'Darling Shabir, no more death, no more revenge, just stop the killing. You and the Jews must learn to live in peace, after all you have lived together for hundreds and thousands of years already. I know little of your place of birth and you little of mine. It does not matter enough to die for. Peace and happiness is in the mind and in the minds of your family, not in a patch of earth. I beg of you, no more killing, just let me love you again. Be a living father to your son, Nicholas, not a martyr to Palestine.' And she looked up brushing the tears away and said:

'Goodbye, my love, come back to us soon. I love you.'

She burst into sobs that racked her body and Nicholas placed a sticky hand on her cheek and tried to talk to her. The screen went dead, then returned to Zuckerman whose face was buried in his hands.

Shabir wept, his helmet wet with tears that ran down his neck and he could not even dry them for the instant he opened his helmet he would die, exactly as his victims Karpov and Tsiolkovsky had died, his blood boiling while his body froze. And so he cried in the utter silence of space as he flew silently towards Dimona at eighteen thousand miles an hour.

But behind him the mysterious target reached the centre of Salyut's radar screen and Shabir Al Timimi began to scream in anguish and terror as suddenly the entire satellite started to spin crazily around him.

59
Claw

Dave Browne held the Claw clamped in a steel grip around the rim of the open airlock hatch exercising his skill to the utmost to reduce the load on the Arm as Michael Allon spun the huge black-bellied Orbiter. In a brain-numbing dance in space his plan had worked. He had moved imperceptibly closer and closer to Salyut as Zuckerman desperately kept the Palestinian's attention. The last few seconds had been a nightmare as he corrected the tumbling, waiting for the golden weapon to swing towards his spacecraft and sweep him and his crew into infinity.

With practiced co-ordination the three men had manoeuvred the hastily strengthened Arm and Claw out of its resting place alongside the left-hand hinge of the cargo bay doors and the fantastic device had hummed slowly, bending at its central elbow joint, then turning through 180 degrees about the swivel joint mounted behind the crew compartment.

Dave Browne had brought it to rest like the lure of a lantern fish, with its Claw suspended high above and ahead of the Orbiter's windscreen where Michael and Pete could line it up with the looming Salyut.

And with brilliant piloting Michael had manoeuvred the Claw until it hovered, open, above the projecting ring.

'Go.' Michael had commanded and Dave had clamped the Claw in a vice-like grip on the ring.

'Got it, she's holding.' And a moment later Michael spun the Orbiter to shake the Palestinian to unconsciousness or death in the spinning interior of the Salyut, with its profusion of projecting instruments, controls and equipment.

Round and round flew the now huge assembly as Dave Browne fought to synchronise the movement of Arm and Claw to follow the tumbling motion of the Orbiter. He was desperately worried that the entire Arm would break off under the inertia of the struggle and leave them to collide with Salyut, killing them all.

Down at the many Norad tracking stations around the world observers saw a sight never imagined before, a duel in space, with its two antagonists locked in mortal combat. The largest space complex ever seen spun and tumbled crazily above the earth at 18,000 miles an hour, flashing white, silver and gold against the sunlight and the blackness of space.

Thousands of miles later and 100 miles above the southern tip of New Zealand Michael slowed the Orbiter down with careful use of the thrusters until finally the incredible object floated silently nose down over the Central Pacific with the Salyut-Zhukov assembly hanging like a dead metal insect beneath it, still held in the grip of the silver Claw.

'OK Pete, she's all yours, here I go,' Michael said, as he quickly unbuckled himself from the left-hand seat, still looking through the windscreen at the incredible sight of Zhukov glistening in the sunlight.

Michael floated to the hatch and opened it, then swam down the ladder to the crew compartment. Within ten minutes he had put on the EVA suit and made straight for the airlock hatch at the back of the crew compartment, floating into its confined cylindrical space. He closed the inner hatch, checked the outer one was sealed and depressurised to match the vacuum of space. He opened the outer circular hatch and looked straight into the cavernous empty space of the cargo bay. He looked up and saw straight into space.

He floated to the right and in a few moments was at the base of the Arm, adjacent to its swivel joint. The Arm was nearly two feet in diameter, smooth and shiny like a polished column of steel. Around it were wrapped, in opposing helices, two nylon tethers which Rockwell had found could give him grip for his next task. Michael was about to do the most dangerous job of all. He was to climb up the Arm, gripping it to his body as he made the long journey to Salyut, without an umbilical tether. One mistake and he would float into space. He wasted no time.

'OK, here we go. I'm on the swivel joint, Dave, she looks good. No obvious signs of damage.'

And carefully, patiently, hand over hand, like climbing a slippery pole, Michael made his weightless way up towards the soaring elbow.

As he moved he gradually looked over the nose of the Orbiter and ahead of him was the weapon, silent and lifeless in the Claw of the Orbiter.

He was also looking straight down at the familiar coastline of California a hundred miles below him.

The sight was breathtaking. The ocean and honey-gold land masses with their canopies of swirling cloud, way, way below him created a fantastic tapestry of coloured light.

'I'm climbing over the elbow, Dave.' He said and sweated with the exertion, pausing to sit on the joint itself, utterly exposed to the vast expanse of earth below and black space above him.

'Just like the simulator, Pete, you're going to love it.'

And all the time Pete Peabody held position as steadily as a rock so as not to shake his friend into oblivion. He switched on the specially mounted TV camera and across the world Norad, Omaha, Jericho, Air Force One and many other locations watched through the Orbiter's windscreen as Michael Allon in his silver and white EVA suit floated slowly down, head first, towards the black hole of Salyut's airlock.

'Nearly at the airlock, fellas. No trouble, just like the simulator, tell those guys they did a great job.'

He smiled, relieved that he had not fallen off, then stopped abruptly as he saw the threads of coloured tapes floating out of the hole to snake like childrens' ribbons over the silver-and-white body of Salyut all the way up towards the charged particle beam weapon.

'Hey, there's something odd here. There are . . . let's see . . . six coloured tapes emerging from the airlock, they go alongside Salyut and . . . yes, they wrap around some sort of antennae on the beam satellite and then . . . oh, Jesus, I think I've got it . . . they're tied to a box on the side of the weapon. I'll take a look later. I'm entering Salyut now.'

But as he pushed his head then chest over the entrance, he looked straight into the visored, manic face of the Palestinian!

With a silent scream of desperation Shabir Al Timimi, now more dead than alive, kicked his way out of Salyut 7 and struck Michael in the shoulder with his helmet. Michael was totally surprised but with sheer reflex grabbed desperately at the waving tapes to prevent himself being pushed into infinity. Down on earth, hundreds of television witnesses screamed as they saw the Palestinian in his space suit strike out of the airlock like a snake after its prey.

Michael gripped the tapes as he felt himself spinning uncontrollably, the earth, stars and the Orbiter flashing across his line of vision. At that instant Zhukov fired as the tapes did their job, a phenomenal shaft of green light swept across space. The observers could see little as the Palestinian floated at the entrance to the airlock, desperately guarding his lair.

Suddenly Michael felt himself slowing rapidly to a halt as the tapes stretched between the airlock and the triggers. He was trapped in them, completely helpless, but the desperate fight was not over yet for the reactions of their movements caused the assembly to tumble slowly.

Then, like the victim of a fly Michael wrapped himself up in the tapes, the beam still slowly tracking across the void of space.

Two of the tapes had come undone from the beam satellite leaving only the red pair firmly attached, the 'Fire' tapes. With a desperate pull as he felt himself floating away again, Michael rolled himself along the white and blue tapes still secured at the airlock and spun towards the waiting

Palestinian whose face was set in mad determination, ready to kick the intruder finally into infinity.

But as Michael rolled and Shabir waited, the rock-hard, ice-cold body of Boris Tsiolkovsky, dislodged from its snare on the Salyut's antennae, sailed towards the airlock, its face bright blue and polished like marble, its eyes totally white in the utter coldness of death. Peabody and Browne with all the other observers watched in horror as this apparition appeared from behind Salyut and silently sailed straight towards the unsuspecting Palestinian. Michael too glimpsed the ghastly sight as he reached almost to the arms of his assailant.

Shabir suddenly screamed inside his visor with terror as he felt something hard push him in the back, off the edge of the airlock and out into space. He clawed desperately, screaming still, until his gloves gripped a strange, hard object nuzzled alongside him. Now, in absolute terror, with his heart racing, he turned slowly to look straight into the ghastly face of the dead Russian.

Michael hung desperately to the edge of the empty airlock gazing in disbelief at the slowly disappearing bodies, one fighting off its lifeless companion, on the long lonely journey into oblivion.

60
Kresta

At that instant, Yigal Beer crossed the north coast of Turkey and thundered across the Black Sea towards his target of Odessa, now only a few minutes away and directly ahead of him. The ship that got him, and which he never saw, was a Soviet Kresta II Class cruiser ordered onto emergency patrol to cover a possible Israeli strike from the south, after the Soviet President had received Stockman's telex on the hot line.

The missiles, four SA-N-3s in two salvoes, appeared suddenly on his missile warning radar and he instantly switched on his electronic countermeasures desperately trying to jam their radar. He almost made it: only one came close, the others hopelessly confused, but that one was sufficient. Its tiny radio-powered proximity fuse detonated the warhead 100 feet from the F-15. At a closing speed of 2,000 miles an hour the metal rods exploded at hypersonic speed into the aircraft's line of flight. Three rods went through the aircraft's electronic coding box while one went clean through Yigal Beer's right leg, quite painlessly at first.

He knew he had been hit as the engines began to lose power and he instantly pulled the nose up to gain height and thus range. He also knew what he would try to do. He would carry out a LABS manoeuvre, literally tossing the bomb up into a ballistic trajectory as he climbed into a loop. That would give the bomb another ten miles range, with luck.

At that instant Rebecca Limpel heard the news from

Zuckerman that Jericho III had succeeded. The Palestinian was dead and Michael Allon was now climbing up towards Zhukov to turn off the mysterious switches. The scene at the War Cabinet was one of jubilation as Rebecca gave the order to cancel Tablet Three.

Landau made the call to IDF Communications Headquarters and got the shock of his life. Nokum 1 could not be contacted. The system was dead. No signals were being received. At least Beer would now turn back according to orders. No nuclear strike could ever occur unless a positive confirmation signal was sent. The pilots were under strict orders to return. But the grim news wiped out the mood of jubilation as the Deputy Chief of the Air Force checked the flight plan.

Ephraim Zuckerman heard the news of the communications breakdown and his face went white as he thought of the possible consequences. He switched on the TV monitor and spoke to Rebecca Limpel:

'Madam, I took a calculated risk concerning Odessa, our agents could still be there now, they have not yet reported back. I'm very worried.'

61
Exodus

The three women, one carrying a little boy, hurried as quickly as they could for the ship to take them to Yugoslavia. It would sail in ten minutes and soon their problems would become easier. They arrived at the customs barrier and joined the queue of tourists, workers, businessmen and others, their hearts beating with the fear of discovery. They need not have worried. The papers Mossad had prepared were perfect and within minutes they were on board. Trying hard to appear relaxed, and obviously looking forward to their trip to Yugoslavia to rejoin their husbands after a visit to the Black Sea resort, they embarked and then gathered at the rail looking out towards the sea.

Around them lay dozens of Soviet naval craft obviously preparing for some exercise in view of the feverish activity they had seen on the quayside. They had been lucky. Their vessel would be the last to leave the port before it was closed by the military, or so they had been told. They had only just made it, in fact.

There was a loud hoot from the ship's siren and suddenly they felt they were moving. They almost cheered as they saw the wash appear at the side of the ferry as she slowly gathered speed.

Just then they heard what sounded like a jet aircraft and they looked up towards the source. Liza Allon basked in the sheer pleasure of not having to appear to be a heavily pregnant woman any more, with the front of her belly strapped up to carry the recording equipment for her interview with Valentina Bykovsky. She was pleased to see Valentina so well and Nicholas also, after all the clandestine preparation to get them out of Russia. But with 'Aliah' by her side she had immense confidence. For 'Aliah' was her Chief's finest agent, and she thought fondly of Ephraim Zuckerman, the grey-haired man in Jerusalem. And he had promised her that soon, very soon, she could return to visit Michael, her brother, in Houston.

Liza could just see the plane now and suddenly she gasped . . . it could not be . . . never . . . but it was. Michael had shown her the photographs many times before. It was an F-15, here, coming towards Odessa!

Yigal Beer felt himself growing fainter as the blood drained stickily into his G-suit but still he climbed and soon there was the target. Obviously now the Russians were at war, they had shot at him over international waters. Israel could very well be under nuclear attack right now but he could hear nothing on the code system. Maybe they had destroyed the communications centre. He flicked the array of switches to Groundburst and kept hauling back on the stick as the twin engines continued to lose power. He had gained 10,000 feet and there, slightly out of his range, was the harbour, full of Soviet cruisers and destroyers. The tidal wave the device would create would probably sink the lot of them. For some reason he was pleased the bomb was a 'clean' one, ideal for a military target.

Beer was climbing at an angle of 68 degrees and travelling at 700 knots when he released the bomb and at that moment he made his final decision. He rolled the aircraft round and followed the climbing bomb. It would be a fitting end to his life—after all, there would be no Israel or family to return to.

Liza saw the aircraft climbing higher and closer, she even thought she saw something falling from it. She turned to Valentina and 'Aliah', worried now, and said urgently:

'I think we ought to take Nicholas into the warm now.' Nicholas nodded in agreement.

'Wave goodbye, Nicholas,' said Valentina, hugging him to her and pointing to Odessa.

At that instant the device exploded a mere two miles out from their ship with a force of more than one million tons of TNT and with a flash of heat at its centre of more than ten million degrees that seared into their faces, followed by a wall of superheated air, igniting every object and person for a distance of over a mile. The heat boiled several million tons of sea water in a second, creating a tidal wave 80 feet high that radiated outwards at over five hundred miles an hour. Among the many ships sunk in the harbour of Odessa was the passenger ferry to Yugoslavia. There were no survivors and only 40 per cent of 500,000 casualties in the port lived more than an hour.

Yigal Beer's last words as he ejected over the falling bomb were:

'For my brother and Israel.'

62
Cargo

The Soviet Union did not react immediately, while it mobilised rescue efforts for the stricken people of Odessa. The world, terrified now by the reports, waited for a nuclear war to begin while all the time the crew of Orbiter 102 worked on the Soviet spacecraft. By their fourth orbit since interception, they had undocked the beam satellite from the Salyut docking port. It had been a comparatively easy job for Dave Browne and Pete Peabody, as Michael waited in the Orbiter.

Wheeler placed a strict embargo on Houston Flight Control not to mention anything of the Odessa explosion in case the tired crew might be too disturbed and start to make mistakes. So the crew of Rocky knew nothing of the bomb and felt the relief and jubilation of their achievement in neutralising the beam.

Peabody had literally sawn off the solar panels of the beam satellite in exactly the same way Pete Conrad had removed metallic debris from the crippled Skylab back in 1972. He used a surgeon's wire saw and carefully kicked the two giant wings away, one by one, watching them tumble lazily in the sunlight out of the Orbiter's path.

Then Dave Browne had returned along the lifeline of the Arm and prepared to exercise his skill again. Orbiter 102 was about to retrieve the Soviet's most sophisticated weapon by putting it into its cargo bay in the specially designed adaptable jig, using the ubiquitous Arm and Claw. Mike watched, fascinated, as the weapon, now devoid of wings and smaller than the cargo bay, was gripped in the silver talons of the Claw. Pete rode alongside it, safely tethered to the satellite, as Dave swung him slowly over the cargo bay.

It took Browne another orbit to manoeuvre it into position until finally the weapon nestled into the arms of the special jig, to which Peabody was making the necessary adjustments, floating over the cargo bay. Within 30 minutes it was done and Dave Browne placed the long Arm back into its waiting clips, where it was also checked by Peabody.

It took him a few minutes to enter the airlock before Dave Browne finally closed the huge cargo bay doors. As he looked through the window he saw the two 60-foot curving interior surfaces and their two silver radiator panels close with a satisfying clunk to conceal the satellite in utter blackness.

As they told Jericho and Houston of their progress they still knew nothing of developments on earth.

'Jericho, this is Rocky, we are ready to return, over.'

'Rocky, this is Jericho, congratulations, you've done a fantastic job, you're go for return on your next orbit. We are handing you over to Houston. Good luck, over and out.'

'Roger, Jericho, Rocky is on his way home.'

At a distance of 4,800 miles from Kennedy Space Center OV-102 started into terminal phase flight at 18,000 miles an hour. It started to lose 272 miles per hour every second after using its OMS, pointing forwards to reduce its speed, before turning nose first towards its direction of return to earth.

The Orbiter's flight path took it on a long descent from 100 miles above the North Pacific, tracking across the Baring Sea and Southern Alaska. It entered North America north of Vancouver in British Columbia, and really started to heat up as it crossed into the United States over Kansas. Here was where the Orbiter Thermal Protection System kept the crew insulated from the fantastic thermal load of atmospheric friction as she heated up to nearly 2,300 degrees C. The entire Orbiter was covered in four different kinds of aerodynamic insulating tiles with the belly and underside of the blended delta wing covered in more than 5,000 square feet of the black ceramic blocks.

Orbiter 102 descended smoothly for the next 30 minutes, burning off orbital speed while Michael and his crew hoped that no other damage had been done to the vehicle. It was pure luck that the beam had destroyed the only part of the Orbiter that was not needed for its return. The main engines were not used on final descent as the vehicle was designed to glide all the way to a safe stop on earth using its shape to control the speed.

'Houston, this is Rocky, we're passing through 150,000 feet, we have 1,000 miles an hour, switching to TAEM at 70,000 feet, everything looks good, over.'

'Roger, Rocky, we have you on Kennedy radar, your computer reads 'go' for terminal area energy management at 70,000 feet, over.' OV-102 passed down through 70,000 feet and went on to computer control for the final landing phase.

Diana Allon at Kennedy Space Center in Florida clutched David to her, as she looked towards the south and anxiously waited for the Space Shuttle to appear out of the sky. Only 100 feet away stood Virginia Kây, tired after her dash from London, many hours before, but now excited at the thought of seeing the Space Shuttle landing. They were but two of the women waiting for the men to return.

Virginia Browne and Martha Peabody had left their tired children at their hotel and prayed silently that nothing would go wrong now. Around them thousands of others stood and prayed, having followed the incredible tenth flight of OV-102 on their TVs and radios.

Suddenly somebody shouted, then another and another and soon everybody was laughing and cheering and clapping. The Shuttle was there, high in the sky, lined up on the runway. There was a fantastic feeling of relief and pride that the crew of OV-102 were coming back safely to their families. It looked very small at 10,000 feet as the microwave scanning beam system installed at Runway 33 switched on to guide her towards the centre of the 15,000-foot-long, 300-foot-wide strip of smooth concrete traversing the swamps of the surrounding Wildlife Reserve.

The Shuttle was coming down steeply on a 22-degree glideslope, Michael maintaining energy to overcome the buffeting from the unbalanced rocket nozzles in the tail. At 900 feet he pulled her nose up for the flare at 6 degrees and at 720 feet and 330 miles an hour he deployed the landing gear. Orbiter 102 touched down in a burst of tyre smoke at 215 knots, its nose held high until it had slowed to 150 miles an hour before rolling to a halt 10,000 feet along the runway.

There was a huge cheer and Diana Allon cried and cried as did the other wives, while little David watched, perplexed at his mother's distress signals. Then they all ran for the courtesy bus to take them to the reception lounge while a convoy of escort vehicles roared out to the big white spaceship, her nose tipped firmly down onto her tiny nosewheel, while at her tail rose the great mass of her fin, OMS fairings and, to the growing amazement of her escorts, a single rocket nozzle where three had been before! They gazed in awe at the coating of metallic particles that covered the entire tail area as if a giant had sprayed her in silver and black. It was incredible what forces the ship had absorbed.

The Shuttle tractor reversed rapidly onto the towing lug and hooked onto its charge. With a grinding mechanical roar it inched forward for the tenth time the ship that had flown at 18,000 miles an hour, but now found itself very much down to earth as it trailed behind the tractor at a mere eight miles an hour, on its one and a half mile journey to the Orbiter Processing Facility by the north-west corner of the Vehicle Assembly Building. The ship swung off left, crossing the marshland until it swung right again and headed north-east for the OPF. The main door of the building stood open, the entire area lit now by floodlights in the gathering dusk. The zone was cordoned off by Air Force and civil police and NASA security guards, while overhead patrolled two police helicopters and two unfamiliar NASA aircraft.

There was a burst of sustained clapping from the waiting technicians and scientists, as Orbiter 102 swung in over the apron and came silently to a halt inside the building. The tractor unhitched and drove out and a handful of white-overalled ground crew approached with a series of inspection platforms. The overhead doors closed, sealing out the crowd of onlookers and there was little conversation as the men by the Shuttle waited for the crew door to open.

General Adam Wheeler, accompanied by Daniel Perès, Bill Kennedy and Gus Lancaster stood by the sealed circular hatch below the flight deck. Their faces were grim but as the hatch eventually swung open they tried to cover their anxiety with smiles of welcome. There was a voice from inside and Wheeler stepped in to the Shuttle, dressed in his full uniform. It was Dave Browne who welcomed him aboard and Wheeler shook hands, now absolutely delighted to see his men back safe and well.

'They're upstairs, General.' Browne said, his face wreathed in smiles. Wheeler climbed the awkward ladder that only hours before had been no obstacle to their weightless manoeuvres.

As he emerged onto the flight deck, Michael and Pete were carrying out the necessary safety checks and turned to greet him, their faces clearly visible through their now open visors. They were both perspiring but were delighted to see him, shaking hands and congratulating each other while down below Dave Browne greeted Kennedy and Lancaster. And so, ten minutes later, a hoard of technicians were invited onto the platforms as Browne opened the huge cargo bay doors.

The scene was amazing, the long curved forms of the doors gaped slowly open until they lay face down, their black inner ribs and hinges now fully exposed to the overhead floodlights. There, lying like some creation of science fiction, lay the golden shimmering form of the world's most powerful gun, the Soviet charged particle beam weapon, named—unknown to them—'Zhukov'.

63

SS14

An hour later, as Diana Allon and her son David comforted Michael after the grim news, Zuckerman quietly put down the phone in his office in Jerusalem. He stopped, took a piece of paper from the telephone pad and wrote his prayer for the memory of Liza Allon, his daughter 'Aliah' and the girl they tried so hard to rescue, Valentina Bykovsky, with her only son Nicholas Al Timimi. Also for his good friends Rabbi Groman and Yigal Beer.

As he did so, President James Stockman received a telex on the hot line from the President of the Soviet Union, as he circled the Atlantic.

TO THE PRESIDENT OF THE UNITED STATES

MR PRESIDENT,

THE SOVIET UNION WAS ATTACKED TODAY IN AN UNPRECEDENTED AND HORRIFIC ESCALATION OF ZIONIST EXPANSIONISM. USING A THERMONUCLEAR DEVICE, THE ISRAELI GOVERNMENT INFLICTED MASSIVE CASUALTIES AND DAMAGE ON THE GREAT CITY OF ODESSA.

THE SOVIET GOVERNMENT HAS THEREFORE ORDERED A LIMITED NUCLEAR STRIKE TO BE MADE ON ISRAEL AS THIS TELEX REACHES YOU. IT CONSISTS OF A SINGLE THERMONUCLEAR WARHEAD OF RESTRICTED CAPACITY AND MINIMAL FALLOUT, BEING DROPPED AWAY

FROM A MAJOR CENTRE OF POPULATION.

THE SOVIET UNION BELIEVES THAT THIS ACTION WILL DETER FURTHER ATTEMPTS BY THE ZIONISTS TO DRIVE OUR GREAT STATES INTO DIRECT NUCLEAR CONFRONTATION. OUR ACTION IS CONTROLLED AND IN ACCORDANCE WITH THE TEACHINGS OF ISRAELI RELIGION, NAMELY 'AN EYE FOR AN EYE'.

THIS ATTACK IS NOT THE PRECURSOR OF A FULL-SCALE STRIKE AND HAS BEEN DESCRIBED AS SUCH TO THE ISRAELI PRIME MINISTER BY DIRECT LINE FROM THE SOVIET UNION.

THIS WILL BRING AN END TO THE CURRENT CRISIS AND WE HOPE WILL LEAD TO A FINAL, PEACEFUL SOLUTION TO THE ARAB-ISRAELI CONFLICT.

SIGNED—ALEXEI BERIEV

THE PRESIDENT OF THE UNION OF SOVIET SOCIALIST REPUBLICS

There was no mention of Shimatov, Al Timimi or the Charged Particle Beam.

Ephraim Zuckerman walked slowly through the mourners and the ring of soldiers until he came into the clear space before the black ruins of the Wall. He carefully took out the little piece of folded paper with the prayer to his now dead friends and walked slowly across to the hallowed stones. Hardly anything remained and he had difficulty finding an unburnt crack in which to place the prayer. He found a likely spot and had to stoop, there was so much damage above him where the Wall had stood before. As he bent, he saw clearly the other holy place, the blackened form of the Dome of the Rock, where the winged horse Erebus had flown with the Prophet Mohammed to Heaven. He heard the doleful bell of the Church of the Holy Sepulchre as he slid the paper into the crack, where it fluttered in the warm breeze.

He whispered his simple prayer, 'Peace for all Mankind.'

Then he kissed the blackened stone before turning away to walk back to his empty house.

At that moment, a single, one-megaton 'clean' warhead on the final stage of a Soviet SS14 'Scapegoat' missile, launched from a wood on the shores of the Caspian Sea, exploded in the most fertile land in Israel, the Jezreel Valley, 50 miles north of Jerusalem.

It landed on the village of Megiddo, the place also known as ARMAGEDDON.

THE END

Postscript

To The Editor
Withering Chronicle
Withering
Northants

Dear Bill

Well, here's the manuscript as promised!

This is my first attempt to cover the whole story of the recent events in Israel. I managed to talk to General Wheeler of the US Air Force, Bill Kennedy of Rockwell and Gus Lancaster of NASA.

Pete Peabody and Dave Browne gave me some good insight into the events during the flight of OV-102. Most of the 'sensitive' technical information came from Gordon Derry and his pupils as well as the various editors of magazines like *Flight* and *Aviation Week*. The British Interplanetary Society were particularly helpful.

Nobody will tell me where Michael Allon and his family are now since his resignation on hearing the news of the death of his sister Liza and his friend Rabbi Groman. I'm sure I'll find him in Israel, possibly Jerusalem, with Daniel Perès and Ephraim Zuckerman. It seems he always was a son of the Abraham Policy.

Ever since Rebecca Limpel's and General Landau's resignations it has been difficult to develop good contacts in Israel. There are calls for Zuckerman to go also.

The Soviet Embassy, Tass and Novosti Press have denied all knowledge of a charged particle beam satellite or the murders of Karpov and Tsiolkovsky.

They insist that all three died as 'martyrs to man's quest for knowledge in the peaceful exploration of space', particularly the Palestinian, and claimed the spacecraft disintegrated on landing after the parachute failed.

They have accused the Israelis of attempting to start a nuclear war between the Soviet Union and America and have claimed that the destruction of the Western Wall was a Mossad bag of tricks to forment trouble between them and the Arabs.

They are demanding that Israel abandons her nuclear weapons but the new head of the Israeli Air Force claims that the bomb that damaged Odessa was a solitary test device and that Yigal Beer got lost on a test flight. It was all an accident. Bullshit!

The Israelis are clearing up the Jezreel Valley after the Soviet retaliatory bomb and claiming that less than 25,000 were killed, because of the low population density, and the fact that it was a 'clean' bomb.

I think I got most of the technical stuff right but I'm sure we'll get the usual schoolboys' letters.

By the way, did you hear that Shimatov is being proposed to become Soviet leader since Beriev's heart attack?

Love,
Virginia Kay.

PS. I overspent my expenses, could I have another £500? I want to go to Israel next.

GENESIS
by W.A. HARBINSON

There is a global conspiracy of such enormity that those who encounter even its outermost fringes are inevitably contaminated. A conspiracy based on incredibly advanced technology of Earthly origin. A conspiracy dedicated to the eventual enslavement and subversion of humanity as we know it. A conspiracy with one man – old beyond nature, powerful beyond measure – at its core. A conspiracy stretching through time – across icy polar wastes and jungle hideouts . . . into the cold vacuum of space itself. A conspiracy poised to turn life on Earth into a chilling nightmare of living death. Unless. . .

GENESIS

is the once-in-a-lifetime novel of searing terror and explosive excitement. Based on little-known but indisputable fact, it is more – much more – than a gripping, frighteningly plausible story. It is the reading experience that will alter the way you look at your world – and your universe. . .

0 552 11533 9 £1.75

THE DEVIL'S ALTERNATIVE
by FREDERICK FORSYTH

'Whichever option I choose, men are going to die'. This is the Devil's Alternative, the appalling choice facing the President of the USA and other statesmen throughout the world.

As the gripping story gathers momentum, the reader is transported from Moscow to London, from Rotterdam to Washingtom, from a country house in Ireland to the world's biggest oil tanker which threatens to pollute the whole of the North Sea. The climax is the most exciting that even this master story-teller has contrived, and the last-minute surprises in the concluding chapters take the breath away.

0 552 11495 2 £1.75

EXODUS
by LEON URIS
Exodus is the story of the greatest miracle of our times, an event unparalleled in the history of mankind: the rebirth of a nation which had been dispersed two thousand years before. It tells the story of the Jews coming back after centuries of abuse, indignities, torture, and murder to carve an oasis in the sand with guts and with blood.
'An epic vision, brilliant, enlightening, horrifying and heroic!'

Saturday Review

0 552 08384 4 £2.50

MILA 18
by LEON URIS
'Uris has created a singularly moving account – a powerful story of people whose personal tragedies make clearer the enormity of Nazi crimes. For all its absorption with the almost unbelievable atrocities which the Nazis inflicted on the Jews jammed behind 'the wall' in Warsaw. *MILA 18* becomes a stirring story of valour, of human dignity, and of love which is able to transcend the bestialities of man. . . .' *Minneapolis Tribune*

0 552 08385 2 £1.75

BLOOD SECRETS
by CRAIG JONES

It starts with a murder.
Then the evil *really* begins. . .

'Simply stunning . . . immaculately constructed to spring shock after shock after shock upon the already fascinated reader . . . unforgettable'.

Brian Levy, Paperback buyer

'Hard to put down'. *The Atlantic Monthly*

'A truly horrendous and yet dazzling climax. . .

about three-quarters of the way through you will begin to think that you have arrived at the most frightening "secret" of all.

There is more in store for you, however, and it won't help solve the ultimate puzzleeeven though you know from the first sentence in the book that the narrator is on trial for murder. The psychological insight here is convincing, the denouement devastating'.

Publishers Weekly

0 552 11290 9 £1.00